How a Monster Is Made

RASHELL LASHBROOK

DEDICATION

This novel is dedicated to the victims of domestic abuse.

Your path is often darkened, your voice silenced, and your story untold.

ACKNOWLEDGMENTS

Thank you, Kris Jackson Keeling, M.N. Pope, Matthew Weller, Steve Litke, Grant Harris, and Michelle Meyer, for your priceless insight on the first edition manuscript of this novel. I am forever grateful for your time, attention to detail, and honest feedback.

Thank you to my family and friends for your steadfast support during this process. You believed in me, even when I lost faith in myself.

Thank you to my children for holding me accountable to my goals and dreams. You are the loves of my life.

CONTENTS

CHAPTER 1

THE END

The jagged edges of the stick burned deep in his throat, but he couldn't turn away. The bitch had his head trapped between her feet. Arms and legs bound; he was at her mercy. No doubt, she loved every second of this. Raine had always been a little off in the head, and this was just more proof.

The seriousness of the situation was sinking in. Randall had a fleeting thought that he might not make it out alive. He stopped fighting back in hopes she might ease up some—but no luck. She pushed even harder, and he could feel the blood trickling down the back of his throat. The damned stick was taking up all the space in his mouth, and swallowing was impossible.

She repositioned the rod, and with a grunt, shoved it in harder. The trickle turned into a gush, and breathing was no longer an option. Panic didn't take over like he'd thought it would. The booze from earlier in the day helped make everything softer.

Strange, he thought; how calm he felt, knowing he was a goner. It was as if he could see everything from a distance. His last thoughts meshed with his first memories.

His mouth was full but not with the hardened, rough edges of the stick. Soft flesh filled his mouth. He suckled furiously, milk from his mother's breast spraying the back of his throat with each swallow.

Her arms were around him, cradling him close. He was safe now. Warm and loved. He reached up for her face, and she smiled down at him, kissing the palm of his hand. Mama pulled the soft blanket up around his shoulder and began to stroke his head gently. When she did this, he could barely keep his eyes open. Drifting off to sleep, he left the cruel stick, the blood, and the last part of his life behind.

CHAPTER 2

HAT TRICK

"Randy," Mama yelled from the front steps, "come here this minute!" Janie stood next to Mama, tears leaving clear little paths down her dusty face.

He hesitated for a second or two longer and continued to scratch in the dirt before standing up.

If Janie was crying, whatever Mama was yelling about wasn't going to be pleasant. His sister was three years older, so she was always the first to get into trouble whenever Mama or Daddy was in a punishing mood.

Daddy liked to punish Janie more. But when Daddy was done and wasn't looking, Mama made it fair and square on Randy. Most of the time, it didn't seem to matter who had done the wrong. The important part was that someone paid for it.

As Randy trudged up the porch steps, he noticed Janie was still holding her schoolbooks. She was six years old now, big enough to go to the first grade.

He missed Janie, and if pressed, he'd have to admit he was somewhat mad at her for leaving him alone with Mama all day.

Janie's shoulders were shuddering from her fresh cry. She refused to make eye contact with him.

"Yes, ma'am?" Randy had already learned to use his good manners when he was in trouble. He did his best to look Mama in the eye.

Daddy swatted him if he didn't and said that a real man ought to look a person in the eye. Daddy made Janie look down at her feet when she was in trouble. He said girls shouldn't be so forward. Randy didn't know what that meant, but he didn't dare ask questions.

"Do you know what happened to your father's best hat?" Mama asked. She picked at her fingernails, something she often did when Daddy was in a mood.

"No, Mama." Randy shook his head and tried to remember what Daddy's best hat looked like. It didn't matter because he hadn't touched any of them.

He cast a sideways glance at Janie to see if she looked guilty, but he couldn't see her eyes.

Janie kept her eyes fixed on her feet. Her cheek had a big red mark on it, and he knew that meant Daddy or Mama had smacked her hard.

"Well, young man, if you don't know, and your sister doesn't know, then I guess you both get it good." Mama sounded like she was about to start bawling.

"No, Mama, please! I didn't do anything to Daddy's hat!" Randy begged, but he knew it was a waste of his time. If Janie had already gotten her punishment, then he was going to get his, too. That was the way it worked in the Carter house.

Mama made Randy pull his pants down to his knees, and she whipped him with Daddy's razor strap until he cried like a baby. He was thankful it was Mama that had done the spanking. If it had been Daddy, he would have swatted Randy again for crying.

Later that night, when Janie was changing into her nightgown, Randy caught a glimpse of the welts that covered her backside from her knees to her shoulder blades.

"Janie?" Randy asked, "Did you take Daddy's hat?"

"No, you big dummy! Why would I do that?" Janie's voice sounded like she'd been eating sand.

"Me, either." Randy thought about Daddy's hat as he drifted off.

Mama's shrieking voice, followed by Daddy's booming one, woke Randy up later that night. He hated it when they fought in the middle of the night. It was scary enough during the daytime.

"You stupid bitch! How dare you tell me how to discipline my daughter!"

"She's bruised so badly; I can't send her to school tomorrow!" Mama cried out, "And for what? You left your stupid hat at your girlfriend's house!"

"Oh, you're so worried about that precious girl of yours, but what about my son? You whipped him for no reason!"

"He's my son, too, Wyatt! And I wouldn't have spanked him if you'd remembered where you left your hat!"

More shouting, followed by banging, and then eventually the sound of Mama pleading for Daddy to stop, terrified Randy. It wasn't the first time he'd woken up to the horrible sounds of his parents going at it.

Randy slid out of his bed and crawled in with Janie, who didn't budge from the movement of the covers. Pressing his face into the back of Janie's neck, he concentrated on the tickle her hair made against his nose with each breath. Eventually, he was able to fall back asleep. She made him feel safe and warm.

CHAPTER 3

REVELATION

Wyatt didn't spend much time around the farm during the month following the hat incident. Janie and Randy might not have understood what happened, but Pearl knew the exact reason his hat was missing.

The worst part for Pearl was the shame that she felt every time she thought about the beatings her children took for that floozie. The pain was nearly physical, a sharp jolt to her shins, as if someone had whacked her with a two-by-four.

When he'd left the house the evening before, Pearl had known he was up to no good. He couldn't get out of the door fast enough. Wyatt had no real friends. His cousin, the only man he ever went drinking with, was out on an oil rig.

***

"See ya later, Pearlie," Wyatt called out. He let the wood-framed screen door slam shut behind him, leaving a cloud of Old Spice.

She watched him strut out to their brand-new Chevrolet truck. He'd surprised her with it a few months before but had yet to let her drive it.

Her pulse quickened as the truck kicked up a cloud of dust down the long driveway.

The sun cast an orange glow over the fields surrounding their old farmhouse. Pearl had a feeling the sun would be lighting up the morning before she'd see Wyatt next.

The night seemed to go on forever. She did a crazy dance in her head for most of it. On the upbeat, she hoped he wasn't home because he'd been in a wreck, and on the downbeat, she prayed he was okay, no matter the reason.

Even though she tried to sleep, the cicadas cajoled her awake through the open windows. She was losing him. Ever since the birth of Randy, things just hadn't been the same.

Making promises to a God that probably wasn't listening to her, Pearl lay motionless in the silvery moonlight. Resorting to prayer was an act of desperation, but it helped to ease the sickening twist she felt in her heart.

Tears ran down her temples into her matted hair. She longed for her mother at times like this. Mama would have known exactly what Pearl should do. Even if she hadn't, Mama's presence would've given the reassurance that Pearl so desperately craved.

The sun rose at its usual time; the rooster crowed at his preset hour, and still no Wyatt. Although she'd yet to get out of bed, her heart raced, as if she'd been running.

Get up, lazybones. Breakfast isn't going to cook itself. Fumbling in the dark for her cotton robe, she slipped it on before she wiggled her legs out from under the bedsheets.

She sat on the edge of the bed for a second or two, thinking about the words she might say to him when he walked through the door. She'd already formulated a tongue lashing.

"Janie, time to get up. I'm going down to start your breakfast." She leaned her head inside the children's bedroom and switched on the lamp.

Out of habit, Pearl combed her sleep-flattened hair with her fingers as she padded down the stairs. A small part of her hoped that Wyatt would be sitting at the table, waiting for her. The larger part knew that she wasn't ready to face him yet. She was too angry.

To her relief, the dark kitchen was empty. She didn't need the light to make her coffee. She'd done it a hundred times in the dark. She lit a cigarette and waited for the coffee to finish percolating.

Stirrings above her head told her that Janie wouldn't need a second waking. She was a breeze. No trouble at home, and never a bad word from her teacher, Janie was a good girl.

Pearl crushed her cigarette out onto the edge of the ashtray and turned the light on above the sink. Distracted by her thoughts, she dumped the entire box of Cream of Wheat into the pan.

Little granules of the dried cereal scattered about the counter and floor. She let out a growl of frustration. It was going to be a long day.

After she put Janie on the bus, she decided to let Randy sleep a while longer. She wasn't in the mood for a rambunctious three-year-old boy's antics. Until Wyatt returned home, the less chaos, the better for her frazzled nerves.

She washed the breakfast dishes first, then gathered up the small amount of dirty laundry. She needed to do something to distract herself from the twisting of her stomach.

Once the few pieces of clean laundry were drying in the morning breeze, Pearl took a stashed pack of Pall Malls hidden behind the bread box and went back outside.

The metal glider sat beneath the most generous shade tree in the yard. Before Randy's birth, Pearl spent many a hot afternoon gliding back and forth, listening to the lazy squeak and watching Janie play with her dolls. Now, she mostly used the space to smoke. Randy was a handful, which didn't allow for much sitting.

Her hands shook as she pulled a cigarette out with her long fingernails. It took several tries to get a match to stay lit long enough in the gusty wind. She inhaled, letting the smoke fill her lungs. Five seconds of peace followed the first inhalation. After that, the anxiety returned swiftly.

Pearl didn't enjoy her cigarette as much as she'd hoped. Fretful thoughts about Wyatt made it nearly impossible. She thought about smoking another one but decided against it. Even though most ladies smoked just as much as their husbands now, Pearl tried to limit herself a bit. Aunt Martha had fallen madly in love with cigarettes. In return, her voice had dropped two octaves to match her newly leathering skin. Certain there was a connection, she didn't want to end up like Aunt Martha.

She'd planned on going to the grocery store, but without Wyatt home to drive her, she'd have to make do with something from the pantry for supper. There was a certain comfort in thinking about her normal routine. If she allowed herself to dwell on the likelihood her husband was with another woman, she might fall apart.

Before tackling the pantry, she went upstairs to check on Randy. He'd kicked off his bedsheets, exposing his bare feet. At three years of age, he still looked like a baby when he was sleeping. She stroked his blonde, silken hair lightly and kissed his forehead. He stirred and turned over to his side. She covered him and said a little prayer he would stay asleep a while longer.

Pearl knew she might be borrowing from tonight's peace by allowing him to sleep so long, but at this moment, she didn't care.

She tiptoed out of the children's room and went downstairs to the kitchen. Out of habit, she glanced at the driveway to see if Wyatt was home. Her heart sank at the sight of the empty place where his truck normally sat.

The kitchen air felt stuffy, so she opened the window over the sink with a shove. The window made a cracking sound as if it were coming apart at the seams. It tended to stick ever since they'd repainted. Lace curtains fluttered in the cool spring breeze, and a clean fragrance from the freshly washed clothes hanging to dry blew in over the bright little kitchen. Pearl began to feel a tiny bit better.

She tugged on the pantry door, and it opened with a sticky creaking sound as well. Inside, the smell of fresh paint blended with the aroma of the herbs she'd hung to dry. As she felt her way to the pull switch, an upside-down dill weed plant entangled itself in her hair. She cringed and hoped there weren't any spiders housing themselves in the branches.

Pearl had only intended to find something for supper in the pantry, but after an hour and a half, she'd completely organized the storage space. She swept the floor of the little room and took her apron off. For lack of anything else to do, she put a pot of tea on the stove to brew.

She could hear Randy crying, so she went upstairs to see what the fuss was all about.

"What's the matter, honey?"

Randy didn't answer with words. Instead, he made a whining sound that always infuriated Wyatt. Whenever Randy had an episode like this in the middle of the night, Wyatt slapped him, which only made Randy cry harder. Pearl was sure he wasn't awake, but she never really knew how to snap him out of it. Of course, she wasn't going to reprimand Wyatt for disciplining his son.

"*Shhh…*" Pearl rocked him back and forth, sitting on the edge of the bed. Randy continued to cry without opening his eyes. After a short time, his cries lessened. Pearl didn't dare stop the rocking motion, even though she could hear the teakettle whistle. She hoped she could calm Randy down before all the water boiled away.

Something was different about little Randy. He was a sweet, intelligent boy, but when he lost control, there was no going back for him. He became inconsolable.

Wyatt hated it when his son behaved in that manner. Instinctively, Pearl did her best to cushion Randy from his father and to protect Wyatt from the irritating presence of his little son. The position she'd unwittingly stepped into, the role of buffer, mediator, was exhausting. She couldn't allow herself to think about the fact that Randy was only three. There were so many more years ahead.

Hopefully, he would outgrow his tendencies to disappoint his father. She looked at Randy's beautiful face and understood she'd never resented and loved someone so much at the same time.

The realization the teakettle was no longer whistling brought her attention back to the moment. It seemed strange all the water would have boiled away, given that she'd filled the pot to its brim. Randy had stopped crying, so she sat still and listened for sounds of Wyatt. Except for the chirping of the birds, everything was silent.

"Are you ready for breakfast?"

Randy smiled at her and nodded his head.

Still holding Randy, she stood up and shifted him to her hip. She could almost hear Wyatt scolding, "He's too big to be carried around. Put that boy down!"

He wrapped his arms around her shoulders and tucked his face into the crook of her neck. Even though he was getting heavier, Pearl liked the way his embrace made her feel needed. She maneuvered down the flight of stairs, through the living room, and into the kitchen while holding her big, little boy.

With her right foot, she slid his chair away from the table and tried to sit him down. Randy held on for a second longer, refusing to let go of her neck.

"Come on." Pearl felt impatient. "Sit down."

He looked disappointed but let loose of her. She scooted his chair up and got a bowl out of the cupboard for his breakfast. While she was getting the Cream of Wheat out of the pantry, she remembered she'd left the teakettle on to boil away. In a panic, she bolted to the stove to turn it off.

The stovetop was empty. She put her hand over the burner that had held the kettle just minutes before. It was still warm. She was relieved because this meant she hadn't completely lost her mind. She was so forgetful that she thought perhaps she'd only imagined putting on the teakettle. Wyatt always said if her head weren't attached, she'd forget it.

"Mama!" Randy complained, "I'm hungry!"

She put her finger up to her lips to signal him to be quiet. His eyes widened, and he stopped protesting. Pearl peeked into the living room, but nothing looked out of place.

Silent, Randy watched as she walked to the back door. She made the motion for him to stay in his chair.

Out in the yard, just past the steps, lay her teakettle on the grass. The handle was splayed sideways, and the lid had popped off. Baffled by the sight of her teapot in the yard, Pearl looked to her right and left for signs of Wyatt. The yard was empty.

With cautious, quiet steps, she walked out toward the shed. Sounds of someone, or something, raffling through the contents of the little toolshed, came through the slightly opened door. As she neared the small building, she could hear Wyatt cursing.

"Wyatt?" She made sure to keep her voice soft. "Is everything all right?"

"Hell no! I can't find my good hat!" His words were sloppy and thick. She guessed that he was still sauced from last night.

"What do you need it for, dear?"

"I don't think that's any of your goddamned business!"

Pearl didn't need to walk any closer to smell the booze on him. She adjusted her countenance and took a step back.

Wyatt teetered about in a ridiculous fashion. "If those damned kids hadn't lost my hat, I wouldn't be late for my meeting."

His words made no sense, but Pearl didn't dare question him.

"Had to come all the way back home and find it!" He mumbled, "Left early this morning and thought I had it with me."

Pearl knew he was lying. She'd barely slept last night. If he'd been home at any time during the previous twelve hours, she'd have known. Her thoughts went back to Randy, likely still waiting at the table for breakfast.

She rushed Randy through breakfast and sent him out to play. Her stomach cramped while she waited for Wyatt to make his way inside. Pearl hated this version of her husband—a filthy, drunken liar.

"Well, did you have any luck?" She pretended to be wiping the counters off.

"No, those damned kids took my hat!" He sat down in his chair and rested his head in his hands. She wondered if he could feel himself swaying back and forth.

"I'm sure it'll turn up," she soothed. "Why don't you go take a little nap, and I'll look for it."

"No!" He slammed his right hand down onto the table and said, "I'm waiting for Janie to get home! She's gonna tell me what happened to my hat!"

Pearl shrugged her shoulders and said, "Suit yourself."

Within a few minutes, Wyatt fell asleep with his head resting on the breakfast table. While he was face down in a puddle of his own drool, Pearl looked in every single place she could imagine Wyatt's hat to be, including his new truck.

If she could find the cap, she reasoned, then no one would get punished. It mattered not to Wyatt that he didn't need the hat, nor did it matter that the meeting he'd missed today wasn't real. He'd created his diversion, and wrath would be bestowed on anyone who questioned him. His hat was nowhere to be found.

Hours passed before Janie's bus dropped her at the end of the long driveway.

"Mama!" Janie beamed at Pearl as she climbed off the old bus. Pearl rarely met Janie at the bus stop.

"Hi, honey," Pearl took Janie's hand. "Have you seen Daddy's new hat?"

Janie lost her smile and shook her head. Pearl led her into the kitchen, where Wyatt sat waiting. She ignored Janie's pleading eyes and went out to the garden. Pearl covered her ears with her palms and prayed to God that she was doing the right thing.

After the spankings had been doled out, Wyatt moved his nap to their bed. Pearl was relieved to be alone with the children. She made their favorite supper and played games with them that evening. It was nearing the children's bedtime when someone knocked on the door.

Pearl considered waking Wyatt. They weren't expecting anyone, and it was getting late. She thought about his temperament earlier and decided to let him sleep.

The girl standing on the other side of the porch couldn't have been much older than seventeen. Because it was dark outside, Pearl didn't immediately see the hat in her hand.

"May I help you?"

"Is this Wyatt's house?" The girl was a pretty little thing. Shy mannered and petite, she spoke softly, as if she were afraid to commit to the words.

"Yes."

"Could you give him this?" She held up Wyatt's new hat.

"Why do you have my husband's hat?" Pearl tried to keep calm.

"Wyatt's married?" Fear flashed over the girl's face.

"Why do you have my husband's hat?" Pearl asked once more, her words coming out jagged and broken.

"I'm sorry." The girl turned and ran off the porch, dropping Wyatt's hat in the process.

"Answer me!" Pearl yelled at the girl's back. "Why do you have my husband's hat?"

The girl jumped into an old Ford pickup truck. She struggled to get the engine to turn over. After a few tries, she gunned the motor and sped out of their driveway.

Pearl stood in the dark, just long enough to catch her breath. The raging of her heart made her feel faint and clammy. She stifled a sob by covering her face with his hat.

"Mama?" Randy called to her from the porch. "Whatcha doin' out here? Who was that lady?"

She sucked the tears in and pasted a smile on her face. "Just someone at the wrong house. Let's get ready for bed now."

Once the children were sleeping soundly, she took the hat and went into their bedroom, where Wyatt was still snoring. He looked peaceful, laying on his back with his arms resting above his head. When he was sleeping, it was easy to forget the bad parts of Wyatt. She debated what to do for a small moment, then tossed the hat onto his chest. He startled a little, and his eyes opened slightly.

"I found your hat." Pearl hoped her voice sounded more substantial than it felt.

"What?" He squinted and looked up at her, confused.

"Who is the little girl that brought your hat?" Pearl couldn't keep the wobbly tremble out of her words.

"What the hell are you talking about?" The confused expression was beginning to give way to anger. Pearl heard the alarms going off in her head, but she didn't heed them.

"I said, who is the little girl that brought your hat home?" Pearl raised the volume of her voice slightly. "Is she your girlfriend?"

"That's none of your fucking business." Wyatt laid back down, turned onto his side, and covered his head with a pillow. Pearl wanted to scream, but she didn't. The children were sleeping.

Her stomach churned as she thought about the punishments both Janie and Randy had been given for a missing hat that had been at some little whore's house. The wise thing to do would be to leave him alone until the morning.

Pearl sat down in the chair next to the bed and watched Wyatt sleep for a while. The hurt continued to expand in her chest, kicking and punching, threatening to squeeze her heart into nothingness. She'd missed out on an entire night of sleep, made herself sick over him.

She'd whipped her three-year-old across his bare bottom and left the room while Wyatt beat Janie, over the missing hat. All so he could tell her it wasn't her business. Tonight would bring no more rest than the last. It was too much.

"Wyatt! Wake up!" Ears ringing hot, she punctuated the words with a sharp kick to the mattress.

After their fight, he'd left. He'd left because the girl was barely old enough to drive the truck that she'd delivered his hat with, let alone spend time with a married man. He'd left because the bruises he'd put on Pearl's face were worse than the bruises on Janie's back. He'd left because Pearl threatened to tell her papa if he didn't go.

CHAPTER 4

THE FISHING TRIP

Daddy left for a while, but Randy didn't know why. In the end, it didn't matter because eventually, he came home. For the first few weeks, even Mama was glad he was back.

"There's my big boy!" Daddy surprised Randy by picking him up and giving him a big hug. Usually, the only sign of affection Daddy gave was a firm smack on the backside. He felt warm inside and wondered what he'd done to deserve such treatment. Mama smiled at him and gave him a nod of encouragement, as if to say, "Go ahead, hug him back."

Reluctant, Janie waited beside Mama. She didn't look happy to see Daddy.

"Hello, Janie," Daddy said with a pat on Janie's head. He quickly turned his attention back to Randy.

"How about you and I go do some fishing?" Daddy asked. "Mother? What do you say about that?"

Mama blushed a pretty shade of pink and said, "That'd be great! Wouldn't you like that, Randy?"

Randy nodded. He did want to go fishing. Butch, his friend from church, got to go fishing all the time with his daddy. A warm sort of happiness swam around in his belly. Not only did Daddy's return bring a bit of long-overdue attention to Randy, but he'd also never seen his parents behave so nice to each other before. He knew they loved each other because they kissed and hugged sometimes, but in the past, their kisses always seemed to turn into slaps. Now, they were going out of their way to be sweet to each other.

"Can I get you more coffee, dear?" Mama stood beside Daddy's chair at breakfast with the pot in her hand. She wore her new yellow apron, and her hair was already fixed up for the day. When Mama sat Randy's plate in front of him, he could smell her perfume. He noticed she had lipstick on, too.

"Thank you, baby." Daddy patted Mama's backside and smiled up at her with a wink. "That'd be nice."

She leaned over and kissed him on the lips, right in front of Janie and Randy. Janie giggled a little.

"You'd better finish up, young lady," Mama warned, "or you're gonna miss your bus."

"Yes, ma'am." Janie shoved the last bite of toast in her mouth and stood up. She took her plate over to the sink to rinse it, just like Mama had taught her to do.

"Janie, did you ask to be excused?" Daddy asked.

Janie's big blue eyes widened with worry over the blunder she'd just made. She shook her head and looked down at her feet. She waited.

"Well, then ask."

"Ma…may I b…b…be excused?" she stuttered.

"Of course," Daddy said. "Now hurry before you miss the bus."

With a look of relief painted all over her face, Mama resumed whatever it was she'd been doing.

Randy paid attention to Janie's mistakes, and he learned from them. After the last bite of bacon, he looked at Daddy right in the eye and asked, "May I be excused, sir?"

Daddy's face cracked into a big grin. "Did you hear my boy, Pearlie? He's turning out to be a fine young man."

Mama smiled and made a sound Randy couldn't understand.

"Of course, you may be excused, son," Daddy beamed. "Leave your plate for your mother. That's women's work."

Mama had taught both Janie and him to rinse their plates after eating, but he wasn't about to argue with Daddy.

"Get your old pants and shoes on. We're going fishing this morning—see if we can't catch something for dinner." He wrapped his arms around Mama's waist and kissed her on the back of her neck as she stood washing up the breakfast dishes.

Randy stood at the doorway for a while, watching his parents standing together. It was how he'd always imagined that people who loved each other acted.

Daddy turned and said, "Well, go on. The day's wasting away, and the fish aren't going to catch themselves!"

He felt very big as he rode alongside Daddy in the new truck through town to Cibolo Creek. The windows had been rolled down just enough to fluff his hair around, and the air smelled clean and fresh. The rain from the night before had washed the dust off every leaf, every single blade of grass, leaving everything shiny and green. It'd been so long since they had rain, Randy had almost forgotten how it smelled afterward. Randy turned to Daddy and smiled.

Daddy tousled his hair and asked, "You ready to catch some fish?"

"Yes, sir!"

"Let's get some nightcrawlers," Daddy said as he maneuvered the truck into the icehouse parking lot. "Watch the truck for me."

Randy scooted over to the driver's seat and wondered if anyone might think he was big enough to drive. He watched as cars passed. Mostly ladies on their way to the grocery store, they seemed too busy to notice him sitting at the wheel. He took a cigarette out of the pack on the seat and pretended to smoke it while watching himself in the side mirror. Randy made sure to hold the smoke with his thumb and forefinger, just like Daddy. He didn't want to hold onto it like a sissy. He was so busy practicing his smoking; he didn't notice Daddy walking up to the truck. Startled by Daddy's booming laughter, Randy nearly dropped the cigarette onto the floorboard.

"Do you want to try one?" Daddy asked.

Randy hesitated. He suspected this might be a trap, but Daddy looked genuinely happy. Mama would kill him if she found out.

"Well? Yes, or no?" Daddy stood outside the truck with a big grin on his face, a proud glint in his eye.

"Okay." Randy shrugged.

"Like this," Daddy showed him.

Randy held the cigarette just like a man, and he took in a big breath while Daddy lit the end of it. All at once, a cloud of dusty smoke filled every bit of his chest. His body rebelled into a fit of ragged coughs. Daddy laughed while Randy fought to hold his breakfast down.

After the hacking and coughing fit was over, Daddy smiled and asked, "Do you want another puff?"

Not trusting his voice yet, Randy just shook his head side to side.

Daddy laughed and said, "I do believe you look a little green around the gills, son. Maybe you'd better wait till you're older before taking up smoking."

"Yes, sir."

He grabbed the supplies he'd bought off the top of the truck and motioned for Randy to slide over. "Here, hold these." With his right hand, he handed Randy a can of worms. Daddy sat in the driver's seat and placed a small cooler of beers on the floor.

The rocking motion of the truck was making Randy sick to his stomach. He didn't want Daddy to think he was a baby, so he swallowed hard and tried to think of other things.

"The water level is down with the drought, so we'll have to go a little farther than normal, I reckon." Daddy said this as if Randy knew where the usual spot was.

Even if he hadn't felt like throwing up, he probably wouldn't have pointed out to Daddy this was his first fishing trip. Instead, he simply nodded in agreement.

Thankfully, a little farther wasn't too far. He could feel the vomit rising in his throat. The truck was barely to a stop before Randy leaned his head out of the window and chucked up his breakfast. Pieces of bacon, mixed with globs of egg, orange juice, and the nasty taste of the cigarette splattered all down the side of the truck.

"Holy hell! Couldn't you hold it a minute longer?" Irritated, Daddy jumped out of the truck and ran to the passenger side. He looked at Randy, and his expression softened a little.

"I'm sorry." Randy couldn't summon much more. The disgusting taste was threatening to cause another round of heaving.

Daddy yanked the door open. "Get out."

He climbed out, carefully stepping around the spots of vomit on the running board. Luckily, he'd leaned far enough out that his shirt had managed to stay dry.

"Here, take a drink." Daddy handed him a beer. "Swish it around and spit it out. Get the taste out of your mouth."

While Randy was gargling beer, Daddy took a pail of water from the creek and dumped it down the side of the truck to rinse off the mess. Randy glanced at Daddy, wondering if he was angry. It was hard to tell sometimes.

"Feel better?" Daddy didn't look mad.

"Yes, sir." Still queasy, Randy wasn't about to let on that he was such a baby.

"That's my boy." Daddy chuckled and patted his back. "Let's get on with it, then."

Daddy strolled for a while along the creek bank until he found a spot he deemed fit for fishing. "That'll do," he said and began to arrange their things.

"Here, hold this still for me." He handed a pole to Randy. After tying a hook on the end of the string, he dug a big fat worm out of the can.

Randy took the worm from Daddy's outstretched hand. It felt cold and squirmy. He'd poked at worms in the yard after a rare rain, but he'd never touched one.

"Take the hook with your left hand, and mind that you don't poke yourself," Daddy instructed. "Now, starting with this end of the worm, push it onto the hook."

The worm began to frantically wiggle as Randy tried to push it onto the hook. "No, Daddy, I can't! I'm hurting it."

"Don't be such a sissy!"

He pushed harder, but the worm fought back and somehow managed to work its way out of his hand. In the process, he poked himself with the hook. All morning, he'd managed to be a big boy, but this was too much. Giant baby tears rolled down his cheeks, and he didn't even try to stifle the sobs.

"I want to go home. I want Mama." Blood was dripping from his finger in a steady rhythm, making big plops in the dirt next to the injured worm below.

Daddy didn't say a word. He opened a beer and swigged half of it back in one drink. He turned to Randy and grabbed the wrist of the hand that was bleeding. He squeezed too hard, and Randy felt his bones separate, but he held his breath. He could see he'd pushed Daddy too far.

"No son of mine is gonna be a pussy!" Daddy forced his bleeding finger up and used it like a paintbrush on Randy's face. He marked lines of blood across his cheeks. Squeezing his finger to force more blood out of the tip, Daddy made more lines on Randy's forehead.

Shaking, Randy tried to make sense of Daddy's actions. He quieted himself inside because it was the only way to stop the feelings. Tears made things worse.

"Now, do it again!" Daddy held up a fresh worm.

Randy made himself not think about the worm he was hurting. He was more scared of Daddy than he was of stabbing the creature. When he'd finished, Daddy patted him on the back, and Randy tried to feel happy.

When they got home that afternoon, Mama seemed pleased with the fish they caught. She didn't say a word about Randy's war-paint.

Daddy bragged, "He's quite the little fisherman, Pearlie!"

He smiled for Mama and pretended he had fun. But later that night, he prayed to God to forgive him for killing the worms.

CHAPTER 5

THE TRAP

Pearl knew within a few weeks that she'd made a terrible mistake in letting Wyatt come back. Her father had begged her to rethink her decision, but she hadn't listened.

"Please Ingrid," Papa pleaded, calling her by her given name, "He's a bad man." At that moment, she hadn't wanted to listen, hadn't wanted to look into his saddened eyes.

"It's the right thing, Papa. There's no good place in this world for a divorcee. And the children need a father."

"He has no God in his heart." Papa was devout, even more so since Mama died. Traditional German people, her parents had never felt Wyatt was good enough for their Ingrid Pearl. He didn't work hard enough, save enough, and didn't provide for her in the manner they'd deemed worthy.

"Your ma and pa have it in for me, Pearlie. They always have." Wyatt repeated this phrase often enough to Pearl that she agreed for the sake of peace. "Damned Krauts, think they're better than everybody else."

The month or so that Wyatt was gone was the most peaceful Pearl had known in years. She and the children were just beginning to breathe easier. No longer did they tiptoe around the house for fear of upsetting Wyatt. Little Janie was starting to smile the kind of smile that reached all the way to her eyes.

Papa was helping her make ends meet, at least until she could find work. In the meantime, she set about training Janie and Randy to clean up after themselves. During the month Wyatt was gone, both Janie and Randy celebrated their birthdays. At seven years of age, Janie had quickly become a master dishwasher. Four-year-old Randy tried to keep up.

20

There were moments when Randy asked for his daddy, but they were few and far between. Janie didn't seem to miss him at all. As each day passed, Pearl became more convinced that making Wyatt go had been the right thing to do. Her head was finally clear.

After tucking the children into bed in the evening, Pearl would switch on the radio and listen while she enjoyed an evening cigarette. These were the only real moments that her thoughts turned to Wyatt. Perhaps it had something to do with the quiet of the evening or the romantic music, but she allowed herself to miss him a little.

The evening Wyatt came back, she'd just switched on the radio and placed an ashtray on the kitchen table when she heard a tap at the back door. Wyatt peered through the window, and her heart did a fearful little skip. She hesitated to open the door but realized he could get into the house if he wanted.

"What do you want?" She whispered loudly. *God forbid the children wake up.*

"I just want to talk to you, Pearlie." His eyes sincere, he rubbed the back of his neck as if it ached. He looked thin, and she wondered if he'd been eating his meals or drinking them instead.

"I've got nothing to talk about."

"Please, Pearlie, just a few minutes." He looked worn-out, beaten down like a stray dog.

She'd never seen him this way before, helpless looking and quiet. Twinges of sympathy nibbled at her heart. *Easy girl,* she cautioned to herself, *don't feel too sorry.* She shook her head and said, "No, I don't think so. If you want to talk, come back tomorrow." *When I'll have Papa here.*

He looked around the kitchen, as if to memorize it, and said, "All right, but can I at least get a cup of coffee for the road?"

Pearl shrugged. "I suppose. Stay on the porch, and I'll bring it to you." Every part of her knew she was playing with fire. Yet, she couldn't bring herself to be rude. And if she were to be completely honest, there was a part of her that was curious, even happy to see him. She'd heard not a peep from Wyatt since the day he left. Why was he on her doorstep?

She filled the percolator up with cold water from the tap and placed the basket filled with fresh grounds into the pot. While she waited for the coffee to brew, she lit a cigarette and leaned back against the counter, all the while watching the door. She could see Wyatt pacing the porch. The coffee seemed to take forever to brew.

"Here," she said as she handed the cup of coffee through the opened door.

"Thank you," Wyatt smiled. "Do you mind if I have a smoke?"

"Suit yourself." She stepped inside and pulled the screen door shut.

"Are you sure you don't want to join me? It's nice out here." He looked at her in a way that still made her stomach twirl around. "I'll leave right after," he reassured her.

She supposed if he were going to grab her and strangle her, he would have done so by now. *No harm in one cigarette. I was going to smoke another anyway.*

He was quick to light her cigarette for her, something he'd not done in years. She remembered how glamourous he'd made her feel, like a Hollywood movie star. She smiled and thanked him.

For a few moments, he said nothing, and she thought he might follow through with his promise to go.

"How've you and the children been?"

"Fine." She knew it was best to minimize the small talk. Talking to him was a trap. It always had been.

"Don't you wonder how I've been?"

Too quickly, she answered, "Of course, I do." *Weak girl! Why are you still talking to him?*

"I'm getting by, but I don't think I can go much longer this way." His voice sounded thick. He turned his face toward her, and in the dark, he looked as if he might be crying.

Pearl was entirely unprepared for this. She'd seen Wyatt angry, mean, passionate, drunk, funny, arrogant, softened, but never tearful.

"I miss you and the babies so much it's killing me. I can't stand being away from you. If I could change the past, I would." He wiped at his eyes. "But I reckon I can't change a thing. And now I've gone and lost the one thing that meant the most to me in this whole world."

Stunned, she reached out to comfort him. He leaned into her neck with his face, and she felt warm inside. His familiar scent reminded her of better days. She sank into the moment, letting the cool night air caress them both.

Wyatt turned her face to his and kissed her in a soft, questioning way customarily reserved for brand-new lovers. It was the kind of kiss that makes no assumptions, and Pearl felt a hungry ache in her heart. A small thought occurred to her that she should push him away, but it'd been so long since they'd made love, her physical desires suffocated any sensible notions she possessed.

Pulling her up with him into a standing position, Wyatt pressed her body into his. Even though he'd grown thinner, his shoulders and arms were still muscular from years of working the ranch. His kisses became possessive. The night air beckoned with seductive whispers, sending delicious chills across her shoulders. An orchestra of breaking glass and sleigh bells, the cicadas played their ancient refrain off in the distance.

"Come with me," he whispered in her ear.

"I don't know," she hesitated, "Maybe we shouldn't."

He slipped his hand inside her panties and slid his finger inside of her. Aching and wet, she could feel her body begin to shudder. The craving was almost unbearable. With one arm around her shoulders, he held her steady as he continued to move his finger in and out of her. She groaned as he inserted another finger and started to thrust more forcefully. He covered her cries of pleasure with his mouth when she climaxed moments later.

"My turn," he said as he turned her away from him, motioning for her to lean over the porch railing.

She placed both hands on the rail and tried to steady her spinning head while he slipped her panties down onto the porch floor. The full moon radiated its sacred, silvery glow over the two of them, giving her the sensation they were in another place and time. She gasped as he lapped at her wetness with his tongue.

"Please," she begged, "I want you inside of me."

"God," Wyatt groaned as he entered her, "you're tight." Threading his fingers into the back of her hair, he stroked her head as he pushed into her.

"I've missed you so much." Her voice came out in ragged breaths. She shoved back into him, forcing him to go deeper.

He twisted her hair up with his hand and pumped harder. "Are you still my girl?"

"I'm still your girl," she cried out. The pain from the hair twisting mingled with the pleasure of his cock driving inside of her. Each savage thrust brought her closer to climax, until she felt like an alarm clock, wound too tightly.

"I'm coming," Wyatt moaned.

Frantically, she rubbed her clitoris, and sweet waves of her orgasm crashed over her.

Still inside of her, Wyatt held her hips firmly, keeping her in a bent-over position. Coming to her senses, she tried to upright herself.

"No, stay." He directed her back down with his hand on her shoulder.

"What if one of the children wakes?" Pearl was appalled at her behavior. She couldn't believe she'd allowed him on the porch, never mind in her undies. "And why can't I stand?"

"I want my seed to stay in you. Don't need some other dog sniffing around, trying to mount what's mine."

"Oh God, Wyatt! I'm not a bitch!" She was disgusted and aroused, all at the same time. Chills traveled up and down her spine as she replayed his words.

He chuckled a little and said, "Yes, you are. You're mine."

As they lay in their bed together that night, Wyatt held her close. With one arm under her neck and shoulders and the other hand cupped in between her legs, he slept guarding his seed.

Pearl knew she would never be able to explain to Papa how she came to change her mind about Wyatt.

***

As all newly reformed criminals do, Wyatt behaved perfectly for the first few weeks. He even apologized to Papa.

"I'm sorry for treating your Pearl that way." He extended his hand out to Papa.

Papa eyed his hand but didn't take it. "Well, son, men shouldn't hit on their women. I ain't got no use for ya."

Wyatt nodded in agreement and appeared to be thinking about Papa's words.

"If I had my way, my Ingrid would have nothing to do with ya either." Papa clenched and unclenched his fists as if they were having an argument with themselves about how best to handle Wyatt.

"And I'm a lucky man, sir. I'll do better from now on." Wyatt managed a humble look and added, "I'll treat her like a lady ought to be."

Papa clearly wasn't impressed with Wyatt's display of good behavior, but Pearl allowed herself to hope it was a permanent change. For a short while, they were about as close to Ozzie and Harriet as anyone could get. Although Papa wasn't coming around in protest of her decision, it didn't matter because she was content in their little oasis.

Untested waters often look smooth on the surface. The new and improved Wyatt was a glassy lake with deadly undercurrents.

When Pearl would look back on the day that she realized taking Wyatt back had been a mistake, she would remember the uneasy vibration in her stomach, like the low rumble warning of a thunderstorm off in the distance.

In the moment, however, she was still under the spell of the con.

"Good morning, baby." She smiled at Wyatt and took his coffee cup out of the cupboard. The coffee wasn't finished percolating, so she set about putting creamer and sugar in the cup.

Wyatt sat quietly, leaning back in his chair. His expression was one she couldn't read.

"Did you sleep well?"

He shrugged and said, "I guess."

"I figured you would've slept like a baby after our..." She giggled and continued, "...recreational activities last night."

The new Wyatt should have winked at her and patted her bottom, but instead, he avoided her eyes and continued to gaze toward the back door.

Pearl poured his coffee and placed it in front of him. "Do you have a job today?" Wyatt was a foreman on a construction crew. Since returning home, he'd had more days without work than ever before. She found it odd that there was any scarcity of work with the number of new houses still being built.

"Why do you want to know?"

"Well, I just was curious." Her gut was humming with a warning, but she ignored the sensation. "No reason," she added.

"Maybe you have plans that don't involve me?" Wyatt still didn't make eye contact.

"No, not at all."

"Let me ask you something, Pearlie." Wyatt put his hands flat together in a mock praying position.

Careful to keep her tone soft, she asked, "What is it?"

"Did you have any company while I was away?" He emphasized the word "company" as if it were code for something.

"Just Papa."

"Hm." Wyatt's face was all-knowing, skeptical.

"What's that supposed to mean?" She was stepping into a landmine.

"Just your papa?" He mocked her tone and wiggled his head side to side, making fun of her mannerisms. "Really? No new boyfriends?"

"God, no! Why would you think something like that?" She did her best to hold her tears in, but her eyes weren't cooperating. She hated being on the underside of things with him. Bullets to her heart, his words took her back to dark days.

"I can tell you've been with someone else, Pearlie."

"No," she argued, "I haven't!"

"You want to explain the way you smell?" Wyatt yelled. "You smell like nasty fish."

Stunned beyond words, she couldn't formulate a response.

"And you don't even deny it." Wyatt shook his head and chuckled.

"I swear to you," Pearl implored, "I haven't been with anyone else." Humiliated, she thought about whether she had an odor. Growing up with boy cousins, she'd heard all the disgusting comparisons between tuna and a girl's private parts. Never had she noticed a bad smell. She was careful to keep clean.

"You probably got a VD from your boyfriend." He smirked and nodded his head, agreeing with himself.

"That's crazy talk!" Pearl cried, "How can you even think something so horrible?"

"Because the rotten smell coming from between your legs is proof!" Wyatt slammed his hand down on the table and stood up, shoving the chair backward in the same motion. He lunged toward Pearl and pushed his forehead onto hers.

"Listen carefully," he said, his breath hot on her face. "Go to the doctor and get a pill for whatever nasty disease you caught while you were out whoring. Then keep your damned legs closed unless I'm around."

Not trusting her voice to work, she simply nodded. Arguing or defending herself would only result in more wrath from Wyatt.

In the first days of their marriage, she justified his behavior by telling herself that a lot of men had changed after the war. She thought she could love him enough that his paranoia and distrust would disappear.

Eventually, she stopped analyzing the moments and directed all hope for change into the trash can.

The only reason this false accusation hurt so badly, she told herself, was that she'd allowed herself hope again. *Foolish girl*, she chided.

Although the new, improved Wyatt was gone, Pearl continued to play the happy wife in front of everyone else. She didn't have the strength to hear an "I told you so" from Papa.

CHAPTER 6

BUNNIES

Randy left Daddy alone unless he was called. But nothing made his little four-year-old heart happier than Daddy's attention.

"Come here, son." They'd been outside since the sun's first glimmer. Daddy was clearing a small field to grow feed for their pigs.

Standing by a small cluster of bushes, Daddy pointed down at the base and gestured with his free hand for Randy to hurry.

"Look," Daddy pointed, "it's a rabbit's nest."

Down at the bottom of the bushes was a pile of soft, brown baby bunnies. Randy smiled. "Can I pet them?"

"Sure, but make it quick." Daddy added, "We have a field to clear, and these pests need to go."

Randy didn't give much thought to his father's words. He squatted down and began to stroke the bunny closest to his feet. It was softer than anything he'd ever touched before. The bunny trembled under Randy's hand. "Don't worry, I won't hurt you," he reassured the rabbit.

"Can we keep them?"

"Hell, no! They're a nuisance. They'll be eating your mother's garden if we don't get rid of them." Daddy scratched his scruffy chin and added, "Wish we could find their mother. She'll make ten more before the month's up."

"Who are we gonna give them to?"

"No one," Daddy said. "Come on."

Randy followed Daddy into the tool shed. He poked around on the top shelf while Randy waited at the door. Finally, Daddy found a mallet. "That'll do."

With giant strides through the grass, Daddy cleared a pathway. Randy tried to step in the same places as Daddy, but his legs were too short.

"Here," he motioned for Randy to kneel beside the bunny nest.

"Like this," Daddy said as he smashed the mallet on top of one of the bunnies. To Randy's horror, the rabbit leaped and flopped all around until it was a good two feet outside of the nest.

"No!" Randy screamed.

"Stop being such a baby." Daddy laughed and handed him the hammer. "Your turn."

Randy sobbed, "No, Daddy! Please!"

Daddy's brow scrunched up into a mad face. He forced Randy to hold the hammer by wrapping his hand around Randy's. With a grunt, Daddy lifted Randy's hand and slammed the mallet down on top of another bunny.

Randy crunched his eyes shut tightly, but he could feel the popping of the bunny's head as the hammer made contact. Refusing to open his eyes, he could hear the baby rabbit thrashing around in the grass. When Daddy let go of his hand, he dropped the mallet onto the ground.

"Mama!" Randy began to scream.

"Shut up!" Daddy clapped his hand over his mouth and squeezed until Randy's teeth dug into his cheeks. "Do you hear me?"

Randy nodded his head, and Daddy removed his hand.

"Don't you dare go crying to your mama!" He gave him a little swat on his behind. "Do you understand me?"

"Yes, sir." Randy hiccupped out an answer. By the time Mama called him for lunch, he'd managed to subdue the sobs still left in his chest.

CHAPTER 7

SILENCE THE SONGBIRD

Sitting crisscross in the rays of sunlight streaming through the dormer window, Janie put the book down in her lap and thought about the lovely words she'd just read. The attic was her favorite place in the house. No one bothered her up here. Randy was too scared to venture into the dusty boxes and old furniture, and her parents had no reason to go into the storage space. She'd made a secret hiding place of sorts, cozy with several patchwork quilts and a few cushions she'd swiped from the old sofa in the corner.

She loved the story she was reading. It was about an orphan child, living in an abandoned apartment building. Janie sometimes wished she had no parents.

"Janie, come here, please," Mama yelled from somewhere below.

She sighed but didn't respond. After marking her place, she stood up and made her way through the maze of boxes. Quietly, she tiptoed down the rickety old stairs. Although Mama hadn't forbidden her to go into the attic, Janie hadn't asked for permission.

Luckily, Mama was in the kitchen and didn't see her coming down the attic stairs.

The radio was playing, and Mama was singing along to "If I Knew You Were Comin' I'd've Baked a Cake."

When Janie was smaller, Mama would pick her up and dance around the kitchen to the music. But that was before Randy. After her pest of a brother was born, Mama acted like Janie didn't exist. Ever since Randy came along, Mama only told her to do her chores or brush her teeth.

Mama smiled and said, "Would you like to help me make jam?" She pointed at a big bunch of strawberries sitting on the table. "It's high time you learn how."

"Yes, Mama," Janie said. She loved strawberry jam, and the chance to do something alone with Mama made her happy.

"First, we pick the stems off," Mama plucked a stem with a knife, "just like this." She handed a strawberry and a knife to Janie and said, "You try."

It took several tries to get just the right amount of stem, but soon, she was working steadily alongside Mama. The sweet smell of the strawberries filled the sunny kitchen, making her mouth water.

Her favorite song came on the radio, and she began to sing along.

"That's nice, Janie." Mama smiled and said, "You sure have a pretty voice. I wish you would sing more often."

Janie stopped singing. Mama's praise made her uncomfortable.

"Oh, honey, don't stop," Mama said. "It does my heart good to hear you sing. You used to sing all of the time."

She shrugged her shoulders. There wasn't much to sing about since Daddy came back home.

"What's wrong?" Mama stopped what she was doing and turned to Janie.

"Nothing." Janie focused on the strawberries.

***

She'd wanted to ask why Daddy was back, but she knew Mama would think she was disrespectful. He was bad enough before. Now, he was worse, treating Randy like a little prince.

She knew it was a sin to hate your parents, but Daddy was so mean. Yesterday morning, Janie had accidentally dropped her plate of eggs onto the floor.

"Nice," Daddy scoffed. "Did you get your grace from your mother?"

Mama, washing dishes at the sink, didn't say a word. Daddy's words must make her sad, Janie thought. She began to pick up the pieces of scrambled egg off the floor.

There were a few splats of egg near Randy's chair, so she crawled on her hands and knees underneath the table to pick them up. Randy giggled and swung his feet, landing a sharp kick on the side of Janie's face.

"Hey! That hurt!" Janie protested and rubbed her injured face.

"Sorry." Randy apologized.

She took a deep breath to keep herself from crying. Daddy hated tears, and she didn't want to anger him.

Randy continued to kick his feet and smacked her again, this time plunking his foot right on the top of her head.

"Ouch!" She slapped his shin in reaction. "Stop it!"

Randy started wailing like a baby. "Janie hit me!"

Daddy scooted his chair back and squatted down under the table. He grabbed Janie by her hair and pulled her out from under the table. He yanked her up by her arm and spun her to face him. "What in the hell do you think you're doing?"

Janie froze like a rabbit in a flashlight beam. It was infinitely better to say nothing than to say the wrong thing. Mama stopped washing dishes and turned around to watch.

"What do you think you're doing?" Daddy repeated himself, more loudly this time.

"Randy was kicking me under the table."

"And you just sat there for it?" Daddy asked. "I think you're lying." He swatted Janie on the bottom.

"I'm not lying!" Janie cried, "He really did kick me! Twice!"

"If you're too stupid to get out of the way, then maybe you deserved it!"

"Wyatt!" Mama exclaimed, "That's enough!"

"No, Pearlie, it's not enough," Daddy sneered. "She's had it in for him since the boy was born. She's jealous! And it ain't pretty on her."

Randy's fake cries had died off. He looked pleased. Ever since he'd been following Daddy around, he hadn't been very nice.

"Come on, son." Daddy motioned for Randy to get up. "Let's go. We've got work to do."

Mama had turned back to her dishes, and Janie had finished picking up her mess. She'd wished Mama would soothe her, hug her, and tell her that she was sorry for Daddy's harsh ways. But Mama acted as if nothing had happened. So, Janie did the same thing she always did. She pretended to be okay.

32

CHAPTER 8

UNTOUCHABLE

The smell coming from the kitchen was delicious. Randy's tummy complained and grumbled about the empty feeling. Mama had told him to stay out until they finished the jam. Janie was lucky. Mama never asked him to help with anything.

"Mama?" Randy called from the sofa. He was supposed to be coloring a picture for the refrigerator. That was what Mama always told him to do when she thought he was in the way. He was getting tired of coloring, and besides, Mama almost never put his pictures up. When she didn't answer, he called again, "Mama?"

"What, Randy?" She used her frustrated voice. "What do you want?"

He took this as an invitation to get off the couch. Peeking into the kitchen, he asked, "When's lunch? I'm starving to death."

"Not for another hour or so," Mama said. "You'll just have to wait. The kitchen is tied up right now."

Janie looked over her shoulder at Randy and popped a strawberry into her mouth. She gave him a mean little smile and turned back to the work she was doing.

"Can I help?" Randy thought it was worth a try. Perhaps he could sneak a berry or two.

Janie took another berry while Mama wasn't looking. She smirked at Randy and chewed it slowly.

Mama sighed, "No, honey, you'll just be in the way. Go find something to do."

"But Janie's eating strawberries! Why can't I have some?"

"Go now!" Mama put her left hand on her hip and pointed toward the back door with her right. Whenever she did this, he knew she meant business.

"All right," he mumbled. He could hear Janie giggle as he pulled the door closed behind him. *What a meanie.*

The bright morning sun hurt his eyes, and his cramping tummy made him feel worse. He didn't have any great ideas about what to do. Daddy was at work, and he'd already played with his trucks that morning.

He shuffled around the yard for a bit in search of something to make the time pass until lunch. The shady spot near Mama's garden was one of his favorite places. He plopped himself down onto the grass underneath the best tree. Even though it was morning, the early summer sun was making him hot and sticky.

A busy ant pile at his feet caught his attention. He wondered what the grainy hill looked like underneath, so he found a small twig and began to scrape off the top. The ants scurried about frantically, and he felt a twinge of excitement. He pretended he was a big giant, attacking a village of helpless people.

"Rah!" He roared as he scraped the stick across a line of ants. "You can run, but you can't get away from me!"

The ants continued their escape route, leaving behind the dead ones. Randy made a game of smashing as many ants as possible. When he'd tired of playing the giant, he stood up and kicked the rest of the anthill flat with the toe of his shoe.

His attention went back to his empty tummy and to Janie, who was eating all the berries she wanted. Randy started to feel mad again.

He noticed the garden gate wasn't latched, so he went over to close it. At the edge, a rabbit perched on its haunches and munched on the newly sprouted plants. He remembered Daddy telling him rabbits would destroy Mama's garden. He imagined how proud Daddy would be if he killed it. His stomach churned at the thought of the baby bunnies.

Maybe I could just chase it away, he thought. There were a few loose bricks next to the walking path that Mama had been creating. He picked one up and chucked it toward the rabbit, hitting a plant instead. Startled by the brick, the bunny ran toward the fence and froze. Randy ran at the rabbit and yelled a battle cry.

The panicked rabbit finally found the open gate and escaped. Randy felt pleased he'd gotten rid of the rabbit without having to kill it. He made sure to latch the gate when he left the garden.

Confident he'd allowed enough time for Mama to finish the jam, he went inside to see if lunch was ready yet.

***

"Do you want to build a fort with me after we eat?" Janie surprised Randy by talking to him. Ever since Daddy moved back home, she'd barely said two words to him.

He studied her face, trying to figure out if Janie was serious. A few days ago, she'd offered a piece of candy, only to clamp her hand shut as he reached for it. Daddy spanked her for teasing him, which only made Janie angry at Randy.

She looked serious enough.

"Okay," he said.

After a minor argument about the best place, they'd agreed on a shady spot in the tree line. They sorted through a pile of wood salvaged from an old shed Grandpa had torn down. One by one, they tugged the boards over to the spot they'd chosen for the fort.

"Don't we need nails and a hammer?" Randy asked.

"No." Janie shook her head. "I have an idea." She smiled and said, "Remember the Lincoln Logs we got for Christmas? That's how we'll do it." She added, "Then, we can take it down if we want to."

They worked together for several hours. The fort was almost as tall as Janie when Mama called for them.

"Who did this?" Red-faced, Mama pointed at the broken plant in the garden.

"Not me," said Janie.

"Not me," Randy echoed.

"One of you is lying. Bricks don't just magically catapult themselves onto a tomato plant!"

"I swear it wasn't me," Janie said with conviction.

Randy didn't say anything.

"Come here." Mama wiggled her finger at him. "I know it was you. Did it make you happy to break my tomato plant?"

"No, Mama. I was trying to kill a rabbit that was going to eat your garden."

"You're lying to me, and I won't tolerate it." She spun him around and proceeded to plant several wallops on his backside. "Go inside and sit in your room. You're grounded."

He stomped through the yard toward the house. The low rumble of Daddy's truck coming up the drive reached his ears as he opened the screen door.

"Daddy!" Relieved, Randy ran to meet him.

"What's the matter?" Daddy asked, "Why are you crying?"

"Mama spanked me 'cause I was protecting the garden."

"Really?" Daddy picked him up. "Let's go find your mama."

Mama was in the garden, kneeled, pulling weeds. She looked up at Daddy. "Hi honey, how was your morning?"

"What's this business about Randy getting a swat for protecting the garden?" Daddy's mouth narrowed down to a thin line.

"He got a spanking for destroying a tomato plant." She stood up and brushed the dirt off her knees. "Chucked a brick right at it—broke it in half," she added.

"Is that true, son?"

"No," Randy said. "I was trying to kill the rabbit that was going to eat Mama's garden."

"And you spanked him for that?" Daddy raised one eyebrow at Mama. "Did you think that was wise?"

Mama's pink face turned three shades darker. "Honestly, Wyatt! You're questioning me like I'm the child!"

Daddy snorted out a dry laugh. "Maybe you should stop acting like a child." He sat Randy down. "If you want this boy to grow up into a man, you'll stop henpecking him over foolish things like this. From now on, you go through me if you think Randy needs punishment."

She opened her mouth, as if she were going to argue, then closed it. Her face looked like she had a sunburn.

"Fine," she said, "but I don't know how he's going to learn respect if everything has to go through you. You're not here half the time."

"He'll learn respect because someone with a solid head will be in charge of his rearing."

Randy didn't understand everything Daddy just said, but he knew Mama was in trouble. And he knew Mama couldn't spank him anymore.

CHAPTER 9

SPARE THE ROD

A mild panic had been shadowing her for days. Wyatt had made it crystal clear she wasn't supposed to exercise any real authority over her own son. Beyond reproach, Randy seemed to be testing her at every turn.

Papa waited until Wyatt was gone for the day before he stopped for his weekly visit. Since his retirement, he had a great deal of free time, so his visits were lengthy. Pearl didn't mind.

"Randy, Janie," Pearl called, "your grandpapa is here to see you."

Two sets of feet thumped down the staircase. The children were supposed to be cleaning their room.

"Grandpa!" Janie cried. Papa was the only person Janie lit up for lately. She threw her arms around him and kissed his cheek.

Papa chuckled, "There's my girl." He hugged her and said, "Okay little lady, let your brother have a turn."

Randy was less enthusiastic than his sister. "Hi, Grandpa."

"Well, come on then," Papa said. "Give your old papa a hug."

He let Papa hug him, then backed away. Papa raised an eyebrow at Pearl, and she shrugged her shoulders. Later, when the children weren't around to hear, she'd tell Papa about Wyatt's new demand. The last thing she needed was for Randy to repeat a conversation to Wyatt.

"Did you bring me anything?" Janie asked, her eyes eager and shiny.

"Let's see," Papa said as he dug around in his pocket. "What do we have here?" He pulled out several wrapped peppermint candies and held his palm out.

Janie hesitated, and Randy grabbed both pieces. Papa looked stunned.

"No, no, son! You have to share with your sister." Papa frowned.

Randy tucked his hands behind his back, his face smug.

"Not fair!" Janie complained, "Give it back!" She reached for his hands to get her piece of candy.

Randy turned his back the other direction and laughed. They scuffled around for a few moments before Papa yelled, "That's enough!"

"Children! Stop this instant!" Pearl was embarrassed. "Your grandpapa was nice enough to bring you candy, and now you're both acting foolish."

"No," Papa corrected her, "Randy is acting foolish."

He leaned forward, tipping Randy's chin up to force his attention. "That's no way to behave, son."

"Fine! I don't want your stupid candy anyway!" Randy threw the mints down at Papa's feet. He defiantly crossed his arms and glared at Janie.

Pearl gasped and clutched her hand to her chest. "Randy! Apologize to your grandpapa."

"No, I don't have to." Randy yelled, "You can't make me!"

"Go to your room!"

"No!" He stomped his feet. "I don't want to."

"Ingrid Pearl!" Papa exclaimed, "Don't let him speak to you this way!"

The screen door made a big bang as Randy shoved his way through it. Pearl didn't try to stop him.

"Why don't you just swat him, Ingrid? You can't let the child act like that." Papa's face was a picture of confusion.

"It's complicated." She argued in her head whether to tell Papa about Wyatt's new rule.

"Daddy won't let Mama spank him." Janie blurted out the truth.

"That's ridiculous!" Papa looked at Pearl, then back at Janie. "Is this true?"

She nodded her head and put both hands over her face to try to cork the tears that were threatening to spill.

"I've never heard of such a thing! How're you supposed to raise a young man without spanking him?" Papa asked. "How are you supposed to teach him right from wrong?"

"I don't know," Pearl cried. "The worst part is Randy knows I can't punish him. I've got about as much control over him as Janie does."

"Sit, Ingrid." Papa patted at the table in front of an empty chair. "Janie, will you please let me talk with your mama alone?"

"Okay, Grandpapa." She gave him a tight hug and left the kitchen.

"Ingrid," Papa said, "I'm trying to stay out of your business." He patted her clasped hands, which were resting on the table in front of her. "I know you want me to think your marriage is perfect."

She didn't bother to protest. Putting up a front was tiring. She was exhausted.

"But," he continued, "it's one thing if you aren't happy and quite another if your children aren't being raised right." Papa squeezed her hands. "Little ones need discipline, and Randy ain't gettin' none of that. You're creating a monster."

"Not me," she vehemently shook her head. "If I had my way, he'd get a good wallop now and then." She pulled her hands away from Papa's and rested her forehead on her palms. "I'm not sure how to make Wyatt see."

"You're not going to make Wyatt see. He's an arrogant fool." Papa pointed at Pearl. "And you're not gonna change him. He's got no business having a family."

Just days before, she would have argued with him, would have defended Wyatt. But that was before he took away her fundamental rights as a mother. She pressed her fingers into her temples to ease the sharp pain in her head. Something had to change, but she didn't have the energy to deal with it right now.

CHAPTER 10

THE DANCE

Summer had seemed to last forever for Janie. The school year couldn't start soon enough. Most of her classmates were the opposite, groaning and moaning about summer's end. Although Janie didn't belong with the other kids, the school provided a break from the darkness at home. Daddy had lost his job mid-summer, and their home had become a scary place.

Janie did her best to stay hidden when he was home. She wasn't sure if it was better when he was drinking or sober. Drunk Daddy was affectionate, loud, and volatile. Sober Daddy was hungover and angry. At least when he was sober, he ignored her, so long as she stayed out of his way.

"Janie," Daddy yelled, "come dance with us." The radio was as loud as she'd ever heard it. "Rag Mop," one of her favorite songs, was playing.

She put her pillow over her head to drown out the noise and hoped he'd forget that he'd called for her. Tired from her first week of school, she'd tucked herself into bed while it was still daylight.

"Janie!" Daddy repeated himself.

She sighed and threw her covers off. There was no use in pretending to be asleep. She slid her feet into her house slippers and shuffled downstairs. The table and chairs had been shoved against the back wall of the large kitchen. Mama was dancing around with Randy, just like she used to do with her.

"Come on, Janie," Daddy held out his hand. "Dance with me." To her surprise, he picked her up and swung her around. One of her house slippers flew off her foot, but she didn't say anything about it. Daddy's breath smelled like booze. It was a smell that she used to like until she'd figured out what it meant.

The song changed to "Chattanoogie Shoe Shine Boy," and Daddy put Janie down. "Like this, Janie." Daddy tapped his feet to the beat, expecting her to follow.

She hesitated. Dancing was hard for her. At recess, other girls bopped around, showing off their fancy footwork. Janie had tried to join in before but gave up because she couldn't seem to make her feet move in the right way. Rather than risk embarrassment, she pretended not to care.

"Come on!" Daddy said.

"I can't." She didn't move her feet.

"Of course, you can! Don't be a ninny!" She could hear the impatience in his voice. Tightening his grip on her hands, he swayed her back and forth, causing her to lose her balance.

"You need to loosen up!" Daddy reached for the glass sitting on the counter. "Here, take a drink."

She obeyed, forcing down the bitter liquor. It burned up into her nose and all the way down into her tummy.

"Wyatt! No!" Mama said, "She's not old enough. You'll make her sick."

"She'll be fine, Pearlie. What do you think cough syrup is made of?" He rolled his eyes.

The room spun around a little, and Janie began to feel warm inside. She paid attention to Daddy's footsteps and tried to mimic him. There seemed to be no real pattern to what he was doing. It was hard to predict his next move and even more difficult to stay out of his path.

"Ouch!" She cried out when he stomped on her bare foot.

"Well, move your feet!" Daddy said.

"I'm trying," she said.

"Come on, Pearlie," Daddy said. "Let's show your clumsy girl how it's done." He grabbed Mama's hands and proceeded to move his feet in the same erratic fashion that he had while dancing with Janie.

Mama stumbled and laughed. "I'm not sure what dance we're doing."

"Swing dance, Pearlie." Daddy snorted, "I guess I know where Janie gets her dance moves from." He let go of Mama's hands and took his half-full glass off the counter. He swigged the liquor down in one big gulp.

Mama's cheeks and ears burned red. "It's not me. You've had too much to drink."

"*I've* had too much?" Daddy's voice raised a little. "I think *you've* had too much, and it's causing you to dance like shit."

Janie's stomach stirred, and she moved over to stand next to Randy, ready to whisk him away. Randy leaned into Janie's side.

"Right, Randy?" Daddy asked, "Isn't Mama dancing like shit?"

Eyes opened wide; Randy slowly nodded his head.

Janie wanted to defend Mama, but she kept her mouth shut. She felt a little angry with Randy for agreeing with Daddy.

"Let's show 'em how to dance." Daddy picked Randy up and rocked back and forth with him in an awkward manner. Randy laughed and stuck his tongue out at Janie.

Mama looked mad but kept quiet. She poured more liquor into her coffee cup and lit a cigarette with shaking hands.

The song faded away, and Mama turned the volume down on the radio. "Janie, Randy, go to bed."

"No," Daddy slurred, "we're just starting to have fun. Aren't we, buddy?"

Randy looked at Mama as if he were unsure about the right way to respond.

"Go on," Mama said. "It's bedtime."

Janie tugged on Randy's hand, and to her relief, he followed her.

"Wait, I need to brush my teeth," Randy said as Janie was pulling his covers back.

"No. Do it in the morning. You're so stupid, sometimes. Can't you tell that they're about to start fighting?"

Small and powerless to stop the battle, she covered her head with her pillow, but the hollow echoes of Mama and Daddy's voices cut through the fabric.

"Janie," Randy yanked on her sleeve.

She took the pillow off her head. "What?" she whispered.

"Can I sleep with you?"

She pulled her blankets back and motioned for him to crawl into bed.

Randy sucked his thumb. If Daddy were to see that, he'd spank Randy for sure. Janie thought about telling him to take his thumb out but decided it didn't matter. Daddy wasn't coming upstairs any time soon. He was too busy fighting with Mama.

She lay awake, praying to God for Mama's safety and waiting for Randy to fall asleep so she could pull his thumb out of his mouth. Maybe if she'd danced better, Daddy would still be in a good mood.

Lulled into an exhausted sleep by imagining the endless possibilities of a bad outcome for Mama, Janie startled awake whenever one of their voices reached an exceptionally high volume. A cycle of dozing off and being frightened awake continued for hours. Eventually, the fighting died down, and Janie slipped into a deep, paralyzing sleep.

At first, Janie wasn't sure whether she was dreaming or awake. It was the kind of dream that meshed into the moonlit bedroom, just as it was. The door opened slowly, revealing the outline of a man. She closed her eyes, willing the figure away.

Quiet footsteps approached the side of her bed and then stopped. Janie breathed slow and shallow. She said a silent prayer for the man to disappear, but she could feel him standing there, even without opening her eyes.

Randy was lifted away from her side, leaving a cold and empty space. She opened her eyes and watched Daddy carry him to his bed. Her nose itched, but Janie didn't dare scratch it until Daddy was gone. Doing her best to look as if she were sleeping, Janie waited for him to leave.

The smell of liquor on his breath hit her nostrils before she felt him pull the covers up around her shoulders. He rubbed her back softly. Out of instinct, she stiffened up. Janie wasn't used to an affectionate touch from Daddy.

"*Shhh*," he whispered and kissed her forehead. "Sleep tight, angel." He gently stroked her hair several times before leaving her bedroom.

Of all the memories that would stand out in her future, this one would remain clear. Her heart would always ache for this Daddy, the one who had tenderly kissed her good night.

CHAPTER 11

FAULT

Pearl knew she should've just ignored Wyatt's insults. If she'd been completely sober, that's precisely what she would've done. The whiskey, with the added humiliation of Wyatt forcing the children to participate, caused her innate restraint to disappear into thin air.

"You embarrassed me, Wyatt! Why are you treating me that way in front of them?" She'd barely waited until the children left the room before confronting him.

"You embarrassed yourself!" He laughed and poured himself another glass of whiskey.

"Stop doing that to me! You're purposely humiliating me in front of the children!" She couldn't swallow the lump in her throat. "How am I supposed to react?"

"Try acting like a grown woman, for a change." He added, "And, stop being so thin-skinned."

Afterward, she lay in bed alone for hours. Ears ringing from the copious amount of whiskey she'd consumed, she wallowed in a swirling mass of guilt and fear. What if she'd gone too far this time? What if he left her for good? Maybe she had been too sensitive and stubborn.

For reasons that made no sense to her now, Pearl had felt the need to continue the argument. Ridiculous, she thought, to try to prove him wrong. They'd been two drunks fighting, both trying to one-up the other. In the end, she always lost. She didn't stand a chance. He was bigger and stronger.

She replayed the scuffle in her mind, trying to recreate the part right before he hit her, wanting to understand how it got to that point. Next time, she wouldn't let it get that far.

Only the humming of the refrigerator broke the stillness of the night. She suppressed the urge to get up and look for him. Humiliation and fear kept her in bed. Hopefully, he'd come to her soon and want to make love. Sometimes, that fixed everything.

The liquor still coursing through her veins produced a torturous state of exhausted wakefulness. Every time she closed her eyes, the room twisted around on her. Her head was beginning to throb, and her mouth felt like she'd just sprayed Stopette in it.

Eventually, the room steadied itself, and she dozed off.

***

When she awoke, mid-morning sun filled the bedroom. For one peaceful moment, she didn't remember the previous night. Her pounding head quickly reminded her of the stupid fight she and Wyatt had.

She sat up slowly and ordered her stomach to hold onto its contents. Thankfully, the bathroom was only steps away. After vomiting, Pearl splashed cold water on her face and brushed her teeth. She sat down on the toilet seat to give her racing heart a chance to calm down. *I must smell like a drunken bum.*

Hesitating to use the last of her favorite perfume for such an occasion, she sprayed a cloud of it on her hair and neck to camouflage the stench. After running a comb through her disheveled hair, she powdered her nose. She wanted to look better than she felt.

"Well, well, she's alive." Wyatt greeted her as she entered the kitchen. "Coffee's ready."

"Thank you." She didn't trust herself to say more. The morning could go either way. At this point, it was entirely up to Wyatt.

"How'd you sleep?"

"Fine." She lied. "How about you?"

Smirking, he taunted, "Wouldn't you like to know?"

Ignoring his jab, she asked Randy, "Are you hungry, baby?"

"He's already eaten." Wyatt said, "That's what good parents do. They feed their children."

His words dashed any hope that she might've had for a peaceful day. The sink was still full of dirty dishes from the night before. Relieved to have a distraction, she filled the dish tub with hot water and began to scrub the crusted plates.

After she'd finished washing the dishes, she turned her attention to the rest of the house. She'd nearly gotten through the first floor when she realized she hadn't seen Janie yet.

"Janie," she yelled, "come here, please."

Pearl finished dusting the bookshelf, and still, there was no sign of Janie. She squirted more polish onto her dusting cloth and wiped the handrail as she went upstairs to check on her.

"Janie?" Pearl leaned her head into the children's bedroom. Janie's bed was tidy. Strange for a Saturday morning, she thought. She usually had to remind Janie.

Randy's bed was a mess, so she tightened the sheets and smoothed his bedspread. Next, she ran the cloth over both headboards and their chest of drawers. Drawings and handwriting practice covered the top of Janie's desk. Carefully, she gathered the papers into a stack and wiped the desktop.

The drawing on the top of the stack caught her attention as she placed the papers back onto the desk. Too sophisticated to be Randy's artwork, it was a picture of a little girl with blonde pigtails. Instead of the usual sun in the corner, the sky was full of black clouds and raindrops. On the girl's chest was a big heart with a jagged line down the middle of it. She considered taking the picture but didn't.

"Janie," she yelled, "Where are you?"

Pearl stood quiet for a moment, straining her ears for the sound of Janie's reply. The house remained silent.

Hoping to see her, Pearl looked out of the window overlooking the garden and tree swing, but the yard was empty.

"What, Mama?" Janie startled her, suddenly appearing in the doorway. Still wearing her pajamas, she held a book in one hand.

"Where were you?"

"In the attic, reading." She'd been crying. Her red eyes and nose gave it away.

"You know I don't like it when you go in there! It's full of spiders and dust."

"I'm sorry."

The hangover prevented her from properly scolding Janie. She was in too much pain to deal with the inevitable tears.

"It's okay." She patted Janie's head and said, "Let's go round up something for lunch."

"Is Daddy home?"

"Yes, but don't worry," she reassured her. "There will be no more arguing today."

CHAPTER 12

1951

Two big things happened to Randy that fall. He started school, and he found out he was going to be a big brother. Going to kindergarten was exciting. He wasn't quite as happy about the news of a baby brother or sister.

***

"Mama!" He had yelled for her two times already that morning. Usually, she appeared at his bedside with a cup of hot cocoa and a hug. Lately, she'd been ignoring him, and he wasn't happy about it.

"Oh, for heaven's sake!" She appeared in his doorway, her cheeks flushed, and her hair stuck to her damp forehead. "What? What do you need?"

"I'm awake!"

"So, get up!" She yanked open his chest of drawers and pulled out a pair of trousers and a white shirt. "You know what to do! You have legs, don't you?"

"Where's my hot chocolate?" He remained under the covers.

"Downstairs, with your breakfast." She glared at him with a look that said he'd better not mess around, or else.

"Fine." He huffed and puffed and threw his bed covers back in an exaggerated fashion.

"Get dressed, and don't mess around." She tossed his clothing on the bed and left the room. Her footsteps made banging sounds the entire way down the stairs.

It didn't take him long to get ready for school, in part because he didn't play around, but mostly because he skipped brushing his hair and teeth.

Janie, of course, beat him to the breakfast table. A boy on the bus had called her a "goody-two-shoes," and although Randy hadn't heard that phrase before, he understood what the boy meant. His sister always followed the rules, and she was always first.

Everyone thought Janie was so great. Except for Daddy. Sometimes Janie made Daddy mad.

"Didn't you brush your hair?" Mama stood above him with a plate of biscuits and gravy.

"Yes, ma'am."

"You're lying," Janie said.

"No, I'm not!" He hated her the most of all when she tattled on him.

"Well, your hair doesn't look brushed." Mama put the plate back on the counter. "Go fix it." She pointed toward the stairs.

"Fine." He shoved the chair away and stomped out of the kitchen. Along the way, he kicked Janie in the shin.

"Ow!" She yipped and rubbed her leg. "You did that on purpose!"

"Randy! Come back here now!" Mama ordered him back to the kitchen. She squatted down and waited for him.

"Yes, ma'am." He covered his hind end to shield it from the spanking he was about to get.

Instead, she put her right hand on his shoulder. "Son, I need you to act like a big boy." She smiled and asked, "Can you guess why?"

"Because I'm going to school now?" he asked.

"No, honey. Because you're going to be a big brother." She raised her eyebrows and grinned. "I'm growing a baby in my tummy, and it makes me very tired. I'm going to need a lot of help from you and Janie."

She tousled his hair and said, "Now, go brush your hair. Breakfast will be waiting for you when you're done."

Later that evening, while he and Daddy were out feeding the animals, he asked, "Did you know Mama has a baby in her belly?"

Daddy laughed. "Is that right?"

"Yup. She needs my help now 'cause the baby makes her tired." He felt proud when he told his father about his new responsibility.

"Well, son, being tired while bearing children is a woman's punishment from the Lord." Daddy shook his head in disbelief. "Your mama shouldn't be complaining about it. And she sure doesn't need any help. Sounds like pure laziness to me."

Randy wasn't sure what laziness was, but he didn't want any of it. And if the new baby meant Mama was too tired to bring his hot cocoa in the mornings, then he didn't want the new baby either.

CHAPTER 13

THE HANGOVER

At first, she'd been sure the queasy feeling was a side effect from all the booze she'd been drinking. Wyatt liked his liquor, and for reasons she didn't completely understand, she wanted to keep up with him. And, when he was home drinking with her, she could keep her eye on him.

With a full hour left before she needed to be awake, Pearl lay in the dark, trying to ignore the vomit gurgling in the pit of her stomach. She'd stayed up too late again, but at least they'd had fun for a change. The hangover after a good time was much easier to handle than the aftermath of a drunken fight.

The wooden floor was chilly under her bare feet. Fall nights were a real treat compared to the sticky summer variety. She closed the bathroom door before turning on the light. It was bad enough to be wide awake at this early hour. The last thing she needed was to have both children awake, too.

In the dingy overhead light, she could see the toll all the late nights had taken on her light pink complexion. She leaned close to the mirror and examined her face. Sunken and dark underneath, her eyes were bloodshot.

The smell of the cold cream soothed her turning stomach as she wiped off the makeup she'd left on the night before. She brushed her teeth with mint toothpaste and felt even better. A smile touched her lips when she thought about the last part of their evening.

She loved it when he was like that—passionate, wild, possessive. She ran a brush through her tangled hair, replaying their lovemaking in her mind. They were in a good spell. It could last a week, a month, or a season. She'd stopped trying to predict. Instead, she'd learned to just enjoy it while it lasted.

Thankfully, they hadn't started their little party until after she'd cleaned up the dinner mess the night before. The only thing worse than waking up early with a hangover was waking up early, still sloshed, to a sink full of dirty dishes.

This morning called for strong coffee. She filled the pot with cold tap water and put three heaping scoops of coffee in the basket. The matches weren't in their regular spot next to the stove, so she rummaged around for a bit in the junk drawer, hoping to find another box.

Cigarettes, she thought—the matches will be with the cigarettes. She laughed at her forgetfulness. *Jeez, maybe I was more soused than I thought.*

On the back porch, neatly stacked atop one another, was a box of matches and a pack of Lucky Strikes. She grabbed the cigarettes and matches off the rail and went back inside.

She slid open the matchbox to find only one remaining. Damnit, she thought, I need this to light the stove. With her left hand, she pushed the burner knob into the ignite position while lighting it with the right hand. She jumped at the whoosh of the fire, even though she knew it was coming.

Before placing the pot on the stove, she put a cigarette in her mouth and leaned over to light it with the burner. Inhaling deeply, she made sure the cigarette was lit before she stood back up.

That was the moment she knew. The smoke tasted awful, just like when she was first pregnant with Janie.

CHAPTER 14

THE CHANGELING

"Oh my God, Pearl," Betty said, making a big deal, waving her hands around. "Are you sure?" She had stopped filing away at her blood-red fingernail and glared at her with an exaggerated expression of shock.

"No, I'm not sure." Betty's reaction irritated her. "I can't remember the date of my last period. It's entirely possible I just have a doozy of a hangover."

Betty laughed. "I keep a hawk-eye on mine." She waved her finger and said, "The last thing I want is a baby."

"Honestly, it's not something I'm hoping for either, but what am I supposed to do about it?"

She wasn't ready. Janie and Randy took everything she had. No one had warned her that having children would empty her so completely.

"Well, you could get rid of it." Betty opened her cigarette case and held it out to offer Pearl one.

Pearl shook her head. "They've been making me sick. Can't stand the taste right now."

"Do you mind if I smoke?"

"No, go ahead. It's only the taste that bothers me."

Betty pursed her perfect, red lips around her cigarette and flicked the lighter. Sucking in, she closed her eyes for a moment, her face an image of ecstasy. Jet black hair, milky white skin, and ice-blue eyes, Betty was the physical opposite of Pearl. Wyatt proclaimed to hate Betty, but Pearl had caught him eyeing her curves more than once when he'd thought she wasn't looking.

She trusted Betty, but Wyatt, not quite as much. It wouldn't be a grand surprise if he thought he'd have an edge with her since her bum of a husband ran off. He'd have to get in line behind everyone else. It was no secret Betty dated lots of different men.

Pearl didn't care what the town's busybodies had to say. Betty had been her best friend since the eighth grade.

"Think about it," Betty continued, "you just got Janie and Randy off to school." She flicked her ashes into the crystal tray sitting in front of her. "Do you honestly want to do it all over again?"

"It's not that I don't love my children—"

"I know you do," Betty interrupted, "but you barely survived Randy. And Wyatt was no help." She held her palms out in a stopping motion and said, "Look, you weren't yourself after Randy. I wasn't sure either one of you was going to survive the baby blues. I was there for enough of it to wonder if they should cart you off to the loony bin."

Betty smashed out her cigarette and glared at her. "Lord, Pearl, why weren't you using a diaphragm, or rubbers?"

Miserable, Pearl rubbed her eyes with the palms of her hands and said, "The diaphragm didn't fit right after Randy was born, and Wyatt hates rubbers. I meant to get refitted but never got around to it."

"You have to decide quickly, honey." Her voice was softer, sympathetic. "If you wait too long, getting rid of it my way won't be possible." She rubbed Pearl's arm. "I'm not trying to pressure you. I just remember how bad it was."

She wanted nothing more than to forget that time. It had been worse than bad.

**

1946

Piercing cries shattered the thin film of sleep she floated on. Disoriented and sweating, her heart raced as she tried to make sense of the frantic shrieks coming from the other room.

Out of habit, she looked at the alarm on the nightstand, but it was still so dark, she couldn't make out the time. No matter because she couldn't remember when she'd last fed the baby. It felt like she'd just fallen asleep. *He never stops!*

Wyatt was lying in the same position as when he'd gone to sleep, snoring and oblivious to the baby's screams. She hated him at that moment. That night, just like every other night for the previous three weeks, had been the same. Pearl was up every two hours while he slept like a log.

Miraculously, Janie was sleeping, undisturbed by the baby's cries. At three years old, it wasn't odd for her to still wake through the night.

Pearl caught her pinky toe on the rocking chair next to the baby's bed and suppressed the urge to yell. Cursing under her breath, she rubbed her wounded toe.

The baby lay on his back, flailing around. In the dark, his gaping mouth and angry face looked nothing like the infant she'd birthed three weeks before. She hesitated, remembering a story about a changeling, a troll baby exchanged for a human infant. *Nonsense.*

She picked him up and held him to her chest. He rooted around, searching for her breast. Pearl sat in the rocking chair and had barely opened her gown before Randy latched on to her nipple. He nursed like he was starving to death. Rocking back and forth, she stroked his downy head. Pearl felt some of her tension dissipate.

Fighting to keep her eyes open, she moved Randy to nurse the other breast. He fussed a little, then settled in, swallowing more slowly this time.

"Time to burp," she whispered. Placing him over her shoulder, she rubbed his back until he'd let out a few big bubbles.

Belly full, eyes closed, the baby was almost asleep. She debated whether to change his diaper or to put him in bed.

Laying him down didn't cause him to wake. Carefully, Pearl eased up his nightgown to his waist and unpinned his diaper. *Only wet, lucky me.*

Holding his legs up, she slid the soaked diaper out, replaced it with a dry one, and pinned it. Not wanting to push her luck, she left his gown above his waist and covered him with a heavy quilt to shield against the night air.

The light coming in through the bedroom window was just turning from black to gray. One more hour of sleep, she prayed as she pulled the covers up over her shoulders.

She drifted off to sleep, much like a feather floating to the floor. She had almost gone all the way down when the baby's frantic yowls interrupted her lovely descent.

Furious, Pearl shoved the bedcovers back and planted her feet onto the floor in one motion. She didn't wait for the room to stop spinning before stomping into the baby's bedroom.

Yanking Randy out of bed, she slammed him into her chest with a tight bear hug. "What is wrong with you?" She squeezed. "Why are you doing this to me?" She patted his back as if she were burping him, only much harder. *Thud, thud, thud.* The sound was horrible.

Little starts of cries came out of his mouth, but he couldn't get enough air to complete them.

A little part of her brain was aware that her vision had dimmed, that she was out of control. Her heart thumped wildly in her chest, and images of throwing the rocking chair out of the window rushed through her head.

Stop squeezing him! She listened to the small voice in her head and loosened her grip. He took one big gasp of air and let out a horrifying shriek, unlike anything she'd ever heard.

"*Shhh, shhh.*" Scared Wyatt would find them, she tried to soothe him, but he continued to scream at the top of his lungs. The more she looked at him, the less he looked like her baby, the less he looked like a human infant. He was frightening.

Oh God, this isn't my baby! Something is wrong with him! He's been changed! She wasn't sure if she'd cried the words aloud or if she'd just screamed them in her head.

Pearl knew she had to get rid of him. He was a danger to her and Janie. To keep him from waking everyone in the house, she smashed his monstrous, little face into the crook of her neck. She could feel his mouth open, gasping for air against the tight seal of her skin. He kicked his legs with a strength that surprised her for his size—more proof that he wasn't human.

"For fuck's sake!" Wyatt's shouting startled her. "What in the hell are you doing? Give me my son!" He yanked the baby from her, and Randy gasped and screeched, terrified.

Pearl crouched in the corner, trying to make sense of what had just happened, of what she'd done. Disconnected from herself, from the room, she watched Wyatt lay the still-screaming creature in his bed.

Only when Wyatt turned around did Pearl feel any fear beyond the baby. She crouched lower to escape his reach, but he grabbed her hair and yanked her to her feet, pulling her inches from his distorted face.

"You crazy bitch! What in the fuck were you doing?" Spittle sprayed out of his mouth, and his chest heaved up and down. "Are you trying to kill him?" He shook her back and forth; his left hand still twisted up in her hair.

"He's not our son!" She begged him to understand, but her words made no difference. Pearl didn't bother to shield herself from the blows. She didn't care. She wanted to die.

"Mama!" Janie's frightened voice rang out in the darkness before she completely faded away.

Someone sat beside her bed. Because her eyes were too swollen to open, she wasn't sure who it was. But she could feel them, the way one senses a wall in the dark without touching it. She lay quiet for a time, hours perhaps, listening to the sound of her blood rushing in and out of her brain. Her wounds throbbed with each beat of her heart. *Pain that I deserve.*

She'd never been smaller in her life. There was barely anything left. Pearl wondered if it was possible just to let go and stop breathing.

"Here," Betty said, soft and low, "take a drink." A gentle hand slid under her neck, lifting her head enough to take a sip from the glass in front of her mouth.

The water went down too cold, and she paused, waiting for the discomfort to pass.

"Come on. You haven't had anything for days."

"It hurts," she croaked.

Betty smoothed the sweat-soaked hair away from Pearl's forehead and shushed her. "Save your strength. Don't try to talk. Just drink if you can manage it."

"How long have I been out?" She opened her eyes a little. The room was brighter than a thousand suns, and she couldn't keep them open for long.

"At least two days." She cleared her throat. Pearl wished she could read Betty's eyes. "Wyatt called the day before last and told me to watch over you or…"

"Or what?"

"Or, you might not make it." Betty's words were soothing as if she were speaking to a wounded animal.

Pearl covered her face with her hands, a half-hearted attempt to hide her tears. She wept without making a sound for a minute or two. To her relief, Betty didn't try to comfort her. There was a reason they had remained friends for so many years. Each knew what the other needed.

After a short time, Betty broke the silence. "I know you probably don't want to talk about it, but what in the world happened?"

"It's bad." Pearl cried. "I can't say it out loud. I don't understand it, and I don't think you will either."

"Try me."

"I tried to kill the baby." There was no other way to say it. "I thought he wasn't my baby, that he was a demon, or…I don't know, a monster of some sort."

"My God!" Betty sputtered, "You don't believe that!"

"No, not now." She shook her head. "I know it's crazy. I'm crazy. But he didn't look like my baby. He was evil." She nibbled on her fingernail.

"Wyatt stopped me." She started to cry again. "If he hadn't walked in, I don't know what I would've done." That wasn't true. She would've smashed his face into her collarbone. Memories of his little legs thrashing against her, fighting the suffocation, sickened her.

"What is wrong with me?" she sobbed. Struggling to sit up, every inch of her body protested in pain. The beating must've been terrible.

Betty helped her to an upright position and looked away. It was a full minute before she turned back and said, "I don't understand what happened. If it were anyone but you, I'd say you should be locked up for good."

Bile welled up into Pearl's throat. Betty was the only person she could call her own. Judging from the look of disgust in her frigid blue eyes, Betty wasn't going to stick through the worst of things. She wanted to explain herself, but anything she could say would only make matters worse. What she had done to the baby was worse than nuts. It was criminal.

So, she said nothing. She wept big tears into the bunched-up bedsheets.

CHAPTER 15

A NEW TACTIC

Hidden by the curve of the china cabinet, he picked at his knee and listened to Mama and Betty talk. The scab on his knee kept growing back, no matter how many times he picked it off.

"Stop that!" Mama scolded whenever she'd catch him scratching at it with his fingernails. "You're going to make it infected."

He hated it when she talked to Betty because she paid him no attention. A visit from Betty meant hours of cigarettes and coffee at the kitchen table, while he was left to himself.

Whenever he'd tried to ask for something, or sit on her lap, she'd push him away, and say, "Go play outside."

Betty would laugh and wink at him, but she wasn't interested in his presence any more than Mama was.

He picked the scab off all the way and put it into his mouth. He liked the taste of it, bitter and a little salty. Chewing it with his front teeth, he broke the scab into tiny pieces and swallowed it down.

With his finger, he stopped the flow of blood from the freshly exposed wound just before it reached his sock. Pushing the trail of blood back up to its origin, he wondered how deep the sore went.

Using his sharpest nail, he scraped away at the whitish flesh until it began to collect under his fingertip.

Intent on seeing the inside, he ignored the pain along with the increasing amount of blood running down his shin. In his deep state of concentration, he didn't notice the lull in Mama and Betty's conversation or the sound of the kitchen chairs moving away from the table.

"What on earth happened?" Mama startled him.

"I fell down."

"Why didn't you say something?"

He studied her face and decided the look was one of worry, not anger. "I didn't wanna make you mad 'cause I was bothering you."

Her expression softened. "I'm not mad." She held her arms out. "Come here. Let's get you cleaned up."

Randy wrapped his arms around Mama's shoulders. His heart felt happy to have her attention again.

CHAPTER 16

OLD FRIENDS

The interior of his truck was immaculate. It always had been. She shook her head and grinned. He never lifted a finger at home, but he made damned sure his truck was spotless. To help pass the time, she opened his dash box and snooped around, searching for signs of another affair.

It wouldn't be much of a surprise. He'd probably had more flings than the number of years he'd been married. She lit another cigarette and yawned. She'd known she would be in for a long wait, but this was ridiculous.

Watching the door of the bar, Betty leaned back against the passenger door and smoked her cigarette. Here and there, a few customers staggered out, but still no sign of him. It was getting close to closing time.

Kicking up gravel all over the place, a Chevy sedan whipped into the parking lot and settled on the spot right next to his truck. She hunkered down, making herself as invisible as possible. The girl's giggle mingled with his deep laughter, the kind he saved for everyone else, to make a song of sorts.

"Good night!" The girl called to him as his footsteps crunched on the gravel-covered parking lot.

Her pulse slightly quickened when he opened the driver's side door. At first, he didn't notice her sitting next to him.

"Oh, shit! You scared me!" He chuckled and asked, "What in the hell are you doing here?"

"We need to talk." His boyish grin didn't impress her nearly as much as it used to.

He turned to her and rested his left hand on her thigh. "I'm a little spent, but I can try to get it up for old time's sake."

He leaned in and kissed her. His mouth tasted of cigarettes, whiskey, and the other girl's lipstick.

Annoyed, she swatted his hand off her leg. "It's not about me, you jackass. It's about your wife."

"Whoa! Too late in the night to talk about her!"

His slurred words told her the conversation would be futile, but there was no other time to talk without Pearl around.

"Did you know she's pregnant?"

"Are ya jealous?" He grinned and said, "I can help you with that."

"What? No! I'm worried about her!" She sighed. Pearl would be better off without him.

"You do remember the last time, don't you?" She studied his face for signs that he was taking in her words, that he cared even the slightest for the well-being of his wife or his children. "She nearly lost it."

"Of course, I do." He clenched his jaw and ground it back and forth as if he were chewing on something hard. The light-hearted tone had left his voice. "I'm not proud of the way I handled any of it."

"If she has this baby, you have to be there for her." She put her hand on his face and turned it gently toward her. "You can't let her get so exhausted. I'm scared she and the baby won't survive it."

"No reason at all for her to be so tired this time." He reached for her pack of cigarettes and slid one out without asking.

"Janie is old enough to be a help, and Randy ain't a baby." He lit the cigarette and leaned his head back against the seat. He exhaled slowly, the smoke making thin swirls against the backdrop of the streetlight.

Remembering things better left forgotten, she watched him as he sat with his eyes closed. Forbidden images of his full mouth on hers, his hands on her body, flooded her mind.

"Am I interrupting something?" He was smiling at her, a wolfish grin.

"No, just thinking about Pearl." Her face flushed hot.

He didn't deserve to know how he moved her still. Neither one deserved Pearl. She was too good for both of them.

"Is that right?" He brushed her hair back from her forehead, his touch soft, sensual. "You were just thinkin' about Pearl?"

She leaned into him, almost meeting his lips with hers. "That's right."

His biceps were still firm under her fingertips. Caressing the familiar shape, she slid her right hand down the length of his arm. When she reached his hand, she took his cigarette. She smiled and put the confiscated smoke up to her lips. Inhaling deeply, she held the smoke in her lungs for a moment then let it ease out of her, soft and slow.

"It's been a while." Close to her ear, Wyatt's words were throaty and raw. He kissed her neck, suckling and biting with each move. She imagined a cheetah carrying a limp gazelle by its neck, still alive but paralyzed.

She was the prey, caught in a delicious trap. Frozen, she didn't stop his greedy hands from traveling underneath her skirt hem. He didn't bother to unfasten her stockings from their suspenders. She didn't care; she was lightheaded with hunger. Pushing the thin silk fabric of her panties aside, he forced several of his fingers inside of her. Her body responded by tightening up around him, begging him in.

"You're so wet," he whispered.

She shook her head and whimpered.

"Been alone for a while, baby doll?" Smothering her soft cries with his kisses, he thrust his fingers in and out in a steady rhythm until she begged him to stop.

"Inside me," she gasped, "I need you inside of me. I can't get there like this." She was so close, but his fingers weren't enough. It was maddening foreplay.

"We need to go somewhere else." Wyatt grinned and pointed at the bar behind them. "The last thing I want to explain to the cops is this."

"My place," she said.

"I'll see you there."

She put the key into the ignition of her old Lincoln and turned it. *What are you doing?*

She wanted to ignore the question. *She's your friend! It's bad enough you did it before. Now? After everything?*

She sighed and got back out of her car.

"What's wrong?" Wyatt's left arm rested on the open window of his truck, a freshly lit cigarette in his hand. His right hand rested casually on the steering wheel.

"I can't." She didn't need to explain. He knew the reason.

"Hey, suit yourself." He waved and drove away.

CHAPTER 17

BIG BOYS DON'T CRY

Mama tore the front of his shirt in half like it was a piece of paper. Stunned, he stood still and silent. Tears mixed up with snot from his nose and traveled down his face, pooling up with the blood dripping off his busted lip.

"You're disgusting." She scrubbed at his face, using a sour-smelling dampened washcloth, without any care for the sore spots.

Randy winced, but he didn't make any sounds. Crying out loud would make her angrier. Instead, he tried to think about how it all happened. She'd gotten mad so fast. He hadn't seen it coming.

***

"Bring your plate to the sink." Mama reminded him as he shoved the last bite of sandwich into his mouth.

Struggling to swallow the last of the crust, he protested. "Daddy says that's women's work."

"Well, I'm your mama, and I'm asking you to take your plate to the sink."

Randy had grinned and said, "Maybe, I'll tell Daddy."

"What did you say?" She'd stopped scouring the dish in her hands and turned to look at him. Her lips were thin and tight.

"Maybe, I'll tell Daddy." He'd repeated himself, less confident the second time.

Mama slammed the plate she was washing into the sink, shattering it. "Come here!"

"No, Mama, I was just playing!" His legs shook when he stood.

Mama grabbed him by the shoulder and yanked him away from the table. His feet couldn't keep up with the upper part of his body, and he stumbled over them.

"How dare you speak to me that way!" Her words came out clipped as if she couldn't take in enough air to carry them.

Frightened by her narrowed eyes and reddened complexion, he'd stared at her face. This wasn't the face of his mama; this was the face of his nightmares.

Her bony hand struck hard against his mouth, twice, maybe three times. There was no time to guard his face, and even if there had been, he wouldn't have tried. It was better to accept the punishment.

Next, she spun him around and swatted his rear-end and legs with a wooden spoon she'd pulled from the kitchen drawer. He'd wanted to shield his legs from the crack of the spoon, but he knew from experience, the spoon was worse on a hand.

"Why won't you cry?" Angry, she'd whipped him harder.

He wanted to cry, but Daddy had taught him crying was for babies.

***

Mama finished cleaning the blood off his face. "Go find a clean shirt and stay in your room." She stood up slowly, using the edge of the bathroom sink to help pull herself up. Her belly was getting bigger every day with the new baby.

He went into his bedroom closet and picked out a shirt. Careful to keep it off his face, he slid it over his head and arms. His entire backside griped from the pain as he sat down on the edge of his bed to wait for Mama. With no one around, he could let some tears slip out.

Hours passed, and still, Mama didn't return. Too afraid to go downstairs or call for her, Randy stayed on his bed.

Crying made him tired. He lay his head down on his pillow and yawned. The awful dream came quickly. Fighting for air, pushing against the pressure over his face with weak arms—it was the same as always.

When he awoke, the light in the room had changed. It was darker. Mama was lying behind him, her arms cradled around him. Her belly was pressed against his back, and he could feel the baby moving around, kicking at him.

"Mama?" Confused, he wondered if it were morning or night.

"*Shhh*, go back to sleep." She stroked his hair, and he relaxed a little into the slow rise and fall of her breath. The warmth of Mama's belly and her gentle touch gave him the comfort he was craving.

"I'm so sorry," she whispered into his hair as he floated off to sleep.

CHAPTER 18

1952

The new baby was smaller than the other two had been. Wyatt held his pinky up to her doll-sized hand, and she curled her fingers around it. She tried with all her pint-sized might to pull his finger to her mouth.

"Hey, look, Pearlie," he chuckled, "she's ready to eat."

He bounced her softly. "There, there, little Rosebud, Mama is right here."

Rose rooted around, as all newborn babies do when they are looking for a nipple to suckle. Wyatt kissed the top of her soft head, inhaling her fragrance. He was a sucker for babies. If he had his way, if Pearl weren't such a fragile thing, he'd have a house full of them.

He two-stepped Rose over to Pearl's hospital bed. "Here she is, Mama. She's all yours."

Pearl turned away. "I don't want her. Call a nurse."

"What do you mean, you don't want her?" The girl rooming with Pearl cleared her throat, reminding Wyatt they weren't alone. He lowered his voice to a loud whisper. "What are you talking about?"

She sighed, but she didn't answer. *Stubborn, moody bitch. Shoulda married Lilah. She might've been a little fat, but at least she wasn't fuckin' crazy.*

Still holding the baby in his left arm, he dug his right hand into her shoulder, forcing her to roll onto her back. Tears rolled down her temples into her hair. Pearl refused to look at him, staring instead at an invisible spot on the ceiling.

"Goddammit, Pearl! You will feed this baby!" The baby began to squirm in his arm. She was hungry, and Pearl was a selfish bitch for not giving a damn. "What kind of mother doesn't care about feeding her baby?"

"Is everything okay in here?" The plump, shiny-faced nurse from earlier poked her head around the curtain divider. She wore a pasted-on smile, but her eyes gave away her concern.

"No, everything is not all right!" Relieved, Wyatt continued, "Maybe you can talk some sense into her. She doesn't give a damn about feeding the baby."

"Sir, we can feed the baby for you." She held her chubby arms out to take Rose. "Most babies do better on the bottle anyway," she soothed. "Plus, the doctor can see how much she's taking."

Wyatt thought about the nurse's words and decided it all sounded like bullshit to him. A baby ought to have their mama's milk. That's how the good Lord created it. He looked at Pearl, laying there like a damned vegetable, and handed the baby over to the nurse.

He waited until the nurse had waddled out of the room before dealing with Pearl. Still staring at the ceiling, she hadn't moved a muscle. Wyatt sat on the side of her bed, leaned over, and put his face right in front of hers.

"Are you listening to me?"

She nodded slightly.

"I don't know what in the fuck kind of game you're playing, but you'd better snap out of it."

Almost unnoticeable, her breath seeped out. Her forehead and nose felt delicate, breakable, beneath his. It would be so easy just to rear his head back and smash his face into hers. Maybe then, she'd respond.

"Do you hear me?" He grabbed her shoulders, needling in harder than necessary, and shook her.

"I hear you," she whispered. "Please just go."

Yes, he thought, *that's exactly what needs to happen*. Pearl disgusted him. He had to get away from her before he did something stupid. *Let the doctors figure her out, old buddy. No sense getting worked up over her like last time.*

The crisp fall air was a welcome change from the antiseptic fog inside the hospital. Leaning against his truck bed, he let his eyes adjust to the bright sunlight while he smoked. He glanced at his wristwatch and thought about stopping at a bar on the way back to Boerne. He didn't venture into San Antonio very often. *Might be nice to be someplace where no one knows my name.*

He tossed the cigarette onto the pavement and smashed it out with the toe of his boot. The truck door creaked when he opened it. Frowning, he tried to remember when he'd oiled the hinges last. It seemed like there was never enough time in the day to take care of all the responsibilities put on a family man. *Must be nice to be a woman, to have everything taken care of by someone else.*

Even though it was mid-October, the interior of the truck was hot. He cranked the window down and relished the cool breeze wafting through his hair. Although he'd intended to find a bar in San Antonio, his truck seemed to have a mind of its own. Before he knew it, he was sitting in the parking lot of his favorite beer joint in Boerne.

He let the truck idle for a minute or so, comforted by the low, loose rumble. Something had to be done about Pearl. She wasn't getting any better. She was a damned liability. A man deserved to have a wife, a partner. Pearl was a spoiled child.

"Hey, buddy!" One of the regulars recognized him. "You comin' in?"

Wyatt waved him on. "Yeah, in a minute." He watched the guy walk up to the front door, and then he put the truck into reverse. The bar might be a perfect place to drink his troubles away, but he needed something else.

Her little house looked the same as always, pink and tidy. She didn't have a regular boyfriend, but he suspected she had plenty of help around the house. A woman like Betty didn't need to pay for favors, at least not with cash.

"We didn't expect you for another day." Flustered, she smoothed her black curls back from her forehead and motioned for him to come inside. "Let me get the children."

"No," he put his hand on her shoulder, "I just want to talk."

"Oh," her brow wrinkled up. "Is everything all right with Pearl? Is the baby okay?"

"The baby's fine." He dismissed her worry with a wave. "But, I don't know how much more of Pearl I can stand."

She held her finger up to her lips to silence him and pointed at Janie and Randy, lost in a game at the kitchen table. After closing the parlor door, Betty asked, "What happened?"

"She doesn't want the baby." Wyatt finished telling her about the day with Pearl. "It was pitiful. I had to leave."

"I tried to warn her." Betty shook her head. "Tried to tell her this would happen. It's beyond me why she wasn't more careful." She clasped her manicured fingers together and cradled them around her crossed legs.

Distracted by her creamy white thighs and red fingernails, Wyatt stopped listening to her words. Betty always was a nice distraction; at least she had been before she decided to go and get a conscience.

"Wyatt," her voice cut through, sharp and irritated. "Are you listening?"

"Sorry," he grinned, "it's been a long day."

Her expression softened. "You must be exhausted. Let me make you dinner. The children will love having their daddy here. They're a little out of sorts." She stood up and walked past him, the perfume from her skirt tickling his nose. He wondered if she wore any stockings and resisted the urge to reach under her skirt as she passed by.

Wyatt waited a moment before following her into the dollhouse kitchen. Betty had already poured two glasses of whiskey. She pointed and said, "Pick one."

"I see you got new appliances." He sat in the chair farthest from her.

She smiled. "I guess it's been a while since you've been by."

He nodded. "They're nice." And they were. Brand new, pink, and electric. *Who did she have to lay under to get them?* Everyone knew Betty's husband hadn't left her a nickel when he ran off.

It was nice to watch a woman in her natural environment again. Pearl had used her pregnancy as an excuse to lie around, always whining about feeling sick. He couldn't remember the last decent meal he'd had at home. And Pearl wondered why he went to the bar every night. At least at the bar, he could get supper on time.

"So, how is the baby?" Betty asked. "You haven't said much about her."

He shrugged his shoulders and tipped his glass back, emptying it. "She's great. She's a real doll, just like the others."

"Need another?" Betty held up the bottle of whiskey.

"Yes, ma'am."

She leaned over the table to refill his glass. He'd forgotten how beautiful she was. It wasn't a surprise that she had a kitchen full of brand-new appliances.

Dinner was ready after two or three more whiskeys. The children were only mildly happy to see him, but he was just snockered enough not to give a shit. It was a strange affair—a peaceful dinner in a pink dollhouse, with his family and a surrogate wife.

After dinner, Betty sent the children to the parlor to watch television. It was a complete novelty to them, so they were happy to oblige. She fussed about, cleaning up the dinner mess. Wyatt sipped on another whiskey and drank in the sight of Betty, pretending this was his life.

"Betty?" His words were slurred a bit, but he didn't try to straighten them. "Are you happy with your life?"

She laughed. "Of course, I am. Why would you ask such a thing?"

"You do all this," he waved his hands dramatically, "so well." He leaned forward and lowered his voice to a whisper. "Your house is clean, the children aren't fighting, dinner was amazing, and you're easy on the eyes."

"Well, thank you." She raised her right eyebrow. "I think…but what does any of that have to do with me being happy?"

"Don't you want all this?" He pointed at his chest with both hands. "The family? The marriage?"

"No," Betty laughed. "Definitely not the family. Doing this for a night or a week is easy enough. But all the time? No way in hell. I'd go crazy! Men and children are too demanding. I love my life just the way it is." She winked and added, "I can borrow other women's families whenever I need a fix."

Don't let the whiskey go to your head. She's talking about your children, not you. Those days are over.

He watched as she put the last of the pots and pans away and kept his mouth shut. If he'd not had an erection, he might have gone to check on Janie and Randy. Instead, he waited and tried to think of anything other than her soft curves and ivory skin.

"I'm going to send the children to bed. There's no reason to take them home tonight. We have big plans for the morning." She smiled and winked.

"Should I go?"

"We can sit out on the porch for a while if you'd like. It's a nice evening." She added, "Give you a chance to sober up a bit."

"Killjoy," he called to her back as she walked away. She was right, though. He could make it home if he had to, but it would be better to wait a while. No sense in risking another wreck.

Betty's front porch was perfectly arranged, just like the inside of the house. He moved a mountain of lacy pillows from her white metal glider and sat down. Rocking back and forth, he struggled to keep his eyes open. The last two or three whiskeys had put him over the top.

The nag inside his head, always looking out for him, always telling him what to do, warned. *Better take care of it now, or you'll regret it later.*

He stopped rocking and stood up. The porch wobbled underneath his feet for a moment. He made his way down the front steps without tumbling and followed Betty's neatly manicured flower beds around to the side of the house until he was out of the view of the street.

Shoving his index and middle finger as far back into his throat as possible, Wyatt forced himself to vomit all the whiskey, along with Betty's delicious dinner. He wiped his fingers in the grass and spat out as much of the nasty taste as he could.

He staggered up the steps and went inside to clean up. Betty's voice carried around the corner from the guest room. She was reading a bedtime story. He wondered if Pearl ever read to them at night.

The bathroom vanity held a display of soaps shaped like seashells. None of them looked like they'd ever been used, and he wasn't about to be the first. He took the bar of soap from her bathtub and lathered up his face and hands. For good measure, he swished around the soapy water in his mouth.

Her lacy towels didn't look any more useful than the soaps, but he grabbed one of them and dried his face and hands. His attempt to hang the towel back the way he'd found it was a failure, and he finally settled on something that remotely resembled her arrangement. *Women.*

The man in the mirror looked tired. *I should go.* He smoothed his dark hair back and examined his scruffy jawline.

"Are you alive?" Betty tapped on the door.

He opened the door to find her posed with her hands poised on her hips, her expression somewhere between amused and irritated. She'd changed into a silky robe with red flowers. The curve of her breasts gave away that she'd removed her brassiere.

"Barely." He smiled. "I overdid it a little. I should go home." Rubbing the back of his aching head, he shrugged his shoulders. "It just feels so empty there."

"You can stay awhile." She bit her bottom lip. "The children are sleeping."

Ol' Betty wasn't as tough as she liked to play. Maybe with a little coaxing, he'd stay longer than a while. "Can I trouble you for some aspirin?"

Every woman had her weakness. On the surface, one might think Betty's weak spot was money. Wyatt knew better. Money was a necessity for her, a rate of exchange, a practicality per se. Betty's weakness was caretaking. She was a sucker for the downtrodden. *Otherwise, how do you explain her marriage to that loser?*

He positioned himself in just the right stance, head weary, chest and shoulders broad, and waited for her in the dimmed parlor. His neck started to ache. Damn, she was taking forever. Any other floozie and he'd be gone already. He'd had a taste of Betty before, though, and she was worth the work.

She returned with a tray of coffee, aspirin, and sugar. "Here." She handed him two aspirins. "You'll feel better."

The pills disintegrated in his mouth before he could swallow them down with the hot coffee. He'd learned to love the bitter taste. It was the taste of relief.

"Thank you, doll." With his right hand, he rubbed the back of his neck, knowing full well that she would follow his lead.

"Let me," she tucked her legs under her and turned him away from her on the sofa. Soft hands massaged imaginary knots on the back of his neck and shoulders.

He groaned. "Thank you. I'm not used to this." *Now for the kicker.* He turned to her and put his hand on hers. "You don't have to. I feel guilty. You're too kind." He let a tear well up in his eye.

Wide-eyed and concerned, she reassured him, "I don't mind."

"I'm sorry," he wiped at the manufactured tear. "It's just been so long. Pearl isn't...affectionate."

She leaned into him, pulling him closer. Her breath smelled like licorice and whiskey. Red lips on his neck, red nails on his back, and Wyatt forgot everything about his troubles.

CHAPTER 19

NIGHTMARE

He kicked and clawed, fighting to breathe. The pillow was smashed onto his face so hard that he couldn't take in any air. Just when his lungs felt like they were about to implode, the pillow was lifted away. He swallowed in frantic gulps of air and put up his hands to fend off the next attack.

"Stop it!" Janie shook him. "Wake up, stupid!"

Confused, Randy sat up and rubbed his eyes. It took him a moment to realize they were at Betty's house.

"Dummy." Janie flopped over, yanking the bedsheets violently over her shoulder. She wiggled around for a second or two and then dozed back off.

Laughter traveled through the small house into the guest room. Randy recognized Betty's voice. The man sounded an awful lot like Daddy. He kicked the sheets down to the foot of the bed and slid down onto the cold wooden floor.

A small lamp lit a window in the parlor, but Betty wasn't in there. Sometimes, grownups liked to sit outside after dark. He pulled the lace curtains back, hoping to see her on the front porch. The seats were all empty.

"Shame on you!" Betty squealed in the other room. She laughed and said something else that Randy couldn't understand.

He followed the sound of her laughter through the dark to her bedroom door.

"Betty?" Afraid to knock, Randy whispered at the door. Save for little rustling sounds, the room was quiet inside. Motionless, afraid to move, he stood covered by darkness. If he were to pass back through the house, a boogeyman might get him. He wasn't comfortable enough with Betty to just barge right into her room and crawl into bed with her. Plus, he was getting too big to do that. Even Mama said so.

Kaboom, kaboom, kaboom, his heart made a hollow echo in his head. He squeezed his eyes shut and held his breath. Willing the monster creeping through the house to go away, he prayed it wouldn't find him.

"Betty!" He whispered again, louder this time. He couldn't be sure, but he thought the shadow at the end of the hallway moved. Once more, he closed his eyes and prayed for the creature to leave. Rickety footsteps inched closer to him. The hairs on the back of his neck moved back and forth with each puff of the monster's breath. Terror won over, and he threw open Betty's door.

"Get out!" Betty screamed at him. She lay on her back, completely naked, legs spread apart.

What he saw with his eyes made no sense to his mind. Daddy lay on his stomach with his face between Betty's legs. The look on Daddy's face scared him more than any monster ever could have.

"Get the fuck out!" Daddy bolted out of bed and chased Randy out of the room.

Randy made it to the end of the hallway before Daddy scooped him up with one arm. Daddy pulled him into the parlor and sat down on Betty's couch without any pants on at all.

He tried not to look at Daddy's private parts, but he'd never seen his father naked before.

"What were you doing?" Daddy shook him by the shoulders.

"I was scared." Randy barely had enough air to fuel his words.

"You little sneaking liar!"

Randy started to cry, even though he knew it would make Daddy mad.

"Bend over!" Daddy shoved him over his knee and paddled his rear-end. Randy was more disturbed by Daddy's bare, hairy legs than the spanking.

"Now, go back to bed!" Daddy swatted him once more as he walked away.

CHAPTER 20

THE ESCAPE

"Pearl, honey?" A sweet, pudgy face peered over her.

The baby, something about the baby. But what was she supposed to do? Oh, yes, she was supposed to help feed the baby.

"Dr. Weller wants you to help with the baby today if you are able, dear." Nurse Pudgy smiled sweetly. "It's necessary to go home."

What if I don't want to go home? Ever? She looked at the baby in the bassinet and felt nothing. Except empty.

Pudgy busied herself, changing the baby's diaper. "So, is this your first girl?"

"Hmm?"

"I asked, is this your first daughter, dear?"

"No, my oldest is a girl." Pearl resented the forced conversation. She was tired in a way she'd never been before. She was scared to go home. At the same time, she was afraid to stay gone from home for too long.

"Here you go, dear." She handed the swaddled-up baby to Pearl. "I'll get the bottle for you."

Rose squirmed a little, not quite awake enough to open her eyes. Pearl wondered if she was capable of feeling love for the baby. She was a fine-looking girl, pretty, with all her fingers and toes. By all standards, there was nothing wrong with her. But this agonizing sense of disconnect was impossible to shake.

She'd be better off without me. They all would be.

"Here, dear." The glass bottle was warm. She'd nursed her other babies. The bottle was a strange thing, and she felt guilty. Wyatt had made it no secret he thought she was a bum mother. Rose readily accepted the nipple of the bottle and began to drink. Pearl felt some of the tension ease out of her shoulders. Maybe this wouldn't be so bad.

Pearl yawned and allowed herself to sink into the comfort of holding Rose's soft, warm body. She watched the baby's eyes close in contentment as she suckled her bottle. Drowsy, she rested her eyes while the baby fed.

"Mrs. Carter!" Pearl jumped. The baby lay on the floor, screaming, with the broken bottle of milk all around her.

"Well, I never…" Nurse Pudgy picked up the baby and began to make soothing sounds.

She glared at Pearl. "What is wrong with you?" She turned toward the door and yelled, "I need some help in here!"

"I don't know…" She stood up out of the rocking chair where she'd been feeding her. "Here, I'll take her."

"No," the nurse spat, "you will not take her." She pointed. "Go lay down." Her pleasant, plump face just looked fat and mad now. "Wait for the doctor."

Pearl lay in the bed, staring at the ceiling, wishing it would swallow her up, while a team of hospital staff examined the baby and cleaned up the mess she'd made.

"Take these." Gone were the niceties from before. Nurse Pudgy held out a small cup with several pills along with a glass of water to swallow them.

"What are they for?" Groggy, she couldn't remember the doctor discussing medicines.

"Never you mind." She pursed her lips and ordered, "Just take them. The doctor will be in later to discuss everything with you."

It doesn't matter. Just swallow them so you can sleep. It's the only place you want to be right now. It didn't take long to fade back into nothingness.

Little whispers gently pulled her out of a dream. Eyes closed, she listened and tried to make out the voices. Who was talking about her? Wyatt, definitely—but who else?

"What's wrong with her?" Wyatt's disembodied voice floated around in her half-dream.

"She's got hysteria," another voice replied.

"So, what in the hell does that mean for me? For the children?" Dream Wyatt sounded angry. "Does she go into an asylum? A nuthouse? How am I supposed to take care of the young'uns?"

"*Shhh.* She's waking."

"I don't give a damn! We don't have time for this!"

Her eyelids were too heavy to push open, and she faded back into the other side.

Spiked with rain, the wind whipped her from all directions. It would have been nearly impossible to stay upright on the roof of the barn, if it weren't for the cross she was tied up to. If she wiggled at all, the baby might not make it.

Bound with baling wire to each of Pearl's hands were glass baby bottles full of milk. Baby Rose hung onto one of the bottles, suckling desperately. The baling wire cut deep into Pearl's wrists, and drops of her blood ran down the bottle onto the sides of Rose's cheeks.

Horrified Rose would fall, Pearl prayed she would continue to suckle the bottle. She screamed for help, but her words were swallowed up by the wind.

With each gulp, the level of the milk lowered. Soon, there would be nothing for Rose to drink and no reason for her to hold on. Gusts of wind shook her tiny body back and forth, and Pearl stifled a cry of fear.

Billowing, black storm clouds were nearing the edge of the property. Although Pearl couldn't see the house, she knew everyone else was safely inside. She was more tired than she'd ever been. No one would blame her if she couldn't save the baby.

Rose turned her head and looked right at Pearl as she fell away. Her mouth was wide open, blood from Pearl's wrist streaked along the sides of her face and neck. Her cries reached Pearl's ears from the jagged rocks at the base of the cliff. *Wait, where is the barn? Weren't we on the barn?*

Two sharp cracks of thunder sounded, and an excruciating white light seared Pearl's eyes. Salty ocean water filled her mouth and nose as the cross plunged into the brine below. Cold liquid filled her ears and muffled all the noises around her.

"Aren't you going back up to the top, now?" A tall, eel-like man asked her. He carried baby Rose in his slithery arms. Content, the baby smiled and put her little chubby hand up to her mouth.

"We'll be just fine, Rosie and I." The eel man smiled.

Rose cooed and smiled, revealing a mouthful of blackish-green seaweed.

"Wake up, Mrs. Carter," Nurse Pudgy shook her shoulder. "It's time for your medication."

Pearl shielded her eyes from the bright morning sun as the nurse slid back the curtains. It seemed later than usual. "Did I miss breakfast?"

"Since when have you cared about breakfast, dear?"

"Oh," she thought for a moment, "I suppose I haven't been eating much, but I'm hungry this morning."

"I'll see what I can find for you." Pudgy shoved a paper cup with pills in front of her.

"How much longer will I need to take these? They make me so sleepy." Determined to keep her voice calm this time, she carried on. "I'm feeling much better now. I'm sure Wyatt and the children are needing me at home."

"You'll need to talk to the doctor, dear," she said as she walked out the door.

Pearl had lost track of the days. When asked about the doctor, Nurse Pudgy would reply, "Sorry, dear, you were sleeping when he dropped by," or, "He'll be around later."

She couldn't remember the last time she'd had a visit from Wyatt or Papa. Instead of swallowing the pills and missing another doctor's visit, Pearl dropped them into the wastebasket beside the bed.

It was time to do something about her situation. She'd been incapacitated for far too long. No one had talked to her about her condition, but she didn't need a diagnosis to know they were treating her like she was a loony.

She lifted her right arm first, then her left, taking a whiff of her underarms. *Ugh, time for a bath.* She considered calling for the nurse but thought better of it. Nurse Pudgy wasn't fond of her, and she didn't want to bother her any more than necessary.

The soap was still wrapped neatly in the cabinet, along with an enamel washbasin and towels. It wasn't a bathtub, but it would do. She wasn't surprised to find the door to her room had no lock. *Crazy people aren't allowed privacy.* She pulled the dressing screen around to the small sink and quickly undressed.

The hot water handle wouldn't budge, and she wondered if it was a luxury not allowed to patients in this ward. *Maybe they're afraid we'll burn ourselves to death.* She shrugged her shoulders and braced herself for a cold sponge bath.

As the day went on without the pills to cloud and confuse, her situation became clear. By the time Nurse Pudgy arrived hours later, she knew exactly what to say.

"Oh my!" The nurse put a hand to her heart. "You startled me!"

"I imagine so." Pearl smiled. "You aren't used to seeing me out of bed."

"No, dear," Pudgy stammered. "How are you feeling this evening?"

"Hungry," Pearl said. "That's how I'm feeling. Hungry."

"Oh, of course, you are. I'll order a tray for you. Let me get your vitals, and I'll make sure the night nurse follows up with the kitchen." She pulled off her stethoscope and began to listen to Pearl's chest.

"I'm glad you're listening up close, so you can hear me when I say this."

The nurse didn't respond, but she stopped moving the stethoscope around.

"You didn't check on me one time today. Not once."

The nurse took a breath as if she were going to say something, but Pearl stopped her.

"You've been doping me and then ignoring me." She stood up and moved away from Nurse Pudgy. "I want to talk to the doctor, and I want my husband. I've been in here for too damned long!"

"Sit down, dear." The nurse reached for Pearl's arm. "You're upsetting yourself."

"Don't touch me!" Pearl pushed Pudgy's arm off and ran toward the door. As she'd discovered earlier, it wasn't locked. She looked behind her, but Nurse Pudgy wasn't following. The nurses' station was empty. Grateful, Pearl walked at a fast pace down the stairwell and toward the front of the building. She thought about running, but she didn't want to draw attention to herself.

Although there were a few visitors in the front lobby, Pearl made her way outside unnoticed. Which was surprising, she realized as she stood on the corner of Morales Street in her hospital gown. Pearl laughed out loud, then began to cry. What now?

The sun was giving way to the soft light of the evening. Street people were starting to appear, ready for a reprieve from the hot Texas daylight. She hadn't a clue where to go, but she needed to put some space between her and the hospital. Nurse Pudgy was out to get her, and the longer she stayed, the more danger she was in.

CHAPTER 21

THE SUBSTITUTE

It was all play-pretend, and she knew it. She watched Wyatt pretending to be a good daddy, threading a worm on Randy's hook, smiling at Janie, while she sat in a lawn chair and held the new baby. She was pretending, too. This baby wasn't her baby, any more than the rest of them. Still, it was nice for a while, to make-believe.

The breeze whipped their tablecloth up, nearly throwing the fried chicken she'd made all over the ground. He laughed and jumped up, plopping his tackle box on the tablecloth to weigh it down.

They'd been playing house just like this for weeks. The children were eating it up like cherry ice cream. She was, too. For however long it might last, she liked being a Mrs. Somebody.

Randy and Janie never asked about their mama. At least not in front of Betty. In the quiet part of the night, when she was alone with her thoughts, she felt guilty. Pearl had been her friend.

It's not your fault she went crazy and left Wyatt with all these babies. You're just helping him out.

But she knew helping Wyatt out didn't include fucking him. Now or then.

It wouldn't last forever. It was just play-pretend. Whenever Pearl was better, she could have her family back.

"Betty, look!" Janie squealed. "I found a shell! All the way inland!"

"Look at you! Using fancy words!" Betty laughed.

Janie blushed. She twisted the hem of her bright yellow skirt into a tight ball. She was an adorable child, especially when someone took the time to fix her hair. Betty had been having a whole lot of fun playing dolly with Janie's wardrobe and long blonde hair.

"Atta boy!" Wyatt slapped Randy on the back and chuckled.

Randy squinted against the bright sun. "Now what, Daddy?"

"Well," Wyatt wrapped his large hand around Randy's tiny one. "We do this." He cast the line far out into the water. It landed with a plop, and Randy beamed.

He looked just like Pearl when he smiled, and her heart ached a bit. Before the children, before Wyatt, Pearl had been nothing but smiles.

Not your fault she's a downer, now. You didn't make her have all those babies, even tried to talk her out of the last one.

"Betty," Randy hollered, excited. "Watch this!" He reeled in the fishing line as fast as his tiny arms could crank. Everyone made a collective cheer as he pulled the smallest catfish Betty had ever seen out of the water.

***

It was a short drive from Cibolo Creek to her house, but all three of the children were passed out cold by the time Wyatt parked her Lincoln in the driveway. The sun had sunk midway down the horizon, and she contemplated skipping dinner altogether.

"Help me get them in?" She called through the open window. Wyatt was already on the first step of her front porch. This wasn't the first time she'd had to remind him to help with his own children. It was moments like this that Betty remembered why she didn't have her own family.

She shoved the passenger door open with her foot and stepped out of the car, careful not to wake the sleeping baby in her arms. The front door was closed. Irritated, she knocked on it with the toe of her shoe.

"Yes?" he opened the door with a mischievous grin.

"Not funny." She stomped past him into her bedroom, where they'd set up a crib for the baby. She laid Rose down and covered her with a knitted yellow blanket that one of the church ladies had made. After the town gossips had spread the word about Pearl's breakdown, little Rosie became the favorite charity for a handful of Good Samaritans. Newly born babies, especially baby girls, were fun to dress up.

Wyatt caught her by surprise by grabbing her from behind and pressing his groin into her rear-end. "How about a little hanky-panky?" he growled into her ear.

"Not now." She shoved him backward with her elbow. "How about you help me get your children out of the hot car before they melt?"

She wanted to scrape that big, stupid grin off his face, in the way one scrapes off mud from the bottom of their shoe on the edge of the porch.

Inside the car, Janie and Randy were leaning against each other, still asleep. Janie's long curls had matted against the side of Randy's sweaty face. Betty gently pushed Janie away from Randy.

"There, there, it's okay. Let's get you inside." Randy was so exhausted from the day he didn't wake when Betty picked him up.

She tossed a cold look toward Wyatt's direction on her way through the parlor. He was sitting on her crushed velvet sofa in his dirty dungarees, reading the morning paper. After depositing Randy in the guest bed, she found Wyatt in the same position she'd left him on the way through—dirtying up her beautiful furniture with fishing stink. The sight of him angered her, but she kept her mouth shut and went back out to the car to retrieve Janie.

"Janie." She nudged her gently. Although Janie wasn't all that large for her age, she was too tall for Betty to carry. "Wake up, sweetie. Let's get to bed."

Janie allowed Betty to hobble her into the house and tuck her next to Randy. She barely opened her eyes.

She studied her guest room, which up until Pearl's confinement had been like a picture out of *Good Housekeeping*. Her darling room, the one she'd painstakingly redecorated with fabrics shipped all the way from Paris, was now covered in an avalanche of toys, children's clothing, and a faint odor of sweaty feet.

Scarlet heat radiated from Betty's neck to her face. How long had it been? Two weeks for Pearl to figure out she didn't want to take care of baby Rose. Then how long? It felt like a month had gone by since Pearl was locked up in the loony bin.

Wyatt hadn't budged from the sofa. She stood in the doorway for a full thirty seconds before he looked up from her newspaper. "Ready now?"

For a moment, the air pressure in the room increased, much in the same way that water pressure increases as one dives deeper below the surface of the ocean. It was difficult to breathe, nearly impossible to speak. Her vision narrowed, and her ears rang with the buzzing sound of fury.

"Ready?" *Don't you dare let him hear your anger, Betty LouAnn.*

He folded the paper up and tossed it aside. "I've been waiting for you to get the children settled." He winked and smiled.

Calm, she said, "What I'm ready for, is for you to go home, feed your animals, and take a night off from me."

"Is that right?" He raised his brow. "You want me to drag them out of bed and take them home at this hour?"

"No." She managed a smile. "Just yourself. They're fine to stay."

"You got it, darlin'." He put his hands up in the air. "Your loss."

"That's right," she said. "My loss."

Just as she knew he would, he slammed the door on his way out— hard enough to jiggle a few knick-knacks loose from a shadow box on the wall. She locked the front door and listened to the sound of his truck as it grumbled away.

The trinkets on the floor hadn't broken. She placed them back into their little compartments in the shadow box on the wall. Looking around her parlor, she realized she'd neglected some things since Wyatt had invaded her home and infected her mind. How was it possible she'd let him inside so readily?

There would be no whiskey tonight. She'd had enough whiskey to last her a while. She started a pot of coffee and lit a cigarette. It was time to rid the house of the dirt that had accumulated during the past month.

She began with the parlor, where Wyatt had sat reading her newspaper. The fishy smell was all but gone, and she was thankful. The sofa had cost a fortune.

One by one, she wiped the built-up dust off her precious keepsakes. Most were gifts given to her at birthdays and Christmastime. A few tokens of affection from smitten lovers were sprinkled into the mix. She gave little thought to the tiny treasures as she cleaned them, until she reached the last item.

It was only half of a set, a porcelain figurine with her hand held out. The other statuette stood in Pearl's china hutch. Were the figurines to be placed side by side, they would appear to be holding hands. She tilted her head and wondered how many different places those miniature china dolls had stood over the past years.

She remembered Pearl's expression as she handed Betty the brightly wrapped package. "Here," she'd said, shy and awkward. Her eyes had shone, her broad smile much like Randy's when he caught that pitiful fish. Eighth grade had just let out for the summer, and they were saying their goodbyes along with all the other schoolgirls.

"But I didn't get you anything." Betty had felt embarrassed. She'd liked Pearl well enough, but the thought hadn't occurred to exchange gifts. And besides, her family was so damned broke she wouldn't have been able to afford a gift anyway. Pearl didn't know that, yet. She wouldn't feel comfortable enough to let Pearl into her home until several years later.

"It's okay," Pearl reassured. "This is for both of us, see?" She unwrapped the gift for Betty. "They're like sisters because you're the sister I wish I had."

Betty had swallowed back her tears and thanked Pearl. Letting Pearl see how touched she'd been by the gesture would've felt worse than playing it cool, so she pretended the gift wasn't that big of a thing. Later that night, though, after she'd washed up the greasy dishes from dinner, and after her parents had wound down their nightly drunken brawl, Betty unwrapped her half of the delicate gift. She traced over the outline of the little figure and thought about Pearl. No one had ever been so kind.

Pearl had always loved Betty the most.

CHAPTER 22

JANIE

"What's he saying to her?" His loud whisper interfered with her eavesdropping, and she motioned for him to be quiet.

Randy frowned, but he stopped talking. Janie could only hear parts of the conversation, and it was frustrating. They always treated her like a baby, making her leave the room anytime they wanted to talk about grown-up things. She'd heard the words, "Leave the room, Janie" a million times already. She was almost nine years old. A boy had already kissed her, so there was no way she was just a baby.

"How long has it been?" Betty's voice cut through the walls.

Grandpa's words weren't clear, but his voice was thick with tears. Janie's tummy twisted with the awful possibilities. She'd been so happy to see his old truck in Betty's driveway. After Mama went into the hospital, Grandpa only came to visit once.

Randy gave up and busied himself in the corner with a pile of blocks. She stayed by the door, hoping to catch a few more words floating through the air. Something terrible must've happened; otherwise, Grandpa wouldn't be crying. Men never cried, except at funerals.

She'd gone to a funeral once before. It was a big affair, like a long church service, only with lots of weeping and pictures of her daddy's friend displayed all around the room. The men had cried as much as the women did, except for Daddy. Daddy never cried.

Unable to stand it a second longer, she opened the door a small crack in hopes of hearing something, anything.

"Just keep them as long as possible." Grandpa's voice was much closer now.

Daring to peek through the tiny opening, Janie could see the backside of Betty, right in front of the guest room. If she shut the door now, they'd know she was spying on them. So, she stood frozen in place and tried not to breathe out into the hallway.

"He's bad off. They don't need to be around it." Grandpa looked worried.

"You know that I can't afford to feed them forever." Betty put her hands up to the sides of her head.

Grandpa dug around in the back pocket of his overalls and pulled out something small. He pushed it into Betty's hand. "Here, take this. Use it for food or whatever they need. I'll bring more as soon as I can."

Betty sighed and said, "For Pearl, I will."

She couldn't see Betty's face, but Grandpa's face crumpled up into something she didn't recognize. "Thank you, my dear. I don't know what I'd do without you. I promise I'll help you as much as I can with the young'uns."

Betty leaned in to hug Grandpa. "It's okay. We'll get through this, won't we?"

She waited, still as a department store mannequin, until they'd left the hallway before throwing herself onto the bed. Mama was dead, and no one was going to tell her.

"What's wrong with you?" Randy called up from the floor.

"Don't talk to me," she muttered, her words muffled, her face smashed into her pillow.

Mama was dead, and Daddy was a stupid drunk. Now, Betty was going to be their new mother. But Betty didn't want to be a mother. She was always telling everyone that she only liked to borrow other people's children.

The beginning of school came and went without much fuss. Months passed, and Betty never said a word to Janie about Mama's death. Janie didn't ask because she didn't want it to be true.

Life felt different at Betty's house than it had at home, especially since Daddy had stopped coming around. Even though she knew it wasn't possible, Janie wished they could stay with Betty forever.

"Dinnertime," Betty yelled from the kitchen.

Janie rubbed her eyes and put down her pencil. Homework was much harder in the fourth grade. "Come on, Randy, let's eat."

"Okay," he said, "let me finish this page." Randy was just learning to read and seemed to like it as much as she did.

"Now, stupid." She hissed, "Betty's waiting."

"Fine."

She could hear Rosie's little warning hungry sounds from Betty's room. "Tell Betty I'm getting Rosie."

Rosie was a good baby, and Janie liked helping Betty with her. She knew that someday when she was all the way grown-up, she'd be a good mother.

"Good evening, sweet girl!" Janie cooed. "Aren't you happy to see your big sister?"

Rosie wiggled with pleasure and grinned at Janie. She was a fat little thing with pretty dimples and blonde ringlets. The doctor was worried because Rosie wasn't sitting up on her own or crawling yet, but Janie knew she was going to be just fine. Rosie hadn't learned those things yet because she didn't need to. She had Janie to carry her everywhere. And when Janie couldn't, Randy or Betty did. They all loved her so very much.

She lifted her out of the crib and breathed in her sweet baby perfume. There was nothing better than the fragrance of Rosie's downy curls. Rosie squeezed Janie's neck with her chubby little arms.

"Hi, baby!" Betty greeted Rosie as Janie was strapping her into the highchair. "Are you ready for dinner?"

Rosie babbled and smiled, revealing two recently cut bottom teeth.

"May I feed her, please?"

"Of course, but aren't you starving? You've had a long day at school." Betty handed a bowl of mashed vegetables to Janie.

"I'll eat, but I can wait." Janie smiled. "She's a baby."

"I want to feed her!" Randy whined.

"You can't," Janie said. "You're not big enough."

"Now, Janie," Betty chided, "he's perfectly capable." She added, "Perhaps, you could take turns."

When Betty turned away, Randy stuck his tongue out at Janie.

"I hate you," she whispered.

"Betty," Randy tattled, "Janie said she hates me."

"Janie! That's out of line!" Betty spun around from the sink.

"He stuck his tongue out at me."

Betty covered her mouth with her hand and closed her eyes tightly. "I don't have time for this shit!"

Rosie started to cry. Betty yanked the dishtowel off her shoulder and threw it onto the counter. She stomped out of the kitchen and into her bedroom, slamming the door behind her.

"Now you've done it!" Janie punched Randy in the shoulder. "Mama's dead, and Betty's going to get rid of us!"

"Take it back!" Randy punched Janie square in the nose.

For a split second, Janie was stunned senseless. Blood trickled out of her nose onto her upper lip. What began as a spark of confusion quickly turned into a white-hot ball of rage.

"You jerk! I hate you!" She shoved him backward with all her might. The chair toppled over, and he landed with a solid thump onto his back.

It seemed like a full minute before he made any noise at all. He just lay there, mouth wide open, eyes round as saucers. When he finally could suck in enough air to breathe, he let out a shrill cry that sounded something like a siren.

Rosie puckered her mouth up and started a new round of crying, only this time much louder.

"Oh, for God's sake! What in the hell is going on?" Betty stood in the doorway, mascara tear stains down her cheeks.

"Mama's dead, and now you're going to make us leave!" Randy wailed. Big tears poured down the sides of his beet-red face.

"What?" Betty sputtered, "Who told you that your mama's dead?" She lifted Randy from the flattened chair and held him to her chest. Rocking him back and forth, she soothed him.

"Your mama isn't dead, honey. She's gone on a trip."

Janie watched, and she knew Betty was lying to make Randy feel better. Mama must be dead. Otherwise, why hadn't she come for them?

"Why didn't she take us?" Randy shuddered and wiped at the snot running down his nose with the back of his hand.

"Your mama is…" She paused and took a deep breath. "She is very sick. She wouldn't have been able to take care of you on the trip."

Betty caressed his hair and kissed his forehead. "She loves you very, very much, and wants you to know she misses you every day."

"But I want her," Randy sobbed. "I want Mama!" He cried hard in Betty's arms for a long while.

Janie lifted Rosie out of the highchair and carried her into the parlor. She nestled her nose into Rosie's silken ringlets. More than anything, she wanted Betty's words to be true.

CHAPTER 23

CASTING PEARL

Insects writhed around in his hair, and he was back in Okinawa. He squeezed the bottle of whiskey in his right hand to make sure it was still there. So long as he had the whiskey, he didn't have to stay in Okinawa for long. He yawned and drifted back into a hazy slumber.

"Wake up, Wyatt." Pearl sat near his feet. "Bugs are crawling all over you." Angelic, her hair was long and flowing, her face clean of makeup. She was still wearing the white hospital gown.

"Where've you been?" Sleep muted his words, but somehow, she heard him.

Pearl smiled. "You're in the hayloft, dummy." And then she dissipated, like a fog in the morning sun.

Wyatt fought gravity to pull himself into an upright position. *How long this time?* It was still dark outside, but the darkness could just as easily be midnight as four in the morning. He held the whiskey bottle up and shook it, determining the contents to be almost empty. Fumbling, he wiggled the cork out and swigged the rest down.

One of the bugs creeping around in his hair made its way out onto his left ear, and he swatted it off into the hay. With both hands, he scratched the stray bits of straw and pests from his head. The hayloft wasn't an ideal bed, but sleeping in the house, without Pearl, was a special kind of hell.

The animals below were quiet, which meant he'd either forgotten to put them up for the night, or it wasn't yet morning. He tossed the empty whiskey bottle aside and crawled toward the ladder. He caught a whiff of his body odor and fought the urge to gag. How long had it been since he'd bathed? As he climbed down the ladder, he counted the days since he'd returned home from Betty's house.

Four days. It had been four days since he'd opened the door to a ringing telephone. He'd thought about ignoring it, but the damned thing continued to ring long after he'd taken his billfold out of his pocket and lit a cigarette.

"Mr. Carter?" Her piercing, thin voice irritated his eardrum. "Is this Mr. Carter?"

"Well, now, who in the hell else would it be?"

"Your wife," she paused, "Mrs. Carter," as if he didn't know his wife's name, "has disappeared."

Wyatt listened to the details as he poured himself a whiskey. "Uh-huh. I see." The amber liquid burned on its way down. "So, what you're saying, is that your fat-ass nurse didn't pay attention to her, and now she's gone."

He'd slammed the receiver down on her excuses and knocked back another shot of relief. *Fuckin' idiots. Every last one of 'em. First, she wasn't sick, and then, she was sick. Now, she's just gone.*

Pearlie's papa had made a visit somewhere around the second day. He didn't bother to bang on the door with his meaty old fist. Flinging it open like he owned the place, the old man stormed in, dripping with sweat.

"I hear my daughter's gone missing. I made it all the way into her room and scared the shit out of some poor old lady."

He took one look at Wyatt, sprawled out on the sofa with a bottle in his hand. "You're soused."

"You think?" He raised the bottle. "There's more in the pantry if you want some."

"No, you fool." Disgust stained the old man's bright red face. "Don't you think you should be looking for her?"

"What for?" He shook his head. "She's gone. Don't want the baby, don't want the children, and damned sure don't want me." Leaning his head back against the sofa cushion, he swallowed more booze.

"Do ya blame her? You did nothing to take care of her. She needed help, and all you could think about was running around sticking your wiener in anything with a skirt on!" Pearlie's papa was hopping mad.

Wyatt chuckled. "You're a funny old fucker. Do ya know that? 'Specially when you're mad."

God, he was smashed. He knew that he was. It took a mountain of effort to get his words out in a straight line. "Nope, I think I'm gonna just sit right here and wait. If she wants to come home, she'll be here."

"What about the children? What'll you do with them?" The old man had started to cry.

"Hmm." He hadn't thought much about the children, not at all, if he were honest. "I don't know. Don't care right now. Do you want 'em?"

Without Pearl, the children were one big hassle. Too much work for him.

The old man mumbled something about kicking the shit out of him in his younger days and slammed the door behind him. Wyatt had laughed.

He'd gone too far. Now, semi-sober, Wyatt felt a small amount of shame. And miserable. Four days of whatever liquor he could get his hands on and no food made for a world-class hangover with a rotten headache. What he needed was more liquor. That'd fix the hangover right up.

"Wyatt," Pearl whispered. "Wake up."

He could feel her sitting on the bed. Surely, he hadn't imagined her voice. Opening his eyes seemed impossible, but if he could, he was sure he would see Pearl right behind him.

Her body weight shifted, and she stretched out to lay next to him, curving her soft body around his. The hairs on the back of his neck stood up from her breath.

"Don't you miss me?" She lightly scratched her fingernails across his chest and shoulders.

God, I miss you. Where've you been?

"*Shhh.*" She slid her hand into his underwear and began to stroke him. "I'm still here."

He groaned. It felt so good. She'd never touched him in that way before. Faster, harder, she manipulated him until he was on the edge of an orgasm.

"How does it feel now?" Something in her voice was wrong. She didn't sound like Pearl at all.

His erection began to fade, and the motion quickly became uncomfortable.

"I said, how does it feel now?" The voice was deep, male, and definitely not Pearl's.

He curled up into a ball to protect himself, but he wasn't strong enough to push her hand away. "Stop it! You're hurting me!" he yelped.

She coughed out a smoky laugh, her breath stinking of old liquor and cigars. "What? You're not having fun?" Pumping furiously with her hand, the sensation was raw agony.

He forced his eyes open and flung his bedcovers back with a start. Blood-tinged spurts of a fresh wet dream stained his sweat-soaked sheets. His limp penis was scarlet red and chafed.

"Where are you?" He screamed into the emptiness, "Come back, goddammit!"

CHAPTER 24

THE PINCH

He'd been waiting in line during the entire recess for a turn on the swings when Billy Caulder barged through and cut right in front of him. Half of a head taller than Randy, and meaner than a bag of snakes, Billy was used to getting his way.

Dressed in dirty denim jeans and a worn flannel shirt, Billy smelled as bad as he looked. Randy glared at the back of his neck for a few seconds before gathering enough anger-fueled courage to speak.

"I was here first!"

Billy turned around and sneered, revealing greenish teeth that likely hadn't been brushed for some time. Sweat dripped down the sides of his face, making dirty paths to his neck. "So? Whatcha gonna do about it?"

Randy hesitated, unable to think of a good comeback.

"That's what I thought. You've got nothing." Smug, Billy turned back around and yelled toward the swings, "Hey Sally, you'd better hurry up before I throw you off!"

"Oh, by the way, loser," Billy added with a grin before he ran to scare Sally off, "I hear your new mommy is a hooker."

Puzzled by the snickering from the children in line behind him, Randy wanted to ask what a hooker was. But he knew better than to talk to Billy unless he had to.

"Shut up," he yelled to the students who were still laughing about Betty. She might not be his real mama, but she took care of him just like a mother would. He loved Betty.

After school, Janie waited for him under the big tree. "What took you so long, dummy?"

He ducked as she swung her sweater toward his head.

They had passed the school grounds by several blocks before he asked Janie. "What's a hooker?"

"What? Who said that to you?"

"It don't matter. I just wanna know what it means." With the back of his sleeve, he wiped at the snot that threatened to drip out of his nose.

"If you won't tell me where you heard it, then I'm not telling you what it means." She flung her book bag over her shoulder and marched past him.

"Janie, wait," he yelled. "I'm sorry, I'll tell you." He ran to catch up with her.

"That idiot!" Janie was furious. "He doesn't know the first thing about Betty!" She poked him in the chest. "Don't you dare listen to him."

"But what does it mean?"

"You sure you want to know what it means?"

His eyes widened as he listened to Janie's graphic definition of the word. No way was Betty that kind of lady. He hadn't known such a job existed, but he was sure Betty would never do something so awful to make money.

Relieved, he skipped the rest of the way home, ignoring Janie's orders to slow down.

"How was school today, sweetheart?" Betty stood in the kitchen with her blue apron on, cutting out cookies on a floured board. "Sugar cookies, coming up soon!"

She smiled and winked. Betty had a way of making Randy feel important.

"Betty?" Randy hesitated. "You look really pretty today."

"Aww, aren't you a doll?" She planted a perfumed kiss on top of his head. "Go change into your play clothes, and check on Rosie for me, would you, love?"

Rosie was sitting in her crib, playing quietly. She never made much noise unless he pinched her. Sometimes, when he was sad in his tummy, hurting Rosie made him feel better.

Janie had only caught him doing it once.

"Stop it!" She'd snatched Rosie up, just after the pinch, but before she'd had a chance to start squawking.

The sight of her breathless crying face, the few seconds between the pinch and the shriek, was the part he liked the best.

Cringing, he expected Janie to yell for Betty. His heart pounded, and his hands trembled like old Mrs. Beasley next door. *Please, Lord, don't let her tell on me. I won't do it again.*

"*Shhh*. You're all right." Janie soothed Rosie, patting her back and kissing away her tears. She glared at Randy over Rosie's shoulder.

Rosie's cries died down to a shaky whimper. She lifted her head off Janie's shoulder and turned to look at Randy. Gone was the smile she usually saved for him. She rubbed her eyes with her chubby little fists and laid her curly head back down onto Janie's shoulder. Shoving her thumb into her cherubic mouth, she sucked until her eyes began to close.

Janie hadn't told on him. He learned a lesson from that close call and made sure no one else was around the next time he gave one of Rosie's chunky legs a little pinch.

"Rosie," Randy whispered to her through the crib slats.

She pulled the stuffed teddy bear out of her mouth, startled by Randy's sudden appearance. A thin string of drool ran down her chin onto the front of her gown. She frowned a little. Rosie didn't seem to like Randy much lately.

"Come here." He held out his hands through the bars of the crib, motioning for her to crawl to him.

Her mouth puckered into a frown, and she looked as though she might start to cry. Rosie used her feet to turn her body away from him.

"I'm trying to be nice to you." Randy could feel his tummy rumbling around. "Come here, dumb baby."

He stretched as far as his arm could reach and grabbed hold of her foot. Pulling it as hard as he could, he managed to yank her over to the side of the bed closest to him. In the process, she fell flat onto her back.

Better hurry before she starts hollering. He glanced at the door to be sure no one was watching. His heart raced with excitement as he slid his hand up her nightgown. He loved the way her skin felt, soft and bouncy. Once he'd reached her armpit, he wiggled his thumb and forefinger just a little further into the opening of her sleeve.

Rosie rolled her head to the side and smiled. She kicked her feet in the way she always did when she was pleased.

"You like that?" Randy grinned back, "Does it tickle?"

Her smiled quickly transformed into a pout, then into an open-mouthed, silent cry as Randy squeezed the plump, delicate spot just under her arm with all his might.

"Betty," Randy yelled over the top of Rosie's shrieks, "I think Rosie is poopy. Do you want Janie to change her diaper?"

He patted Rosie on the head, a little too hard, and waited for Betty to respond.

"Quiet! I can't hear Betty!" He slapped Rosie on the belly, which only upset her more.

Tired of waiting for Betty and sick of the crying, Randy reached through the bars and squeezed Rosie's mouth hard for a second before leaving the room.

"Betty?" Randy called for her through the house. Freshly baked cookies rested on the table to cool in the empty kitchen. Her bedroom door was wide open, but she wasn't there either.

Tinkling laughter wafted through the open parlor windows. The front porch—that was where the sound was coming from. She was out front. Relief washed over him.

"Oh my!" Betty teased her faceless visitor, "You are a mess!"

"So, around what time would be acceptable for you, doll?" The man added, "Now that you're an upstanding woman, you know, with children and all."

Both Betty and her visitor laughed over this as if it were the cleverest thing to say in the whole wide world. Randy didn't think the man was funny at all.

Randy couldn't understand her hushed words. He considered peeking through Betty's lace curtains but decided against it. Snooping was bad enough, but getting caught for snooping was even worse. His throat was tight, and he could barely swallow, but he wasn't going to cry just because Betty had a new boyfriend.

His legs couldn't carry him away fast enough from the sounds of them mooning over each other. The potting shed in the back corner of the yard seemed like as good a place as any to hide. He banged the door shut behind him, stirring up a cloud of cobwebs and dust.

He swiped away the angry tears that streamed down his dirty face. Betty had no right to get a boyfriend. Daddy was supposed to be her boyfriend.

But if Daddy is married to Mama, how's that gonna work? Can Daddy have a girlfriend?

It was all very confusing.

CHAPTER 25

DISCOMBOBULATED

She had strategically placed her dressing table in the corner of the room, where the natural daylight from windows on both sides would illuminate her face in the vanity mirror. Doing double duty as a mother was beginning to take its toll on her complexion. The morning light wasn't as kind as it used to be to her freshly washed face.

She dipped her fingers into a pot of cold cream and began to smear it all over her face, examining for signs of wrinkles, searching for reasons her dates hadn't gifted her as much as usual.

Gifted? Is that what we're calling it now?

Of course, she never called the gifts what they really were, not even to her dates. For the gifts were not gifts at all. Instead, they were cold hard cash, payment rendered for services provided.

Betty had been in the business for just long enough—long enough to get past the moral dilemma, long enough to build a small reputation, and long enough to develop the necessary skills.

One of her dates had made the mistake of calling her a prostitute. She'd made sure he regretted his words. Prostitutes walked the streets and turned their money over to pimps. Prostitutes were dirty people. She was none of those things.

Betty gave something to her dates they couldn't get at home—affection, undivided attention, and, more importantly, desire. In Betty's boudoir, a date knew he was the only man that mattered to her. At least for the moment.

She replayed the evening before back through her mind, as if it were a movie. Unless she missed something, some big clue that he hadn't been satisfied, everything had seemed swell. She shrugged her shoulders and decided the amount had been a mistake.

She dipped her puff into a pot of loose powder and shook the excess off. Closing her eyes, she covered her entire face with a thin layer. As she built her face for the day, Betty thought about the dates she had scheduled for the rest of the week.

Early on, before she'd adjusted her mindset, she'd used the morning hours to berate herself for her low station in life. As the years wore on, Betty realized her position wasn't lowly. It was honest.

Rosie's waking cry from the other room reminded Betty she had bigger things to worry about than her dates for the week. Pearl was still missing.

"Randy, Janie, hurry up, or you're going to be late!" She called as she walked through the house toward the kitchen. "Breakfast will be ready in five minutes."

She popped some bread into the toaster and pulled out several eggs from the icebox. The tasks of caring for them was easy enough. It was the way they were always underneath her feet that was beginning to suffocate her.

After the children were off to school, Betty bundled Rosie up. "Do you want to go see your grandpa?"

Rosie grinned and pulled her finger out of her mouth long enough to reach for Betty's face.

"If your grandpa wasn't so stubborn and old, he'd have a telephone," she crooned to Rosie, "yes, he would." She touched the tip of Rosie's perfect nose. "And then we could just call him."

***

Rosie kicked her feet and said, "Mama."

She beat on his front door until she nearly bruised her knuckles, but he didn't answer. She tested the knob, and it was unlocked.

The inside was typical of an old man who had lived through the Great Depression. Full of salvaged items—empty cans, jars, and other things saved for "just in case," the home was somewhat disorderly but clean enough. She looked around for a spot to put Rosie down and found an area that was clear of clutter. She dug around in her diaper bag, pulled out a few toys, and placed them in front of Rosie.

Rosie's face lit up, and she grabbed a rattler.

"Hello?" She walked through the house. "Are you in here?"

The house was still. From the kitchen sink, she could see movement near the barn. He was a damned fool, too old to be out working like that. She grabbed Rosie from the parlor and went out to talk to him.

"Don't you know you're too old for that kind of work?" She held her hand over her eyes to shield them from the bright morning sun. Rosie squinted and turned away.

He wiped the sweat from his brow and smiled. "Never too old for this work. This work keeps me from getting too old." He pulled a handkerchief from his pocket and wiped his hands. "What brings you all of the way out here?"

"If you had a phone, I would've just called."

"Eh, phones are for lazy folks." His blue eyes twinkled under white, bushy brows. "How're my grandchildren?"

"They're well." She wanted to choose the right words. "But we need to talk. Do you have some time?"

His smile faded. "I can make some time." He pointed toward the house. "I'll meet you inside."

Gesturing for her to sit at the kitchen table, he said, "So, what is it?" His tone was abrupt. "What do we need to talk about?"

She bounced Rosie on her knee for a second or two before answering. Everything she'd rehearsed on the way out to his farm sounded selfish, cruel even, now that she was sitting in front of the old man.

"How much longer do you expect I'll have the children?"

His pale blue eyes misted with tears. "I don't know. How can I know when my Ingrid is still missing?" Resting his head in his hands, he lamented, "That son of a bitch isn't even looking for her. Doesn't care that she's gone."

"I understand." She placed her hand lightly atop his forearm. "But I can't keep them forever, you see? I have a life, too."

"I'll get you more money," he promised.

"It's not about the money." She hoped her voice sounded kind, gentle. "I didn't have children of my own because I don't want the hassle of taking care of them."

"What am I supposed to do with them?" The red rims of his eyes emphasized the blue centers. Seeing an old man cry had to top the worst of experiences she could recall.

"I don't know." She shook her head. "But you're going to have to figure out something soon. Rosie thinks I'm her mama. It's only going to be more difficult the longer they're with me."

CHAPTER 26

THE FINAL STRAW

"Please, just let me get you back into the mood." She did her best to keep the desperation out of her voice, but it was there.

He cocked an eyebrow and finished threading his belt through the last loop. "Sorry, doll. No can do. The sounds coming from the other room are too distracting."

He leaned over and gave her a quick peck on the nose. "If I want to hear a baby squawking, I'll go home."

She nodded and pulled her silk robe around her shoulders. "Are you leaving anything for me?"

"Here's a little for your time." He tossed a few meager bills onto the foot of her bed. Nothing close to what she'd expected.

She waited until he'd gone before getting up to quiet Rosie. The other two had managed to stay sleeping through all the fussing.

Little Rosie stood holding onto the edge of her crib. "Mama," she said, reaching for Betty.

"Not your mama," she whispered and lifted her out of bed.

Rosie leaned into Betty and relaxed. The last of her tears subsided, and she yawned.

With each bouncing motion Betty made, Rosie became heavier, limper. Soon, her breathing was that of a sleeping child, slow and shallow.

Taking great care not to wake her, Betty placed her into the crib and covered her. Although the room was darkened, she could see Janie had kicked her bedsheets off. She tucked them back around her thin shoulders and kissed her on her forehead.

Randy was sleeping soundly. In the dark, he looked like a perfect angel. During his waking hours, he was beginning to show signs of trouble.

She ran her fingers through his downy hair and wondered what disturbing dreams his mind played for him at night.

The poor little guy doesn't stand a chance.

Betty closed the guest room door quietly and padded softly to the kitchen. Since the children had come to stay, the night had become her favorite time. Her days were filled with their messes and noises, and she could barely think.

The familiar process of making coffee gave her a sense of security. It was the same routine every time—rinse the pot, fill the pot with water, put the coffee in the basket, put the basket in the pot, put the lid on, put the pot on the burner, and wait for the coffee to percolate. She liked things that gave her a sense of security.

Cold, hard cash also gave her a sense of security. She lit a cigarette and thought about all the money she was losing thanks to the children.

Tonight's date was the second one that ended short this week. Tonight was Rosie's fault. Monday night's date had ended early because of Randy.

When she thought about that disaster, she wasn't sure whether to laugh or cry. *Poor man, he'll probably never come back.* She'd just begun what she liked to think of as her grand finale when catastrophe struck.

"Oh God," he moaned. "It feels so fucking good! Don't stop! Please don't ever stop."

Buck naked and straddling him backward, she faced the foot of the bed. She'd bound her date's hands and feet to the bedposts with silken ties, which was meant to be pleasurable. And of course, it was, right up until the part where Randy barged into her room holding a dead frog.

"My frog died!" He screamed at Betty, thrusting the lifeless frog in her direction. "I woke up to go pee, and he's dead!"

"Get out!" She yelled at Randy but continued to ride her date like a Comanche on a wild mustang. It hadn't occurred to her to stop.

"Hey!" He bucked her off him. "What the hell? Is that your brat?"

"I'm so sorry!" Only then did she think to pull a sheet up to cover her nakedness.

Randy didn't budge. His eyes were stuck wide open, his mouth gaping. The frog dropped to the floor with a splat.

"Go, Randy! Go back to bed!"

She took a long drag off the cigarette and exhaled a laugh. The laughter turned to tears, which quickly changed into heaving sobs. She fumbled around in her robe pocket for her handkerchief and dabbed away at the salty drops puddling out of her eyes, smearing mascara all over the white cloth.

"Oh, Pearl," she cried out, "where are you? And what am I supposed to do with your babies?"

She wondered, for what seemed like the hundredth time, whether her childhood friend was even alive. "Don't you know they still need you?" She whispered to the empty chair where Pearl had sat for so many talks.

Betty had a decision to make. And no one, not Pearl, not Wyatt, not even the old man was there to help her figure it out. Emotions didn't pay the bills, and she'd worked too hard to let feelings put her out on the streets now. She wasn't getting any younger. She might only have a few more good years left before she'd have to settle on one fellow. One fellow would equate into less income and more work in the kitchen.

There was no way around it. It was time to give them back to their father.

CHAPTER 27

GOING HOME

The new toy Betty had given him was missing. He'd looked under the bed, under Rosie's crib, inside the closet, and everywhere else he could think to look.

It was a simple model car—the kind that could be painted. He'd begged for it each time they'd gone to the store. When she'd finally given in, he hadn't let the thing out of his sight.

"Betty?" He yelled for her, even though she'd told him never to wake her on Saturday morning. "Have you seen my new car?"

He stopped abruptly. Several suitcases were stacked up by the front door. Outside, Betty was busy loading boxes into the trunk of her car. She didn't notice him at first.

"Betty? Are we going for a drive?"

"Good morning." Red-faced, she looked like she'd been crying all night.

His tummy started to hurt. Scared that she was leaving them, just like Mama had, he asked, "Where are you going? Can I come with you?"

"I'm not going anywhere, honey." Her smile was thin and not at all real. It was the same kind of smile his teacher made when Principal Ballard visited their classroom. "You're going home to your daddy."

"Is Mama back?" He felt a spark of hope. It'd been so long since he'd seen her, he was having trouble remembering what she looked like.

"Not yet," she said, "but your daddy is there. And it's time you go home."

On the drive to the farm, Janie picked at a hangnail while she stared out of the window. Her jaw was thrust forward in the way she did when she was mad and pouting.

"Janie," Randy whispered and reached for her hand. "Do you think Betty's mad at us?"

Janie wrenched her hand away. "I told you she'd get rid of us." A tear dropped into her lap.

Rosie sat in her car seat, busy chewing on the corner of the blanket. She didn't seem to notice Randy's or Janie's sadness.

"Must be nice to be so dumb," he whispered to her.

She cooed and offered her slobbery blanket to him.

Randy pushed the blanket, along with her hand, away. Rosie was lucky. She didn't know what it felt like to be so sad. It wasn't fair that she was so happy all the time.

Betty rolled her window down a crack and lit a cigarette. He watched her from the backseat, trying to read her face. If she loved him, all of them, as much as she said, why was she leaving them with Daddy?

With her cigarette in her hand, she turned the radio on. In a mellow, rich tone, she sang along to a song by Perry Como.

He loved to hear Betty sing. Most days, he would join in with her, but his throat felt too tight to let his voice squeeze through. Instead, he leaned back into the seat and let the air wipe the tears away from his eyes.

The drive to Daddy's house didn't take nearly long enough. Even a five-hour drive would've been too soon. Janie looked a lot like the stone statue of Mary, the mama of Jesus—serious and a little sad. He'd seen Mama Mary at the graveyard when Daddy's friend died.

"Come," Betty ordered. "Help carry your things." She opened the trunk and handed a suitcase to each of them. "Well, go on. Say hello to your daddy."

Janie rolled her eyes at Randy, and he couldn't help but smile. She flipped her hair, angry, and turned away from Betty. Since Betty's announcement this morning, Janie hadn't said a word to her.

He waited for her to go up the steps before following her. It was strange to walk into the house after being gone for so long. He sat his suitcase down in front of the sofa and examined the parlor. Other than a few empty cups and plates sitting around, not much had changed. The smell in the house, however, was a lot like the dead opossum he and Janie had found by the garden last summer.

"Ugh." He scrunched up his nose. "What's that stink?"

"How am I supposed to know?" Janie snarled and asked, "Does it look like I'm the expert?"

Betty stormed in with Rosie perched on her hip. "You two need to finish carrying the rest of your things."

"Oh, my Lord! What is that God-awful smell?" She made a sour face, sat Rosie down in the middle of the parlor floor, and went into the kitchen.

Randy shrugged his shoulders. "Come on, Janie."

Janie lifted one box from the trunk, then another. "Here, this one's light enough for you to carry."

"What do you think is in them?"

"Probably everything she gave us." Janie's voice was strained. "What difference does it make?"

He followed behind her, their shoes making a crunching sound on the gravel drive.

This wasn't fair. First, Mama went away, and now, Betty didn't want them. Even worse, Janie was mad at him for it all.

Inside, they sat the boxes next to their suitcases and listened to the noise coming from above. Betty was angry. There was no mistaking the sound.

"Because they're your children," Betty yelled. "Not mine!"

Daddy said something back and laughed, but Randy couldn't make out his words.

"You piece of shit! How dare you talk that way to me! I've done nothing but help you while you went on the bender of your life! You have no right to judge me!" A loud slap punctuated the last word of her sentence.

Her high-heeled shoes were hammer strikes across the floor above them and then down the stairs. She seemed startled to see Janie and Randy.

"I have to go." Shaking and thin-lipped, she said, "Tell your grandpa if you need anything."

Rosie puckered up and began to cry. "Mama!" She reached up for Betty, bouncing up and down, begging to be picked up.

"I can't take you," Betty said. "You're not mine. You never were." She held Rosie's little wrists to prevent her from latching on and leaned down to kiss the top of her head.

Rosie screamed even louder when Betty slammed the door shut behind her.

Randy watched the fog of dust stirred up by her car as she sped down the driveway. He wished he could cry for Betty, but he knew it wouldn't make her come back for them.

He sneaked a look at Janie. Consoling Rosie by walking and bouncing, she wore the same angry look as before. Once his big sister got mad, she usually stayed that way for a while.

"Come on, dummy." Janie smacked him on the arm and said, "Let's go figure out what died in the kitchen."

She grinned at Rosie and poked her gently in the tummy. "Should we go figure out what died in the kitchen?"

Rosie babbled and smiled through her tears.

"Maybe it's Mama!" Janie laughed as if she'd said the funniest thing in the world. Rosie giggled with her.

CHAPTER 28

POLLY

Perhaps the baby had been born months ago, or, just as easily, a year before. Time passed by erratically since she'd been on the streets. The first few weeks had been hell.

Huddled in small groups around the embankment and under bridges, the homeless flocked near the river at night. Made up of mostly older men, there was a pecking order amongst them.

Pearl kept to herself, deferring to all but the youngest for shelter under the bridge.

The nights were growing colder, which presented a dilemma. Fire was quick to warm a cold body and just as quick to alert the police of their presence.

Pulling the tattered blanket tightly around her shoulders, she scanned the horizon for signs of intruders. New faces sometimes meant trouble.

She kept a close eye on her neighbor. The woman was a newcomer to the group. It was difficult to guess her age. Life on the street was harsh. Food was scarce, and bathing was reduced to a quick splash of the face and underarms in the bus station restroom.

Whenever she bothered to look in the dingy restroom mirror, Pearl realized she looked much older than her own years.

She guessed the newcomer could have been anywhere between thirty and fifty years old.

A yellow crocheted hat covered the woman's dirty blonde hair, except for a few curly strands peeking out of the bottom. Her worn, double-breasted woolen coat fit as though it had been tailored for her.

Rocking back and forth, the woman held a worn-out book close to her chest. It was her prop.

It was important to have a prop, something to pretend to be doing, while barely existing out on the streets. Pearl's prop was a half-empty sketch pad she'd found while scrounging through a bus station dumpster.

Sometimes, she made pictures in it. Mostly, she sat with a pencil in hand, posed on the blank sheet of paper, and watched for intruders.

"What're you reading?"

"*The Catcher in the Rye.*" The woman's voice came out in a whisper of sorts. "Have you read it? It's by J.D. Salinger."

Pearl shook her head. "I don't read much."

"Holden," she blurted out, "he's a lot like me."

"Who's Holden?"

The woman shook the book in front of Pearl's face. "The book, the fellow in the book!"

She took a deep breath as if she were trying to calm herself down. "The book—it's good. You should read it sometime. He speaks to me."

"Sure," Pearl nodded to be agreeable. "Thank you for your offer."

"No!" She clutched the book tightly to her heaving chest. "Y-y-you have to g-g-get your own!"

The last word was emphasized in such a way that left no confusion for Pearl. It was not intended to be a loan, merely a recommendation.

Pearl wanted to laugh. She imagined what her reaction to this type of treatment would've been before, when she was a real person, living in a real house. With every fiber of her being, she would have been mortified, angry perhaps. But, in this new world, female companionship was rare. She wasn't about to run off the only woman, crazy or not, remotely close to her own age.

"Of course," she reassured. "I'll get my own."

The world's biggest J.D. Salinger fan began to breathe more easily. She turned her soft brown eyes toward Pearl and smiled. "Maybe, when I'm done, I'll let you read it."

Pearl shrugged and said, "If you feel like it."

"What are you writing about?"

Pearl glanced down at the blank tablet in her lap. "Oh, just sketching. You know, flowers and things. Nothing, really."

"I see," the woman whispered. She covered a giggle with her grimy hand and looked away.

Pearl suppressed the urge to laugh out loud and asked, "Where are you from?"

"That depends on who you ask."

"Who should I ask?" She decided to play along. It seemed harmless enough.

"Well," the woman paused, "you could ask me. I'm Polly." Cupping the side of her face with her hand, she added in a loud whisper, "Or, you could ask him." She pointed to the empty space behind her shoulder.

Chills traveled up from Pearl's toes to the top of her head. She cleared her throat. "I think I'd rather ask you, Polly."

Don't be silly. There's no one there. She's a loony.

Polly cocked her head to the side and squinted her eyes, as though she were telling a secret. She nodded her head and grinned. "I'm from Boerne—same as you."

"How...who told you that?" She'd told no one where she was from. Beyond her first name, she hadn't shared anything personal with any of the other street people. She examined Polly's face, trying to remember if she'd seen her before.

Pointing behind her shoulder with her thumb, she said, "He told me." She scratched at the rim of her crocheted hat for a second or two before opening her book.

It didn't take much time to gather her belongings. The sun was fading, and she'd rather not spend the night next to Polly and her invisible friend. "I need to check on someone."

"See you next time, then." Polly waved.

She set off walking along the river, away from her usual encampment. Someone had decided to brave a fire in a small trash can under the Houston Street bridge. She thought about joining them but decided against it. As much as she wanted to warm up, drawing attention to herself was the last thing she needed. No way was she going back to that place again.

"Hey, good lookin'!" A man from the nearby gathering shouted in her direction. "Hey! I'm talkin' to you!"

She kept her eyes cast down and prayed the attention was meant for someone else. Women were few and far between in this underground world, and to be alone was asking for trouble. Each footstep would take her farther away from the voice, so she focused on the number of them. *Nineteen, twenty, twenty-one, twenty-two...*

"Don't you know it's rude to ignore someone when they're speaking to you?" Something between a snarl and a smile crossed his scarred-up face.

He'd crossed the distance more quickly than seemed possible.

Startled by his sudden presence, she wanted to scream, to slap at him, but she knew better. She took a step away from him and said, "I'm sorry. I didn't realize you were talking to me."

"Where are you heading to this fine evening?" His hand was on her arm, preventing her from moving forward.

"I'm going to meet my husband at the next bridge over." She forced herself to smile. "He's waiting for me."

Squinting, he examined her face for a moment before releasing her arm. "Have a good evening, ma'am." With a tip of his frayed hat, he was done with her.

She watched him walk away and exhaled the shaky breath she'd been holding in since her lie. The next bridge over didn't feel far enough away from the man, but she wouldn't be able to travel much farther in the dark. Better to settle in for the night. Polly's invisible fellow didn't seem so bad after all, and she found herself wishing that she'd stayed.

The sounds of the street people faded as she neared the next bridge. In contrast, only a few were camped out for the night, most already sleeping.

She imagined that the crowd back at the Houston bridge were the more robust men, still wishing for whiskey and women. This group, she thought with a smile, was the elderly sort—yearning for a hot meal and a warm bed.

She squatted behind a spot sheltered from the view of the street and peed. Careful not to disturb any of her neighbors, she found a safe space near a thick shrub and unrolled her blankets.

Curling up on her side, she quietly unwrapped her only meal for the day. She'd learned to eat when the others weren't watching. It saved her from harassment and guilt. A little stale, but still better than nothing, the Moon Pie staved off her hunger pangs.

She'd watched a child throw it defiantly onto the grass earlier that morning. When his parents weren't looking, she'd snatched it up and tucked it away. He'd hollered something fierce about the pastry after she'd picked it up. The parents had been too busy talking with their friends to notice. She hadn't felt bad about taking it. Maybe, she thought, he won't act so spoiled next time.

She scrubbed her teeth with her fingers and wondered if Wyatt was reminding the children to brush their teeth every day. She tried not to think of them too often. This was the kind of guilt she couldn't easily push away.

They were better off without her. She cleared her mind and let the river's night songs lull her to sleep.

"Where's that husband of yours?" A rough hand smelling of stale tobacco clamped over her mouth. "Make one sound, and I'll snap your neck, little birdie," he hissed in her ear. His hot, liquor-soaked breath made her skin crawl.

Looking side to side, she scanned her surroundings as best she could without moving her head. Save for a few dim streetlights, the sky was black. Laughter from the party one bridge over had died down. The bundle lying near her was gone, and she had no idea how close her nearest neighbor was. Even if she were to call for help, she wasn't sure anyone would stick their neck out for her. There was no place for ladies on the street.

"I knew you was a liar." He dug around in his satchel and pulled out something soft shaped. The darkness made it nearly impossible to see details, and his hand held her head still, preventing her from looking directly.

She had the notion she should be crying, but the tears weren't there.

He lifted his hand long enough to shove the soft thing into her mouth. It was fabric—a dirty, sweat-soaked sock.

She bullied the urge to vomit. Instead, she focused on his movements, his appearance. He was one she'd better memorize.

When he had finished, she did not give him the satisfaction of a single tear. He took his dirty sock and left with a mumbled threat about keeping quiet. She lay motionless for a long while afterward and stared into the starless sky.

When the light began to seep into the dark, the homeless started to gather their things and head out to wherever they spent their days.

"I knew that was going to happen."

Behind her, carrying her book, Polly appeared to be tagging along for the journey to Pearl's regular post.

"Pardon me?" Pearl spun around. "What are you talking about?"

"The man, last night." She looked sympathetic enough. "I knew that was going to happen. He told me."

She pointed to the air behind her.

"No one's there!" she snapped at Polly. "You're crazy!"

"If you say so," Polly sniffed and walked around her.

Several of the group chuckled. Someone muttered under his breath, "Who in the hell is she talking to?"

CHAPTER 29

1955

Sweat dripped down her brow into her eyes. She used one of the red handkerchiefs to wipe her face and went back to the tedious work of handwashing their laundry. The washing machine had been busted since Christmas break.

"What do you think I'm made of? Money?" Daddy grumbled the last time she'd asked him to fix it. But he was the first to ask about clean clothes every Monday morning.

She consoled herself with the fact that the weather was getting warmer, which meant drying on the line took less time. Laundry was an all-day affair to begin with. It would be nice to be done with the ironing before Sunday evening supper for a change.

"Rosie!" She yelled toward the direction of the house. "Come here, please."

Three-year-old Rosie peeked her head around from the front porch where she was playing with her dollies. "What?"

"Come help me wring out the laundry!"

Rosie disappeared behind the silhouette of the house.

Janie grinned. "Come on, Rosie! Help me so we can bake some cookies!"

The cookies always did it. Rosie had a sweet tooth to be reckoned with. Baby doll in hand, with her lopsided blond pigtails flying behind her, Rosie ran at full speed over to the makeshift laundry room Janie had set up near the clothesline.

"What kind of cookies are we gonna make?" Her blue eyes were wide with excitement. She grabbed on to the other end of the sopping wet shirt and began to make twisting motions.

"No, Rosie." Janie had a reservoir of patience for her baby sister. "Your hands are too tiny still. Remember? Just hold it steady while I twist."

"Oh, yeah." She crinkled up her nose and said, "I forgot. But, what kinda cookies are we gonna make?"

"Lemon."

Although the laundry would've gone a lot faster with someone taller, Janie was thankful for another pair of hands. Randy was never around when she needed help. Asking Daddy would be unthinkable.

After she'd hung the clothes on the line and dumped the tubs of water, Janie poured a glass of cold water from the almost empty icebox. Soon, she'd have to talk to Daddy about some grocery money.

In the pantry, she kept a stash of cigarettes she'd tapped from Daddy after he'd passed out. He'd never said a word—probably thought he'd smoked them all. She didn't do it often. Just in the evenings or after a big chore, such as the laundry.

She waited until she was outside before lighting up. Daddy always smoked in the house, and it made Rosie cough. It made their clothes and hair stink, too.

She was getting quite good at the whole match-lighting part. At first, she'd wasted six or seven matches just to light one cigarette.

The first drag was always the nicest. She let the smoke fill her lungs and held it for just a second or two. Now, she understood the satisfied look on Mama's face. Mama crossed her mind often. A part of her wondered if Mama's ghost was there with her, smoking a ghost cigarette.

"Hey!" Rosie startled her. "Aren't you supposed to be a growed up person before you do that?" She winced against the setting sun.

"It's grown-up," she corrected Rosie. "And I do plenty of grown-up things, so I think I'm entitled to a grown-up cigarette." She inhaled, holding the cigarette, just the way she'd seen Mama do hundreds of times.

"When are we gonna make cookies?"

"Soon. Just let me have a minute to myself."

Rosie walked away, shoulders sagging, head tipped down. She was easy to read. Janie liked this about her. No guessing what Rosie thought or felt. If it weren't for Rosie and Grandpa, Janie would hate everyone on the face of the earth.

The yard was quiet. There were no signs of Randy or Daddy. That was fine with her. If both of them disappeared, she wouldn't miss them much.

She stamped out the cigarette on the side of the back porch and tossed the butt into an empty can. The recent rains had caused the weathered screen door to swell up, and she had to give it a tug to open it. It needed painting, along with the rest of the house, but Daddy was too busy with working and drinking to even think about it.

She'd thought about volunteering for the job, but she could barely handle the house and school. And besides, getting extra money from Daddy was like squeezing blood out of a turnip.

Rosie was already inside the pantry, making a big racket. "Janie?" She appeared at the pantry door with an armful of canisters. "Do we need vinegar for the cookies?"

Janie laughed. "How did you manage to get flour in your hair? We haven't even started!"

"Do we? Need vinegar?" Rosie tilted her head to the side and grinned. Spending her days with Grandpa had given her some very unusual mannerisms for a three-year-old girl.

"No, silly! Vinegar would be disgusting!" Janie tousled some of the flour out of Rosie's hair. "Put that stuff down, and find an apron."

She wiped Randy's toast crumbs off the table and arranged the ingredients in order of the recipe. Janie liked things to be orderly. "You can smash the oleo with the eggs." She handed Rosie a potato masher.

Rosie climbed onto a chair and sat on her knees in front of the mixing bowl. She struggled to peel off the wrapper and turned to Janie. "I can't do it."

"Of course, you can. Just peel the edge like this." Janie took the stick of margarine from her and carefully peeled back at the edge. "See? Not so hard."

Rosie frowned. "Can we turn on the radio?"

"If it'll get you to work faster," Janie teased. She poked Rosie in the ribs.

"Hey!" Rosie smiled and threatened to fling margarine and eggs onto her.

"Put that down and dance with me." Janie held her hands out.

Rosie squealed and jumped off the chair. Her hands were soft and warm inside Janie's. "We're gonna rock around the clock tonight. We're gonna rock, rock, rock 'til broad daylight." She danced a crazy twist while singing along. "Hey, Janie, this one's my favorite song!"

"Mine, too!" Holding Rosie's hand like a tether, Janie tapped the beat with her toes. Moments like this, everything bad just disappeared. She could forget Mama was dead, Daddy was a drunk, and that Betty had thrown them away. Rosie was her special person. Mama used to say that everybody had at least one. Rosie filled her heart with sunshine.

"You know what, Rosie?"

She stopped twirling. "No, what?"

"Our mama used to dance around the kitchen with me, just like this."

"I remember that," Rosie smiled and resumed spinning in circles.

"But you couldn't. You weren't there."

Rosie's brow crinkled. "Yes, I was!" She nodded her head and insisted, "I 'member her dancing me 'round when I was little."

She looked around the kitchen. "The stove and 'frigerator was pink back then. I know 'cause pink's my best color."

"No," Janie argued, "we've never had a pink—" She stopped. Rosie was too little to remember Betty.

"I 'member it!" She stomped her foot on the floor. Her smile was gone, replaced by a defiant jut of her jaw.

"You're right, I forgot." Janie hugged her and said, "Let's get those cookies into the oven."

The kitchen was dark and cool. Monday mornings were always the same for Janie. She was the first to wake, even before their old rooster. The pot of coffee she made was a top priority, more so for the scent than the taste. It reminded her of Mama, and if truth be told, of Betty, too. The aroma of coffee was a symbol of comfort, a sign the storm had passed. Sometimes, it was a welcome to a new friend or a peace offering to an old one. And, at the beginning of the day, coffee was always the smell of hope.

Once the coffee was percolating, she scrounged around for something to feed Randy and Rosie. For a day or so after Daddy's payday, there would be a box of Sugar Smacks or Trix cereal in the pantry. Beyond that, breakfast would be something that required a little more effort than pouring into a bowl. This Monday was a week and two days after Daddy's last paycheck. If it weren't for the chickens, they would be in bad shape.

She tugged at the sticky refrigerator door handle and cursed under her breath. No doubt, Randy was behind the gluey mess somehow. He rarely thought of washing his hands.

The egg bowl was almost empty. She growled and slammed the door. She hated digging for eggs in the dark.

Daddy's truck wasn't parked in the driveway, which wasn't all that unusual. She breathed a small prayer that he wouldn't come home until they'd gone for the day.

She rummaged around under several of the roosting hens until she found enough eggs for breakfast. For the most part, the chickens didn't protest much. Because she was the one who fed them every day, they trusted her. Randy would never have been able to get that close without creating a big uproar. Even though a chicken's brain is the size of a peanut, she figured they hadn't forgotten all the times Randy had pestered them.

"Randy! Rosie!" She yelled up to the ceiling—something she'd never do if Daddy were home. "Breakfast is ready."

A thump sounded above her head, followed by crying.

"Get up, I said!" Randy yelled.

Janie dropped her fork onto her plate and scooted her chair away from the table. She grabbed the biggest wooden spoon out of the drawer next to the stove and ran up the stairs.

Randy was towering over Rosie, where she lay next to the bed, wrapped up in her sheet.

"What happened?"

"H-h-he pulled me outta the bed," Rosie hiccupped through her tears. "An' he jus' kicked me in m-my bottom!"

The light dimmed, and all the sounds in the room had been sucked into the tunnel inside her head. "What in the hell for?" She cocked back the hand, holding the wooden spoon, and whacked at Randy's head with every ounce of strength she could muster. "She's still a baby!"

Randy screamed like a pig, but she didn't stop with his head. He dropped down to the floor to escape the thrashing. She smacked his back and shoulders at least twenty times.

"No, Janie!" Terrified, Rosie covered her face with the sheet.

"I hate you!" Janie shouted. "You're the reason Betty got rid of us, and it's your fault that Mama died!"

"Take it back!" Randy's arms were covered with red marks from the spoon, and blood was running out of his nose. The backs of his hands were splattered with welts from shielding his body from the beating.

"Everything's your fault! Mama was happy before you were born!" She didn't care that her words were hateful. He deserved it.

"You're a mean, horrible sister! And you have flat titties! So, there!" Randy ran out of the bedroom and slammed the door behind him.

"I wish you were dead!" She threw a shoe at the closed door.

Rosie had completely covered herself in her sheet. Sobbing, she sat on the floor in a pile where Randy had pulled her off the bed.

Janie lifted the sheet off her head and said, "Come here." She picked her up and swayed back and forth, quieting her. Rosie was over half her height, and her toes scraped Janie's shins with each rocking motion.

She pressed her face into Rosie's soft neck and breathed in her scent, a mixture of soap and sunshine. "I'm sorry he hurt you," she whispered into her hair. "I don't know why he does that."

When Rosie had calmed down enough for the shivering to stop, Janie sat her on the bed. "Let's get you dressed for Grandpa. He's gonna be here any minute now."

"Hop on in." Grandpa said the same thing every morning. The inside of Grandpa's truck smelled like grease, gas, and chewing tobacco, and she loved it. Plus, it was better than riding the bus.

Rosie scrambled up into the spot right next to Grandpa and wrapped her arms around his neck. "Good mornin', Grandpa." She wriggled into the seat, nearly sitting on top of him.

"How's my girl?" He chuckled and squeezed her. Janie suspected Grandpa loved Rosie the most, but that was fine. After all, she loved Rosie the most, too.

"I'm jus' fine, 'cept Randy yanked me outta bed and kicked me right in the bottom."

"He did what?" Grandpa cast a glance at Randy, sitting on the outside, next to the window.

Randy stared at his feet and remained silent.

"That's right. An' you know what else he did?"

126

"I'm afraid to ask." Grandpa shook his head and rubbed his brow with his left hand.

"He told Janie she has flat titties!"

A hot flush spread from Janie's stomach up to her face and ears. She pulled her book close to her chest and stared at the stick shifter. It was bad enough to have a flat chest, but to have Grandpa's attention drawn to it was the most embarrassing thing she could imagine.

"Well, I reckon Randy needs a good whippin'." Grandpa spat some of his chewing tobacco into an old tin can. His face, ordinarily kind, turned angry.

"Is that what you need, son?"

Randy turned to Grandpa and said, "Janie already gave me a good beatin'."

"I see that!" Grandpa frowned, looking more closely at Randy. "Janie, don't you think you went a little hard on him? He looks like someone threw him in a rock tumbler."

"Yes, sir." Janie knew she'd done wrong. She still didn't feel bad about it.

"Where was your daddy during all this fuss?"

Janie shrugged her shoulders. "Your guess is as good as mine."

"He doesn't come home sometimes," Randy added.

Grandpa shoved the gear into reverse and backed the old truck up to turn around. He stopped and turned to Janie. "You keep track of when your daddy's gone. I want to know how much this goes on."

"It's okay, Grandpa," Janie reassured him. "We don't mind."

"Well, I do." He slammed his big hands onto the steering wheel. "A man oughta keep an eye on his young'uns."

Janie didn't respond. She'd never seen Grandpa so mad. Everyone was quiet on the drive to school, even Rosie.

Grandpa pulled into the drive next to the school office. He said the usual thing, "Soak some knowledge into those heads, and have a good day," but his face was still mad.

A nervous butterfly flitted around in the pit of her stomach.

CHAPTER 30

THE PRINCIPAL

Randy hoped he wasn't in trouble. He sat in the waiting chair and watched Mrs. Meyer typing furiously, her spectacles perched on the edge of her pointy nose. Free to stare at the school secretary undetected, he noticed her hair was two different colors. Most of her short, curly hair was a bright shade of reddish-brown. The part closest to her head was silvery-gray. *Interesting*, he thought.

A buzz sounded, and Mrs. Meyer answered, "Yes, Mr. Schmidt? He's waiting now." She motioned to Randy to stand up. "I'll send him in."

His heart beat a little faster as he approached her desk. He thought about the ornery things he'd done over the past week and wondered if any of them were deserving of a spanking. Although he'd never been on the receiving end of the principal's paddle, rumors spread like wildfire amongst the fourth-grade boys about the size and the bite of Mr. Schmidt's paddle.

"Go in there, dear." She pointed to Mr. Schmidt's closed door and went back to her typing.

Mr. Schmidt sat behind his tidy desk, waiting for Randy. Younger than Grandpa, but older than Daddy, Mr. Schmidt wore the same suit jacket every day. His mousy brown hair was slicked back with a shiny lotion, and his face sported a pair of thick, outdated black-rimmed glasses. Randy could tell his left eye was worse off than the right because the lens was twice as thick.

"Have a seat, son."

Randy's pulse settled a bit. He guessed if he were going to get a whipping on his rear-end, Mr. Schmidt wouldn't ask him to sit down on it. He sat in the chair closest to the door.

Mr. Schmidt rearranged some papers on his desk and cleared his throat. Finally, he said, "Son, how are things at home?"

Randy shrugged his shoulders. "Fine, I reckon." His feet wanted to tap, but he made them stay still. Avoiding Mr. Schmidt's gaze, he directed his eyes to the picture frames on the wall.

Mr. Schmidt cleared his throat once again and said, "Look, son, I'm not going to beat around the bush. I think you're old enough to talk to me about your situation."

What situation? Randy wasn't sure what the principal was talking about. Uncomfortable, he waited.

Mr. Schmidt rested back in his chair and tapped his ink pen onto the edge of his desk. "Is someone hitting you?" He leaned forward again. "You can talk to me about it."

"Yes, sir." Randy was happy someone cared. "My sister, Janie. She hits me all the time, sir."

"Is that right? And what does your…" Mr. Schmidt looked down at the papers in front of him. "What does your father say about that?"

"Well, Daddy's not home when she does it."

He examined the paperwork again and asked, "Your sister, Janie?"

"Yes, sir."

"Would you like to tell me about the marks you've got? What'd she hit you with?"

Randy told him how mean Janie had been while Mr. Schmidt wrote in his notebook. When he'd finished, he felt happy. Maybe now, she'd get in trouble. He wondered if Mr. Schmidt was going to spank her. Looking around the office, he searched for the signs of the infamous paddle.

"Get yourself back to class, son." Mr. Schmidt pointed to his door. "And don't forget, if you ever need to talk, my door is open."

Except it wasn't, Randy thought. The principal's door was always closed. He thought about asking when Mr. Schmidt was going to paddle his sister but changed his mind. Mr. Schmidt had picked up the telephone and began dialing a number.

CHAPTER 31

THE VISIT

The bus smelled like sweat and dirty feet. A pack of high school boys tossed back and forth some poor square's shoe from side to side. Miserable looking, he gave up trying to grab it and sat down in his seat.

"Hey, Harvey!" The one with the most pimples teased, "Better get your shoe before I drop it." He dangled Harvey's shoe outside of the open bus window.

Harvey started to stand up, then sat back down. This wouldn't be the first time he'd gone home with one foot bare.

Janie hunkered down into her seat, making herself as small as possible. After the boys got bored with Harvey, they'd be looking for a new victim.

"Sit down!" The bus driver yelled to the back and pulled the door shut.

The old bus jerked forward with a start and a grind. Janie gripped her book bag tightly.

Once the bus was moving at a steady pace, Janie placed her book bag onto the seat next to her. She sat alone, watching the other girls whisper and giggle secrets to each other. Sometimes, she thought it would be nice to have a friend, but the other girls had nothing in common with Janie. They went home to freshly painted houses with mothers and fathers, and cookies baking in the oven. The other girls wore shiny, black Mary Janes and new dresses.

Janie's dresses were hand-me-downs from a cousin, and her shoes were of the scuffed, brown variety. If a classmate had thought to invite Janie over, she wouldn't go anyway. Someone had to watch Rosie, and she didn't trust Randy.

Her stop was one of the first along the route. She was thankful the driveway was so long. Their old farmhouse was an eyesore, with peeling paint and overgrown flower beds. She gathered up her bag and stepped over the assortment of feet, legs, and duffels sitting in the aisle. The tittering and whispering grew louder as she made her way to the front of the bus. She pretended not to notice.

Randy had already reached the front door by the time she climbed off the bus. She stopped at the mailbox because she knew her brother never bothered to check it. He would have grabbed a cookie or two from the jar and plopped himself down in front of their television before she even got to the front porch. She didn't mind. It kept him out of her hair while she did her homework. Grandpa would bring Rosie home by supper time. The hour or so between the bus drop off and supper was the only time Janie had to herself.

She dumped her bag onto the kitchen table and took off her sweater. Beads of sweat dripped down her back. Although the afternoons were growing warmer, the cardigan stayed on for the entire bus ride home. She had yet to think of a better way to hide her budding breasts from the mean high school boys.

There was only one assignment to complete: an essay for English class. If she hurried, she'd have time to read for a while before Grandpa arrived. She examined her pencil and decided it was sharp enough to get through the essay.

The first two paragraphs went quickly. Writing was easy for her. It didn't seem all that different than talking. She was just about to start her third paragraph when Randy shouted for her.

"There's a lady at the door!"

Butterfly wings tickled the inside of her belly. Even though she mostly knew Mama was dead, there was a small part of her that still hoped. She tucked her hair away from her eyes and wiped the wrinkles out of her skirt before going to the door.

The woman on the other side of the door looked nothing like her memories. A drab felt hat sat atop her light brown curls. A thin coat of the same color skimmed her shapeless figure. "May I speak with Mr. Carter?"

"He's not here right now." *Big dummy—Mama's dead.* She knew better than to hope. If Mama were still alive, she would be home already.

The woman put the toe of her right shoe over the threshold. "May I come in and wait?" She took another step inside, preventing Janie from shutting the door.

"I…I don't know when he'll be home," Janie said. She wasn't sure if it was okay for the lady to wait. Whenever people talked about bad guys, they were never women.

"I can tell him you were here," she offered.

"I'll just wait." She smiled and said, "My name is Ms. Crable. And you are?"

"Janie," she stuttered. "I'm Janie." Unease surrounded her. She shouldn't have let the woman in. Daddy might be mad to come home to a strange person in the house. He liked talking to ladies, but this one wasn't very pretty.

"Is your brother home?" She unbuttoned her coat and slipped it off. Instead of hanging it on the coat tree, she folded it over her arm.

Janie nodded.

"Could I speak with him?"

***

Janie was sitting in the kitchen, trying to hear what Ms. Crable and Randy were talking about when Grandpa brought Rosie home. She'd watched the clock over the breakfast table, counting the minutes. Exactly thirty-five had passed since Randy had been called down.

"Who's here?" Grandpa whispered. He sat a gallon of milk fresh from his cows on the counter.

"Missus Crable. But I don't know who she is."

"Stay here." He pointed to an empty chair and told Rosie to sit.

Moments later, Randy came into the kitchen and joined them at the table.

"What did she want to talk to you about?"

"You." A smug grin flashed across his face. "She wanted to know about you. I told her all about how you beat me with a spoon."

"That was your fault! Did you tell her about throwing Rosie onto the floor?" Anger buzzed in her ears to the rhythm of her heart.

"They're young'uns! They're supposed to fight with each other!" Grandpa bellowed at the woman in the other room.

"Go on out of here! They're doing just fine without you nosing around."

The front door banged shut. Janie ran to the window facing the driveway and watched the woman get into her car and slam the door shut.

"She looks mad," she said to Randy. "What else did you say to her? Why was she here?"

He smiled and shrugged his shoulders.

CHAPTER 32

BAR FIGHT

"Come on," Bogey bellowed. "One more round." He clamped his massive paw onto Wyatt's shoulder. "What's five more minutes?"

Wyatt glanced at the neon-framed clock over the pool table. It wasn't as late as he'd thought. "Sure, what's one more?"

He was venturing into the gray area. The gray area was a state of being somewhere in between the sweet spot and fall-down-drunk. The problem was, whenever he got to the sweet spot, he wanted to keep drinking. He knew he was getting into the gray area because the room looked darker than usual, and his face felt numb.

The bartender raised an eyebrow at him and said, "You sure about that?"

"Of course, I'm sure. Just get me my drink." He laughed and said, "What are you? My mother?"

Bogey wheezed out a wet laugh, followed by a fit of coughing. Wyatt's newest drinking buddy, he was easily impressed. "My mother," he repeated. "That's some funny shit."

Wyatt liked Bogey well enough, for now. Eventually, he'd annoy him enough that they would part ways, and either Bogey or Wyatt would move to another bar. It was always like that with bar mates. Good fun, for a while.

"Cheers!" Wyatt tipped his glass and swallowed. The whiskey went down like water. It always did after the first few.

Someone opened the door, and a slice of daylight poured into the dim bar. The traffic was beginning to pick up as men stopped for a beer before heading home. Wyatt turned to see who the newcomer was. He hoped it would be the little blonde dish from several nights ago. She'd given him the doe eyes the whole evening, but the big fellow next to her had blocked him from even thinking about buying her a drink.

Disappointed to see an old man, he turned back to the empty glass in front of him. He rattled his drink at the bartender and said, "I'll have another."

The bartender shook his head and took the glass. "I'm thinking you've had enough."

Wyatt was about to give him a piece of his mind when a familiar voice interrupted. "That's right. You've had more than enough."

He spun the barstool around to find Pearlie's papa standing directly behind him. Even in the dim light, his rounded cheeks sported a bright shade of red. With his silver-white hair and white beard, he looked like an irritated Santa Claus. Wyatt laughed. "Hey, old man! What brings you here this evening?"

"Your children." He frowned and said, "There was a goddamn social worker at your house this afternoon poking her pointy nose into everything."

"What for? Nothing wrong at home as far as I can see." He knocked back the fresh whiskey. "Got a roof over their heads and food in their bellies."

"And no parents around to watch over them."

Wyatt waved away his words. "They're fine. Janie's old enough to mind them all."

"Janie's old enough to beat the hell out of Randy. And Randy's old enough to torture Rosie." He pointed his finger at Wyatt's nose. "And you ain't around for none of it."

"Go away, old man. Get your finger outta my face!" *Damned old fool—always meddling.*

"They're my grandchildren. My Ingrid's babies. You're gonna lose them to the state if you don't take better care!" He shouted out the words loud enough to be heard across the room. The other patrons in the bar stopped talking to better hear the show that was about to happen.

"Your precious Ingrid Pearl," he mocked the old man. "She might be something, but my Pearlie is a worthless piece of shit who forgot she had babies."

With enough strength to knock him backward off his barstool, Pearlie's papa smashed his fist into the middle of Wyatt's face.

Too stunned to react, Wyatt watched the room spin a full turn before sliding onto the ground. A collective gasp sounded around the bar.

"What the hell!" Bogey could be heard above the other voices. "That was a sucker punch if I ever saw one!"

"Back off, mister! Or you're gonna be next." The old man's voice was laden with fury.

"Leave him be," Wyatt mumbled from his spot on the floor. "Just let him be." *Didn't know the old man had it in him.*

"You'd better find a way to be home at night, 'cause that social worker's comin' back soon!" He shook his fist at Wyatt. "There's more of that for you if you don't make this right. I've lost enough because of you."

The front door slammed, and Wyatt assumed he'd gone. "Is it safe to get up?" He chuckled, and the entire room roared with laughter.

"He sure kicked your ass!" Bogey laughed.

"Yeah, well, I let him, you dumb shit! I'm not gonna beat up an old man." He wiped his bloody nose on a napkin.

Bogey raised his eyebrows. "If you say so, boss."

"Fuck you." He spat a blood clot out of his mouth into the napkin. Slapping his hand on the bar, he said, "I'll take another whiskey—double this time."

CHAPTER 33

1960

"See ya," Beau yelled and waved his skinny arm out of the window as he made a U-turn in the driveway.

Randy waved back and turned to the house. He hesitated before opening the back door. Going home was the worst part of the day.

The kitchen smelled from the stale bacon grease left sitting in a frying pan on the back of the stove. Dad never washed the pan. He just heated the fat until it was smoking and cracked a few eggs onto the mess. Lately, Randy lived on peanut butter and jelly sandwiches. It was the only thing he knew how to make, and Dad's eggs made him want to puke.

He tossed his backpack onto the table and tiptoed up the stairs. The sound of Dad's snoring greeted him at the top. He stopped in front of the open bedroom door to look at him. Flat on his back, Dad lay with one hairy leg sticking out of the sheets. A fly buzzed around Dad's face, landing periodically on his forehead or his nose. Dad didn't seem to be bothered by it. The room stunk of sweat and old liquor oozing out of his pores. He would lay there for most of the evening.

In contrast, Randy's bedroom was neat and tidy now that he no longer shared it with anyone. He'd given his toys away shortly after his twelfth birthday. They'd sat untouched for a year or more before then.

He shut the door behind him and threw himself down onto the bed. There was a mountain of homework in his backpack, but he needed a nap first. The noise had kept him up for most of last night.

He turned onto his side and tucked his hand under his cheek. Put up long before his birth, the floral wallpaper was faded and water stained. *Roses*, he thought, but maybe it was a different kind of flower. For as long as he could remember, he'd stared at the wallpaper while falling asleep. He looked for images in the pattern and the stains. Sometimes, a face would appear to him. This scared him because the face seemed to be hurting or angry. Other times, he would see images of landscapes or animals. When he was younger, the wallpaper had seemed magical, ever-changing. Once, he'd dreamed his mama had stepped out of the wallpaper to visit him in the night. Now that he was older, he understood it was all tricks of light and perception.

Relaxing his eyes, he watched the paper for the changes. At first, nothing happened. As he drifted off to sleep, the flowers and the stains began to move. When they were done rearranging, a smiling face manifested itself. The face was neither of a boy or a girl. He smiled back and wondered if it would stay or go.

He blinked several times and watched some more. Yes, he decided, the face was repositioning. The eyebrows appeared smaller, more tilted. The delicate nose turned up slightly over a rosebud mouth.

When it had finished moving, Rosie stared back at him.

"Rosie," he mumbled. "What're you doing here?"

She smiled but said nothing. She never spoke.

Strains of music nudged him awake. Dusky-gray light came in through the window. He guessed he'd been asleep for several hours. Stretching, he yawned and turned onto his back. He sat up and rubbed his eyes. Homework wasn't going to do itself.

Dad sat in his easy-chair, nursing a glass of whiskey. The living room was dark, barely lit by the lamp next to his chair. The same old song was playing on the record player.

"I'd rather die young than grow old without you." Dad crooned along, his expression melancholy. He acknowledged Randy by raising his glass toward him.

Randy rolled his eyes and continued walking toward the kitchen. It was the same thing every night. *What a drip. She's dead—and you're not young. Should've been you dead—not her.*

He pulled out the crumpled-up answers for his math homework. Linda was sweet on him, and she'd do just about anything to talk to him, including giving him the answers to copy. She was the smartest dumb bitch he knew. Most of the girls were too busy giggling and flirting to pay attention in class.

Linda was different. Awkward and plain, she didn't stand a chance of being a cheerleader or any of the other things that girls dreamed about. Instead, she tried to outshine all the boys in the academic department. While the other guys ignored her, Randy saw an opportunity to get something from her. Pretending to like her a little bit was worth the easy school work.

He packed the homework away and opened the refrigerator—a stupid old habit leftover from the days before Janie left. He didn't miss her, but he did wish the fridge had food in it. At least she'd cooked for them. He slammed the door harder than necessary and took the loaf of bread off the top of the refrigerator. Peanut butter and jelly for supper it was, again.

"Hey, Randy." Rosie flitted around in his head. "Will you make me a sammich?" He wished he could stop thinking about her, but the last memories always nagged at him.

"It's sandwich, not sammich," he'd scolded. "And no, I won't. Make it yourself." He'd pushed his way past her in the kitchen doorway, knocking her over in the process.

"Hey!" Rosie had protested. She stood up and rubbed her sore bottom. "That hurted!" Tears welled up in her blue eyes.

If Janie had been home, she would've yelled for her. Instead, there was no one home to coddle her. Janie had stayed after school to finish a science project.

"Yeah, well, try staying out of my way!" He'd knocked her down again, on purpose that time.

Even though her head hit the door frame hard, she hadn't cried as he'd anticipated. Stunned, she sat still. He'd never forget the bewildered look in her eyes.

· Something about that look had angered him deeply. He remembered thinking she should be crying.

***

"Randy!" Dad yelled across the house. "Come here!"

He sighed and hesitated. Dad was already sloppy drunk. He wished once more that it was his father who had died instead. Mama wouldn't have annoyed the shit out of him as much. He fantasized about knocking Dad's block off, but he doubted he could do it without getting clobbered.

Dad was still in his chair, looking through a newspaper. He looked up at Randy and said, "Did you hear about that satellite? The one we sent to take pictures of the earth?"

"Yeah, we learned about it two years ago in science class."

"Two years ago?" Squinting his eyes, Dad looked down at the paper. "Oh. Guess I'm reading old news." He laughed and tossed the newspaper onto a pile next to his chair.

"Did you want something?" Randy hated being near him, especially when he was drinking. Every word exchanged was pregnant with the possibility of a fight.

The first time Dad forced him to duke it out, Randy lost something fierce. After throwing a punch that had knocked him on his ass, Dad had said, "You gotta learn to fight like a man, not like a sister."

Now, at the age of fourteen, he'd finally hit a solid growth spurt. His return jabs and punches were respectable.

Of course, there never would be a win for Randy, and he knew this. Dad would always throw the last blow.

"Have a seat," Dad slurred. "Talk with your old man for a while."

Randy sat in the chair that used to be Mama's. It still smelled like her perfume.

"What do you want to talk about?" His heart beat faster.

If the booze had gone down the right way, the conversation would be harmless, easygoing. But, if the liquor had gone down the wrong way, talking would be a minefield. It would only be a matter of time before he stepped on a bomb.

Dad chuckled. "Don't worry, son. You're not in trouble." He uncorked the bottle of whiskey sitting on the side table and dumped more into his glass. "How's school going?"

"Fine," he answered.

"Got a girlfriend yet?"

Would it be better to tell a lie? He wasn't sure which way to go. "No," he answered truthfully. "Not yet." He stared at his feet, hoping Dad would tire of the conversation and let him leave.

"Why not?" His smile was more of a grimace. "Nothing sweeter than a piece of fourteen-year-old tail." He tipped his glass to his mouth and drained the last of his whiskey. "That's assuming you can find one who's ready for it." He wiggled his brow up and down in a lecherous way.

Disgusting. Talking about girls with Dad was the last thing he wanted to do. Even if he had done it, he wouldn't want to tell his old man.

"What? Cat got your tongue?" Dad laughed. "Don't tell me you don't like girls. What are ya? A faggot?"

"No." He shook his head vehemently. "I like girls."

Dad nodded his head. "Good. No son of mine is gonna be a cocksucker." He pointed his finger at Randy and added, "Just remember, all girls say 'no' at first. Most of 'em really want to say 'yes.' You gotta overcome their objections."

Randy thought about Linda. He wondered if she'd have any objections.

CHAPTER 34

AFTERMATH

It was a chill she couldn't shake. Three years had gone by since Rosie died—three years since she'd left the farm. The cold stayed with her, a reminder of the empty place in her heart.

Rosie's death had almost destroyed Grandpa. He was a shadow of a man. She was a shell of a girl. Together, they were alone.

She wrapped an afghan around her shoulders and sat in the chair closest to the light. Worn around the edges, the old lounge chair was her favorite place to do homework. Covered in a rose-print fabric, the soft chair reminded her of Mama. Roses had been her mother's favorite flower. The chair also reminded her of Rosie.

Grandpa snored in his rocking chair, head back, mouth open, and eyes shut. He slept nearly all the time now. It was better that way. Finding comfort in his dreams, he often smiled or laughed in his sleep.

She finished an assignment for government and tucked it inside of her book bag. School wasn't difficult. Her studies were a welcome distraction from the memories. Graduation was only three months away. While most of the other girls were planning their weddings, she was on track to go to college—something that wasn't common in her graduating class. Especially for a girl.

Leaving him to nap a little longer, Janie went into the kitchen to cook supper. The outdated kitchen was tidy, thanks to Janie. In it were remnants of a grandmother she'd only known through Mama's stories. She liked to imagine Mama and Grandma were there, cooking and cleaning with her, sharing stories of their day. Rosie would be there, too, laughing and getting underfoot.

Tears stung her nose and eyes. Rosie, she missed most of all. Not a day went by that she didn't think of her, didn't regret staying late after school on that day. Whenever she wasn't ear-deep in a book, the aftermath of the accident replayed in her mind.

A boy from school had driven her home. She remembered feeling shy and deliriously happy. He wasn't just any boy. Jacob had dreamy blue eyes and thick, wavy brown hair. All the other girls had a crush on him, too. But he'd offered to drive her home. She'd tried to look cool and collected as she climbed into the passenger seat of his dad's car. She pretended not to notice the other girls' envious glances.

Parked in front of her house, Jacob had stared at her for a minute. He looked as though he wanted to say something to her. She didn't make it easy for him. Truthfully, she had no idea what to say or how to act around a boy. In retrospect, he probably hadn't known what to say either.

She went first. "Thank you for driving me." Her lips quivered as she forced them into a shaky smile. "And for the help with the project."

He leaned toward her and tilted his head slightly. Her heart thumped wild. She was terrified and excited all at once with the thought he might kiss her. She wondered if she should close her eyes.

A faint mewing sound blew in through the open car windows. For a moment, she'd dismissed it, thinking it to be one of the barn cats. Then, the mewing twisted into a human cry.

Accurately remembering the moment, just as it had happened, wasn't possible. She'd never been able to comprehend it clearly. Perhaps she never would. Depending on the day, she remembered the accident from different perspectives. For the most part, the moment when she shoved the back door open replayed in the same way.

Randy stood at the base of the stairs leading up to the second floor. "No, no, no!" He screamed again and again.

"Stop it!" Janie yelled over his words. "Leave her alone!" He was at it again, bullying Rosie. She'd dropped her bag and ran toward them.

Facedown, Rosie lay motionless, her right arm mangled into a position that shouldn't have been possible. Blood trickled out of her nose and dripped into her long blonde hair.

"What in the hell did you do to her?" She shoved Randy backward, screaming in a voice that she didn't recognize as her own.

"Nothing!" Randy cried, "She fell down the stairs!" Sobbing, he placed his hands over his face.

Janie knelt by her tiny body. She caressed Rosie's cold forehead and fought off the urge to straighten the pink satin bow she'd put in Rosie's hair that morning. "Where's Daddy?" Her chest was caving in. She could barely speak.

"I dunno," Randy wailed. "I've been yelling for him for hours."

She didn't remember making the phone call, but she must have. The rest of the day and night was a blur. Daddy had to be found at the bar, but by then, Rosie had been pronounced dead.

Like debris, floating on the sea after a shipwreck, bits and pieces of memories appeared at will in Janie's mind. One image haunted her more often than the others.

After the medics had come and gone, after the coroner's department had taken Rosie away, Janie sat on the bottom step. In the corner, next to the staircase, was a tiny, single shoe. The thought of Rosie tucked away in a morgue drawer, with one shoe missing, was more than she could bear. She cried until there were no more tears.

For all of Rosie's five years, Janie had made sure she was clean, clothed, and fed. Somehow, she'd managed to let her go with one foot bare.

The first night without Rosie, she wanted to die, too. No bath to run, no soft, blonde locks to braid, no bedtime story. And the worst of all, no small set of knees and elbows poking into her back during the middle of the night.

She'd refused to wash the bedsheets after Rosie died. Rosie's scent and the fragrance of Johnson's Baby Shampoo lingered on her pillow for weeks. She slept every night, cradling the pillow. Over time, the smell faded, leaving nothing but cotton and feathers.

CHAPTER 35

HELEN

While waiting underneath the awning for the rain to let up, she scanned the obituaries, looking for familiar names. It was late April, and the heat was already beginning to feel like summer. A few patrons waited with her, enjoying the cooler air the storm had brought with it.

The lunch counter at Woolworth's was busier than normal. Her manager had been worried the voluntary integration would cause their best customers to leave. In reality, it had the opposite effect.

In hopes of avoiding the disruption created by the sit-ins in North Carolina, the city conspired with church leaders and the like to convince businesses and citizens to support desegregation. Every pastor, minister, and reverend were encouraged to preach the values of an integrated lunch counter. This was accomplished by a certain amount of pressure from the NAACP.

San Antonio was now reaping the benefits of progressive thinking. For the most part, except for the loss of a few cranky white customers, business increased as colored folks could eat lunch with their white counterparts.

To Helen, it made no difference. She wasn't used to serving lunch to anyone darker than a peach, but other than the widening of the color scale, her job was no different. She kept quiet and did her work, the same as before.

The downpour lessened to a light sprinkle, and she set out on foot to the apartment she shared with two other women. It was a twenty-five-minute walk to Victoria Courts. Constructed in the early 1940s to provide adequate housing for low-income families, the apartments were in mild disrepair. She'd been at Victoria Courts for a year. Her roommates complained about the conditions, but to her, the little one-bedroom apartment was a vast improvement over life on the street.

She opened the main entry door and tried not to breathe in the mixture of cigarette smoke and cooking grease. The stairs were cluttered with discarded candy wrappers and cigarette butts. She stepped over a tricycle and a baseball bat dropped in front of the door of her third-floor apartment.

The lock was difficult to turn unless one knew how to wiggle it just so. She jimmied it open, shoving it with her hip and shoulder. As usual, she was the first one home. She went about turning on the lights. Without artificial light, the place was dim and dingy.

The small amount of clothing she owned took up exactly one-third of the tiny closet she shared with the other two girls. She took off her work dress and hung it next to her robe. With any luck, the dress would stay relatively clean until next week when she could afford to go to the laundromat. Should she splatter food on it before then, she'd have to handwash it in the sink and hang it to dry.

The recent rains caused the building to feel like a swamp. To cool off, she liked to stay in her underwear until her roommates got home.

She'd gotten the idea from them. Much younger than Helen, they were free spirits who didn't mind walking around in their undies all evening. Helen, on the other hand, wasn't all that comfortable being practically naked in front of other people.

She opened the icebox and was happy to see no one had taken her last soda. Rummaging through the silverware drawer, she found the bottle opener and popped off the cap. Tipping her head back, she swallowed the icy-cold cola and smiled. There was nothing as good as the first swig.

The fan in front of the window was still. She pushed the window open and switched it on to the fastest setting. Standing in front of the mechanized breeze, she drank the rest of her soda. Delicious goosebumps formed across her abdomen and back. For a moment, she felt happy in the most perfect way.

Christina, the youngest of her two roommates, had been given an old television by her boyfriend. Helen turned it on and waited for it to warm up. She turned the fan to blow at the shabby sofa and sat down to watch the five o'clock news.

The anchors went through their routine, dropping hints at the most sensational pieces which would be saved until close to the end to keep the viewing audience watching during the entire broadcast.

After the weather segment was over, the view cut away to a field reporter covering a music festival. Helen stood up, intending to use the bathroom. She glanced once more at the screen, realizing the background behind the journalist looked familiar. Boerne Gesang Verein, the singing club from her hometown, was performing in front of the common area next to the Dienger Building.

Frozen, she stared at the crowd behind the reporter, scanning for familiar faces.

Would I recognize them? She realized she imagined them as she'd left them—Janie as a nine-year-old and Randy as a six-year-old. Rosie was still faceless, an unformed baby in her mind's eye. She tried to envision Janie, nearly grown, and Randy at fourteen. She wondered what his changing voice would sound like, what his angelic face would look like with the influence of testosterone. *Boys change the most after puberty,* she thought.

Many nights, she'd lain awake contemplating, planning her return. Each time, by morning light, she'd lost all courage. There would be no place for her in that house. Eight years had passed. Eight years was long enough for nature to swallow up a garden, left unattended. It was long enough to undo her existence in their lives. *They're better off without me.* In the end, she consoled herself with the knowledge that going back would be selfish.

Several years had passed since she'd gotten off the streets. She wanted to believe she was well—capable of a normal life, but she didn't trust herself. The shame of her actions, and the fear of repeating them, kept her away. Hidden in plain sight with a new identity, she stayed small and quiet.

The broadcast transitioned to world news, and Helen went to the bathroom. She examined her face in the chipped mirror. A permanent smattering of freckles danced across her nose and cheeks—a souvenir from her time on the streets. Thankfully, she hadn't been out there long enough to get a leathery hide like so many others.

Greta, her other roommate, could be heard through the thin bathroom door. She finished peeing and flushed the toilet.

Time to get dressed.

Her pajamas, a luxury that hadn't existed on the street, were tucked under her pillow. Now that she had a home, she wore them every chance she got. Both Greta and Christina teased her for lounging around in her pajamas so often. Their good-natured joking didn't bother her a bit. Neither knew about her past, and Helen didn't feel like sharing it with them.

"Hey, Helen." Greta looked up from painting her nails and asked, "How was work?"

"Good," Helen answered to her stolen name. "How about your day?" She stifled a yawn and nodded, pretending to listen to Greta's recanting of her workday. Greta liked to gossip about people Helen had never met.

"So, whaddya think?"

Helen realized she'd lost track of the conversation. "Sorry, what?"

"About the date?" Greta smiled. "He's really nice, and around your age."

"Your date?"

"No." Exasperated, Greta groaned. "Your date! Please just say yes. I promise you won't regret it!"

"I don't think so."

"Why not? You sit here night after night, bored to death!"

Helen shrugged her shoulders. "Not interested. Sorry."

"Suit yourself. I think it's a shame for you to miss out." Greta blew on her fingers to dry the fresh nail polish. "You're lonely."

Helen agreed. Greta had no idea just how lonely she was. She couldn't risk it, though. Letting a man get too close would only cause problems. Better to stay single.

CHAPTER 36

NO MEANS YES

He watched as she scribbled on the notebook in front of her. Her breasts were bigger than he'd realized. Her face wasn't great, but that didn't matter.

She looked over at his blank paper. "What did you get for number three?"

"Can we get out of here?" The library was too quiet. The prune-faced librarian, Miss Cowen, shot suspicious glances in his direction every few minutes. He was out of his element.

"Where do you want to go?" Her voice was hopeful.

He shrugged. "Anywhere but here."

"How about the soda shop?" Smiling, she revealed crooked teeth.

"Nah, let's just go for a walk." He didn't want to be caught anywhere that one might go on a date. Linda was nice enough but too ugly to be seen in public with.

They packed up their books and breezed past Miss Cowen. She made an expression he assumed to be a smile.

It was late spring, but the air was already heavy with summer. She took off her cardigan and tied it around her waist. "It's so hot out." Fanning her face with her hand, she asked, "Where do you want to walk?"

"Let's check out the river." There would be plenty of privacy if they went far enough.

She boldly reached for his hand. He prayed no one was watching and allowed her to hold it.

Don't be such a pussy, Dad's voice echoed.

He wasn't a pussy. And getting laid shouldn't be difficult. She practically drooled every time he walked by.

There for the taking, boy.

They followed the river until the manicured banks disappeared, and wild shrubs and vines took over.

"Here," he said. "This is perfect."

"Perfect for what?" She genuinely looked confused.

"For this." He kissed her, clamping his eyes tightly shut. He pretended he was kissing someone else, someone prettier.

She allowed him to do it, kissing him back.

He pressed his lips onto hers again, this time sticking his tongue in her mouth. She tasted like toothpaste and cookies. Wrapping his arms around her, he cupped her bottom.

She stiffened and said, "Stop it."

Randy moved his hands back up to her waist and kissed her again. Standing so close to her made him hard. She was teasing him.

That's what girls do—they say "no," but they mean yes.

He pulled her to him and slid his hand back down.

"Seriously," she shouted, "stop." She wriggled around to squirm away.

He kissed her, harder this time, pressing his lips into her crooked teeth. He managed to catch her left arm with his right hand before she smacked him.

Pissed off, his adrenaline surged. "Ungrateful bitch," he seethed in her ear. "You're lucky I pay any attention to you at all."

She kicked up against his crotch with her thigh, almost knocking him in the balls. Shaking her shoulders side to side, she almost broke loose from his grasp.

He let go of her hand, and she shoved against his shoulders. She was no match for him. Knocking her down was as easy as pushing over a kitten. Pinning her down with his body weight, he reached between her legs with his right hand and tore at her thin panties. He felt resistance, then a pop, as he forced himself inside her.

She gasped and began to cry. He clamped his hand over her mouth to shut her up. Tears rolled down the sides of her temples, and snot from her nose pooled on his hand.

Aroused by her fear, he moved in and out of her as hard as he could, excited by each muffled groan.

When he'd finished, she lay motionless, staring up at the trees. A perfect imprint of his hand covered her face.

"Tell anyone, and I'll say you wanted it."

She closed her eyes and turned her head farther away from him.

"Hear me?"

She nodded.

Dad was right. She did want it.

CHAPTER 37

TRUTH AND THE RUMOR

She wasn't surprised by the rumor. Once again, she found herself wishing they weren't related. Without Mama to interfere, Randy had taken on all of Daddy's bad qualities. Randy owned his traits like a prince.

He was good-looking enough now, sandy blonde hair and blue eyes, just like their daddy. That was part of the problem. Confused by his handsome face and easy smile, he was generally regarded as a good guy.

The tale was spreading like wildfire around the school. The poor girl, labeled as a liar, a floozy, had gone to great lengths to avoid the curious stares and gossipy whispers. It was said she had a thing for Randy and gave it up willingly. Her few remaining friends continued to insist he'd raped her. Like all gossip, the story would die down as soon as the next titillating bit came along.

A nice girl like Linda surely had parents that gave a damn. Janie wondered where her parents were in the situation—if they even knew about it.

Although she passed her brother in the hallway from time to time, Janie didn't speak to him. For that matter, she didn't talk to anyone else either. Graduation was just around the corner, and she couldn't wait to get as far away as possible.

All around her, in the typical end-of-the-day hubbub, the other students laughed and shouted at each other. Practically invisible, she stuffed the books she wouldn't need into her locker and buttoned her book bag. As she moved through the clusters of kids, bunched together in groups, talking about their day, the pangs of being alone needled at her.

She'd never had many friends, but when Rosie died, the few she did have eventually disappeared. Rosie's death aged her. It put a burden on her soul. No one else could grasp the pain she felt. It was much easier not to talk than it was to explain.

Outside, cigarette smoke wafted through the trees lining the edge of the school property. Rebels and wannabes huddled together, just outside of the watchful eyes of the few teachers that still cared. Had she still been twelve or thirteen, she would've tried to bum a cigarette off one of them. Partly to fit in, mostly because she'd been hooked.

As did so many other things, her smoking habit went away with Rosie. The first time she'd lit up after Rosie's death, all she could think about was her baby sister's distaste for the smell. Smoking felt like blasphemy.

She climbed behind the wheel of Grandpa's old truck and put the key in. With no small amount of effort on her part, the engine roared to life. Paint faded and dinged from years of weather, the truck looked like Grandpa—gray and worn. She revved the motor long enough to warm it up and shifted into reverse.

As she left the school parking lot, she noticed Randy, laughing and flirting with a cheerleader. He lifted his hand into a wave as she drove past him. Her heartbeat sped up. She pretended not to see him.

She stopped at the grocery store to pick up something for dinner. The responsibility of cooking and cleaning had fallen on her shoulders, but she didn't mind. Grandpa was easy to please. She suspected he would live on tinned sardines and crackers if she weren't around.

Doing the math in her head, she decided on the Kielbasa. It was a better deal. She opened her pocketbook to see how much was left of the money Grandpa had given to her.

"Janie, is that you?" A familiar voice called to her from behind.

Wishing the floor would swallow her up, she hesitated to turn around.

"Janie! Oh, my! You're all grown up!" The woman was unmistakable.

Stunned, Janie said nothing. Except for a longer hairstyle, Betty looked virtually the same as she had seven years before.

"How've you been?" Betty smiled. Her voice was bright. "How're Rosie and Randy doing?"

She wanted to scream at her, to tell her that it was none of her business. At the same time, she wished she could hug her. Could Betty even guess how many times Randy had cried for her in the beginning?

Instead, she smiled back. "Randy is a bully."

Betty's face deflated. "Oh, I see. Tell me about Rosie. I'll bet she's a pistol."

Unable to smile this time, she said, "Rosie died." Her voice was flat. "Three years ago. Surely, you must have heard."

"But how?" Betty stammered.

Janie grabbed another package of sausages, bratwurst this time, and left Betty standing in front of the butcher's counter, mouth wide open. She'd almost made it up to the cashier when Betty grabbed her arm.

"How can you just walk away?" Shaking, Betty's eyes flooded with tears, her nose reddened. "What happened to her?"

"How could you just walk away?" One ounce of emotion was more than Betty deserved, and she hated herself for showing weakness. She couldn't stop the tremble in her voice. "How could you leave us that way? What did you think would happen?"

This moment, confronting Betty, had happened many times over in her mind. Strange, she didn't feel the satisfaction she'd hoped for. She needed more. She needed a bigger release.

"You're a whore!" There, that was it—the words that would crush Betty. Furious, she waited for a reaction.

"Well, I've been called worse." Betty smiled thinly and sniffed her tears back. She took her purse out of the shopping cart and walked around the counter toward the front entrance.

Motionless, the cashier stood with an expression of shock frozen on her face. Janie was reminded she was in public. Embarrassed, she looked around to see if anyone she knew had witnessed her outburst.

Tossing the sausages onto the checkout counter, she apologized to the cashier. "I'm sorry. That was inappropriate."

"Definitely the most excitement we've had all week." The girl smiled and took a deep breath. She rang up the sausages and said, "That'll be one dollar and three cents."

As usual, Grandpa was sleeping in his chair when she got home. She'd finally gotten used to this pale version of the grandpa she remembered from her childhood.

"Hi Grandpa, I'm home," she called from the kitchen while she gathered ingredients for their supper. His lack of response wasn't surprising. Some days, the most she heard from him was an occasional loud snore.

She set about chopping the onions, cabbage, and garlic. Cooking soothed her soul. It was a connection to Mama and to Rosie.

She scooped some bacon grease out of the mason jar and tapped it into the cast-iron skillet sitting on the back of the stove. Fumbling around on the shelf above the range, she found the box of matches and lit the burner. She watched the grease change from a white blob into clear oil, filling the kitchen with a delicious aroma of bacon. After dumping the vegetables into the skillet, she chopped the sausage into small, bite-sized pieces.

"Grandpa? Are you getting hungry?" She wondered if he'd eaten anything while she was at school. The living room was dim, and she guessed he'd been sleeping most of the day. Knocking on the door frame connecting the kitchen and living room, she repeated herself. "Are you hungry yet? I'm making your favorite—fried cabbage."

Something wasn't right. *He shouldn't be so hard to wake.* Closer, she shook his shoulder. His flesh was eerily firm under her fingertips.

She turned on the lamp next to his chair. There was no mistaking his appearance. She thought of her kitten, years ago, lying under the sofa, frozen stiff with Rigor Mortis. She hadn't understood what it meant until they'd buried it next to Mama's rosebushes.

Images of Rosie, angelic in her little coffin, her body frozen in death, flooded her mind. Next, she thought of Mama and wondered who had touched her rigid, cold body. Now, Grandpa had joined them.

Strangely, she had no tears for Grandpa, her last special person. Calm and logical, Janie dialed the number penciled in by the phone for the doctor. Then, she turned off the burner under the scorching cabbage and sat at the breakfast table to wait.

***

Bright rays of spring sunshine warmed the shoulders of the small group of mourners at Grandpa's funeral. She'd chosen a graveside service, partly because of the cost, but mostly because she didn't think she could bear to sit through another service in the church. Barely an adult, now that her eighteenth birthday had passed, the burden of planning had rested on her shoulders. It was okay, though. She wouldn't have considered involving Daddy, and there was no one else. Randy didn't count. Fifteen years old and too stupid to think for himself, he wouldn't have been any help at all.

She sat in one of the folding chairs placed beside the coffin. The simple wooden casket, the least expensive available, was suspended over an open grave by a series of straps attached to a frame. Morbidly, she imagined the straps breaking and the casket falling into the abyss.

The preacher stood near the coffin with a sympathetic smile on his thin face, patient, waiting for last-minute funeral-goers. Janie kept her eyes on the coffin, occasionally looking at the preacher to pass the time.

Out of the corner of her eye, she could see Daddy and Randy. Almost late, they took seats on the front row, next to Janie. She didn't acknowledge their presence. She could only hope they would ignore her.

The whispers and rustling of funeral program pamphlets died down as the preacher took his place in front of a small wooden podium. He cleared his throat loudly and placed his spectacles on his nose. "We meet here today to honor and pay tribute to the life of Frederick, and to express our love and admiration for him."

"Also, to try to bring some comfort to those of his family and friends who are here and have been deeply hurt by his sudden death." He continued to orate to the small group huddled together under the tent.

Grandpa was one of the old-timers. Most of his friends had been gone for years now. She wondered if the tearful ladies seated behind her, sniffling into their handkerchiefs, had known him, or if they were just busybodies cashing in on the event. During the three years she'd lived with him, no one had been out to visit.

Tuning out the preacher, she thought about Rosie. She conjured up an image in her mind of what Rosie would look like now. Blonde hair, a little darker and slightly longer, in pigtails. Her arms and legs would be thin. Her fingers would be like those of a pianist, long and delicate.

Imaginary Rosie smiled at her, revealing partially grown-in adult teeth. At eight years old, make-believe Rosie was somewhere between child and teenager, too big for nursery rhymes, too small for lipstick. She grinned at Janie and held out her hand. Janie wished she could hold it once more, aching to smell her sunshine soaked hair.

Rosie faded away just as quickly as she'd appeared, leaving Janie ransacking her memories for just one more clear picture.

"Let us bow our heads in prayer," the preacher warbled. Janie bowed her head while he pled for comfort to a God she hated. "Amen."

"Amen." Hushed voices agreed.

Daring to sneak a sideways glance, she caught Daddy's eye. He smiled, barely, and tilted his head back down, seemingly fixated on his lap. Randy stared straight ahead; his hands clenched into tight balls. More man than child, he strongly resembled their father. Scared he would catch her studying him, she quickly looked away.

After the brief service, she stood in the receiving line and accepted condolences, delivered by strangers, built from words that meant nothing. She nodded and pretended to be thankful. As was customary, Daddy and Randy stood next to her in the line and accepted sympathies for the loss of a man they hadn't spoken to in years.

The small group of people dissipated, leaving the three of them alone with the casket. Uncomfortable, Janie turned away, hoping to catch sight of the preacher. Instead, she noticed a woman standing underneath one of the nearby oak trees. Something about her stance was familiar.

The woman wore a simple dress, not the typical black, but close—dark gray. Covered by a matching gray scarf, it was difficult to know the color of her hair. She watched, still and quiet. When she noticed Janie studying her, she took a step forward, then back again.

Good, Janie thought. She'd had her fill of strangers for the day.

CHAPTER 38

THE RETURN

Helen watched from a distance. When she read the obituary, she'd immediately ruled out going to the funeral. As she lay in bed later that night, sleepless, agitated, Helen realized she would never forgive herself for not going. She kept enough layers of guilt as it was, and she didn't need to add another.

She hadn't given considerable thought about what she'd do should someone spot her. After all, the children were a lot older now. Likely, they'd forgotten her. And even if they hadn't, the elements had stomped all over her face, making her nearly unrecognizable.

Standing back as far as she could without losing sight of the service, she strained to listen to the minister's words. Although no mention had been made of his wife or his daughter, at least not that she could hear, it was a nice funeral, simple and kind.

Janie hadn't changed, not much anyway. Older, taller, but still the same. Randy was a younger version of his daddy. Her heart ached as she watched them. Wyatt matched up with her imagination—older, worn-out, but still handsome.

She wondered about Rosie. Had Wyatt remarried? Perhaps, they'd left her home with the new wife, had decided Rosie was too young for a funeral. Wherever Rosie was, she was thankful they'd spared her.

For a moment, she thought Janie might have seen her. Instinctively, she took a step forward, wanting to run to her. It was foolish thinking. *What would I say?*

After the service, Helen sat in the car for several minutes and contemplated waiting until everyone had gone. It had been years since she'd visited her mother's grave, and she had no intention of returning.

Boerne was Pearl's hometown, not Helen's. In the end, she chickened out and started the drive back to San Antonio.

At the very edge of town, at the familiar place where the highway barely touched, she stopped her roommate's car. She needed to go back. Backing up into a field entrance, she wrestled the big steering wheel around. She wanted to take everything in, one last time.

Boerne hadn't changed much. She noticed a few new gas stations and an unfamiliar diner. Her heart ached. This was the town in her dreams. It was her beginning and her ending. She'd left Pearl behind in this small place.

It only took a few minutes to get out to the farm. *What could it hurt? He's gone. No one will be there.* She wanted to see it one last time, to say her proper goodbyes.

Papa's truck was sitting in the same place he'd always parked. Comforted in a small way, she fantasized that she would open the back door, and the aroma of coffee and cabbage would greet her.

She opened the heavy door to her roommate's old Cadillac and got out of the car. Listening, she waited for a moment.

Don't be silly. No one is home.

Soft clucking came from the chicken coop. Helen wondered who would take over the farm. Most of it had been sold off years before, but there would still be responsibilities. Without her in the way, it would fall to the children, she supposed.

The sunroom screen door squawked as she opened it. The old springs needed replacing. Papa was frugal. The springs would stay until they turned to powdered rust. *Would have stayed,* she reminded herself. A lump swelled up in her throat. She hadn't cried yet, hadn't allowed herself to feel the pain of a missed goodbye.

She wondered how it happened. The obituary had made no mention of the cause of death. Did he cry out for her? Ask to see her in the end? She hoped he hadn't been alone.

Stacks of newspapers lay in heaps around the sunporch, along with empty jugs and cans. Papa hated to waste anything. Unfortunately, he never seemed to find a use for all his saved trash. She mentally calculated how long it would take to clear the mess. Probably days, she decided.

The metal knob to the kitchen door was cold to the touch. The paint had worn off many years before. The door wasn't locked. It never was.

The kitchen light had been left on. Instinctively, she turned it off. The room wasn't nearly as messy as she'd anticipated. The small breakfast table was clear of the usual clutter, newspapers, and empty coffee cups. On the stove was a cast-iron skillet. It was clean, not a speck of grease in it. Someone had washed the dishes. She wondered if Papa had help in the last days.

She sat her purse down on the counter and went into the living room. Papa's chair was in the same place as before. Her favorite chair was still in its spot, too. She sat down and turned off the lamp. It felt good to be home. She tucked her feet up under her legs and leaned her head on the wing of her chair. As she dozed off, she was comforted by the smell of coffee and cabbage.

CHAPTER 39

TRICK QUESTION

They rode home in silence after the funeral. He hadn't wanted to go, but Dad said he'd regret it if he didn't—said the heirs to Grandpa's estate ought to be there.

Janie had ignored him. It wasn't surprising. At school, she acted as if he were invisible. He still couldn't figure out why she hated him. After all, she couldn't know everything.

He tried not to think about the last time he'd seen Grandpa alive. It had been at a different funeral. Rosie's funeral.

"Want one?" Dad slipped a smoke out of the pack sitting between them on the seat and put it into his mouth. He held the cigarettes out.

"Sure." Randy took one and waited for the lighter.

"What did you think about the service?" Dad dropped the lighter into his hand.

He shrugged and lit his cigarette, cupping his hand around the flame to prevent the wind from blowing it out. "It was nice."

"Did you notice anything strange?"

He sighed. "Like what?"

He hated the guessing games that Dad made him play. Always on edge, he prayed he'd give the right answer.

Dad turned and sneered at him. "I want you to think for yourself, son." He chuckled and took a long drag off his cigarette. "Just replay the funeral in your mind. Tell me what you noticed."

There would be no getting out of the game today, at least not during the ride home.

Resigned, he narrated the funeral. "There was almost no one there." He glanced at Dad to see if he was on the right track.

"Uh-huh, go on," Dad urged.

"Okay, um," he fumbled, racking his brain for something unusual. "Let's see; the preacher didn't say anything about Mama, or Grandma."

"Why would he? It wasn't their funeral. Go on, what else?"

"I don't know."

"I'm not surprised." He scoffed, "The brilliance in this family is astounding."

Randy hung his head. He never got it, never understood what Dad wanted from him.

Irritated, Dad continued, "Did you like the part where he talked about your grandpa's military service?"

"Yeah." Pretending to remember, he nodded.

Dad took another puff off his cigarette and grinned. "Is that right? You liked that part, did you?"

Warning bells went off in his head. He'd just stepped on a tripwire, and there was no turning back. He was being tested. There were two choices at this juncture; own up to his lie and admit he hadn't heard anything about Grandpa's military service or forge forward and pray Dad had liked that part, too. Either choice had as much of a chance of being wrong as the other. He smiled in hopes Dad would interpret it favorably.

"Did you really hear something about your grandpa's time serving our fine country?" His smile resembled a grimace. He tossed his cigarette butt out the window. "Because I didn't hear a damned thing about it."

"I m-must've remembered it wrong."

"That's right. You must have remembered it wrong." Dad taunted him. "Any thoughts on why your grandpa didn't have a military funeral service?"

"I dunno; maybe Janie forgot to plan it?"

Dad laughed. "It doesn't work that way, son." He shook his head. "If your grandpa had actually been in the military, he'd have a military funeral. Don't matter which branch; Army, Navy, Air Force, Marines, you name it—they take care of their own."

Randy stayed quiet and scrambled through his mind, sorting his thoughts.

"So, with that information, why do you think your Grandpa didn't have a military funeral?"

"But he told us about it."

"That don't mean shit." Face hardened, and eyes narrowed; Dad pointed at Randy. "You can bet your ass that your grandpa was a liar."

"I don't think he'd lie about it, Dad," Randy insisted.

"Where do you think your mama learned it from? She was a liar, just like her precious Papa."

Randy grew silent. Any conversation that veered off in the direction of Mama wasn't going to end well. He prayed for an intervention of some sort. A wreck, a tornado, even a Russian invasion, would've been better than another conversation about Mama.

He had no good defense for her. He was mad at her for leaving them. But, when Daddy started in bashing her, Randy wanted to make excuses for her. After the last time, he knew better.

Turning his face away from Dad, he took the last drag off his cigarette and tossed it out the window. His reflection in the side mirror, the scar above his brow, gave witness to how wrong a talk about Mama could go.

Randy would never forget how he got the scar. Dad had been drunk for most of the day, not his typical sort of drunk, but magnificently, rip-roaring, fall-down-dead drunk.

Randy had been searching through the attic for something he could use in a history project. It was Saturday afternoon, and he was proud of the fact that he wasn't waiting until Sunday night to start his homework.

"What's all the ruckus?" Red-faced, Dad wheezed and panted from his trek up the stairs.

Randy sat in the middle of the dusty floor, surrounded by boxes full of cast-offs and keepsakes. He'd just opened one full of Mama's stuff, things she'd saved from her childhood. A framed sketch lay in his lap, a picture of a vase of roses. In the corner was a childlike version of Mama's signature.

"Sorry," he apologized. "I'm looking for something for a history project. It has to be a piece of family history."

Dad staggered over to Randy's side. "What's that in your lap?"

"It's a picture. Made by Mama, I think."

"And you wanna use that?"

He should have known by the tone of Dad's voice, but he wasn't paying attention. "Probably."

"Lemme see if I understand," he slurred. "You wanna use something for history class from your mama because she's history?"

"No, because she's family," Randy explained quietly. "We're supposed to bring a piece of family history—something passed down."

"And of all the things in this house, you wanna bring something from your mama? The woman who left us?" Bulging veins on his forehead and temples threatened to burst through the skin.

"No, Dad," Randy argued. "It's not like that."

"Not like what? She didn't leave us? Am I confused?"

"That's not what I meant." He forgot to keep his words calm. "What I'm trying to say is—"

"It don't matter what you're trying to say," Dad yelled. "What you're doing is putting her on a pedestal! You do realize she left you, don't you? Abandoned her newborn baby, too! What kinda woman does that?"

"Something might've happened to her," he offered.

"Something happened to her, all right! She was a piece-of-shit mother! She didn't give a damn about you or your sisters!"

"That's not true!" His chest heaved with raw emotion. "She loved me." He stood up quickly, dropping the sketch out of his lap onto the floor.

Dad swung his fist at Randy, connecting with his right eye socket. "You'd better not come at me like that again, boy!" Dad towered over him.

Hot blood oozed out of the spot above his brow, where Dad's Lions Club ring made contact. Searing pain radiated into his eyeball and down the side of his face.

"I wasn't coming at you!" Knowing full well Dad would make fun of him, he couldn't stop the tears running down his cheeks.

"Don't be such a pussy!" Dad hollered, "Fuckin' mama's boy!" He stomped the glass out of Mama's sketch with his dirty boot.

CHAPTER 40

THE INTRUDER

Exhausted, she climbed into bed and pulled the blankets up to her neck. The funeral had been a blur of unrecognizable faces and polite sympathies. Forced conversations left her head aching.

She closed her eyes and hovered somewhere between asleep and awake. Letting her thoughts go completely, she gradually slipped into the deep.

When she awoke, the light coming in through the window had faded to a smoky gray. She sat up with a jolt. Dinner should've been started hours before. Grandpa would be starving.

Her heart sank when she remembered Grandpa wasn't a worry any longer. Janie lay back down to give her pulse a chance to slow down. She'd dreamed Grandpa had come home, even heard his footsteps in the kitchen below. Tears dripped into her hair and onto the pillow.

Although she'd been taking care of Grandpa and not the other way around, the knowledge that she was alone in the world terrified her.

Days before, her plan had been crystal clear; finish high school, work the summer, and start college in the fall. Our Lady of the Lake had accepted her, and although it was a slap in the face considering her grades were good enough to get into Yale, she was thankful to be accepted just the same.

Now, she wasn't sure what she wanted. Grandpa had promised he would help her get through college. What if she couldn't do it on her own?

Don't borrow tomorrow's troubles. Grandpa had said these words to her many times over the last three years. She would miss his twinkling smile and his calm spirit.

She took in a deep breath and sat up, swinging her legs onto the floor. Better to do something, she thought, than to lay around moping.

The stairway was cluttered with things that needed to be either carried up or taken down. She carefully stepped to one side or the other to avoid tripping. It was a miracle Grandpa hadn't broken his neck. She couldn't help but think of Rosie each time she used the stairs. When Janie was in a morbid mood, she fantasized about tripping and joining her baby sister.

She didn't bother to switch on a light in the darkened living room. The furniture had been arranged the same for the entirety of her life. No danger of walking into anything—she could navigate the room with her eyes closed.

The refrigerator was full of food, brought by well-meaning do-gooders, meant to ease the pain of Grandpa's death. She probably wouldn't have to cook for a week. Even though she didn't feel particularly hungry, she knew she needed to eat something. Without turning on the kitchen light, she opened the refrigerator and pulled casserole dishes and foil packets out and placed them onto the counter. She lifted the lids of each, trying to decide which, if any, appealed to her non-existent appetite. The fried chicken looked decent, even cold.

With a bit of struggle, she managed to rearrange everything back into a pile that wouldn't topple over. She poured a glass of milk and carried it, along with the chicken, into the living room. She hadn't watched television for days. It would be a welcome distraction.

Left out from her search for memorial photographs for Grandpa's obituary, a stack of photo albums covered the coffee table. She sat her plate and glass next to Grandpa's chair before turning on the lamp.

She let out a huge scream.

Startled, the woman sitting in her chair jumped and shrieked.

Janie backed away and tripped over the rug, barely catching herself on the stone fireplace mantel. "Stay away!"

"Janie! It's me! It's Mama."

The words didn't register at first. The face belonged to someone much older than Mama. Wisps of blonde hair streaked with silver surrounded the woman's freckled face. Clothed in a simple gray dress, she sat barefoot. Her shoes, black pumps, rested on the floor in front of the chair.

"Janie, it's Mama," she repeated, gently this time.

Her chin quivered, and tears stung at her eyes and nose. "Mama?"

She could see the resemblance now that she was looking for it. *Am I dreaming?* She wasn't sure how to react.

"I don't understand." On the verge of tears, Janie swallowed at the lump forming in her throat. "You were dead."

Mama sat quietly.

"Why?" A single word uttered, pregnant with so many different questions. *Why did you leave? Why did you stay gone? Why now?*

"Where've you been?" She demanded, "All this time? Where?"

"Oh, honey," Mama whispered. "It's such a long story." She looked down at her clasped hands. "I don't know where to begin."

"Start somewhere!" Janie half-begged, half-demanded.

Mama smiled weakly. "I think your life was better without me."

"How can you say that?" Janie cried, "You have no idea what our life was like! Randy, Rosie, they're not better!"

She put her hand to her heart. "Randy—he's so handsome. And Rosie? How is she? I don't think she was at the funeral, was she?" She added brightly, "I'll bet she's getting big."

Janie wanted to throw up. Her legs turned to gelatin. She sat in Grandpa's chair for fear she might fall over. The wound was wide and deep, and it threatened to swallow her up. She covered her face with her hands and sobbed.

Warm hands, strong and small, wrapped around her shoulders. "*Shhh*, it's okay," Mama soothed.

She shrugged Mama's hands away. "It's not," she cried. "R-R-Rosie is dead!"

Pale, shaking, Mama stared blankly at Janie for a few moments after learning how Rosie died. It would have been better if she would've said something, no matter how meaningless the words would be.

Janie waited, wiping away at her tears with the palms of her hands. She wasn't sure whether the tears were for Rosie, Grandpa, or Mama. Maybe she was grieving for all three.

"Oh, God." Mama whimpered, "I don't even know what to say. My baby is gone."

"Your baby?" Janie managed to croak out a few words through her aching throat. "You left her. She was *my* baby, not yours." Sucking up tears and snot, she continued, "Who do you think took care of her when you left? Changed her diapers? Held her when she cried? I taught her to use the toilet, tie her shoes, brush her teeth! Where were you?"

"Janie, please." Mama begged, "I was sick. I wasn't good for Rosie, or you and Randy, for that matter."

"Neither was Daddy," she choked out. "He wasn't good for us, either!"

"Honey, please just let me explain." She pressed her palms together in an unspoken prayer. "There's so much you don't know about."

Janie wrapped her arms around herself and rocked back and forth. Prickly cold nipped at her skin from the inside, and she couldn't stop shaking. She managed to utter the words, "N-Not now!"

"Okay," Mama backed away. "I'll give you some time." Barefoot, she went into the kitchen.

Even though Janie didn't want to hear her excuses, she felt relieved Mama hadn't put on her shoes. This meant she wasn't leaving yet.

Her thoughts slithered about in her head, like a pile of snakes, difficult to separate, impossible to control. Less than one week before, Grandpa had been alive, and Mama had been dead.

***

The rundown apartment building that Mama had lived in with her faceless roommates left Janie feeling off-balance. It had been strange enough to find out Mama wasn't dead. Seeing the place where she'd lived, only miles away from her children, the family that she'd abandoned, was too much. It was a betrayal.

"Do you want to come inside?" Mama asked. "I'll just be a minute."

"Can I help you carry anything?" Her words were polite, but she didn't mean them, at least not yet.

"No," Mama shook her head. "I'm going to leave the car keys and grab a few changes of clothing. I won't be long."

The old steering wheel, petrified from years of the sun beating down, felt cold under her grip. Resting her hands on the top, she was ready to leave at a moment's notice. She sat, watching tenants come and go across the sparse grounds.

She knew it was hypocritical of her, given the neglected condition of Grandpa's yard, to feel disgusted by the overgrown shrubs and untrimmed pathways.

Litter, a combination of empty cigarette packs and scraps of paper, got caught up in a strong gust of wind. For a short second, it looked as though the refuse might be carried away to another plot of grounds. Just as quickly, the flurry dropped the trash back down in a slightly rearranged position.

Wasn't it this way with Mama? She thought about her mother, being dropped back down into the same place as before, somewhat battered and worn from all the swirling around but virtually in the same position as before she'd been taken up and away.

A smile touched the corners of her mouth. Grandpa would tease her a little, had he been around to listen to her thoughts.

"My goodness, Janie! You're so full of big ideas." Which is what he would say whenever she got carried away with her notions. He almost always followed with, "You're too smart for your own good." Or something of the like.

She'd never minded the teasing because he'd believed in her. When she'd announced that she was going to college, he'd bragged about it to everyone, friends and strangers alike. Although she pretended to be embarrassed, secretly, she'd liked the attention.

Still not used to Mama's present-day appearance, she watched her hobble down the walk for a half-minute before recognizing her. Up close, her features were the same. The rest had been replaced by an older, tattered version of the mother she remembered.

Before she could climb out of the truck, Mama had thrown a large bag into the back. Feeling a bit stupid for not offering to carry the suitcase, Janie leaned over and shoved the passenger door open as wide as her reach would allow.

"Thank you, dear."

"Welcome," she mumbled. "Where to now?"

"Grandpa's will be fine."

Mama fixed her gaze on the building as they drove over the broken pavement. "I won't miss it."

She didn't talk on the way back from San Antonio. Mama didn't say much, either. She didn't trust herself to respond. Undoubtedly, she didn't trust Mama. Should she say anything, this would seep into her words. She'd prefer to remain respectful.

In the absence of spoken words, her brain filled the empty space with thoughts of the past.

How many times, she wondered, had she and Mama made this long drive home from the big city? Ten times, perhaps one hundred times? When she and Randy were still very small, Mama and Betty would drag them for hours through the fancy department stores. Frost Bros was her favorite—Mama's, too. And even though she rarely bought anything at Frost's, it seemed as if they spent the most time there.

"Oh, my! Isn't this charming?" she'd ask of Betty, caressing some shiny trinket. Betty would squeal with delight and shake her head over the price.

Feeling impatient once, she'd asked her mother, "Aren't we going to buy anything?"

"We're just window-shopping, dear." Mama had smiled.

Were there windows for sale? Confused, Janie kept her questions inside and followed along, contenting herself to look for pretty things and, of course, for windows.

Hoping for a reward, in the form of sugared nuts or an ice cream cone, she and Randy kept their hands to themselves and tried not to complain.

What should've been a pleasant remembrance only angered her, left her feeling bitter. The voyages to San Antonio had stopped with the disappearance of Mama.

While her classmates still shopped in those stores with their mothers for school clothes, *quinceañera* dresses, and prom gowns, Janie picked out her things from the Sears catalog in Grandpa's kitchen.

CHAPTER 41

LESSONS

"Thanks, man!" He raised his hand as he reached the back porch.

Beau always gave him shit about mooching rides, but that was just for show. He was damned lucky to hang with Randy, and he knew it. Taking Randy home was a small price to pay for all the chicks flocking around. *Let's face it; without me, the dumbass would never score.*

Randy hated the bus, so he let Beau think they were tight. In truth, Randy was close with no one. Most people weren't worth his time. If they didn't have something to offer to him, he didn't bother with them.

Dad was snoozing in his chair, empty glass in his hand. He'd missed three days of work this week, so far. Although Dad always drank, he had been loaded non-stop since the funeral. *Probably gonna lose this job, too.*

Randy couldn't keep up with Dad's jobs, or lack thereof. He'd lost track of the number of times Dad had been fired. Some type of money, from the Veteran's Administration, he thought, kept them afloat each time Dad lost a job. Dad didn't discuss these things.

Beau had paid for his burger at the diner, so for once, he wasn't starving. Good thing because there wouldn't be food in the fridge unless whiskey could be considered food.

"Hey, Dad, I'm home." Randy nudged Dad's foot as he walked by.

"Hmm?" He mumbled and opened his eyes for a moment before nodding back off.

Randy scoffed and flipped on the television. He had homework, but who wants to study all day, then come home and study some more? He had yet to find a replacement for Linda, so the work was all on him.

He grabbed Dad's pack of smokes and tipped one out into his thumb and forefinger. He picked up the lighter from the side table and flicked it. The first puff was always the best part. He deeply inhaled while keeping one eye on Dad to see if he'd wake from the smell. Sometimes, Dad offered him a cigarette, but that wasn't to be construed as permission to smoke any time he wanted.

Out cold, Dad didn't notice a thing. Randy placed the lighter back onto the table and went out through the front door. The front porch didn't get much use. They generally went in and out of the house through the back, and company was rare.

He sat on the weathered railing, savoring the cigarette. It was an exceptionally warm day. School would be out in a week's time, which meant Janie would be graduating. He wished she'd at least acknowledge his presence once in a while. It stung to be ignored.

Of course, Randy couldn't tell her that he missed her. She didn't deserve to know how he felt. It had been a long time since he'd felt anything other than bad. Trapped in a life that didn't feel like his own, he wondered what would be better.

As if he could summon her with only his thoughts, Janie turned into the drive. Gravel crunched and popped underneath the tires of Grandpa's old truck as she inched her way to the house.

He took the last drag off the smoke and stamped it out onto the railing. Keeping his eyes on the truck, he flicked the butt into the yard and waited for her to get out.

Confusion set in as both the driver and passenger doors opened. *Does she even have friends?*

Always alone in the hallways at school, Janie wasn't the type to drive around with other girls. And besides, the passenger was far from a girl.

Janie and the woman, grayish-haired and leathered, walked through the sparse grass, skipping the concrete path altogether.

"Hey, Randy," Janie called. "Is Dad inside?" Something between a grimace and a smile was glued onto her face. The woman stared at him.

Uncomfortable, he nodded.

He studied the woman's appearance. She looked familiar, but he couldn't remember where he'd seen her before.

Tears glistened in her eyes. Her reddened nose gave away that she'd been crying.

"Randy," the woman said. "Do you know who I am?" Her voice, he remembered. It was the voice he'd longed to hear during the nights he was alone and terrified.

"Mama?"

"Yes, honey." She swallowed a sob and held her arms open. "It's me."

He stopped himself from running to her.

"You were dead."

"No, not dead," she corrected him. "Just sick."

"Sick? Too sick to come home?" He didn't bother to disguise his disbelief.

"Yes," she nodded, "in a way that you might not understand, I was."

He'd prayed for this, begged, and made deals with God for Mama's return. Now that she was standing before him, he wasn't sure what to say. Hell, he had no idea how to feel. If he were a small child, he'd have run to her. But too many years had passed, too many tears into his pillow, for him to let her back just like that.

"What do you want?" He struggled to keep his voice cold and collected. "I mean, what're you doing here now, after all this time?"

She stuttered something about needing to see him, and her words hit him like raindrops on a plastic coat. He heard them, and felt their impact, just a little bit, but they didn't soak through.

"Well, well, look at what the cat dragged in." Dad's slurred words cut through the silence, startling Randy. He hadn't noticed Dad standing behind him on the porch.

Mama's face crinkled up into the beginnings of another crying jag. "Wyatt, it's been so long. Can we not do this now?"

"Do what, my dear?" Dad sniggered. "Did you expect to show up after all this time without any ramifications?"

Mama opened her mouth to say something, but Dad interrupted her.

"Of course, you did." Hate was smeared all over his drunken face. "What? You wanted a queen's reception?"

Dad did a deep bow, tipping an imaginary hat. "Oh, welcome home, our queen! We've missed you ever so much!"

Randy squirmed at the sound of Dad's exaggerated British accent. He cast a glance at Mama, afraid to make eye contact with her.

Through pale lips, she whispered, "Please, Wyatt. Not here."

"I'll be at Grandpa's if you want to talk," she said to Randy.

As she walked away, Randy noticed her gait was staggered, as if she had been injured.

"That's right. Walk away," Dad yelled at her back. "Just like you always do."

Mama surprised him by flipping the bird at Dad over her shoulder.

Dad responded with a belly laugh, something Randy hadn't heard for a long while.

"Are you hungry, son?" Dad startled him for the second time that day.

The television was on, but Randy wasn't paying attention. Eager for a distraction from the thoughts spinning around in his head, he'd switched over to the evening news, but none of it was getting through.

"Huh? Oh, no, thank you." *Since when did you start caring about whether I've eaten or not?*

Holding a plate of fried eggs, Dad sat in his recliner. "So, what do you think about your mama's visit?" He stabbed an egg with his fork and shoved the whole thing into his mouth.

Randy tried to ignore the way Dad chewed with his mouth open. One of the many reasons he didn't like eating with Dad.

He shrugged. "I dunno."

"Oh, come on. You must have something to say about it." Dad grinned, revealing bits of egg yolk stuck in the cracks of his teeth.

He took in a deep breath. "I thought she was dead."

Dad chuckled. "I told you she'd run off." He pointed his empty fork in Randy's direction. "That one's a quitter. Never did have a backbone."

"Mama said she'd been sick."

"No, not sick—just weak."

Dad was adamant, so Randy didn't argue. Instead, he turned his attention back to the television, pretending to watch.

"Seriously, son, think about it. What kind of sickness could keep a woman away from her husband and children?" He paused, but Randy knew he wasn't waiting for an answer. "None, that's what! She never wanted children, and she's weak. No spine, no commitment."

He closed his eyes, wishing he could shut out Dad's words. When he was younger, these words had made him cry. Calloused by repetition, he'd grown numb over time. Now, Dad's rants triggered black, moldy thoughts.

"The nerve of her, showing up after all this time. What in the hell is she thinking?" He impaled the last egg on his plate and shoved it into his mouth.

The conversation had only one direction to go—downhill. An invisible claw gripped at his intestines and twisted them around. If he chose not to respond, Dad would construe his silence as disloyal. Equally, if he were to agree, Dad would meet his words with suspicion. There was no win to be had, and he was a seven-year-old little boy once again.

Even though Mama had been gone for a year, he didn't always recall her absence first thing in the morning. The night had been longer than most, full of dream monsters and sad things that he couldn't quite remember once fully awake.

He'd cried out for her in the early dawn.

"*Shhh*," Janie had soothed him. "Go back to sleep."

He remembered being inconsolable. Only Mama would do.

"Shut up! You're going to wake Rosie!" Janie's voice had changed from comforting to irritated.

Disturbed by the commotion, Rosie broke into a startled cry and stood up in her bed.

"Now you've done it!" Janie shoved him onto his pillow as she stormed past to get Rosie.

"What in the hell is going on in here?" Dad had appeared at their door, hair disheveled, brow furrowed.

"Randy was crying for Mama." Janie rocked from side to side, bouncing Rosie back and forth. "And he woke up Rosie."

"Come here," Daddy pointed to the spot right in front of him.

Randy obeyed. Shaking, he stood in front of Daddy and awaited his fate.

He gripped the underside of Randy's chin and forced his face up. "Why are you wasting tears on your mama? She's never coming back. You know that, right?"

"No," he shook his head. "That's not right."

"Excuse me?" Dad had raised one eyebrow.

"Maybe she will." He couldn't have been prepared for Dad's reaction.

"You're telling me I'm wrong?" Dad ground his teeth back and forth between clenched jaws.

"No, Daddy! That's not what I was gonna say!" He shielded his face from the blows with the palms of his hands.

He managed to protect himself from the first few blows, but they came too quickly to stop the rest.

It was the first of many lessons. Eventually, Randy learned how to keep his mouth shut.

CHAPTER 42

BAIT

His chest had tightened at the sight of her. She looked almost the same, a little grayed and weathered, but still like herself.

He might have been too hard on her, but what did she think would happen? What he'd said to her and what he'd thought had been worlds apart. Now that he'd had some time for her return to sink in, there was a lot more he planned to say.

Standing on her papa's porch, he waited. He ran his fingers through his hair, still damp from the shower, and debated ringing the bell. He thought better of it and knocked again, harder this time. Footsteps grew louder from inside.

"Not now," Pearl said through the partially open door. "It's been a long week. I'm not up for a battle with you tonight."

"Just give me a minute of your time. No need for a battle."

She didn't open the door all the way, but she didn't slam it in his face either. A gust of air blew through the door, carrying her scent with it.

God, she still smelled the same. He'd missed her fragrance, a delicious blend of her natural body oils and the same perfume she'd worn for as long as he could remember. The smell left behind in her pillow, her chair, and her clothing had haunted him for years.

She sighed and opened the door wider. "Five minutes. That's it."

"Thank you." Best to be polite. No need to start out with force.

He stepped inside, half-expecting to see the old man sitting in his chair. Instead, Janie sat under the lamp, reading a book.

"Hey, Janie."

He wasn't surprised when she didn't bother to look up.

Silent, Pearl stood with her arms crossed and waited for him to speak.

"Can we go in the other room?"

She shrugged her shoulders and said, "Sure."

He followed her into the kitchen, trying to formulate what he was going to say. An apology felt like too much, and yet he knew he'd better offer something if he wanted to get more than a few minutes with her.

"I was a little hard on you," he said, "and I'm sorry for that."

Thin-lipped, she remained quiet.

"How have you been?"

"Fine."

God, she's tough to crack. "You look great."

She laughed. "Really? Because the last check in the mirror, I saw a tired, old woman." Still smirking, she asked, "What do you want?"

He kept his face relaxed, and he smiled. "Nothing much. Just wondering what happened to you."

Reaching out, he caressed her shoulder. "Where have you been all this time, Pearlie? Where'd you go?"

Tears pooled up in her eyes, and he knew he'd found a vein.

Softly, he said, "We missed you. The children, me, we all missed you."

"Don't," she warned. "Don't go there. You've done nothing but badmouth me to the children." Her voice thickened. "I know. I heard all about it."

"You walked out on us. What did you think I would say to them? That it was okay for their mama to desert them? That it was normal?"

"I was sick," she whispered. She pushed her hair back from her eyes with shaking hands. "You couldn't possibly understand."

"Oh, I understood, all right! I witnessed it. You weren't sick. You were a quitter!"

He did what he'd promised himself he wouldn't do and raised his voice. "You left them. A newborn baby, a six-year-old, and a nine-year-old. What'd you do that for? Huh, Pearlie? Did you run off with your boyfriend?"

"You're out of line! Get out!" She pushed her hand against his chest, and it took everything in him not to shove back at her.

"Whoa! Did I touch on the truth?" He knew it wasn't getting him anywhere with her, but the gloves were off now. "Why else would a woman leave her newborn baby?"

"I didn't leave her! She was taken away from me. I was the one who was left!" She shoved him again. "You left me in the loony bin to rot!"

He stifled a growl. "What else was I supposed to do? You were acting crazy!"

"Because I was sick," she insisted. "And you just left me! You never came back." Tears dripped down her freckled cheeks. "Papa was the only one who ever checked on me." Her words came out in staggered, hiccupping sobs. "They were doping me and leaving me alone for days. I begged for you, but you never came."

He'd been so focused on the wrongs done to him that he'd never contemplated what she might've gone through. He held his expression firm. He didn't want her to see signs of weakness. Pearl didn't deserve a free pass.

But something in the way she wrapped her arms around herself moved him, put a twinge in his heart that felt remotely like regret. And besides, no matter what she'd done, she was still his wife.

"*Shhh*," he quieted her, wrapping his arms around her shoulders.

She let him embrace her. He noticed how fragile her frail frame felt, and he was reminded of their barn cat after it had been accidentally locked in the tool shed for nearly a week. Her shoulders trembled as she cried silently into his chest.

His groin tightened in response to the closeness of her body. It had been a long stretch since he'd held a woman. After Rosie died, he'd found it difficult to converse with a strange woman, much less impress her into bed. His smile didn't come easy anymore.

Tempted to run his hands down the full length of her back, he restrained himself. Now wasn't the time. Instead, he contented himself with kissing the top of her head and breathing in the scent of her hair.

She relaxed a little, and her sobs began to subside. "Sorry about that." She leaned back and half-smiled. "It's just a lot to take in. Thinking about the past."

"Could I trouble you for a cup of coffee?" Sensing she was about to close back up, he grasped at something to prevent her from telling him to leave.

She bit her bottom lip, the way she always did when she was unsure of something. "Sure, no problem."

He sat at the small kitchen table and watched her familiar movements as she started the coffee. It occurred to him that he wasn't nearly as irritated with her as he'd expected to be. Her presence was comforting.

"How did you hear about your papa?" No topic of conversation was truly safe with her. He figured he'd start with the one that had nothing to do with the two of them.

She pulled the chair out directly across from him and sat down. "The obituaries."

"I thought maybe you stayed in touch with someone here in town. Betty, maybe?"

Her expression clouded. "Betty? No, not Betty."

He'd struck a nerve. *Of course, it was Janie. She must have told her.* "So, the obituaries? Where've you been staying? I figured you'd up and left the state."

"No, I was close enough."

She wasn't going to tell him shit. "Are you going back? Or have you decided to stay awhile?"

Shrugging her shoulders, she said, "I'm not sure. I'm not in a rush to decide."

He opened a new pack of smokes and held it out toward her. "Want one?"

"No, I stopped a long time ago."

"Yeah? How come?"

"Didn't have the money." She'd fixed her gaze on the spot over his shoulder. The conversation was going nowhere. He'd always been the one to ask the questions, to initiate things. Not much had changed.

"Speaking of money, how have you been making it?" He wouldn't be surprised if she'd shacked up with someone. How else would she survive?

"Work. Waiting tables."

He had always been able to tell when she was lying. This time, he wasn't sure. It didn't matter anyway. Water under the bridge, so to speak. Even if she had another man, she was here now.

The coffee pot sputtered out the last few drops of coffee. Pearl pulled two cups out of the cabinet and set them on the table. She poured the thick black liquid into the cups. "Cream and sugar?"

"Yes, please."

The first sip was delicious. No one made coffee as good as Pearl. Rather than continuing to carry the conversation, he slowly drank his coffee. He could see she was worn, nervous. Assuming it was because of his presence, he did his best to keep his expression kind.

She refilled his empty cup and stirred in more cream and sugar.

He had no idea how to cut through the wall. Scared to push too far, especially since he no longer had a hold on her, he remained quiet.

The silence was awkward, and he was tempted to fill it with trivial talk. Listening to his gut feeling, he considered the words he wanted to leave her with, the words that might touch her cold heart.

"I'm gonna leave you be for now." He leaned over and brushed his fingers lightly along her forearm, which was resting on the table. "If you want to see some pictures of Rosie, feel free to stop by."

CHAPTER 43

KITTY

He was a giddy, strange sort of happy. She was there, her voice filling the house. For a time, he stared up at the ceiling, tucked under the covers, pretending she had never left. The only thing that could possibly make him happier would be to smell her French toast, drifting up through the beams, just like when he was a little boy.

After a while, he dared to creep down the stairs. He suspected he was dreaming and that by the time he reached the source of the sounds, she would be gone. It was often this way for him, a dream of a cake in the icebox, or of his favorite ice cream, gone by the time he reached it, waking at the very moment he was just about to take a bite.

There she was. Sitting on the floor in front of the sofa, legs tucked under her, Mama sorted through photographs spread all around her.

"Oh my! Wasn't she beautiful!" It was hard to decide whether she was about to cry or getting ready to laugh.

More softly than normal, Dad said something he couldn't quite make out.

Afraid to interrupt the dream, he sat on the third step, content to watch her from a distance.

It was a bizarre sensation, to know his parents were together, talking without any discord. It brought about an unease. Every memory he had of the two of them was contaminated with conflict, anger, and fear.

Yes, he decided, this must be a dream. Wishing to leave before she vanished like all the other good things in his dreams, he stood, intending to go back to his bedroom.

"Randy," she called from the living room. "Come join us."

The drum inside his chest thumped a mad, uneven rhythm. He'd been spotted. Either she was indeed real, or this was the most convincing hallucination he'd ever had.

"Hey, there." Dad waved from his chair. "You plan on sleeping the whole evening away?" Instead of reclining, Dad sat perched on the edge.

Mama smiled. "Sit." She pointed to the spot next to her on the floor. "We were just looking through pictures of you all."

Wary, he sat down beside her.

She reached out to pat his leg, then pulled her hand back, as if she had changed her mind.

Not ready for her to be real, not sure he could stand for her to touch him, he exhaled relief.

"Your daddy was just showing me pictures of Rosie." Tears brimmed at the edge of her lashes. "You must miss her very much."

Did he? He wondered what it would feel like to miss Rosie as much as he'd missed Mama. Shrugging, he said, "Yeah, I guess."

Silence filled the room, the kind of awkward stillness that made everyone uncomfortable. He'd said the wrong thing, but there was no taking it back.

Fixing his gaze onto the floor, he wished he'd stayed in bed. The whole situation was surreal—everyone going about their business as if Mama returning from the dead was no big deal. Dad sat in his chair, docile, grinning like a goon. Mama giggled like a schoolgirl from time to time. *I must be stuck in an episode of* The Twilight Zone.

Once again, he was forced to think about Rosie. In the days following her death, it was all he could think about. Revolting images had mucked about in his head, and bile burned at his throat, rendering him incapable of swallowing anything.

It was a memory that he would never be able to wipe from his mind.

"No!" A fusion of fear and disbelief distorted her tiny features as she clawed at the air.

He'd reached for her, his hands grasping at the space she'd been a split second before. In the short time it had taken him to react, her body was already gone, lying in a mangled mess at the base of the stairs.

His own flight down was a blur. *Please, God,* he'd prayed, *let this be a nightmare.*

A terrifying bubbling sound came from her mouth, but her eyes remained closed. Shaking her, even yelling at her to get up, didn't wake her.

"Daddy!" He screamed over and over, but Dad never came.

By the time Janie got home, the gurgling had stopped, and Randy had reduced his words to one raw, ragged syllable.

The remainder of that awful day was swallowed up by a sea of confusion. A police officer asked him questions, but he was so distracted by Rosie's body, still lying on the floor, he couldn't respond.

This horrible thing he'd done could never be undone. He reasoned that telling the truth about it wouldn't have changed a thing. He carried it inside like a lump of burning coal, pushed it away when it got too close to his edges. Eventually, it had become easier not to think of it at all.

Now that Mama was back, the truth was tickling at the edges. He wouldn't be able to hide it from her. This thought made him feel panicked.

"Randy?" Dad's voice startled him. "What do you think?"

His cheeks flushed hot. "Sorry, I wasn't paying attention."

"Would you like me to cook my fried chicken?" Mama asked.

"Sure, whatever." He stood up, "I've got homework to do."

Mama whispered something unintelligible as he was leaving the room. Dad snickered and said, "He'll get over it."

Randy pulled his bedroom door shut with a slam. *Get over it? Just like that? That's some fucked-up shit!* Chest heaving, he huffed into his pillow.

Once he'd gotten his breathing under control, he squatted down beside the bed and felt around for the old cigar box stashed underneath. He took a cigarette from his collection of pilfered objects, which consisted of a handful of smokes of various brands, a box of matches, and a small bottle of half-drank whiskey.

Using both hands, he shoved the window up as wide as it would go. The night air, chilled by the setting of the spring sunshine, blew in. He perched himself in the open window, with his feet resting outside on the gable of the porch roof. The wind blew out the first match, and he tossed it out onto the overhang.

Cupping his hand more closely around the second match, he was able to keep it lit long enough to ignite the cigarette. He sucked in the first lungful and held it for a second.

A faint, mewing sound caught his attention. One of the barn cats had climbed onto the roof. It wasn't uncommon. Nearby tree branches gave easy access. Getting back down had proved to be difficult for a few of them over the years.

"Here kitty, kitty." He called to the cat perched near the edge.

The cat took a few tentative steps toward Randy.

"Come on. You can do it." Leaning back against the siding to stabilize himself, he knelt and held his hand out to coax the cat toward him.

He stroked the cat's silky fur until it began to purr loudly.

"You're a pretty little thing, aren't you?"

The cat continued to weave in and out of Randy's caresses, tipping its nose into his palm each time.

Randy chuckled. "You wanna come inside with me?"

He tossed his cigarette out onto the shingles and grabbed the cat around its midsection.

The cat tensed up and frantically clawed at Randy's chest, trying to cling onto his shirt.

"Hey! That hurts, you little shit!" He clamped harder around the cat.

The cat reacted, digging deeper into his chest.

"You fucker!" Randy moved a hand up to the cat's scrawny neck and squeezed.

The cat thrashed around, shredding Randy's arms in the process.

White-hot rage seared the back of his eyes. He clenched his jaw and tightened his grip around the cat's neck. Relief washed over him as he felt bones snap beneath his fingers.

The cat grew limp, save for an occasional jerk of a leg or twitch of its tail. He dropped the body and shivered with a mixture of horror and fascination as it slid down the gentle slope of the roof.

CHAPTER 44

ONE MORE TIME

She hadn't planned on moving in, but after a month or so, she realized she'd been there more often than not. Against her better judgment, she'd let her guard down.

Wyatt seemed different now. Of course, he hadn't stopped drinking, but he was gentler than before. She would've gone so far to say he was kind.

And, she was tired. Tired of running, tired of working so hard, tired of pretending to be someone she was not.

"What're you thinking?" Janie had refused to look up from the bowl of snap peas she was sorting through, but Pearl could see the disgust written all over her face. "Why are you even considering going back to him?"

She struggled to give an explanation that seemed valid. "I don't know. I guess we've both been through hell. Maybe we've beat each other up long enough."

"Ha," Janie uttered. "Is that what you're calling it? Beating each other up?" She shook her head and threw a pea pod into the colander. "Seems like I remember Dad doing all the beating."

"I don't expect you to understand. Where else should I go?"

"You could stay here at Grandpa's house. It's yours now, you know?"

"I could. Just the same, I'd like to try to make things work with your dad." She smiled, but it was lost on Janie.

Silent, Janie didn't look up from the peas.

"Think how much better it'll be for you and Randy," she added.

"You must be joking." Janie frowned. "Please don't do us any favors."

Pearl gave up trying to convince Janie. She didn't need her permission. After all, Janie was the child, not the other way around. She thought about placing the blame on Janie, telling her that she couldn't stand seeing the disapproval in her eyes every day. Partially true, it would've been wrong of her to say such a thing.

What she didn't know how to say was that life had lost its intensity. Although she'd felt more secure without Wyatt, even during her time on the street, the highs and lows were gone. She missed him, missed the colors. She reasoned, wasn't taking the bad along with the good a part of anything worthwhile?

They fell into a routine rather quickly. While she cooked their meals, Wyatt drank. When she cleaned the house, he drank. It didn't matter much to her because the present-day-Wyatt wasn't nearly as ferocious as the Wyatt of yesteryear.

She bumbled around with the children, trying to find her place with them. In a way, Janie was easier. She didn't live in the same house, and now that she'd started college, she wasn't around much at all.

Barely visible, Randy skulked around the house all summer long.

On the rare occasion that she found herself in the same room at the same time as him, the silence between them was profound. In her thoughts, she practiced what she might say to him, but everything she formulated seemed inadequate. Unfortunately for her, Emily Post didn't have a chapter in her etiquette book on how to speak to the child that you abandoned. *What should I say? "I'm sorry I left you alone, but I lost my mind"?*

She began most mornings out in the garden before the air grew heavy for the day.

"Isn't it a little late in the season to plant?" Leaning against the garden fence, Wyatt had watched her while she poked green bean seeds into the ripe soil.

"Maybe." On all fours, she'd pushed up and rested her weight onto her heels. Careful to keep the dirt out of her face, she pushed her hair away with the back of her wrist. "But it's a gamble how the garden will do most of the time anyway."

She'd made it a practice to pull weeds every day, and four weeks into it, the garden was coming along nicely. It was an interesting thought to her that a person could do everything out of order and still have success. What is it, she wondered, that determines the outcome of our efforts?

The creaking of the garden gate steered her away from her philosophical thoughts. Expecting to see Wyatt standing behind her, armed with a smart-ass comment, she was surprised by Randy's appearance.

"Good morning." On the inside, she vibrated with hope. Praying it didn't show, she kept a casual expression on her face. "How are you?"

He shrugged his shoulders and did a quick nod to flip his hair out of his eyes.

She hadn't adjusted to the longer hair—always hiding his eyes, a curtain designed to keep others out. It wasn't unusual, though. The whole generation was wearing their hair this way. Were they hoping to keep "the man" or their own parents away? She could guess all day long and still be wrong. The only thing she was certain of was that she missed her little boy—the shiny-eyed one who'd been happy to see her.

"Would you like to help pull weeds?"

He snorted. "No, thanks."

She waited for a second or two before turning her attention back to the tiny blades of grass emerging from the soil. Afraid to run him off, she decided to wait for Randy to reveal in his own time the reason for his presence.

From very early on, it was clear that he liked things to be on his terms.

Randy had been around two years old, just beginning to talk in full sentences.

"Put on your shoes, Randy." She'd been in a bit of a hurry to get to the market. The meat selection would be picked over by noon, and it was already eleven.

"You do it." He jutted his bottom lip out in a gesture of defiance.

"No, you're a big boy." She'd smiled. "You can do it."

He'd crossed his chubby little arms and stared at her. She remembered feeling amused. Janie's disposition was completely different—obedient, eager to please.

Of course, he'd won. She'd caved and put his shoes on.

Afterward, he'd slipped his warm, tiny hand inside hers. Randy was sweet as pie during the entire trip to the market. She'd thought she'd figured out how to control him. Little did she realize; he was learning how to control her.

Nothing had changed. It was a relief to think that all she need do was to figure out what he wanted. He was older now, but the behavior was the same.

"Will you be home for dinner?" It felt like a safe question.

"I dunno."

A flash of irritation over his lack of emotion caught her off guard, leaving her vulnerable. She regretted the words the very moment they escaped her. "Look, I'm trying to connect with you in some way, but I don't know what you want from me."

His lips curved into a tiny smile. "What I *wanted* from you," he corrected. "It's too late now." A sharp glint crossed his eyes, making his smooth face look hardened, older than his fifteen years.

"I've been trying to figure out why you're here." He chewed on the inside of his lip and waited for a second before finishing his thought. "I know why Dad wants you here. Simple—you're a piece of ass that cooks and cleans. But why in the hell would you want to be here? What're you getting out of the deal?"

"Please don't say that. We made some big mistakes, but we're trying now. Doesn't that count for something?" She wrenched her hands together, rubbing the drying dirt off her fingers.

"Sure." He shoved his hands deep into his pockets and rocked from heels to toes. "That counts for something."

She watched him walk to the house. He didn't look back. How was it possible that their first real conversation in ages had left her more confused than before?

CHAPTER 45

PARTY

Beau's old man was out of town for the entire week, so there was no good excuse for the party to be as lame as it was. The music had stopped, but no one seemed straight enough to change the record.

Randy sat in the corner, perched on the edge of the credenza. He occasionally took a swig out of a small bottle of whiskey he'd stolen from his old man. He watched all the girls, but one held his attention.

She was a pretty little thing, blonde and fair-skinned, not tanned like all the other girls. It wasn't her looks that caught his eye. She moved differently—smooth and deliberate, as if each action were thought out.

The squad of girls surrounding her burst into laughter. Polished, adult-like in contrast to the others, she smiled but didn't join in.

He held off until she was alone before braving a conversation. She'd gone to the bathroom. He waited for her outside the door.

"Oh! You scared me!" She laughed and clutched her hand to her chest. The sound was musical.

"Sorry about that." He held his hands up in mock defense, and she laughed again.

"I'm Peggy." Sticking her hand out for a shake, she smiled.

"Randy." He took her hand. It felt strange to make such a grown-up gesture, but he liked it.

"So, are you from here?"

"Yeah. Good ol' Boerne," he chuckled. "It's home." He raised an eyebrow. "But you're not from here, are you?"

"No, sir." She winked and said, "I'm a college girl."

He wasn't sure what the wink meant, but he liked the way it made him feel. Hell, she was probably humoring him with this conversation. "So, what're you doing at a high-school party?"

Pointing out the slightly plump girl on the sofa, she said, "My cousin, Lucy, lives here. She's a senior."

"I know Lucy," he lied. Lucy had a forgettable face.

"So, what grade are you in?"

"I'm a junior." Another lie. *Oh well, I'm probably not going to see her again after tonight.*

Her face darkened a bit. "Well, I'll let you get to it." She waved toward the bathroom.

The bathroom had been a ruse, but he went inside anyway. He examined himself in the mirror. His hair was still strategically messy. Grinning at his reflection, he whispered, "You've got this, man."

Just in case she was waiting outside the door, he flushed the toilet and turned on the faucet. *Only a girl would primp in the mirror this long.*

The hallway was empty. Randy followed the sound of high-pitched squeals and giggles into the kitchen, but Peggy wasn't there.

Traces of smoke from stolen cigarettes beckoned to him through the open windows. Outside, it took his eyes a few seconds to adjust to the darkness.

She was sitting on a metal glider, surrounded by a group of boys, each vying for her attention.

Ridiculous, he thought, *what a cat will do, just for a piece of ass.* None of them stood a chance with her. She was way out of their league.

He sat on the edge of the porch and leaned back on his hands. The edge of Beau's yard met up with fields of corn. Their farm was one of the few in the county that grew crops instead of livestock. Corn smelled a lot better than hogs and sheep, he decided.

Pretending to stare at the night skies, he let their boastful, competitive words fill his head.

After a time, he glanced her way. Her head was turned in his direction. Although it was difficult to see in the dark, he was certain she was looking right at him. It felt like an invitation.

Afraid to seem too eager, he took his time joining the group. The guy sitting closest to Peggy glared at him. He didn't mind. They would all scatter soon enough.

She turned her face up to him and smiled.

"Ready to get out of here?" He knew it was strong. Wasn't that what girls want?

She raised both eyebrows, then laughed. "Are you talking to me?"

"I'm not talking to any of these losers." He grinned.

"Um, no." Her smile disappeared, replaced by palpable irritation. "Not interested."

Flames of humiliation caught wind in the center of his chest and traveled up to engulf his neck and face. Beyond the rushing in his ears, the guys chuckled and snorted.

"Your loss, baby." He forced himself to smile. Pretending not to notice the jeers and wisecracks, he casually strolled back to the house.

He uncorked the bottle and finished it off in three big swallows. The whiskey burned all the way down to his gut.

In contrast to the cool night breeze, the inside of the house felt dank and smelled of smoke, as if it were a magnet, drawing in all the impurities from the outside air. On the ceiling, left uncovered, the bulbs cast harsh shadows around the room. He wondered what had happened to all the shades.

She was sitting by herself on the sofa, right where Peggy had left her.

"What're you doing here, all alone?" He smiled down at her.

Tears glistened in her soft, brown eyes, but she smiled back. "I don't really know anyone." Playing with the buttons on her pink cardigan, she added, "I'm not much for parties."

She's not bad looking, he thought. A little fat, but her face was all right.

"Whatcha drinkin'?"

"A soda." She smiled again. "I know, I'm a square. But I don't like the taste of liquor."

He sank into the seat next to her. "Nothing wrong with that."

"It's Lucy, right?"

Nodding, she looked pleased that he knew her name.

"I've seen you around at school." He slipped his arm behind her back, resting it on the sofa. "Always wanted to say hello, but I was shy."

She laughed, but the sound wasn't musical like her cousin's. "I didn't take you for the shy type."

"You're so pretty, how else am I supposed to feel around you?" He let his arm slide down around her shoulders. She didn't flinch. Her cheeks turned a shade of hot pink under her makeup.

He buried his nose into the top of her hair and inhaled. "*Mmmm*, what's that perfume? Smells like roses."

Lucy shivered and giggled. "It's my shampoo."

"Oh, I guess your perfume would be here." He put his face in the curve of her neck and breathed her scent in. She smelled like a powder that reminded him of the old ladies at the grocery store.

Turning in to him, she wrapped her free arm around his back.

They made out for a few minutes on the sofa, right in front of everyone. No one seemed to care.

"Wanna go somewhere else?"

She nodded. "But where?"

"Come with me." He stood up and held out his hand.

She followed him into Beau's bedroom.

Afterward, he lay on his back with his arms above his head while she dressed.

"That was my first time," she said.

"Me, too."

The soft glow from the nightlight reflected onto her face. She was smiling.

"Do you want my phone number?" Eager, she waited.

"Sure."

"That's swell! Maybe we can go to the movies or something tomorrow night?"

Even in the dim light, he could see that awful, mushy look in her eyes.

"Yeah, sure." He pulled his jeans up and turned his shirt right-side out. "I mean, I'll have to check with the old man to make sure he doesn't have plans for me." *As if he ever has plans other than getting soused.*

She'd managed to scribble her number on a scrap of paper from Beau's dresser during the time it took him to get dressed. "Here, call me tomorrow."

"Okay, will do."

"Well, I'd better get back. Peggy might be looking for me." She kissed him on the cheek.

He crumpled up the paper and tossed it into Beau's trash can on the way out.

CHAPTER 46

YOU CAN'T GO BACK

It was late autumn, the best time of the year in her book. Mornings were cool, but not cold. Days were a mild version of the scorching summer, sunny but not nearly as harsh. Walking from room to room, she opened the windows to let in the fresh air. The morning breeze smelled more like spring than fall. It was deceiving, making her feel that summer, rather than winter, was coming.

Randy slept, covered by a mound of blankets.

She tiptoed to his window, hesitant to wake him even though he needed to be up for school. She pushed the window up carefully, but there was no avoiding the squawk and rattle of the old frame.

He rolled over with a muffled protest and covered his face with his pillow.

"Randy," she whispered. "It's time to get up. Don't want to be late." She held her hand above his shoulder for a second before gently shaking him.

"Stop," he grumbled and turned back the other direction.

She turned to the window and breathed in the clean air. A dark lump of something lay at the edge of the roof, resting on the gutter. She squinted to see it better. *A dead squirrel? No, too black. Squirrels are brown.* Must be a cat that got stuck, she thought. It happened sometimes.

"Honey, you're going to be late for school." She didn't touch him this time; just spoke more loudly. "I'll make your breakfast."

He kicked his covers back and sat up. His muscled, bare chest reminded her that he wasn't a small child any longer. She turned away before he stood up. It'd been too long since she'd been in his life. Privacy seemed important now.

She rushed through the cooking, turning the burner on high. By the time he reached the kitchen, she had managed to put a full plate of French toast and a couple of fried eggs on the table.

He glanced at the plate but continued his path to the back door.

"Don't you have time to eat?"

"I hate eggs, and I'm not in the mood for French toast."

"But French toast is your favorite!"

"Was my favorite. Isn't now." He slammed the door behind him.

Tears prickled at the back of her eyes. She picked the plate up and thought about throwing it. Instead, she covered it with tin foil and placed it in the refrigerator.

"*Mmmm*, something smells good in here!" Wyatt shuffled into the kitchen, scruffy from sleep.

"Breakfast for Randy," she struggled to speak through the threatened tears. "He didn't want it, so you're welcome to it."

"Still not talking to you?"

"No, he's not. I don't know what to do about it. I feel like I've lost him forever."

"What'd you expect? You've been gone for years." He laughed and shook his head. "Do you blame him? What kind of mother leaves her children?"

Cold pumped through her veins. She knew better than to broach this subject with Wyatt. It was off-limits. They'd made it through the entire summer without speaking of it. She'd managed to convince herself that he'd let go of his judgments.

She turned away from him and began to clean up the mess from cooking. Damning the tears leaking from her eyes, she wiped them away with the back of her robe sleeve.

Wyatt poured himself a cup of coffee, sat at the table, and lit a cigarette.

She pretended not to notice, but she could feel him watching her.

"That was a serious question." His voice startled her, and she jumped.

"I don't want to rehash this." She didn't turn around.

"When? When are we going to figure it out?" She could hear him take a drag off his cigarette. "I've been patient up till now."

She spun around. "Is there no forgiveness? I guess you think you had no part in all this?" She gestured back and forth between herself and him. "You're blameless?"

"They're fucked up because of you!" Wyatt thumped his hand onto the table. "I didn't leave. You did!"

She was slipping off the edge of a cliff. There would be no return if she took one more step toward the great divide.

"And we are *all* fucked up because of you! You're still a drunk! Nothing's changed here. You're a lazy con artist!" She tossed the dish towel onto the table, wishing it were a grenade. "I can't believe I fell for your act. I'm such an idiot!"

He snorted. "That's an understatement!"

"I'm done. I don't care what happens to you. Don't call, don't come by. In fact, if you see me on the street, don't even look at me."

"Don't worry. I don't pay attention to old whores on the street."

"Fuck you!" she screamed at him.

"Not in a million years, baby," he laughed. "I don't want my dick to rot off!"

"You're vile. Filthy!" She stomped up the stairs. It didn't take long to gather her things. Leaving was different this time. She had a place to go. Janie wouldn't mind. She might rub it in her face a little, say, "I told you so," but that would be nothing compared to facing Wyatt's scorn every day for the rest of her life.

He was waiting on the porch when she left. "Need a ride?"

"No, thanks. I'll walk."

"I guess that's what streetwalkers are best at," he yelled as she walked away from the house. "Walking. And hoeing around."

By the time Pearl reached the end of the drive, she could no longer make out the names he had continued to shout at her.

She turned to take it all in, one last time. The house was no longer white. Most of the paint had peeled years ago. Bare timbers, exposed season after season to the rain and temperature changes, jutted loose from their fastenings. The shrubs, once manicured and green, were now small dead trees that twisted over the windows.

He belonged there. Decaying, filthy, falling down around his ears, the house looked just like him.

CHAPTER 47

NO SURPRISE

She was gone by the time he got home from school. He'd known she wouldn't stay, and it hurt a little less because he'd predicted it.

Dad was three sheets to the wind. Why wouldn't he be? That was his answer to everything. Hard day at work? Get drunk. Lose a job? Get really drunk. Hangover? The hair of the dog to take the edge off.

He went straight to his room and kicked off his shoes. He unbuckled his belt, slipped his jeans off, and climbed into bed.

The Vaseline was still wedged between his headboard and mattress. He scooped out a good amount and slid his hand into his underpants. Moving his hand slowly up and down, he made himself hard.

There were several different things he liked to think about when he jerked off. Sometimes, he thought about photographs in a nudie magazine from Dad's stash. Other times, he imagined a girl from school. But by far, the image that came to his mind most often was a memory.

Rosie was around four years old. He would've been ten. Janie wasn't home that afternoon, and Dad was supposed to watch them. He was drunk, of course, oblivious to everything and everyone.

She was outside, poking around in the little sandbox that Grandpa had made for her.

He watched her pouring the sand in and out of empty cans for a while before he said anything.

"Wanna go exploring with me?"

Her face lit up. "Okay." She smiled and dropped the cans.

She'd followed him into the tree line at the edge of their field. "Where're we going?"

"I dunno. Just exploring."

It took him a little while to get up the courage to make her do it. Scared that Dad or Janie might find them, he walked until he couldn't see the house.

"But why?" she'd asked when he told her to lift her dress up.

"Because I want to make sure your undies are clean."

Her blue eyes clouded, and she hesitated.

"Come on. You don't want sand bugs in your bottom, do you?"

Alarmed, she shook her head. "What's that?"

"Mean bugs that'll climb up inside your butt and eat your tummy out." The fear on her face thrilled him.

Her eyes puddled with tears. She lifted her dress.

"Higher," he said.

She complied, and a rush of power coursed through his veins.

"Take them off."

She didn't move.

"How're we supposed to check for bugs if you leave 'em on?"

Reluctantly, she pulled her panties down.

He could see the shame in her eyes, and this excited him.

This memory of Rosie, burned into his brain, was the one he used the most when masturbating. Numbed by the repetition, he'd long since gotten past the shame.

When he'd finished, he wiped his hand off on the washcloth that he kept in his nightstand.

Lying still, he listened to the rushing of the wind through the tree branches outside his window. Dad was right about Mama. *She's a quitter.*

He dozed for a while, dreaming of Rosie and her last day. When he awoke, the sun was gone.

Sappy, stupid music drifted up through the floor. It was a sure sign that Dad was not only drunk but sad—the worst combination. Sad could quickly turn to mad.

Standing up into a stretch, he yawned. If his stomach weren't growling, he'd stay in bed and avoid Dad altogether.

Not worried about Dad hearing him over the music, he didn't bother to tiptoe as he walked down the stairs.

The kitchen was still orderly from her daily cleaning. He opened the icebox and smiled. *Thank God,* he thought, *we're not down to just eggs, yet.*

A variety of leftovers sat neatly wrapped in tin foil. He wished she'd bothered to label them. Picking one packet at a time, he jiggled them around like a Christmas present, as if he could decipher the contents just by shaking them. Finally, he settled on one that felt like meatloaf. Just to be sure, he put his nose up to it and sniffed.

"Yep, meatloaf," he said to the empty kitchen. "Thanks, Mom."

He turned the oven on to heat up the mystery package and tossed it in. Unopened mail sat in a pile in the middle of the kitchen table. Bored, he rifled through it to pass the time until his dinner was ready. Sorting through the mail by the recipient, he made little stacks for each person. In the end, Dad had the lion's share.

Mama only had one piece of mail, a small envelope with no return address. He held it loosely in his hand for a while and wondered who it could be from. The handwriting was neat, flowery.

He held the envelope up to his face and breathed in. Disappointingly, it only smelled of paper, not of perfume as he'd expected. Such elegant handwriting should have a fragrance, he thought.

The envelope made a satisfying zipping sound as he sliced open the side with a steak knife. He squeezed it open and dumped the letter into his hand.

Dear Helen,

(Sorry, but I will always think of you as Helen.)

I was surprised to get your letter. We worried so after your disappearance! Greta thought to call the police, but I was afraid to get you in trouble somehow, so we waited.

Your boss called a couple of times to check on you. The last message from him was, "Don't worry about coming back!" What an asshole! It sounds like you don't have to worry about work anymore. I'm so jealous!

I'm sorry to hear about your father's death, but I'm happy that you are back with your family. I had no idea that you had children! I'd love to meet them someday.

Thank you for giving us your things. You know that we'll use them! (We already did when you were here—haha)

Don't be a stranger—we're only half an hour away!

Love,

Christina

His chest tightened, and a lump formed in his throat. Mama had been close. He'd imagined that she'd been miles away during all the years she wasn't home, that coming to see him had been impossible. And now this. Proof that she had stayed away because she'd wanted to. Evidence that he'd mattered so little to Mama that she hadn't bothered to tell her friends about her own children.

Fighting the urge to cry, he crumpled the letter with both hands and tossed it toward the trash like a basketball.

"Bitch!" He didn't care if Dad heard him. He wanted to scream at the top of his lungs. He was filled with the worst kind of fury, and he had no place to put it.

Stupid, girly tears filled his eyes. Which made him angrier, at Mama, and especially at himself for crying over her.

CHAPTER 48

A FATHER SON MOMENT

At first, he wasn't sure which direction the sounds were coming from. He'd fallen asleep in his chair again. Earlier, the afternoon sun had baked a sweat out of him. Now, the cooler evening temperature had rendered him into a cold puddle of damp. He pushed the footrest down and peeled his bare back off the vinyl.

Disoriented, he listened for a bit to the sound of glass breaking. It was coming from the backside of the house.

"What the hell," he mumbled under his breath. Using the back of his forearm, Wyatt swiped away at the cold beads of sweat dripping from his brow. He shoved himself into a standing position using the arms of the chair and waited for the room to steady itself before attempting to find the source of the commotion.

Randy stood about ten feet away from the old oak near the garden. With an arm that would make Babe Ruth proud, he smashed plate after plate into the tree. Hunks of bark were missing off the trunk, and shards of glass and stoneware lay all around the base, glittering in the moonlight.

"Hey!" He shouted from the edge of the porch. "Knock it off!"

Randy turned to him and dropped a bowl from his hand.

"What in the hell are you doing?"

"I hate her!" he bellowed.

"Who?"

"Mama." His words came out in ragged gasps. "You're right. She doesn't give a shit about me."

"Come here." He wiggled his finger at Randy, summoning him to the house.

Randy looked as though he were expecting an ass-chewing.

Wyatt wrapped his arms around him. "Son, I wish I could argue that. But her actions show otherwise." He moved his hands to Randy's shoulders and took a step backward to get a better look.

He was a good-looking kid. Already over six feet tall at fifteen years old, he had a fierce look in his eye that women would someday swoon for, and other men would fear. His soft cheeks gave away his age, but that would soon change. There were only a few years left before he'd be turned loose on the world. Wyatt had a fleeting feeling of panic that he might not have prepared his son for this momentous event.

"We don't need her." He cupped his hand around Randy's neck and jaw. "Right? We've been just fine without her for all this time."

Randy nodded. For the first time in ages, he looked Wyatt directly in the eyes. "Yeah, we don't need her."

"That's my boy." He slapped him on the back and steered him into the house.

He switched on the light over the kitchen sink and opened the cupboard. Only a few dishes remained after the smashing party. Grumbling under his breath, he debated ripping Randy a new asshole.

He stretched his arm to the dark corners of the cabinet and managed to swipe at something made of glass. No matter how much he reached, he couldn't quite grab onto it.

"Randy," he yelled. "I need your long arms!"

He pulled the bottle out of the freezer, took a swig, and waited for Randy.

"What took you so long?" He grinned and said, "Were you taking a dump?"

Randy rolled his eyes and groaned, "God, Dad, that's gross."

Pointing up to the cabinet, he said, "Can you reach that glass in the back?"

"Doesn't look like you need one," Randy scoffed.

"Watch it now. You're getting close to the line." He thought about knocking him in the shoulder but didn't. He'd cut him some slack, this one time.

"Sorry," Randy mumbled and grabbed the glass out with no effort.

"Thank you, son." Wyatt poured the booze into an old beer mug that he'd taken from the bar—walked out with it in his hand, half full of beer for the drive. No one had said a word about it. He figured it was a well-deserved souvenir after all the dough he'd dropped at that dive.

"You want some?"

Randy shook his head. "No, thanks."

"Aw, come on. Don't be a pussy." He held the glass in Randy's direction. "A little won't hurt. It'll put hair on your chest."

He took the glass and put it to his lips. Handing it back, he said, "It's not my first time, you know."

Wyatt grinned. "Oh, yeah? Do tell."

"It's no big deal." He shrugged. "Just a lame party."

"All this time, I thought you were turning into Carrie Nation." He pushed the glass back to Randy.

"No, just don't wanna get drunk." Randy took another sip.

"All you got to do is control yourself," he said. "Just like I do."

Passing the glass back, Randy smiled. "Sure."

"Isn't this nice? Father and son, sharing a drink?"

It was one of the moments he'd looked forward to since Randy was a baby. He wondered why he'd waited so long. He was nearly a man—looked like one, already.

"Want a smoke?" Reaching into his pocket, he tipped a cigarette out and offered it.

"Thanks." Like a pro, Randy lit it and took a deep drag.

"How's school going this year?" Small talk, he knew, but where else could he start?

"Good, I guess." Randy pushed his hair back from his brow and looked away.

"Got a girlfriend?"

"Geez, Dad. Is that all you ever think about?"

He chuckled. "What else is there worth thinking about? Women, booze, and smoke—makes the world go 'round. Right?"

Randy raised an eyebrow. "Yeah, I guess so. Seems like more trouble than they're worth. Look at how women have turned out for you."

"Well, you can't judge all women based on your mama. She's a pain in the ass." He swallowed the last of the booze and filled the glass again. "Don't fool yourself, though. We had some good times."

Randy frowned. "Didn't look so great from here."

"I never figured out how to keep her in check, that's all. You have to control them. Most of 'em ain't got enough sense to do that for themselves."

He pointed at Randy's heart. "Can't let a woman get in there. If you do, she'll be the boss of you. I always loved your mama too much for my own good—let her get under my skin."

Randy listened but said nothing.

He hoped he was taking it in, this lesson he was leaving his son with. Life would damn sure be a lot easier for him if he did.

"Learn from my mistakes. That's all I'm trying to say."

CHAPTER 49

OLD FRIENDS AND THE TRUTH

She had just taken off her nightgown and turned on the bath when a succession of frantic knocks sounded at the door.

Damn it. Every time! Who now? Last time, it'd been a powdered and perfumed church lady trying to sell tickets to a fundraiser.

She considered ignoring the person, but the banging continued. She picked her gown off the floor and slipped it back over her head. If she'd been certain that the front door was locked, she might have climbed into the tub, instead.

"Hold your horses! I'm coming!"

A glance through the sheer curtains revealed a woman, but she couldn't make out her face. No matter, at least it wasn't the bogeyman.

"Can I help you?"

"Betty, it's me—Pearl."

She examined the middle-aged woman standing on her porch. A freckled, leathering face, surrounded by wispy locks of blond and silver hair, stared back.

"Holy shit! It is you!"

Pearl's mouth curved into a weak, sheepish grin. "It's me."

Dumb, Betty continued to stare at this shabby version of the woman who used to be her best friend.

"May I come in?"

"Of course!" She held the door open wide and ushered her in. "I don't know what's wrong with me. It's just that I feel like I'm seeing a ghost!"

Pearl looked around the parlor. "It's all the same, but it's been so long that I feel like I'm seeing it for the first time."

"Sit, please."

Her eyes flitted from sofa to chair as if she wasn't sure where to place herself.

"Anywhere is fine," she reassured Pearl.

"Thank you." She chose the chair closest to the front door.

"Where are my manners? Can I get you something? Coffee? You do still drink coffee, yes?"

To her relief, Pearl laughed.

"Of course, I still drink coffee! I'll take something stronger if you have it."

"Oh, good!" Betty chuckled. "I think we may need it."

Pearl followed her into the kitchen, as she'd done so many times in years past. "This room looks the same, too. I thought you'd have remodeled since…" Her voice trailed off, an indecisive tendril of smoke.

More cheerful than intended, she answered, "I don't quite have the funds that I did before. I'm older now, and there isn't a market for this." She swept her hand up and down her body.

Pearl giggled. "No, I guess not. We're older now. You're still beautiful, though," she reassured. "I'll bet men still fall all over themselves when you're around."

"Sure, they do. Especially the men that need canes and walkers."

They both broke into a fit of roaring laughter, the kind that made them both tear up. For a moment, it felt like the old days.

Pearl dabbed at her eyes with a thin handkerchief. "I've missed you, Betty." Her chin quivered, and her eyes pooled with more tears.

"I've missed you, too. For God's sake, what happened to you? Do the children know you're here?"

She cleared her throat and nodded. "I've been here all summer."

"Since your papa's death?"

A sob escaped from Pearl's mouth. "Yes, since then." She rested her forehead against her clenched fist. "I don't know if I can forgive myself for missing his last days."

"He never stopped looking for you."

She could say this truthfully. On more than one occasion, Betty had bumped into him at the filling station. He never failed to ask, "Have you heard from Ingrid?"

"Whiskey, or vodka?" She held up a bottle in each hand.

"Vodka, I think. Just a splash will do."

She placed a juice glass full of the clear, bitter liquid in front of Pearl. "Do you still smoke?"

"Not anymore." Smiling, she added, "But, seeing you is making me crave one—just for old times' sake."

"We'll have to go buy some." She took a drink from her whiskey-spiked coffee. "I gave up the things a few years back—couldn't stand the coughing."

"Wasn't it the worst?" Pearl agreed. "I don't miss the ashtray breath, either." The tremble in her voice gave away her nervousness.

Both nursed their drinks in a moment of uncomfortable silence. She was afraid to go deeper into the conversation for fear of saying the wrong thing.

"Tell me," she said. "How've you been?" It was the only question that felt safe.

Pearl hesitated. Looking down at her half-empty glass, she pursed her lips together, in the same fashion as always.

It was unreal, watching this stranger making expressions that belonged to the woman she knew so long ago. Pearl is tucked inside of this impressionist, she reminded herself.

"Honestly, I don't know. My life has changed so much that I don't recognize it. Hell, I don't recognize myself."

"No matter how many ways I tried to look at it, I couldn't understand why you left." Tears welled up in Betty's eyes. "Where in the world did you go? And more importantly, why?"

Pearl sighed. "I don't know where to begin."

"But you left on your own? No one forced you?"

"No, no one made me leave." She swallowed the remaining vodka. "Things were so bad at the hospital that I didn't feel I had a choice." She ran her finger around the rim of the empty glass.

Betty wanted to bombard her with all the questions she'd stored up for nearly a decade, but she restrained herself.

"I knew the longer that I stayed, the worse I would become."

"Couldn't you have come home? At least have let us know you were alive?" Her words were edgy, angry, and she could see Pearl react to them.

"I didn't want to hurt the children," she murmured. "I was afraid I'd…well, you know."

Betty did know. She remembered all too well what had happened after the birth of Randy.

"What were they doing for you? At the hospital? I mean, how did they treat you?"

"Are you familiar with electroshock treatments?" Her lips stretched into a thin smile.

"They electrocuted you? How is that supposed to help?"

She chuckled. "It's a painful exorcism. That's what it feels like."

"Oh, God! That's awful!"

"It was. And each time afterward, I would lose another piece of myself." She held out her glass for another.

Betty filled the glass halfway. "Did it help at all?"

"With what? It was a punishment. My nurse hated me. She kept me unconscious. I went days at a time without eating. I lost so much weight that I must've looked like a Jew in a concentration camp."

"I don't know what to say. I'm so sorry." Cynical thoughts crept into the back of Betty's mind. What if she were lying? Wouldn't the hospital have needed permission from Wyatt?

"I had to leave. Everyone stopped coming, and I was terrified I'd completely disappear." She nibbled on her pinky nail, a nervous habit carried over from her childhood.

"Where did you go? Who helped you?" She'd been Pearl's only friend, at least so far as she knew.

"Some of the others, the ones out on the street."

Betty dumped more booze into a cup of coffee and let Pearl's story sink in. She had the same sickening feeling in her gut as when she ran over the neighbor's cat.

Barely alive, and mostly unrecognizable, the cat demanded she do something, just by the fact that it wasn't dead. She remembered wishing for the cat's death because there was no way that she could help it.

Although she didn't wish for Pearl's demise, there was no way to undo the damage that had been done.

Her memories of the friendship they'd once had were tainted beyond repair by this broken creature in front of her. Just as leaving the cat to die alone would've been cruel, sending her away would be unkind, unthinkable. What to do with her, she didn't know.

So, she listened, and offered coffee, all the while willing her to leave.

***

How many different ways could I have said it? Hours had passed since Pearl had left, yet she lay wide awake, questioning her choice of words.

It wasn't my fault. She shouldn't have kept pushing if she didn't want to know the truth.

Twinges of unwanted guilt irritated her gut as she reran the conversation through her mind again.

All the niceties and polite chatter had been exhausted. Betty knew there must have been another reason for the unannounced visit beyond catching up with an old friend.

"What exactly is it that you want to know?"

Pressing her fingers against her mouth, Pearl had hesitated. She scrunched her eyes shut and sighed. "I guess I wanted you to tell me what happened after I left."

"Why not ask your family?" Betty chuckled softly. "I doubt I can tell you as much as they can."

She shook her head gently. "I don't know. Janie said enough."

Betty exhaled, shaky and slow. "Naturally, at first, everyone was worried about you. I tried to help out with the children as much as possible."

Pearl smiled. "Because Wyatt couldn't handle it?"

"You know as well as I do, he's not capable." Afraid to be offensive, she added, "After all, you did manage everything for the children. Plus, his head wasn't right after you disappeared."

"I see." Pearl nodded. "That's interesting. Janie told me they lived with you."

A flush crept up the back of her neck and spread around the sides of her cheeks. She prayed her unease wasn't obvious.

"That's true," she admitted. "They did stay with me for a while."

Her gut told her to say as little as possible, but the urge to explain took control of her mouth. "Wyatt was...well, you know what he's like when things go south."

Pearl smiled weakly. "Of course."

In the past, Betty would've been able to see Pearl's thoughts run across her face like a flashing billboard. *Mysterious, this new Pearl.*

"I couldn't let the children fend for themselves. And, your papa asked me to take them in. After you ran…" she corrected herself, "after you left the hospital, he went off the deep end."

"Really? Janie had the impression that Wyatt lived with you, also."

She answered too quickly. "I'm sure that's what it looked like. At first, before you disappeared, he'd come over for dinner with the children. He'd tuck them into bed, too. I'm sure he was worried about their feelings, with you away and all."

"But he wasn't staying with you?"

A surge of anger festered somewhere in the back of her head. Being cornered in this way brought out the animal in her. "Why all the questions?" she snapped.

"I'm just trying to understand what happened after I left."

Betty imagined slapping the suspicious expression off Pearl's face.

"Is it necessary? I mean, what good will it do now?" Once more, she wished for a cigarette. "Shouldn't you focus on the future?"

"How can I fix things with them if I don't know what they went through?"

"Fair enough." She took a sip of her coffee, now gone cold. "What exactly do you want to know?"

"I don't know." She fixed her gaze away from Betty's eyes. "They're so angry at me. I guess I need to know what happened while I was away."

To pace herself, she took in as much air as her lungs would hold, and let it seep out slowly. "Can you handle the truth of everything?"

Pearl held her bottom lip between her teeth and closed her eyes. She shrugged her shoulders and said, "I don't think there is any other way."

"I don't owe you anything."

"I know. I'm begging you as nicely as I can."

She put both hands up, surrendering. "You want the truth? Well, you can have it."

Dumping everything at once onto Pearl's frail lap, she proceeded to bombard her with the truth. As she took Pearl back through the past, beginning with the day Rosie was born, her heart raged. She hadn't realized how that time stayed with her, still.

Pearl sat through it all, silent and pale.

"Don't you have anything to say?" Betty didn't bother to disguise her anger.

She covered her face with both hands, but Betty could hear the tears in her voice. "I didn't realize."

"How could you? You weren't here for any of it!"

"You're absolutely right." Pearl stood and pushed the chair back into its place, underneath the table. "Thank you for your honesty. And, thank you for helping in the only way that you knew how."

Betty wondered if this was a sarcastic reference to her fling with Wyatt, but she held her tongue. Already, the guilt was sinking in.

Now, in the early morning hours, regret had wrapped around her with the voracity of a boa constrictor, threatening to squeeze her in half.

CHAPTER 50

RESOLUTION

The glass was a filter of sorts. Warped, faded, and flecked with black spots where the backing was worn, the mirror transformed her reflection into a creature that was deserving of the emotion her heart encased.

None of them, not even Janie, had been truthful with her.

Betty had been, though—brutally honest. Her words might have felt cruel, but it was right of her to be so frank about the past. Pearl deserved to know all the ways she had destroyed her own family.

Only now, Pearl was unsure how to proceed.

It wasn't that she questioned what to do with herself. It was simply a matter of how—how to leave without inconveniencing anyone.

Oh, but you aren't that concerned with the inconvenience part. Really now? Aren't you more worried about how they'll discover you? The ugly voice in her mind taunted her. *Worried they'll find you in a pile of your own shit?*

"Shut up!" She put her hands over her ears. The wraith living in her thoughts was right. The idea of being found in soiled clothing disturbed her.

She needed to prepare. Everything must be meaningful.

"That's right," Polly mocked her through the mirror. "Make it all count for something."

"Go away!" She shouted, "I don't need you anymore."

She walked from room to room, looking for items to bequeath to Janie and Randy. There wasn't much left of her in Papa's house.

"There isn't much of you left anywhere," the nasty voice taunted.

Once her mind was made up, relief set in. The worst part had been the uncertainty.

It took a while to find the good stationery in Papa's desk drawer, tucked away behind the collection of pencils and scraps of paper.

The words didn't come easily. Feeling lightheaded, she fought the urge to vomit. A solid brew of fright and exhilaration danced around in her head. She wondered what had taken so long for her to reach this conclusion. After all, there was no reason to continue this charade. She'd simply outlasted her time.

First, she penned a note to Janie. Questioning if it was substantial enough, she read it aloud. It sounded nice enough, and she hoped Janie would interpret it just that way. One never knew how words would be received.

Randy's letter proved to be more difficult. Not surprising, since Randy had always been more difficult. In the end, she chose to keep her words generic, loving. Pearl reasoned, there was no sense in burdening him with every little regret.

Although she'd made her mind up, she found herself wandering from room to room, tidying up her messes and those left before her arrival.

The bully in her head picked at her. *What're you waiting for? Scared? Get it over with, already.*

In the bedroom that had been hers before Janie had taken possession, she undressed. Several minutes passed while she stood motionless, examining her image in the vanity mirror. Stretch marks reminded her of the vessel she had once been. Gravity had left its unkind marks in the form of loose skin and useless curves.

She stilled the sob before it could escape her lips. *What a waste of flesh.* Shame burned its way through her core.

Aware that someone would be required to clean up the mess, she chose her attire carefully. A simple button-front robe would be the kindest thing—nothing to peel off afterward.

Pearl brushed her hair, one last time, with the same brush that her mother had used on her as a small child. Ivory handled, cool to the touch, the brush reminded her of the beginning, long ago, when she was still clean.

She pulled the linen bedspread off. Remembering how she'd begged Mother; it was everything that her fourteen-year-old heart had desired. Dreaming for weeks of the delicate rose print, she'd been overjoyed when it had finally arrived.

Wrapping her shoulders with the thin, heavy spread, she paused at the doorway and let the room leave its lasting impression in her mind. She wanted the room to be the last thing she thought of when she left.

Careful with her footing, she descended the stairs at a rather slow pace, taking in the dust-covered photo frames along the staircase. It'd been years since she'd taken notice of them.

Knowing that she wouldn't return, the urge to preserve everything about her childhood home momentarily consumed her.

Once she'd had her fill, she went to the kitchen. Out of habit, she opened the box of matches to light the pilot with. "You won't be needing those," the voice reminded her.

It took less time than she'd imagined, for the invisible fog to fill her lungs. Inside her rosette covered tent, she pushed away from the sensations and allowed herself to be lulled into the forever after.

CHAPTER 51

A LIE AND THE GOODBYE

"Hey, Janie!"

At first, Janie couldn't make out which direction the voice was coming from. October winds had a way of shifting sounds from one path to another. Squinting, she used her hand as a makeshift shelter against the mid-morning sun.

She waved to Janie, separating herself from the crowd of students traveling from one class to the next.

Janie raised her hand in acknowledgment and waited. She was invisible to most of the other students, but not to Hildy.

Hildy was an unusual bird. Dressed in men's trousers and a button-up shirt, she managed to look every bit a girl. Hildy roomed in the dormer one over from Janie's. She always seemed to have an entourage with her.

Janie had yet to figure out what Hildy saw in her. Impulsive and full of energy, Hildy was the polar opposite of her conservative, quiet nature.

Long curly hair stuck to the perspiration on her neck, gasping from the quick jog, she caught up to Janie. "Did you finish your psych homework?"

"Yeah, it wasn't too bad." Suddenly shy, Janie smiled without looking into Hildy's eyes. "How about you?"

With a dismissive wave, she answered, "Nah, but I'll do it this afternoon." Brightly, she added, "It's easy enough."

Everything seemed to be easy for Hildy. Rumor had it that she was from old money. Her brand-new convertible certainly appeared to confirm it.

"What's your weekend look like?" She tossed her hair away from her face and grinned. "Any chance you want to go away with us?"

"I dunno, I'm supposed to go home." She frowned. "I haven't been for a while." She wasn't sure why she made up a lie. Many nights, she'd lain awake, wishing for an invitation. *You're chickenshit—that's why.*

She was surprised to see the disappointment on Hildy's face.

"Oh, well. Maybe next time?" Hildy flashed another brilliant smile and pushed her unruly mane back from her eyes. "Gotta run!"

A tornado, that's what Hildy is, Janie thought, *a damned tornado.* A smile touched Janie's lips as she watched Hildy twist away.

As she trudged to class, the realization sank in. She'd have to go home. She couldn't be seen in the dorm lest she be caught in her fib.

After her classes were over for the day, Janie went back to her room to pack. Dragging her feet in hopes that everyone else would leave for the weekend, she took her time filling the small suitcase. There would be no reason to go home if she were the only student left in the dorm.

Gradually, the number of housemates dwindled down to a few stragglers, including her roommate, Amy—none of whom appeared to be leaving.

Sighing, she latched her case, put on her coat, and grabbed her purse and keys. "Have a nice weekend," she called to her roomie.

Buried in her magazine, Amy grunted a goodbye of sorts.

The old Studebaker was cold-blooded. It took a while to warm up, but she wasn't in a hurry to leave, so she didn't mind. Wishing there was some other place to go, Janie put the car in gear and crept out of the parking lot.

She made it to Boerne by eight o'clock, well past dark. Reminded again of the smallness of her little hometown, she noticed that the streets were nearly empty. San Antonio wouldn't be quiet for hours, she thought.

All the lights were off at the farm. It was too early for bed, even for Mama. Janie wondered if she'd gone back to Dad again. It wouldn't be surprising. After all, Mama wasn't the most resolute person in the world.

The smell, rotten, like sulfur from the pits of hell, punched her in the nose as soon as she opened the car door. Passed down for a generation or more, the stories of the New London schoolhouse explosion came to mind.

As a small child, she would think about their deaths with horror, too frightened of the gas stove to even consider touching it.

She put her key back into the ignition and hoped like hell that the spark of the engine wouldn't ignite the cloud that seemed to be surrounding the old house.

For once, she was relieved to see the lights on at Dad's.

He was right where she'd imagined, sitting in his chair. "What brings you here, stranger?" Grinning big, he was already half shit-faced.

"Grandpa's house! It's full of gas! It's going to explode!"

"Are you serious?" His eyes sobered in an instant, and he slammed the footrest down on his chair. "Is she there?"

"I have no idea. I just got into town, and Mama didn't know I was coming." Her words came out in gasps. "What do we do?"

"Call the fire department." He stood up and pulled his keys out of his pocket. "I'll meet them there."

Petrified with shock, Janie tried to comprehend his words. There was no way this could be happening.

"Call now!" Dad raised his voice, but it wasn't out of anger. He sounded terrified. "Do you hear me?"

She nodded dumbly.

"And wake your brother up!"

Confused as to whether she should call for help first or wake Randy, Janie hesitated.

Dad shook his head and said, "Never mind." He cupped his hands to the sides of his mouth and yelled for Randy.

"Meet me there after you've called," Dad said and shut the door behind him.

She'd already made the call when Randy appeared in the kitchen.

"What's going on?" He rubbed his eyes, sleepy and confused.

"Grandpa's house. It's full of gas." She noticed he'd grown taller since the summer. "I'm going back. Are you coming?"

"Is Mama inside?" His voice cracked.

"I have no idea."

The mile and a half between Dad's house and Grandpa's seemed like ten. The fire department had already arrived, along with the gas company. Men bustled back and forth between the house and vehicles.

Dad was leaning against the side of his truck, parked on the road, far away from the house.

She stood next to Dad, closer than she'd been in years. His scent, a familiar mixture of liquor and aftershave, struck a sentimental chord. She watched him from the side, noting the agonized arrangement of his features. Did he still love Mama?

"Is she here?" Randy was the first to ask.

"I still don't know." Dad rubbed his forehead with his hand. "They won't let me near the place."

Off in the distance, flashing lights grew closer. A police car, followed by the town's ambulance, turned into the long drive, and her heart sank.

"They wouldn't call the police for a gas leak, would they?" Randy asked.

Dad put his hand on the back of Randy's neck and rubbed gently. "No, son. I don't believe so."

Nodding, Randy seemed to comprehend. He covered his face with his hands and sobbed.

Red lights from the police cruiser mingled with that of the firetruck, transforming the yard into a hellish scene. Nothing seemed real. Shivering, Janie wrapped her arms around herself.

CHAPTER 52

TOO LITTLE—TOO LATE

The funeral had been a disaster. Only a handful of people attended, and Dad had been rip-roaring drunk. Embarrassed by his old man's ridiculous behavior, Randy had slipped away before the service was finished.

To make matters worse, his teachers were overly nice. It didn't cushion the pain. If anything, their pity angered him.

Drinking helped to squash the fury, most of the time. Randy found he could stay on the bright side of numb, so long as he kept a nice even supply of alcohol trickling into his veins. Maybe Dad had the right idea, all along.

It was a learning process, figuring out how to walk the line. He'd gone over the limit a time or two at school. Mr. Belvin, the gym teacher, had steered him into the locker room to sleep it off.

Even though he'd gotten away with it, after that, he made an effort to control himself. In his eyes, ending up like the old man would be a disgrace.

Mama was in his head most of the time. In a million years, he still wouldn't understand why she killed herself.

The note was worn around the edges from his fingers. He'd read it at least a hundred times, looking, hoping for something different. Her words gave nothing. He damned sure didn't feel the love that he hoped she'd intended.

Dearest Randy,

I am sorry for what I couldn't give to you. It's not your fault. You were a good son, and I know that you did your best to please me. I want you to have the rocking chair. Please think of me when you hold your children.

Love,

Mother

It wasn't right. She'd signed it, "Mother." He'd never called her by that name. She'd always been "Mama." And why would she give him a stupid chair? He didn't want children, and he didn't want the damned rocking chair.

He crumpled the note into a ball and tossed it onto the floor. Using it as a punching bag, he let his rage loose on his pillow until the feathers burst out.

CHAPTER 53

HILDY AND THE KISS

The sky had already darkened. Campus lights cast a soft, yellow glow over their conversation.

"Are you sure you're okay?" Using her ring finger, Hildy had brushed a caramel-stained curl from the corner of her own mouth. "Losing your mom is about the worst thing I can think of. Should you even be here?"

"I'm fine, really," she lied. She'd resisted the urge to smooth away the rest of Hildy's hair from her face and asked, "What else should I be doing?"

Hildy's concern was touching. None of her other roommates had even so much as acknowledged Janie's loss.

"Staying home with your family?" Her answer had been half statement, half question. "Is your dad still around?"

Janie wanted to say that her dad hadn't been around in ages, but that would've started a conversation that she wasn't ready to have, so she nodded. After all, he was still alive, even though he'd been dead to Janie for years.

Although her focus should've been on her mom's death, all she could think about was Hildy.

Now, she sat with her legs tucked under her, staring at the same tree through her dorm window for hours, replaying the kiss many times over. It wasn't something that she'd anticipated.

Had she wished for it, though? Perhaps.

She wondered if Hildy had planned to kiss her, or if the kiss was a result of an impulse, a spontaneous urge.

Easily, if she wore the question out, she would be able to convince herself that the kiss meant nothing more than a gesture of sympathy. And that would be easier, wouldn't it? To think of the kiss as an act of comfort.

"Come here," she'd whispered. Pulling Janie into her, she'd pressed her soft, full mouth onto Janie's.

You didn't resist. You kissed her back, all the way.

It was true. She hadn't tried to stop it.

Instead, she'd welcomed her, letting Hildy's tongue caress and explore the sensitive places inside her lips.

The kiss made her forget everything. It left her wanting more.

***

Winter moved into autumn's space, and the kisses continued. Neither had given their relationship a name, but Janie was sure that they were in one.

"Going home?" Janie hoped she sounded casual. She would be humiliated if Hildy knew how hollow she felt when they were apart.

"I thought I might go with you this time," Hildy cast a sideways grin. "See your world for a change."

"I don't know." Horrified at the thought of taking Hildy to her decaying home, Janie faltered.

"Come on," she coaxed. "We'll go incognito."

In truth, they were always in disguise. No one knew.

"What?" She pulled Janie close. "Are you embarrassed by me?"

"No, of course not!" She kissed Hildy square on the mouth, without checking first to see who was looking. "It's just that…my family isn't exactly friendly."

"I know all about your dad." Hildy sighed. "You don't have to be ashamed. Can't we just go to your grandpa's house? Think about it. We'll have the entire weekend alone."

Janie knew that she was acting ridiculous, worrying about the condition of either house. Hildy wouldn't care so long as they had a roof over their heads. She was the most nonmaterialistic person that Janie had ever known. An ironic twist, considering that Hildy came from wealth.

"Why Our Lady of the Lake?" she'd asked during one of their early marathon conversations. "Why not some Ivy League school? Your family can afford it."

"I don't need a pedigree. Our Lady of the Lake is just fine." She'd flashed one of her famous smiles. "Plus, I wouldn't have met you."

Janie lived in a state of euphoric disbelief of Hildy's general existence in her life. Although she didn't dare tell Hildy, she was completely prepared for the spell to break.

"Doesn't it sound divine? Just you and me? Alone, all weekend?" She waggled her eyebrows up and down provocatively, making Janie laugh.

"Oh, all right!" She pretended to be exasperated, but it was all for show. The fantasy of living like a normal couple was always in the back of her mind.

They stopped at a small diner along the way. The other customers paid them no mind. Why would they? To unknowing eyes, they were two college girls, heading away for the weekend, maybe looking for a little fun in the form of boys.

Feeling brave, Janie reached across the table and touched Hildy's hand. Delightful sparks danced up her arm.

Hildy reciprocated, tracing the veins on the back of Janie's hand with the tip of her finger.

Daring not to linger too long, lest someone notice, Janie pulled her hand away and busied it with her fork.

Hildy leaned across the table and whispered the word "chicken."

She smiled and stuffed a bite of actual chicken into her mouth, all the while looking into Hildy's tiger-hued eyes.

A secret conversation happened between them, promises of unconcealed passion away from the watchful gaze of others.

Hildy was the first to stand. She tossed a handful of money onto the table and said, "Let's hurry."

Something in her expression liquefied Janie through to her core.

In the car, Hildy reached over and caressed Janie's knee with her right hand while she guided the steering wheel with her other hand. In a maddeningly slow progression, she moved her hand toward Janie's inner thigh, one inch at a time.

"Which way?" Hildy chuckled softly. "Right or left?"

"What?" Distracted by the caresses, she wasn't paying attention to their surroundings.

"Do we turn right or left at the stop?"

"Oh, sorry—right."

Hildy used both hands to make the turn, then resumed the torture with her long, delicate fingers. By the time they reached Grandpa's house, Janie's panties were soaked.

"Where should I park?"

In a breathy voice, Janie answered, "It doesn't matter."

"Everything all right?"

"I'm just feeling impatient." She laughed softly. The drive had taken forever, and the aching sensation in between her thighs was threatening to push her over the edge of sanity.

All the other encounters had been stolen and instantly gratifying. None had the luxury, or agony, depending on which way she chose to view it, of this tantalizing, slow build.

"Show me inside, already." Hildy whispered, "What are you waiting for?"

Shrunken by the cooler air, the back door of the house opened easily. She hadn't expected the inside to be the same temperature as the outside. The furnace hadn't been lit since Mama's death.

"It's so cold," she apologized.

"Shush." Hildy winked. "It'll make everything more stimulating."

She followed Hildy through the old house, trying to see it through her eyes as if it were for the first time.

They passed through the clean, outdated kitchen into a cozy parlor stuffed with mismatched chairs and various books stacked within arm's reach of every sitting position.

Above the small fireplace hung an old mirror, encased in a wooden frame with the gilding softly worn off the edges. On the mantel sat a collection of dusty figurines, none of them appearing to belong to the others in any particular sort of way.

Beyond the fireplace, a staircase led them to the former attic, turned into the second story. Faded portraits, some marked with water stains, others encased in fancy frames and bubble glass, lined the ascent up the stairway to the small landing.

Worn and smoothed from the brushing of hands over many years, the rail was marble-like beneath her palm. Treads creaked lightly under their eager steps.

"Not that one." She stopped Hildy from opening the door to the room her mother had last stayed in. It felt wrong, somehow.

With everything in her, she wanted to hide the sudden dampening of her desire. Which would have been better? The room that her deceased mother had occupied, or the bed that her darling, dead grandpa had slept in over the past forty years? It was a whopper of a dilemma and one that she decided not to burden her lover with. *Not exactly fantastic foreplay.*

The door to Grandpa's room groaned as it had always been prone to do in the winter, what with the shifting of the house and such. The modest room was just as he'd left it. Not keen on décor and excess personal things, Grandpa's was the neatest room in the old home.

Hildy seemed to sense her need to slow down and stopped to notice her surroundings.

Running her fingertips slowly across the length of the mirrored bureau, she said, "It's peaceful."

Janie nodded, caught off guard by the lump in her throat.

"Come here," Hildy beckoned with her finger.

She allowed Hildy to embrace her.

"Hey, relax." She scratched Janie's back lightly. "I won't bite."

"Maybe I'm not cut out for this." *Goddammit, I sound like a baby!*

Hildy laughed and backed away. "Cut out for what?"

"Whatever this is." Janie made an invisible line back and forth between the two of them. "I don't know how to do this."

She was aware that her words had a hysterical edge to them. The monitor in her head warned her to stop before she revealed too much. No one had gotten this close before.

"You're doing just fine." Hildy held her arms out and let them drop to her side. "Honestly."

She nodded and swiped away the tears that had begun to fall. Humiliated, betrayed, by her brokenness, Janie turned away.

"Aw, come on, Janie," Hildy whispered. "It's not that bad."

"You don't belong here." Janie sobbed into her hands. "You're gold, and caramel, and electricity, and…and everything beautiful. This place—it's dead. Just dust and echoes."

Soft, warm hands cupped her trembling shoulders. "This place has you." Hildy smiled and dipped her head low to connect with Janie's eyes.

"I shouldn't have brought you here. We should go."

A thin smile crossed Hildy's face. "If that's what you want, but I think you're overreacting."

Sick to her stomach, all she could think about was Grandpa and Mama. It had been wrong to bring her here. She'd shown her too much already.

At the side of the car, Janie stood, awkward and tense. "Can you open the trunk? I want my bag."

"Aren't you coming? How're you getting back to school?" Wild-eyed, Hildy asked, "What in the hell did I do wrong?"

"Nothing. It's not you." She squinted her eyes to combat the sting of tears. "I don't think I'm ready for this. Can you please open the trunk?"

Hildy unlocked the trunk and jumped into the driver's seat. She slammed her door shut.

Through the open window, she said, "You're obviously not ready for anything. I don't know what you had in your mind, but I thought we had something special."

Janie grabbed her bag and stepped away from the car. Everything she wanted to say would've come out wrong, so she stood and waited for Hildy to leave.

Hildy shook her head in disbelief. She backed the car up and stopped. "You don't know what you're missing out on. We could've been great."

Janie watched the road until the plume of dust following the little car disappeared.

Numb to the cold, she sat down on the weather-worn metal glider that had rested in the same place in the yard for as long as she could remember. When she and Randy were young, the glider served as a makeshift car, or sometimes a church pew, for their play-pretend.

The glider squeaked and squealed under her weight as she rocked back and forth.

It had been a stupid idea to bring her here. It was probably a stupid idea to get involved in the first place. Mismatched, it would've never worked. Even if they'd managed to get past their social differences, the world would never accept them. She would've just been another of Hildy's eccentric flings.

Chicken shit—that's not why you made her go, and you know it.

It was true. She wouldn't be enough. Hildy would grow tired of her.

It was more than that, though. Wasn't it? In her Papa's little room, she was afraid Hildy would see her for what she was. A fraud—an empty soul. It would've been a matter of time before the real Janie revealed herself. Then, Hildy would've gone away, just like everyone else she'd ever cared about.

It would be more than she could bear.

CHAPTER 54

GOING STEADY

He'd spent most of the fifth hour staring at her legs, occasionally glimpsing at her face. She was a cheerleader, which gave her extra points in his opinion. When she smiled, even the teacher looked smitten. Blonde, petite, and aloof, Susan was a challenge to the rest of the pack.

Typically, all he had to do to get a girl's attention was to make a wisecrack and give her a look. Then, he'd let her make the next move. Girls were easy.

Susan, on the other hand, was anything but easy. Randy was starting to feel like a sucker. The only person that seemed to take notice of his efforts was the teacher. More than once, he'd shot a glare of disapproval in Randy's direction.

He'd toyed with the idea of cornering her after the game to show her what she was missing. The crowd that always seemed to surround her made this tactic impossible, so he'd let the thought go.

What're you wasting your time on her for? There's other fish in the sea. The rational voice argued with the jilted one. *Find a girl who'll be grateful.*

So, he lowered his sights.

She wasn't as cute as the cheerleader, but she'd laughed at all his jokes. When he gave her that look, her cheeks turned a pretty shade of pink. He began to feel more like himself.

"Are you going to the game tomorrow?" Her shy, brown eyes radiated hope.

"Maybe," he shrugged. "You?"

She nodded and smiled. "Maybe I'll see you there."

"Sure." It was easy to play it cool with her. She didn't give him the same kind of fluttery feeling in his stomach as Susan did. Just the same, she was into him. And, that was what really mattered.

The next night, she found him on the bleachers. "Is this spot taken?"

He liked that she didn't assume he'd saved it for her. It was proof that she wasn't too sure of herself.

"No," he smiled and winked. "Have a seat."

Although he couldn't have cared less about the game, he pretended to be interested. He didn't want her to think that he was only there to see her.

Sandra sat next to him, just the right distance away—not too close, not too far.

She untied the scarf wrapped around her hair and folded it neatly in her lap. He noticed her hair was styled differently than her usual ponytail. A faint scent of her hairspray tickled his nose.

He could feel her eyes on him through most of the game. Stifling a smile, he trained his gaze on the field.

They were getting pulverized by the other team, and by the third quarter, he'd had enough. He could barely stomach watching a winning game. A losing game felt like pure torture.

"This is bullshit," he yelled over the ruckus of the crowd. "Wanna get out of here?"

Happiness washed over her face. "Of course!"

He opened the door of his dad's truck and helped her climb into it.

The delicate structure of her hand excited him. Something about her reminded him of a helpless baby bird. He could protect her, or he could just as easily break her.

"Are you hungry?"

She smoothed the hem of her skirt with trembling hands. "Not really, but if you are, we can go eat."

"No, I'm not either." He was relieved since he didn't have enough money to buy a soda, never mind dinner for two.

"We could go watch for shooting stars." She dared to look at him. Her full lips twisted into a nervous smile. "If that seems boring, we can do something else."

It was perfect. He'd been racking his brain to figure out a way to lull her out to the windbreak by the house. Not wanting to appear too eager, he waited a few seconds before responding. "Sure. Why not?"

She was quiet during the drive, but this wasn't disappointing. Randy knew that she liked him, and he liked the absence of forced conversation.

The dirt road along the windbreak was empty. It was private property, but that didn't stop other kids from using it to make out.

He doubted that his dad was still awake, but he turned the headlights off, just in case. Nothing would ruin his plans faster than his drunken father with a shotgun.

The worn-out truck rumbled and squeaked drudgingly over the ruts of the dirt path. By the time they'd passed the perimeter of the yard, his eyes had adjusted to the moonlight.

"We'll need something to sit on. I think Dad keeps an old blanket in here for emergencies." He put the parking brake on. "Let me check behind the seat."

She nodded and slid out through the driver's side.

For show, he dug around behind his side of the seat first. "Hmm, maybe it's on the other side."

"I don't mind sitting on the grass."

"No way. Too many stickers. You'll never get them out of your clothes."

He opened the passenger door and reached behind the seat. Pulling the blanket from the spot he'd placed it earlier in the day, he said, "Found it!"

She helped him spread the blanket out in a patch just beyond the little road. "It's nice that the sky is clear."

"That's right. Good for stargazing."

He slipped his shoes off before stepping onto the old quilt. She did the same.

Every so often, he peeked in her direction to see if she was looking at him.

Still as a statue, she remained in the same pose. Resting on her arms, she leaned back, head tilted up to the stars.

After a time, he lay down. "It's easier to see the stars this way. Less strain on the neck."

She didn't lay down immediately, but once she did, he knew it was only a matter of time.

***

The weeks passed by rather quickly after their first time. Randy had grown accustomed to having her by his side in the hallways of the school.

He didn't mind having her around. She was easy to be near. Expecting little from him, other than his presence, she wasn't like the other girls. If she'd had her way, she would be with him all the time.

They'd already settled into a routine. Friday night was spent sitting in front of the television with her parents. Saturday night was for cruising the main strip of Boerne. And Sunday was church with her mother.

Sandra's daddy never went to church, likely because he was still sozzled from the night before.

Although her daddy had a love of the drink in common with Randy's own father, that was where the similarity ended.

Wyatt Carter was a mean drunk who couldn't hold a job down longer than several months at a time. In contrast, Sandra's father worked his family's sheep farm and came home every evening by six o'clock.

Her mother was a soft-spoken, graying, little bit of a woman. With a determined stoicism, she doted on her family. It was clear they were her world.

At first, Randy had thought her to have a sour disposition. Years of work and worry had left their mark on her once pretty face. She didn't smile much, save for Sunday morning after-church-service greetings.

Over time, he changed his mind about her. She simply cared so much about her family, that her expression was one of permanent burden.

What would his life have been, had his parents loved him as much as Sandra's parents loved her? A small, envious pang snaked up from his belly whenever he asked himself this question.

He was left with conflicting feelings. The security of guaranteed tail was welcome, but the boredom was a growing mold, creeping into all his edges.

CHAPTER 55

WHIPPED

Randy and Sandra were a full-fledged item now. Since he'd gotten a steady girl, everyone—even the teachers—seemed to treat him with a little more respect. He liked this part of things.

What he hadn't been prepared for was the way his heart felt pinched when Sandra was upset with him. It was disgusting. His happiness was dependent on her notice of him.

He tried to recall when the dynamic had shifted. He'd lost control, and it wasn't good for him.

If Dad were to find out about Randy's feelings, he would call him pussy-whipped.

Months before, in the very beginning, it had been so easy to make her smile. The smallest of gestures, opening her door, helping her with her coat, bringing her a wildflower—these little things had caused her to look at him as if he'd hung the moon.

And now, for reasons unknown to him, Sandra was a cold bitch.

"What're you thinking about?"

Her blank expression stoked the unsettled quiver that lived, dormant, in the pit of his belly.

"Nothing."

Her parents weren't home, and the night was supposed to play out differently. By his calculations, they should've already been upstairs, stripped naked, and going at it.

She was riled up about something. Anger, he could deal with. Anger had been served to him for breakfast, lunch, and dinner nearly every day of his life.

Only, Sandra didn't come right out and say that she was mad. The lack of emotion, her empty eyes, this was a different animal. It felt deceptive.

The script wasn't his, and he was off-balance. Pissed off at himself for begging like a dog for attention, he stood up and said, "I'm going home."

He glanced to see her reaction.

Sandra's expression didn't change. It was as if he hadn't spoken at all.

"What a waste of time," he said. "I'm out of here."

"Suit yourself." She continued to stare at the television.

His vision narrowed, and an annoying buzz burned in his ears. *Fucking, ungrateful bitch. She's forgotten that she's lucky to be with me.*

Aware of the vibration in his hand as he yanked his jacket off the branch of the coat tree, he glared at her.

Still fixated on the television, her jaw jutted out defiantly.

With two long steps, he moved directly behind her. Squatting down, so his head was level with hers, he whispered in her ear, "Better get your shit together."

He meant to frighten her.

Instead, she smiled.

No, he thought, *smile* is the wrong word. It was a smirk.

He twisted his hand into the back of her hair. He wasn't aware of the movement until he was already in the middle of it.

She let out a gasping squeal when he tugged harder.

Cruel satisfaction drenched his brain. He felt more like himself and less like a dog begging for scraps at the dinner table.

"As I was saying," he paused, distracted by the exquisite feel of her scalp stretched by the hair pulled tight in his hand. "As I was saying, you'd better get your shit together."

She nodded as much as his hand would allow.

Releasing her twisted hair, he stood up and put on his jacket.

Muffled sobs told him everything that he needed to know. He hadn't lost control of her.

***

Hot under the collar over Sandra's mood, he paid no mind to the grinding gears in the old truck as he barreled down the dirt road. It wasn't until he reached the farm that he noticed the burning smell of the clutch. If his old man were to catch on, he'd have his ass.

Randy kicked his shoes off just outside the back door and padded softly through the kitchen. Avoiding the loose boards, he managed to make it to the top of the stairs before Dad bellowed from his recliner.

He froze, hoping that would be the last of it.

"Randy!" More urgent than the first call, Dad wasn't giving up.

"Coming!" He yelled back a little louder than necessary.

He took his time down the stairs, making each step purposely forceful.

This blatant act of defiance would've earned him a whipping when he was a small child. A fairly large portion of him hoped his old man might think it fitting to pull his leather belt off and lay into him.

The very thought of punching Dad, square in the face, gave rise to the kind of anger that excited him.

In his usual spot, Dad was melted onto the worn-out recliner, courtesy of Jack Daniels or whatever liquor was on sale that day. Yellow light from the smoke-stained lampshade flooded over him, making a spotlight of sorts in the otherwise darkened room.

He'd been summoned to this scene at least a thousand times since Mama left. Bristles of unshaved hair stood up on the back of Randy's neck.

"Yeah, what is it?"

"You talk with rep—respect when you're talkin' to me, boy." Eyes barely open, Dad attempted to bring him in line.

Randy crossed his arms, fighting the urge to walk away. He could hardly stand to look at Dad.

"Wanna try that again, son?"

"Sure," he said through gritted teeth. "What can I do for you, sir?"

Randy emphasized the word "sir" with a small bow. He was asking for it, but he didn't give two shits.

Dad struggled to push himself into an upright position. It was comical. Too drunk to sit upright, too shit-faced to complete a sentence without fucking up at least one word, Dad was pitiful. It was true, the gossip going around town—Wyatt Carter was a waste of flesh.

It had been two full months since Dad had even tried to pretend that he was looking for work. He contributed nothing. The only food in the house came from Dad's latest piece of ass, desperately trying to wiggle her way in as the woman of the house. What kind of trash viewed his dad as a prize catch?

Rage coursed through his veins. Dad had ruined everything, and everyone, that was good in Randy's life. He clenched his fists, fighting the urge to smash his fist into the old man's slack jaw.

"Got a phone call from your little girl's parents. You're not playing it too safe, boy." Dad frowned.

It would've been better to keep his mouth shut, but he couldn't stop himself. "What are you talking about?" He knew full well what was coming next.

"Beating on a girl is unacceptable."

The arteries in Randy's neck pulsed with each thump of his heart. Cotton-mouthed, he spat out the words, the things he knew better than to say. "That's hilarious, coming from you. You gave it good to Mama at least once a month, you drunk fuck!"

He was stunned by Dad's sudden burst of agility. The force of Dad's fist connecting with his jaw knocked him flat onto his ass. Replaced by burning rage, gone was his childhood reaction—to cower in fear.

Shoving himself backward and upright in one fluid motion, Randy found his feet. His chest threatened to burst with gasping breaths. His fists were wrecking balls. Muffled by his own raging pulse, the only sound he heard was the popping of his knuckles against Dad's face and chest.

He didn't stop until Dad lay on the floor.

Randy knelt beside his unconscious body and examined his bleeding face. Dad was almost unrecognizable.

The silence was deafening.

He frantically shook Dad's shoulder. "Dad! Wake up!"

His body wiggled like one of those fancy gelatin desserts that Betty used to create for them.

"Dad!" He shrieked, "Wake up!"

He stood up and kicked his dad on the side. "Get up, you piece of shit!"

Fury erupted from every molecule of his existence. He kicked his father's motionless body until his legs gave out. He kicked for Mama. He kicked for Janie. He kicked for Rosie. Lastly, he kicked for himself and all the years he lived in terror.

Randy crouched in the corner of the room and watched for movement. He wasn't sure which frightened him more; the thought that Dad might wake, or the idea that he might never.

Tears ran down his face. He wiped his nose with the back of his hand. The patterns created with his snot and Dad's blood reminded him of finger painting in Mrs. Howard's second-grade class.

***

He couldn't say how long he stayed in that corner, looking around at the room. Every place had a bad memory attached to it. The velvet settee had the image of Mama, with her head in her hands, sobbing like there was no tomorrow. The corner held the thought of Janie, standing still with fresh welts across her bare legs. An apparition of Rosie, bare-legged and chewing on the end of a blonde pigtail, sat on the floor, lost in the evening show.

After a time, he crawled to the small table that held the telephone and dialed the number to Papa's house. Janie would know what to do.

Randy moved back to the safety of the corner and waited for a change.

He hadn't expected her to come. But there she was, kneeling in front of him. He'd never seen such a welcome sight.

"Randy?" Her voice was weak, frightened.

At first, he thought her to be another vision.

Her hand, strong and warm, touched the crown of his head. "What in God's name happened?"

CHAPTER 56

CLEAN UP

Like tendrils of ivy, invading the mortar of an old building, the ringing worked its way into her dream.

She was back in the dorm, reading a book written in a language that she didn't recognize.

The report was due soon. Panic welled up into her throat. She'd already stayed longer than she should have.

It was impossible to concentrate with the shrill sound of the phone ringing off in the distance.

"Can someone please answer that?" She shouted to an empty room.

The thin jangle of the phone continued.

Cold air rushed through her hair in the empty, darkened hallway. She fumbled for the light switch, but it wasn't where it should be.

Janie flattened her palm and slid her hand up and down the drywall until the switch appeared. Overhead, bulbs slowly warmed to a dingy glow.

At the end of the hall, the phone waited for her, still ringing. With each step, the phone moved farther away from her.

She tossed and turned into a state of uneasy wakefulness. Her eyes adjusted to her unlit bedroom. Concentrating on her breathing, she forced her heart to slow down.

The phone continued to ring. Beneath her bare feet, the time-worn floorboards felt cold.

"Hello?"

"Janie, you have to come now."

Papa's old truck deserved a proper warm-up, but the fear in Randy's voice had told her there wasn't time.

Thin moonlight projected spidery shadows of winter's leafless trees onto the dirt road between Papa's house and the farm. An involuntary shiver traveled up her spine into her tightened shoulders and neck. The possibilities of what she might find terrified her.

***

The house was quiet. As she'd learned to do when she was a child, Janie paced her movements soft and slow.

The only light came from the living room. Dad's chair was shoved away from the accompanying end table, which held a nearly empty bottle of whiskey and a glass of melting ice cubes.

Motionless, Dad lay, arms flailed out, on his back. A trickle of dried blood ran from his nose down to his matted hair.

The putrid odor of liquor, smoke, and feces hit her nose before she got to him. She knelt and gingerly examined his still body.

He was dead. She could be sure of it because she'd done all the things that she knew to do. It was impossible to find a pulse on his already stiffening body.

At this moment that she'd wished for, more times than she could count, Janie didn't feel what she'd imagined. She pushed away at an unwelcome memory, an image of Daddy stroking her hair, telling her how much he loved her.

In the corner, Randy cowered in an upright fetal position. Splotchy patterns of blood covered his face. His hands, coated with dried blood, gripped tightly around his knees.

"Randy," she whispered.

He tilted his head up but looked right through her.

She wiped away the cold sweat from her brow. "What in God's name happened?"

"He hit me."

She didn't need to hear any more to know the rest. The old man had finally met his match. She listened as her brother babbled a confession.

Janie knew what had to be done.

"Please, no!" Randy begged like a child. "Please don't! They're gonna lock me up!"

"Don't say anything! You'll make everything worse for yourself." She pointed a finger at her chest. "You let me do the talking!"

The phone call, the interview with the police, the carting away of Dad's body, all of this was blurry.

"Don't leave, okay?" Randy begged, "I can't be in this place alone tonight."

"I won't." No matter how she'd despised him when growing up, he was still her brother. She'd been there, had witnessed the torment. Something like this was bound to happen.

The soft, gray light of the early morning had just begun to seep in through the cracks as she finished cleaning the mess in the living room.

She'd just sat down at the kitchen table when Randy came downstairs, hair still wet from a shower.

"I made coffee." She gestured for him to sit.

Randy slid the chair out and sat. His expression blank, his slow, measured movements matched that of someone with arthritis. His coffee remained untouched.

She studied his face and tried to remember what it had looked like before when he was a little boy. When was the last time she saw him smile?

"Do you remember playing in the sprinkler?"

Wary, he met her gaze. "Not really."

She took a cigarette out of his pack and put it in her mouth. "Want one?"

He nodded. "I didn't know you still smoke."

"I don't." She lit a cigarette and smiled at the irony of her statement. "This one doesn't count."

Janie watched the match flare as he lit one. The moment of combustion had always fascinated her. A chemical reaction caused by simple friction. It was nothing more and nothing less. There wasn't much difference between the igniting of the match and the igniting of human rage.

"Are they going to arrest me?"

She shook her head. "I don't think so."

He seemed to be reassured by this and took another drag off his cigarette.

"He attacked you. It was self-defense." She reminded him of her statement to the police.

"It's a good sign," she added, "that you're sitting here instead of jail."

"How can you be so sure?"

"I'm not." She crushed the cigarette out in the little ceramic ashtray. She tried to remember watching Mama do the same.

It had been effortless, at first. Every part of the house had an image of Mama attached. Stirring dinner in front of the stove with her apron on, reading a magazine in the sunny spot by the window, washing laundry in the old washer on the sunporch—all of these had been easily conjured.

She'd faithfully practiced seeing Mama, much in the same way a good Catholic prays the rosary.

Moving in with Papa had taken away the compulsive need to look for her mother in every nook and cranny. Without Janie's presence, Mama's ghost had faded away.

In the present, it was rare to see anything other than a wisp. And sometimes, when she could recall a moment from childhood, she couldn't honestly say whether it had been Betty or Mama.

"Do you ever think about Rosie?" She still couldn't speak her name without tearing up.

"Why are you bringing her up now?" His lips tightened into a hard line. He stood up with a start, knocking his chair off-balance.

She flinched. "What are you mad about?"

"I'm not!" He growled, "Just don't wanna talk about the past. There's no damn reason to go over it again."

"Fair enough," she conceded. "I didn't want to relive it, either." Damning herself for the lump in her throat, she said, "I miss her. That's all."

Not a day went by that she didn't think about Rosie, didn't try to picture her all grown up.

He shoved the empty chair up to the table. "We can't bring her back by talking about her, can we? I mean, what's the point?"

What was the expression on his face? Fear? Anger? Guilt? She had never been good at reading him.

"I'm going to bed."

"Yes," she agreed. "You need to rest."

She sat a while longer, imagining what her life might look like—had she been born into a different family. As she tallied up the tragedies, the hard truth struck her; she and Randy had no one left.

CHAPTER 57

THE BREAKUP

Fear scratched at the pit of his stomach. What if Janie was wrong? What if they put him in jail? He wanted to lock this up in the same place he'd put Rosie, but the fight with Dad replayed over and over.

Downstairs, Janie messed around for a while. He closed his eyes, pretending to sleep when he heard her footsteps in the hallway by his bedroom.

Eventually, the only sound in the house was that of the bedroom clock, ticking in the reliable fashion that had comforted him as a small child.

Tuning his ears to the steady rhythm, he timed his breathing to one complete breath every eight seconds. It helped to smother the babble in his head. In—one, two, three, four, and out—five, six, seven, eight. He'd learned to do this when he was smaller. Eventually, he would fall asleep.

It wasn't working. The room was too bright. Wide awake, his thoughts turned back to Dad and then, eventually, to Sandra.

Sandra. He needed to see her.

Papa's truck wasn't in the driveway. He was relieved Janie had gone.

He realized halfway down the stairs that there was no longer a need to tiptoe. Dad wasn't home, sleeping off his booze.

He listened to the dial tone for a while before getting the courage to call her.

The phone rang for some time, and he was just about to hang up when her mother answered.

"May I speak with Sandra, please?" He hadn't expected to feel so nervous.

A silence followed. Randy waited for her, not yet sure if he would apologize.

Muffled sounds came through the receiver, and he pictured her mother cupping the mouthpiece, telling Sandra what to say to him.

Instead, her father's gruff voice came on the line. "Is this Randy?"

"Yes, sir," he croaked. "May I speak with your daughter, please?"

"Absolutely not! You will never speak to her again!"

Caught off guard, Randy said nothing.

"Do you hear me, boy?" her daddy shouted. "Am I making myself clear? If you ever come near my girl again, I'll end you with my bare hands!"

***

Suffocated by the looks of pity, the whispers in the school halls, and the condolences from his teachers, he got through the following days by sheer determination to see Sandra.

He waited near her locker after the first hour. She was the only reason he'd bothered to show up.

"Hey, have you seen Sandra?" He cornered her best friend, a mousy little thing.

Peering over the glasses perched at the edge of her long, thin nose, her eyes darted back and forth as she seemed to be gauging which way best to escape. Finally, she sighed and said, "No, I haven't heard from her."

She skirted around him and began to walk faster.

"Can you give her a message?" A full foot taller, he had to jog to keep up with her.

She spun around, gripping her books so tightly that her knuckles had whitened. "No, I can't. Her parents don't want you to have anything to do with her," she sighed. "Honestly, Sandra doesn't want to hear from you, either."

"That's bullshit! You're lying."

The normal chatter of the other students passing died down to complete silence. Embarrassed, he was aware of their stares.

Loud enough that everyone could hear, her friend said, "You're bad news, Randy. She told me what happened. I wouldn't blame her if she never wanted to see you again."

"You can go to hell, you little mouse!"

"Is there a problem?" The math teacher poked her gray head out of the nearby classroom.

"No, no problem." What else was he supposed to say? *Yes, ma'am, this entire school is full of idiots, and this little rodent is the ringleader.*

He threw his books onto the floor at her friend's feet. It gave him a mean kind of gratification, to see the shock in her face, to hear the accumulation of gasps from the other students.

"The show's over, everyone! Go back to your little lives."

Cutting through a dodgeball game and knocking one of the players down in the process, he sprinted through the gymnasium toward the exit door.

With both hands, he shoved the door open to the sunlit parking lot. He didn't break speed until he'd reached the truck.

Resting his hands on the steering wheel, he sat for a moment, staving off the urge to cry. Now, he understood what Dad had meant; why he'd warned Randy not to let a girl into his heart. It was the worst possible thing—to love a girl too much.

She'd gotten under his skin. This dreadful feeling of losing, of wanting, was more than he was willing to pay. Sandra had made a fool of him, and even worse, the whole damned town knew about it.

He turned the key into the ignition, pumping the gas pedal until the old truck came to life. Snorting and coughing, the beast complained a bit, then settled into a steady rumble.

Sandra's house wasn't far from the high school. She wasn't going to break up with him—not without telling him to his face.

Neither of her parents' cars was in the driveway. Right about now, her daddy would be knee-deep in sheep shit. It was the normal time that her mother might be grocery shopping. Out of respect, he parked on the street.

When he rang the bell, his sweaty hand trembled. Restraining himself from ringing a second time, he waited and imagined Sandra, frightened, hiding from him.

Soft movements sounded from the inside. This gave him hope that she might open the door.

"Sandra," he called to her through the closed door. "It's me. I just wanna talk with you."

"Go away." Small and quiet through the thickness of the door, Sandra's voice was strained.

"I won't stay. I promise. Can't we talk about this like reasonable people? I don't want it to end like this."

"Mother's coming back soon. You can't be here."

The frantic edge that colored her words told him everything he needed to know. It wasn't Sandra keeping him away; it was her parents.

He pondered this new information for a bit before saying to her, "My dad is dead. I can't talk about it to anyone else."

She fumbled with the lock and opened the door to expose a small sliver of the inside.

His eyes adjusted to the interior light, and he could see that she'd been crying.

"I heard. I'm sorry." Sandra blotted her tears with the sleeve of her sweater. "They're saying you…that you…did it. Is that true?"

"Please, don't make me stand out here," he pleaded.

"I don't know." She hesitated. "I shouldn't."

He reached toward her, his only intention to touch her face.

Sandra flinched and shrank away from his caress. "Don't," she whispered.

Randy fought the impulse to yank her through the door. "What's with the act? Your mother's been filling your head full of shit, hasn't she?"

"You scare me!"

He pushed the door open against her resistance and mocked, "Aw, do I frighten you? I'm not scary!"

The danger point had been reached. His ears flushed hot with anger.

She backed away and put her hands up in defense. "Get away from me!"

Did she actually believe he was going to harm her? This notion infuriated him.

"Come here!" He grabbed her shoulder with his left hand and pressed her into his chest to quiet her struggle.

"You're hurting me!"

"Calm down!" He squeezed tighter, wanting to crush her into him. "You hear me?"

Shaking, she nodded.

"Are you done?" He took a deep breath and started again. "Are you finished with the act?"

"Yes," came her quiet response.

"I'm not going to hurt you." He released her from his squeeze and took a step backward. "We'd be fine if your parents hadn't gotten in the middle of our business."

He'd expected that her expression would be one of remorse. He'd even hoped she would apologize for her overreaction.

"You need to leave," she shouted.

The eruption startled him. Confused, he tried to make sense of the outburst.

"Go on! Get out!" An angry flush stained her cheeks.

He imagined slapping her across the face, just to see if he could deepen the red.

Dad's voice filled his head. *The bitch ain't worth your time, son. Stop being such a faggot.*

"No problem. I'm done with you," he hissed with a grin. "Don't come crying to me when you realize how much you fucked up."

All the way home, he rehearsed the devastating things he would say to her when she came begging for him to change his mind. The thought of watching her face twist up into an ugly cry made him feel a whole lot better.

CHAPTER 58

CLASS CLOWN

Stuck halfway between the dream and the light of the day, Randy awoke in the same manner as he did most mornings. Drenched with sweat, exhausted by the restless sleep, he groaned and sat upright to force the start of his day.

There was no escaping him. No longer contained in a physical body, Dad rattled on incessantly, scolding, berating, and giving his opinion about Randy's actions. Even his private thoughts weren't safe from Dad's scrutiny.

He rubbed the sleep from his eyes and chuckled. He had a drunken ghost living in his head—a poetic punishment for beating one's father to death.

Standing up into a stretch, he roared out a yawn and hoped he had something clean, or at least passable, to wear to school. So far, no one had seemed to question the wisdom of letting him live alone. He wasn't going to raise suspicions by skipping school.

In the days following Dad's death, Janie had reassured the principal of Boerne High that she was more than capable of managing him. She continued to surprise him with her protective goodwill.

He supposed that she was just doing what came to her naturally—bossing him around. It didn't annoy him as much as it had before. And besides, there was no one else. He'd be free of her henpecking soon enough. In the meantime, he'd decided to make the best of it.

At least there was food in the house again. Once a week, Janie dropped off a bag or two of groceries.

He never thought to ask how she paid for them. He didn't care, so long as the refrigerator had more than a bowl of eggs. Eggs were all Dad ate in the end. No shopping required. He hadn't given two shits about Randy's needs.

Janie might be a bitch, but at least she didn't come empty-handed. Although it went against his grain to play nice with Janie, he understood the currency required to get the things that he needed. Small luxuries— gas money, food, electricity, and such—might stop if he forgot to be a loving brother. So, he played along.

In less than two years, he'd be done with school, Janie, and all the bullshit on the farm. After that, he was going to get as far away from this place as possible.

Rifling through a small mountain of clothing piled in the chair, he began the morning routine of smelling the garments to determine his best options. Deciding on a pair of Levi jeans with questionable scent, and a shirt that didn't smell of anything at all, Randy dressed for the day.

There was no time for a shower, so he splashed a copious amount of Old Spice on his neck and face. For good measure, he rubbed a bit into his hair. It would do for the day, but a shower was in order, soon.

He grabbed a pack of smokes off the table and lit one while shoving the screen door open with his foot. Making it all the way to the truck before he remembered the chickens, he sighed and cursed, "Damned birds!"

Tempted to skip them for the second day in a row, he thought better and jogged to the coop to let them out.

The flock clucked and swarmed around him, waiting for their breakfast. No doubt, they were hungry. He scooped a pail of feed and scattered it about. The famished hens scurried to peck at the feed, allowing him a clear path out.

"Cold bitch," he muttered at the old truck as he held the ignition and pumped the gas pedal. She was always slow to start, but worse so in the wintertime.

After a bit of cranking and pumping, the engine roared to life. He tapped a series of shorter thrusts on the gas pedal to wake her up fully. Finally satisfied that she'd make it down the drive without choking, Randy set out for school.

Morning sunshine sparkled on frosty branches and blades of grass. Ghosts on the water, wisps of fog floated just above ponds and streams, giving an otherworldly feel to the land.

The parking lot was full of cars and empty of students. He'd missed the first bell. Jogging through the lawn, he took the chance that the gymnasium door wouldn't be locked. Mr. Johnson, the decrepit old janitor, more often than not, forgot to lock doors or to unlock doors. There had been a solid week last fall that the students arrived each morning to a locked front entrance.

Slowing to a fast walk once inside, he took the shortest route to the office for a pass.

"Good morning, Randy." The fresh-faced secretary was a vast improvement over the grouchy old hag that had reluctantly retired last year. She smiled at Randy and slid a pass across the counter.

He liked that she didn't give him any hassle. It didn't hurt that she was easy on the eye, either.

Built like a brick shithouse, son. She'd be a fun roll in the hay. Ignoring Dad's disembodied voice, he grinned and wished her a good day.

The first period was well under way. Slipping into class as quietly as possible, he took a seat in the back. Mr. Klause flashed a disapproving glance for the interruption but continued with his lecture.

Randy suppressed a sigh and leaned back into his seat, resting his forearm on the desk. Already bored, he struggled to keep his eyes open.

"Mr. Carter," the teacher's voice startled him out of the sleep he'd fallen into.

Snickering and tittering broke out in the class as he snapped his head back into an upright position.

"Am I interrupting your sleep?"

Randy grinned, "Actually, yes, you are." As soon as the words rolled out of his mouth, he knew he was going to pay for them.

"Quiet!" Mr. Klause ordered the class to stop laughing.

"Out in the hall, now!"

"Yes, sir!" Randy stood into a salute, inciting another round of laughter.

He followed Mr. Klause into the hallway, quite enjoying the looks of admiration from his classmates.

"Mr. Carter, I don't know what you think you are up to, but that behavior is unacceptable. Am I clear?"

"Yes, sir. I apologize." It was a struggle to keep his face straight.

Mr. Klause locked his eyes into a standoff with Randy's.

What the hell is he doing? You don't have to tolerate this bullshit.

A frustrated sigh escaped his lips. Dad had an opinion on everything.

Puffed up, red in the face, Mr. Klause squinted his eyes as a final threat and ordered him back to his seat.

Pussy! Are you just gonna let him talk to you like that? A real man doesn't take orders from anyone, son!

It was a struggle to maintain his composure. He was getting it from both ends. He imagined feeling a connection between his fist and Mr. Klause's face, but he'd rather deck his dad, square in the mouth.

They're not laughing with you, son; they're laughing at you. Don't go getting all high and mighty on yourself.

CHAPTER 59

FREE PASS

The pretty secretary paid him no mind while he waited. He would feel less agitated if she would smile at him in the way that she had earlier in the morning.

Tight-lipped, head tilted down so far that she had a double chin, her fingers clicked a furious beat on the typewriter.

Jesus Christ, what is she working on—a damned novel? Irritated by the sound, angry that he was captive until the principal decided it was convenient to see him, Randy struggled to sit still.

Opening his sore fist into a wide stretch, he winced and wondered if it was broken. It had been an impulse, one that he'd been unable to control.

"Randall Carter?" The principal stuck his head out of his office to summon him.

"Have a seat, please."

Randy sat in the seat closest to the window and waited.

"It's my understanding that you punched a desk. Care to explain?" Staring at Randy, he leaned into the back of his heavy leather chair and tapped on the arm.

Tendrils of darkness rose from the base of Randy's neck and threatened to swaddle his entire head. "Mr. Klause is a liar. My hand slipped when I sat down."

It was plausible. He could've whacked his hand on the desk when he returned from the ass-chewing in the hallway. Rubbing his sore knuckles with his left hand, he watched the principal's reaction. Was he buying it?

The principal pursed his lips and remained silent for a long second or two. Resting his elbows on his desk, he picked up a folder and cradled it loosely with both hands.

"Mr. Carter, this isn't your first outburst." Rearranging his face into a half-assed expression of sympathy, he carried on with the rest of his lecture—the part where he would give Randy an out.

He hoped his amusement wasn't apparent. They, the powers that be, always made an effort to understand his suffering. It was tedious, their do-gooder sympathy. Did they get off on feeling better than him?

"I know," the principal's voice took on a soft, caring tone, "that your life has been difficult...with your mother's...passing."

He cleared his throat and continued. "It's my understanding that your father had some...trouble with the bottle and . . ."

Randy smiled at the principal's discomfort but kept his mouth shut.

He didn't have to say anything. He never had to say anything at all. They always managed to talk themselves out of their original line of action.

This is a learning moment, son. This dumbass doesn't know the first thing about your life, but don't let that stop him. Folks see what they want to see.

"And if you need to talk, my door's open. You can't go around beating up desks. You're a smart young man. Use your head instead of your fists. You don't want to end up like your old man."

The principal paused, seemingly expecting a response.

Randy nodded. "Thank you, sir." He stood up to offer his hand for a shake. Grownups ate up that shit like candy.

Taking his hand, the principal reciprocated with a firm grip. "Anytime, son—anytime."

End up like your old man? Dad ranted on. *Don't listen to that malarkey, son! The only thing wrong with your old man was a lack of opportunity. No one in this fucking town ever got me. I could've been someone if your mama hadn't opened her legs. Fucking viper, that woman was.*

He was getting better at tuning out Dad's constant jabbering, but at times, it was downright entertaining.

For the remainder of the day, Randy ignored the intrusive stares and hushed whispers. He couldn't wait until the last day in this hell hole they called school.

More than a few times, he'd given serious consideration to dropping out. He could always work the oil rigs, but a little voice in his head—not his father's—told him to steer clear of that mess. It was dangerous work, or so he'd been told, and he wasn't keen on the heavy labor.

No, he decided, there was something better. Whenever he envisioned the future Mr. Randy Carter, he saw a suit and tie. Something respectable—something that would impress.

***

"Why not college?" Janie asked during one of her mother-hen visits.

"Why aren't *you* in college?" He turned the question back onto her.

Irritation danced across her face. She took in a deep breath and exhaled slowly. "Hand me the milk, please."

Avoiding his question, Janie busied herself with putting the groceries away.

In part, he'd asked because he wanted to needle her a little, but he was genuinely curious. She'd always been the smart one. He wanted to demand an answer. Out of fear that she might grab the sack and leave him with an empty refrigerator, he didn't.

"Okay, smart-ass." Janie spun around and tossed the empty grocery sack in his direction. "If you must know, I dropped out because I couldn't deal with the load after Mama…did what she did."

"Did what she did?" He grinned, but it wasn't a smile. "Just say it. Call it like it is. She killed herself. No need to tiptoe around it."

"Jesus, Randy!" Her eyes crinkled shut and her chin quivered. "Don't be such an insensitive bastard."

He chuckled and said, "Well, she did." He'd never understand girls. Dad might've been an asshole, but at least he didn't try to pretend that nothing had happened.

That's right, son. I was always honest with you.

"I'm such an idiot. Every time I think you might have an ounce of decency in your body, you prove me wrong. Don't you ever get tired of being so calloused? Do you hear the words that come out of your mouth?" She pinched her thumb and forefinger together. "I'm this close to being done with you!"

She was shaking, hopping mad. He wasn't surprised.

"Stop being so *sensitive*," he sneered. "You've always taken everything the wrong way. Don't you ever get tired of being a crybaby?"

"I'm done. I can't take it anymore. Have fun taking care of yourself!"

"Don't go," he chuckled. "We were just getting to the good part."

After she'd gone, he finished putting the rest of the food away while replaying the argument. It felt good to push her buttons once in a while.

CHAPTER 60

GRADUATION

The handkerchief in her hand was damp from her sweaty palm. Spring rains had soaked the football field just that morning, turning the event into an enormous steam bath. Drenched in perspiration, the portly woman sitting next to her fanned her face with the ceremony program.

It was a big day for Janie. On more than one occasion over the past two years, she'd doubted that he'd finish. Pushing him through was her biggest accomplishment to date.

Caught up in a sea of caps and gowns, Randy blended in with his classmates. She scanned the rows, searching for his face. Eventually, she spotted him on the third row from the back.

A stark contrast from the eager faces of his graduating class, Randy's expression was aloof, irritated. A storm was brewing.

A knee-jerk reaction, Janie's gut tightened. *Does it matter anymore? Not your problem after today.*

Turning her attention back to the principal's rambling address, she wondered if he used the same speech year after year. She speculated that the audience paid little mind to the blabbering. Self-serving, it was human nature to focus on the individual point of interest. Holding out for the announcement of their graduate's promotion, the crowd simply tolerated the formality.

Once the principal's speech was over, the remainder of the ceremony went by quickly.

"See you at the house?" Janie interrupted a conversation between Randy and a group of his classmates.

"Later." He nodded in her direction and turned his attention back to the excited chatter of the group.

She was surprised to see him interacting with other students. Randy was a loner. Although he'd managed to make a friend or two through the years, he didn't spend much time with them.

That's the pot calling the kettle black. When's the last time you had a friend? You can't count Hildy.

It was true. Being a loner had always been the way to go. It didn't bother her as much as it had. She remembered the wistful longing to be a part of something, a part of anything. Giggles on the playground, whispered plans for slumber parties, secret notes passed just out of range of the teacher's watchful eye—she'd pretended not to notice her exclusion from the interactions that created a friendship. Being an outsider hadn't been a choice. At least not her choice.

And now? What's the excuse now? There's nothing to hide from the others—no drunken father, no absence of a mother, none of the things that humiliated the girl trying so hard to fit in.

All around her, friends and family congratulated the new graduates. Laughter, hugs, and good-natured teasing created a jubilant symphony that only served to heighten her unadulterated loneliness.

The soggy field gave way beneath her high-heeled pumps with each step. By the time she reached Papa's truck, clumps of mud with bits of grass stuck in them had covered the shoes. She leaned against the fender of the dusty old truck and took her right heel off. Not wanting to ruin her best handkerchief, Janie scraped the excess mud off on the edge of the wheel well. She repeated the process with her left shoe.

"Janie, is that you?"

Focused on her shoes, his voice startled her. It took a moment for her to recognize his face.

"Richard!" Too brightly, she asked, "How have you been?" Damning the flush spreading across her cheeks, her mouth twisted into a ridiculous attempt of a smile.

"Good," he grinned at her. "And you? What've you been up to since graduation?"

"Oh, you know," she stammered, "just taking care of Randy since..." *Stupid, stupid girl. What are you mumbling about?*

"I heard." He hesitated, seeming to search for the right thing to say. "You've had your share of bad shit over the past few years."

She examined his face to gauge his intention. It wasn't like her to air her dirty laundry. Relief settled over her when she realized there was no sign of pleasure in his demeanor over her misfortune.

"I'm hanging in there." A wane smile touched her lips. "It's not so bad."

An uncomfortable silence filled the air as he seemed to struggle for a response.

Compelled to change the direction of the conversation, she asked, "So, who are you here for?"

"My little brother, John." He chuckled and said, "My mom didn't think he was gonna finish, and my old man was threatening him with an ass-kicking almost every day."

"I know exactly how they felt! I didn't think Randy was going to make it either. I kept him going with the promise to cut off the food supply if he didn't get his rear end up and go to school."

It was amazing—laughing in the parking lot with a boy that she'd barely known in school. She felt...normal.

"You're..." his voice trailed off. He took in a deep breath.

"I'm what?" She prompted him to continue.

"You've really held it together."

"Not in the way I wished I would've. I dropped out of college when my mother passed." She wrapped her arms around herself in a protective hug.

"You did what you had to do. Hell, half the people in our class didn't make it to college in the first place." He reached out and gave her shoulder a sympathetic pat.

Janie nodded.

"You could go back."

"I don't know...It was a time in my life. I'm not sure I belong there now."

She was stuck in a purgatory of sorts. She imagined that time had stopped for her, and that she was trapped until a penance could be paid to free her.

"You're too smart to give up. If I had half of your brains, I wouldn't be working for my old man."

He said this with a grin, and she guessed he wasn't unhappy with his lot in life. His family owned a large insurance agency that paid for a big house on a hill and brand-new Cadillacs every other year.

"And if I had your old man to work for, I wouldn't need to finish college," she teased. "You're not exactly digging ditches."

"You have no idea." His laughter erupted from his belly. "My father is a slave driver!"

Never one to joke around with others, the foreign sensation of sheer amusement was alluring.

The sun had set on the nearly empty parking lot. She glanced at her wristwatch and said, "I'd better get home. I have a cake for Randy. It would be rude of me to skip his celebration."

"Oh, Lord, my mom will have my ass! I was supposed to help set up the food for John's party!" His eyes widened under his raised brow.

The thought of a grown man, still afraid of his mother's wrath, made her giggle. "Yes, you'd better hurry! Your father might make you dig a ditch."

He touched her shoulder once more. "It was really good to run into you. Maybe we could have dinner sometime."

Suddenly shy, she nodded. Was it too much to hope this was a date? She didn't dare to ask for fear of being the fool.

Janie smiled and said, "I'd like that."

"It's a date, then!" His expression was that of an eager child on Christmas morning.

Along the drive to the farm, she replayed the conversation with Richard. She'd give just about anything to feel that way again.

***

She'd already waited for several hours for him. Barely able to keep her eyes open, she yawned again. There was no reason to stay.

Fighting the heaviness of her heart, she tucked a handmade card under the edge of the cake.

It was graduation night, and he'd found a better way to celebrate than eating a piece of cake with his big sister. Disgusted by her self-pity, Janie reminded herself that he was doing just as he should—having fun with friends.

CHAPTER 61

THE PRANK

Consciousness seeped in bit by bit as a squadron of gnats carried out a dive-bomb attack at his eyes and nose. Swiping away the sweat from his brow, he opened his eyes to the bright sunlight. Blood rushed in and out of his ears with the racing of his heart.

Disoriented, he pushed himself upright from the lounge chair. The world spun around a time or two before righting itself. Empty beer bottles and cigarette butts littered the pavement. A lone shoe floated in the water.

His mouth was the Sahara Desert. He had the overwhelming urge to stick his face in the swimming pool and drink from it. Scanning the remains of the party, he realized that he couldn't remember most of it.

Flies buzzed around a picked-over display of appetizers and desserts. Several bottles of soda floated in a melted bucket of ice. He took one and popped the top off. The morning sun had heated the soda to an unsatisfying lukewarm temperature. Fizz welled up in his throat, making it painful to swallow.

He let out a large belch and felt better. Patting his pockets, he discovered his key was missing. Hesitant to walk in unannounced, he tapped on the patio door. He wished he could remember whose party it was.

Cupping his face with both hands, he peered through the glass. There didn't seem to be anyone inside. He knocked again, more loudly. Hopeful his key might be inside, he tugged at the door.

"Hello?" He called out to the empty house before stepping in all the way.

When no one answered, he pulled the door shut behind him and began to ransack the clutter on the kitchen counters. It took a minute or so to get through it all. The search turned up a handful of beer tabs and the occasional soda lid, but no key.

"Well, shit!" He cursed the empty house. "Guess I'm walking."

If he hadn't been so hungover, his predicament would be downright funny.

Keenly aware of his full bladder, Randy decided to take a piss before hoofing it home. The layout was typical of most newer ranch-style homes, and the bathroom was easy enough to find.

His headache diminished as he relieved himself. Imagining he'd been so full of urine that it caused his brain to ache, he fought the urge to laugh.

The stench of alcohol oozed out of his pores. He lathered a rose-shaped soap between his hands until there was a good amount of suds, then proceeded to scrub his face and neck. Cold water from the tap felt like heaven as he splashed the soap away. He considered wetting his hair down, but he'd taken long enough already. Blindly, he fumbled to find a hand towel.

The soft towel smelled of laundry soap—a sharp contrast to the stale, moldy-smelling one hanging in his own bathroom. Enjoying the comfort, he rubbed his face and neck longer than necessary to dry.

Next, he searched the kitchen again, but for food instead of his key. The refrigerator was stuffed to the brim with Pyrex dishes. Lifting the lids, one by one, Randy couldn't remember the last time he'd seen so many different meals in one place. He contemplated taking a slice of meatloaf before discovering a large dish of fried chicken. Saliva welled up under his tongue.

A long-forgotten memory pushed its way into the front of his mind. Barely tall enough to see over the kitchen counter, he'd watched Mama, or perhaps Betty, pack a picnic basket with loads of chilled fried chicken. His hunger pangs had threatened to do him in.

He took several pieces before leaving the house. With a refrigerator that full, they wouldn't miss the chicken. He was sure of it.

The truck was sitting alone. All the other party guests had long gone. Worried that it might rain before his key was found, Randy crossed the street to roll the windows up.

He opened the passenger side door, and the rotten odor of excrement hit his nose.

"What in the hell?" Randy stared at the mound of shit in the middle of the driver's seat.

His initial thought was that a dog had somehow climbed into the truck and relieved itself.

Wake up, idiot. No way in hell that's dog shit.

A growl formed in the back of his throat. White-hot pressure pushed against the backside of his eyes. He kicked the side of the truck, which only served to increase his anger.

Torn between screaming at the pile of crap in the middle of his seat and crying like a baby, Randy felt around behind the passenger's seat for something to pick it up with. He fished out a brown paper sack from the burger joint that had slid under the seat.

He slammed the passenger door shut and walked around the truck to the driver's side. Using the sack like a makeshift mitten, Randy fought the urge to vomit as he picked up the shit. He looked around to see if anyone was watching before dropping it on the freshly mowed lawn next to the truck.

It broke into several pieces, revealing a shiny object stuck in the middle of it. He realized it was a key—his truck key.

"Assholes!" he bellowed. He wanted to beat the hell out of someone, but there was no one to take it out on.

Chickenshit cowards, son! That's what they are—chickenshit. They're probably having a good laugh right about now.

He used the bag to pick the key up and wipe it in the grass. It was no use. Shit remained in the grooves of the key. If another key existed, he would've left it.

The headache was back, and he wasn't up for a long walk in the bright noon sun.

With the key still gripped in the paper bag, Randy crossed the street. Praying that no one had come home unnoticed while he was cleaning the mess, he opened the back gate to the swimming pool.

He placed the key onto the pavement and dropped the bag. Kneeling at the water's edge, he whisked the key back and forth until it looked clean. Using a damp towel left behind in a lounge chair, Randy dried the key. He tossed the towel over his shoulder and grabbed the last soda out of the bucket.

The towel served as a makeshift barrier over the spot where the feces had been left. It did little to get rid of the stench, but he'd worry about that later.

First, he was going to find the asshole that left a hot dump in his seat.

CHAPTER 62

THE PAYBACK

Squinting in the bright sunlight, Randy rubbed the aching spot between his eyes. He wasn't delusional enough to think that everyone in his class was a friend, but there were only a few possibilities for the culprit.

It was Sunday, and the herds of worshippers were beginning to pour out of their respective churches. Shaking his head, he pondered the ridiculous amount of churches in the little town.

The party, at least the parts that he remembered, had been uneventful. He replayed the night, frame by frame, up until the point that things got fuzzy.

There had been a moment, a small interaction, that gave him an uneasy feeling as he got to it. Was it over a girl? He couldn't recall that part.

Think harder, stupid. You know.

He did know. The only thing that he didn't know was where to find the bastard.

Figure it out, son. Use your noggin. Who does the asshole run with? What about his girlfriend?

Cold sweat drenched his head and chest. He wished Dad would shut the hell up. It was worse than ever—his non-stop commentary on Randy's every thought. There was no escaping him now that he wasn't limited by a physical body.

The girlfriend, Stacey, was a sweet little dish. She also happened to work at the burger joint. Randy knew this because he'd sat at her booth more than once, trying to picture her big tits without the constraints of a brassiere.

The diner wasn't open yet. Nothing in the entire town was open on Sunday, at least not until the churchgoers had a chance to finish their "praise Jesus—Hallelujah" bullshit.

He drove to the diner, parked under the only tree, and resigned himself to a long wait. The truck still smelled of shit, so he rolled down the window. Partially to mask the stench, but mostly to past the time, Randy lit a cigarette.

The owner of the diner shuffled up to the front door, unlocked it, and turned the open sign around. Although it was sunny outside, Randy could see the fluorescent lights brighten one by one.

His patience paid off. At a quarter after one, Stacey arrived late for work, delivered by none other than the asshole from the party. She got out of the car and blew a kiss goodbye.

Randy turned the ignition and gunned the engine several times before putting it into drive. With a jolt and jut forward, he blocked Stacey's ride from moving.

A surge of excitement rushed through his entire body when he saw the loser's pimpled face morph from confusion into alarm.

You've got him now, son. Don't make it easy for him.

He slammed the truck into park. In one fluid motion, he jumped out of the truck and grabbed the shit-stained towel that he'd been sitting on. Sour fumes of drying crap wafted up to his nostrils, giving fuel to his anger.

"Get out!" he screamed. "Now!"

"Why? What for?" Pimple Face stammered. "I didn't do anything!"

He didn't wait for him to open the door. With as much force as he could summon, Randy crammed the towel over his face through the open window.

The horn blared as he struggled to turn away from Randy's grasp.

Randy had a death grip on his face as he shoved his head into the back of the seat. Hatred deafened his ears, and his vision narrowed into a predator's sight. He imagined smashing the towel into his face until his tiny brain oozed out of his ears.

"Stop it!"

The command cut through the fog of rage, but Randy didn't ease up. He couldn't stop himself. Every sensible part of his existence had been crippled.

"Stop it!"

This time, the order came with a sharp thump to the back of Randy's head. It was just enough to cause his attention to shift.

Fists cocked, ready to hammer into the owner of the voice, he spun around.

The moment was a kaleidoscope, fragmented by broken screams of the asshole, the face of the police officer that had dealt the blow, and the sound of Stacey, sobbing.

"Get on the ground!"

Randy dropped to his knees, instinctively throwing his hands in the air.

"You're nothing but trouble, Carter! Just like your old man!"

The officer huffed and wheezed as he cuffed Randy's wrists behind his back. Another blow, with what felt like a boot, struck between Randy's shoulder blades, causing him to fall forward onto his chest and belly.

Flashes of lights peppered his vision. Bits of sand collected in the pool of blood gathering in his mouth. He tried to spit them out, but with each effort, more debris entered his mouth. Chunks of stolen fried chicken danced at the back of his throat like baby spit-up. Swallowing hard, he focused his attention on his breathing to steady his stomach.

CHAPTER 63

CONNECTION

"I guess he had it coming." His lips hinted at a smile.

"Surely, you don't find this amusing." Rubbing her temples, Janie frowned. "He's going to end up behind bars for good if he doesn't change his ways."

Richard leaned across the table and placed his hand over hers. "Not amusing, just...seems like a reasonable reaction to finding a pile of poop in your car seat."

"I'm sorry," she said. "I didn't mean to ruin this nice dinner by bringing up my stupid brother." She had the urge to pull her hand out from underneath his and tuck it into her lap. Not because his touch made her uncomfortable, but because it felt right.

"Are you kidding me?" He winked at her. "Your brother is the talk of the town, right now. If you hadn't brought it up, I was going to ask!"

"I was afraid of that," she groaned. "This town is full of busybodies."

Nodding, he said, "It is that, chock full of gossips. And that's not counting the nosy old church ladies." He raised his water glass in a mock toast and said, "Here's to the most interesting conversation I've ever had on a first date."

Wishing to hide the flush spreading across her cheeks, she poked around at the carefully arranged lettuce on her plate.

"How's your salad?"

"I'm not sure this can legally be called a salad." She grinned and stuffed a small glazed piece of carrot into her mouth.

"It sure is fancy, though!" He chuckled and said, "Blame my mother. She said this was a perfect place to take a nice girl for a first date."

She had the urge to pinch herself just to make sure she was awake. How was it possible that a boy like Richard would consider taking her on a date, to begin with, much less find her conversation interesting?

"I was being a smart-ass. Your mother has great taste. The restaurant is perfect."

"You're funny." He grinned and said, "It's a nice change from most girls."

After the waiter refreshed their glasses, Richard changed the subject. "What's your brother going to do with his life now that high school is over?"

"Other than going to jail? I don't know. The house is free and clear, so he's not desperate." She blotted the corners of her mouth with her napkin and said, "He wants to do a job that allows him to wear a tie every day. Doesn't want to get his hands dirty."

"My dad is looking for a new agent. He wants someone that he can train from scratch—pliable, as he likes to say." He tilted his head and raised one eyebrow. "I could talk to him."

"Maybe. I'm not sure he's cut out for anything that requires him to be polite to other people." She imagined Randy wearing a dress shirt and tie while telling some poor old woman to go fuck herself.

"You might be surprised. Sometimes a little guidance is all a boy needs." Richard smiled and said, "You should've seen me in my first few days on the job. I was all thumbs and elbows. I told Mr. Krebbit that he was probably too old to buy life insurance."

Janie covered her cheeks with her palms and laughed. "No! You didn't."

"I did. And it took everything in my dad not to drag me out by the scruff of my neck."

"That's terrible…and funny. Terribly funny." She grinned from ear to ear.

"If I'm salvageable, then Randy probably is, too."

CHAPTER 64

SUIT AND TIE

She took long enough to get to the point that he'd begun to imagine taping her mouth shut.

"Well, what do you think?" She chewed on her bottom lip and waited for his response.

"How much money would I make?"

"For Christ's sake, Randy. I don't know! Does it matter at first? It's a chance to wear a tie every day—just like you wanted." She turned away and wiped at invisible crumbs on the kitchen counter.

He lit a cigarette and stood for a moment, watching her from the doorway. There was a large part of him that enjoyed her angst.

"What do you get out of it?"

She spun around fast enough that he was surprised her head didn't twist off. Fists clenched, Janie looked ready for a fight.

"What do *I* get out of it?" She echoed his question.

Her eyes, shining glints of blue ice, met with his. He didn't look away.

"Wipe that mean smile off your face! I get nothing out of it, other than I might stop worrying about your selfish ass."

She was quite ugly when she was mad. He thought about telling her this.

"You don't have to worry about me. I'm just fine on my own." He took a deep drag off his smoke and blew it out forcefully, in her direction.

"You're not fine. The electricity has been off for a week. You don't have anything other than this piece-of-shit house. Where are you getting money for cigarettes?"

"That's none of your business." He cocked his head to the side and watched her face. "What's Dick get out of this? A piece of your tail?"

"You're despicable!" she spat. "You don't have the God-given sense to know your ass from a hole in the ground! And it's Richard, not Dick!"

"I guess Dick knows *your* ass from a hole in the ground, though. Don't he, sis?"

Janie grabbed her purse off the table and dug around. Hands shaking, she slapped a scrap of paper onto the table.

"There! That's the number and address. Do whatever the hell you want with it! I don't care anymore. I'm done babysitting!"

She slammed the door behind her hard enough to rattle the glass panes in their casings.

Randy waited in the doorway between the kitchen and the parlor until the rumble of her car disappeared into the evening air. He unfolded the slip of paper and stared at the foreign handwriting.

Dick's chicken scratch—son of a bitch must want in your sister's pants real bad. Who does she think she is? She's not your mama, son.

He opened the glass shade and lit the wick, bathing the kitchen in the soft orange glow of the kerosene lamp.

The bottle was stashed far in the back, where she would never find it. He pulled the cork, and the familiar, bittersweet oak fragrance filled his nostrils. All his best and worst memories of childhood were bound to the smell of whiskey.

He poured the amber-brown liquid into Dad's favorite glass and swirled it around. "This one's for you, Dad," he said to the empty room. It had become a way to honor him, a ritual of sorts.

The first glass seared a fiery path down into the pit of his gut. The second went down smooth and sweet. An easy calm settled over him. He poured a third glass and lit a cigarette.

Now, the world was straightening up right.

The world's your oyster, son. That's what it is—your goddamn oyster.

Dad's recliner remained in the position it had been for as long as he could remember. He stood in front of it, and imagined for a moment that Dad was upstairs, passed out.

The dark brown leather was stiff in the spots that had been exposed to years of sunlight, soft in the places his body had touched most often. Randy lifted the handle and stretched until the chair had fully reclined back.

How in the hell had Dad managed to stay in this chair for so long? There was nothing to see from this perspective. The television, the curtained window, and a portion of the doorway—that had been his entire view for most of his life after Mama had gone.

He tipped the glass to his mouth to swallow the last drop. He reached for the bottle and twisted the cork until it made a pop. As a boy, he'd learned to fear the sound. Now, he associated it with the relief to follow.

Was there a sign? A magical moment that he would know what to do with the rest of his life?

CHAPTER 65

THE INTERVIEW

He damned near hated Janie, but she was right. He intended to wear a tie to work. One way or another, the world was going to respect him.

Sandra would respect him. He smiled at the thought of her, begging him to take her back. It was enough to give him the guts to open the door to the insurance agency.

Inside, cool air blew across his face. He'd forgotten how nice air conditioning felt. It took a second or two for his eyes to adjust to the dimly lit reception area.

"May I help you?"

"I'm here for the interview." Unsure what to do with his hands, he stuffed them into his pockets.

She pushed her glasses from the tip of her sharp nose against her face and peered at the appointment book on her desk. "And your name?"

"Randy…Randall Carter."

"Have a seat. He'll be right with you."

While he waited, he picked at a loose thread on the edge of the upholstered chair.

Poorly lit and quiet, the office felt more like a morgue than an insurance agency. Hushed voices, punctuated with the occasional ringing of a telephone, traveled through the hallways. He tried to imagine the occupants of unseen offices, but the only scene to come to mind was that of rows of books, policed by a crotchety librarian.

"Mr. Carter? Come this way."

He followed the man, presumably Dick's father, through a side door into a conference room.

"Have a seat." The man didn't gesture toward any particular chair but instead stood to wait for Randy to sit.

Randy wondered if it was a test.

Show him who's boss, son.

He pulled the chair at the head of the table and sat down. Heart racing, he cranked out a rusty smile and hoped that he'd gotten it right.

"Richard tells me that you've had no experience in the workplace."

Flashbacks of sitting in the principal's office, waiting for punishment, swam around in his head, and he suddenly felt nauseous. Hidden under the table, he pressed his clammy palms together in his lap. It occurred to him that he was unprepared for the questions. Fighting the urge to bolt out of the room, he answered, "No, sir. I just graduated from high school."

"Relax, you're not in trouble." He chuckled and wrote something on the paper in front of him.

By the time that the interview was finished, Randy's head was a spinning mass of mush.

"Thank you, Mr. Carter. We'll be in touch."

Dick's father extended a hand, and Randy resisted the nervous impulse to wipe the sweat off his palm before taking it.

"Thank you, sir." He cleared his throat and stammered, "Do you know how soon you'll know…I mean…when you'll make a decision?"

"I like your gumption." He smiled. "Soon."

CHAPTER 66

FIVE YEARS LATER

The office was empty, for the most part. It usually was when he arrived. The new secretary scurried about making coffee and leaving memos on desks.

"Good morning, Mr. Carter." Her cheeks flushed a pretty shade of pink whenever she saw him.

She was barely eighteen, he guessed. He liked this one. She had a softness about her. She wasn't like the others.

"Morning, Genny."

"Good morning." Giggling, she added, "I guess I already said that to you."

Something was endearing about the way she fiddled with the neckline of her dress whenever he spoke to her. She was unsophisticated in the purest of ways.

Fresh out of high school, Genny had started with the agency just weeks before. A sharp contrast to her predecessor, she was open and willing to learn. And so far, she didn't seem offended by Randy's attention.

Richard's dad had been furious with him.

"Single-handedly, you ran off my best secretary! What were you thinking, son?" Veins had threatened to pop out of the old man's forehead. "You're lucky she didn't sic her husband on you!"

Randy had waved away his words. "She was a tease and a liar. She wanted it."

"Carter, if you weren't my best producer, you'd be gone!" Storming out of the office and slamming the door behind him, he'd left Randy sitting speechless.

The temptation had been to get angry, indignant even, but in truth, Randy had been relieved that the old man hadn't canned him.

Now, just weeks later, all was well again for the agency. The arrival of the new secretary had fixed everything. She was good at her job, attractive, and she knew her place.

***

"Meet me at the Watering Hole? Five o'clock?" George poked his head into Randy's office. "One last appointment and I'm out of here for the day."

A few years older than Randy, George had taken him under his wing in the beginning, had given him a template to copy.

He liked George well enough. A bachelor, just like Randy, George was not only a mentor but one hell of a drinking buddy.

"You know it! I'm ready for this day to be done. Just finishing up this proposal, and I'll be right behind you."

The Watering Hole was perfectly dark inside. Lit by a few neon signs over the bar and small fixtures above the tables, the bar was his oasis after a long, stressful day.

Two drinks ahead of Randy, George sat at the bar—bending Mac's ear. Mac had acquired the patience necessary to listen to a bunch of drunkards for ten hours every day. Judging the expression on Mac's face, he guessed that George was already testing it.

"Hey, pal," George slurred. "You finally made it! I was starting to think you weren't coming."

Randy glanced at his wristwatch and chuckled. "I'm only half an hour late. You must be on bar time."

"What'll you have?" Mac asked. "The usual?"

He liked that Mac remembered his drink of choice. It made him feel important.

"You got it, my man. Whiskey—neat."

Mac nodded and poured.

"What took you so long? Did you get caught by the boss-man?"

"No, not this time." He shook his head and grinned. "A pretty little birdie delayed me."

"Oh Lord, Carter." George covered his forehead and eyes with his hand and said, "You're asking for trouble again."

"She's different than the last one."

George snorted. "She's also a baby. Is she even full-grown?"

"Jesus! I'm not an old man like you!" Randy laughed.

"Twenty-five? That's too old for her."

"Twenty-four," Randy corrected. "And that's a perfect age for her."

"And you know this how? Did you ask her?" Squinting, George waited.

"Knock it off. I'm working on it."

He downed the whiskey in one swallow and held his glass up for Mac to fill it again. George was getting under his skin, and he didn't care for it.

"This one's different." Gritting his teeth, he struggled to keep his voice level.

"How so?"

"I'm gonna marry this one."

"You don't know her."

"Enough to know that she's the one."

CHAPTER 67

GENNY

He buried his nose into her hair and breathed in the scent of honeysuckle and soap. Delicate and small, she felt fragile in his arms. He was going to make her his. A familiar stirring ached in his groin, but he ignored it. She was worth the wait. He would keep her pure.

"Would you like that?"

Tipping her head up to meet his gaze, her eyes shone like blue pools of water in the moonlight. She smiled shyly and nodded.

He cupped her face with his hands and leaned back. "I want to take care of you. Do you understand? I'm going to make sure that you'll never want for anything again, Genny."

She sighed as he pulled her back into his arms. This felt right.

"I've never...had anyone take care of me before." Her voice trembled with emotion. "I'm the luckiest girl in the world."

He squeezed her tightly. "Let's get married tomorrow."

She giggled. "I don't think it works like that. Don't we need to find a church? Get a license?"

Randy frowned. "I guess we should. I haven't been in a church for years."

"My grandma still goes to the church I grew up in." Her eyes widened as she waited for his reaction.

"I don't know...doesn't that seem a little far away?"

"It's Kerrville, not New York City."

She giggled again, and he felt irritated. Was she making fun of him?

"Okay." She backed off. "Does your mama go to a church here?"

He swallowed thickly, his mouth suddenly dry. She didn't know about his mother—didn't know anything about his past. He needed to keep it that way.

"She did. Years ago." Lightheaded, his pulse pounded in his ears. "After my dad died, she couldn't stand to be in the house. Said it didn't feel like home anymore. She moved into town."

"But why did she stop going to church?" Puzzled, she studied his face.

"I don't want to talk about it." His chest tightened, and his stomach churned. He let go of her and stepped away.

"I don't understand."

"She's not the same. After Dad died, it was like she died, too."

Genny reached for him, and he instinctively pushed away.

"Don't," he warned.

Tears collected in her eyes. "I'm sorry. I wasn't trying to upset you."

His heart softened a little. Perhaps, he had it wrong. She wasn't like the others.

"Come here," he soothed. "I'm sorry. It's just hard to talk about. I can't stand to be around my mom since Dad died. She's not the same. It's like she doesn't exist."

Genny wrapped her arms around his waist and pulled him closer. "I don't care where we get married," she whispered. "It doesn't matter. The important thing is that we're together. We'll make the house feel like home again."

He closed his eyes and took in a deep breath through his nose. A calm feeling filled his soul. She believed him. More importantly, she believed in him. That mattered most of all.

CHAPTER 68

EXPECTING

"Genny," Randall yelled through the screen door. "Come down here."

She appeared almost immediately. She'd been crying again. He was beyond tired of it.

***

George had tried to warn him several months before.

"Pregnant women are crazy," George had said with a smile. "Better get used to it, buddy." He'd held his glass up in Randy's direction and said, "Welcome back to the Watering Hole. You'll be spending a lot of time here during the next nine months. After that, you'll come here to get away from the screaming baby *and* the crying wife."

Randy had shaken his head and laughed. "No, I'm happy at home. Just not up to dealing with the waterworks tonight."

So far, George had not been wrong. Last night, he'd reached his limit in the patience department.

"Now, what's the matter?" He hadn't tried to hide his irritation.

"I don't know." She'd sobbed and wiped the snot from her nose with the back of her hand. "I guess I feel so…alone."

He'd struggled to remember what about her face had ever made him think she was pretty. Swollen and red from days of crying, her expression more closely resembled that of a troll's than of a young girl's.

"It's just that… I have no one. Grandma's too far away. I don't know anyone here." She broke into another round of shuddering sobs, struggling to finish her sentence. "You're always gone, and I don't even know my mother-in-law."

"I'm having a real hard time understanding what my mother has to do with any of this." He took in a deep breath. "Seriously, what does my being gone at work have to do with my mother?"

"I've never even met her!" she wailed. "Why haven't I met her?"

"I told you, I can't be around her!"

"My mom is gone, and you don't talk to yours!" She'd slapped her hands together in a ridiculous motion. "And our baby won't have any grandparents! Don't you think that's terribly sad?"

She was irrational. It was impossible to talk to her.

Women are irrational by nature, son. Don't you remember your mama? This is what you signed up for. I tried to tell you.

He groaned inwardly. It had been a long while since Dad had put his two-cents worth into the mix.

At a complete loss of what to do to make the crying stop, he'd gone to bed. It wasn't until the next day, after the whiskey had worn off, that he'd figured out what to do.

***

"What do you want?" she sniffled. She was still dressed in her housecoat and slippers.

"Hold the door open."

He picked up the rocking chair with both hands, maneuvered through the door, and plopped it down in front of the stove.

"What is this?"

"It's a rocking chair from my mama—it's for the baby." He took a deep breath and said, "She wanted you to have it."

"You saw her?" Her brow furrowed into deep creases.

"Yes, for you. I figured you'd be happy."

"I'm glad to have the chair, but I still want to meet her."

"She doesn't want to meet you."

Genny recoiled, visibly struck by his words. "But why?"

"I tried to tell you before, but you don't listen!" He smacked his hand against the door. "You never listen! She isn't the same, Genny! Don't you get it? She's dead to me." He thrust his finger toward the rocking chair and bellowed, "*This* is all you get. This is all you're ever going to get from her! Are we clear?"

"But I thought maybe…." she whimpered. "Maybe she would get better if she knew that we were happy."

"It doesn't matter," he hissed. "Why can't you get that through your thick skull?"

Her eyes widened, and she took a step backward. "I just wanted…"

"Just wanted to *what*? Piss me off? Is that what you wanted? Because that's exactly what you're doing!"

He grabbed her shoulders and shook her. "Damn it, Genny! Why can't you just leave shit alone?"

"Please, don't," she begged. "I'll stop. I'm sorry."

He pulled her against his chest and squeezed, hard. After a moment, he loosened his grip and held her. She had deceived him. She wasn't different than all the others, after all.

But she's yours, son. Bought and paid for. I told you not to let a woman get under your skin. Better keep yourself in check.

CHAPTER 69

ALLEY CAT

He was blitzed, as in a numb-faced, blurred vision, slurry drunk. It was dark inside, which made it difficult to decide whether she was pretty or just made up that way. He looked at her painted face and struggled to remember her name.

None of this mattered. There was only one reason he was still sitting in the booth with her, watching her chew gum, like a cow with her cud.

Fighting the urge to bite her, he covered her sticky, red lips with a rough kiss.

She moaned, inviting him into her wet, sloppy mouth. The taste of Juicy Fruit chewing gum mingled together with stale cigarette smoke and bourbon.

Provoked by the dirty flavor, he bit her bottom lip just a little, imagining how it would feel to chomp down all the way through.

Oblivious to his anger, she stroked his crotch. "Wanna get out of here?" she whispered into his ear, each word punctuated by the squishing sounds of the chewing gum lodged between her jaw teeth.

He slipped his hand under her skirt. Her panties were wet through. She didn't gasp when he shoved three fingers into her. This could be fun. It had been too long since he'd been able to let go.

"Yeah, let's get outta here." He let her kiss him once more, squashing his distaste for her.

A tap on his shoulder startled him. Instinctively, he jumped up, ready for a fight.

"Whoa, easy there, fellow!" Sergeant Williams led him away to a spot near the john.

"Your sweet little wife is looking for you. She's worried something awful. I think you ought to head home." The sergeant shot a judgmental glance toward the bimbo waiting in the booth.

He gritted his jaw. "That's none of your business," he hissed under his breath.

The officer took a step back, allowing Randall to return to the booth.

"Let's go."

She laughed and nodded.

He wondered what in the hell was so damned funny. Some women laughed just to fill in the empty space, an annoying punctuation to each uttered phrase. Images filled his head of pounding the cackling right out of her.

"Am I following you?"

"I don't have a car," she giggled.

He wasn't surprised. She was an alley cat, looking for any morsel of food she could get her claws into. He knew her type.

"Over here." Pointing toward the direction of his car, he said, "The orange Chevy."

"Nice!" she squealed. "I dated a guy with one just like yours, except it wasn't orange."

"Then it wasn't just like mine, was it?" Not waiting for her, he made it to the driver's side door before she'd managed to get halfway.

Revving the engine, he realized that she was waiting outside the passenger door. Was she expecting him to open the door for her?

Leaning across the seat, he pulled the handle and shoved the door open.

Disappointment registered across her face, making her painted-on features seem garish in the dimly lit parking lot.

She isn't giggling now, he thought.

"Where to?" He kept his eyes on the road.

"Um," she hesitated. "The trailer park just south of town. You can get to it by taking—"

Cutting her off, he said, "Yeah, I know where it's at."

"Look, we don't have to do this if you're not into it." Her voice trailed off. Her hands were clasped around her knees. She wasn't so sure of herself now. Her discomfort was palpable, and this made him feel better.

"No, I'm good." He grinned and winked at her. "Want one?"

She took the pack of cigarettes from his outstretched hand and said, "Thanks."

"Light one for me?" It was easy to gauge a woman's nature by asking her to do something for him.

"Of course." Her words were followed by a small burst of laughter. "I'm the last house on the right."

Makeshift wooden steps groaned and cracked beneath his feet while she fumbled with her key. Using her shoulder and hip, she shoved open the door.

The off-putting odor of rancid grease, cigarette smoke, and moldy laundry assaulted his senses. He wasn't surprised by the condition of the tin box she called home. His drunken high was beginning to wear off, and the surroundings were only fueling his annoyance.

"Want a drink? I think I have a bottle of gin." She began the process of opening and shutting the flimsy, rusted metal cabinet doors lining the wall of the cramped kitchen.

"I've had enough." Perched on the edge of the stained sofa, he tapped his toes.

"Oh." She left the cabinet door open she'd been rifling through and turned to face him. "Do you want to talk?"

Disgusted by the eager shine in her eyes, he shook his head. "Come here."

She smiled and complied with his demand, kneeling before him.

"Good girl." Women's lib was a hoax. They really just wanted to be treated like children. Time and again, he'd found this to be true.

Something in the way she gave in so easily disturbed him. Bored already, he smashed his mouth onto hers in a brutal fashion. She had the decency to play along and pulled away. His groin ached in acknowledgment of his excitement.

Pulling her back into him, he wound her hair into his fingers. When she groaned with pleasure, he twisted a half-turn tighter. The groaning became more guttural, and her features distorted in pain.

"Ouch!" She cried out, "That's too rough!"

"You like it that way, don't you?"

She nodded against the tension of his hand in her hair.

Smothering her protests, he kissed her in the same way as before. His mouth watered with the salty, metallic taste of the blood he'd drawn.

Cuffing her wrist with his free hand, he forced her to feel his erection. "See what you're doing to me?" he growled.

"You're hurting me!" She pleaded with him to stop, but she didn't pull away.

After he'd finished, she lay face down on the matted carpet in front of her sofa. He gave an inner prayer of thanks that she didn't try to reach for him or to make small talk. Nothing was worse than pretending it had meant something.

Motionless, she remained silent as he belted his trousers. He noticed the graying roots where her hair fell to each side of the back of her head. Under the harsh glare of the overhead light, he allowed himself to take in her age.

This whore is old enough to be your mother, son. You're not that desperate.

A wave of revulsion sloshed around in his gut.

He nudged the side of her thigh with his foot. "Hey, I'm leaving."

A shuddering breath escaped her, but she said nothing.

"Are you okay?" he asked.

What the fuck do you care? You scared she'll tell on you? It's not like she's gonna stick around. She'll burn through the pool of scumbags and move on. Beggars like her always do.

Lost in the nest of ratty locks surrounding her face, she mumbled something unintelligible.

He ran his fingers through his hair. If he'd wanted drama, he would've stayed home. Unsatisfied and spent, he slammed the door shut behind him.

CHAPTER 70

FAMILY MAN

It was her fault. Genny never should've sent the cops looking for him, should've known better than to lunge at him the minute he'd walked through the door. She'd pushed him to do it. She came at him, not the other way around. Her act of aggression—grabbing at him like that—set off a motion of events that he had no control over.

The darkness had taken over—caused him to overreact. Worst of all, he was forced to break the vow that he would never, ever, in a million years, beat on his wife. Randall resented her for that. He was better than his old man. He had to be.

He promised her it would never happen again. He believed his words, and she did, too.

He needed to feel connected to her, but the life growing inside of her changed things for him. The grotesque belly and bulging veins that seemed to increase by the day were a turn-off. She wasn't the pretty, young girl he'd married just months before. To override his aversion to her pregnant body, Randall focused on himself, and the power he felt over her, the sensation of owning her. It was a necessary sacrifice.

The baby was born in September, and he found himself mildly fascinated by her perfect, miniature features. He hadn't anticipated that she would be so small.

Although he felt a certain amount of disconnection from Lillian Grace, he pretended to be overjoyed because he knew that was expected of him—not only by his wife but by the busybodies from church that turned out in droves.

Besides, the new status of family man wasn't hurting his career in the least. The role of bachelor had been fun while it lasted, but his newfound position gained automatic respect from his colleagues and clients alike.

He was on top of the world, and for a moment, everything lined up perfectly. It was too good to be true.

***

"Genny, I'm home," he announced.

The kitchen was void of the fragrance of his supper on the stove. Dishes, leftover from breakfast, cluttered the table. The dark mood that he'd managed to keep at bay slithered from his chest into the cavity behind his eyes. He inhaled through his nostrils and exhaled slowly through his mouth.

He placed his briefcase on the countertop and yelled for her once more.

"*Shhh!*" Genny whispered loudly from the top of the staircase. "She's finally sleeping."

He waited until she made it down the stairs before asking, "What's for dinner?"

"Nothing. I haven't had time to start anything." Her bottom lip quivered.

"What have you been doing all day? The house is a mess." Randall pointed at the table.

Genny burst into tears. "She won't stop crying. I can't get her to nurse, and I don't know what to do!"

"If she's hungry, she'll eat. I don't know what the big deal is. This place smells like dirty diapers and nothing cooking."

"You're insensitive, Randall! I haven't had time to do anything today. I just told you that!" She smacked her hand onto the tabletop, causing the dirty dishes to rattle.

Piercing cries sounded from above, and Genny forced out an exaggerated sigh. "Now you've done it!" She stomped up the stairs, mumbling something that he couldn't make out.

"Where were all your church friends?" he yelled.

"Visiting a new baby!" she screamed. "And now I have no help around here! You're gone all day, and you sit on your ass when you come home."

The ringing noise in his ears drowned the rest of her words. By the time he reached the nursery, Genny had picked up the baby. A hollow thumping sound resonated through the room with each whack of her hand.

"Stop patting her so hard!"

"I'm burping her, you idiot! You would know if you ever bothered to help!"

"That's enough! I'm the one supporting you. You have some ridiculous, fairy-tale princess idea of how it is. You shouldn't need help taking care of your own baby!" He shook his head. "For Christ's sake, Genny! Pull your head out of your ass!"

***

"I wondered how long it would take for your 'happy home' illusion to disappear." George patted the empty barstool next to him and welcomed him back to the Watering Hole with a smug grin.

"Fuck you, George." Randy chuckled and took his spot.

"Care to talk about it?"

"Wipe the shit-eating grin off your face, and I might do that."

It looked to be a struggle, but George managed to straighten his mouth into a stoic position. "I'm all ears, man."

"It was all good, at first." He shook his head in disbelief.

"She's ignoring you now," George offered. "That baby's her whole world."

Waving away his words, Randy said, "No, it's not that. She's just so goddamn…" He rummaged around for the right description of Genny's state. "So needy, selfish—actually had the nerve to accuse me of not doing anything to help."

George scoffed and knocked back the rest of his glass. "Go on."

"Another, please." Randall held his empty glass to the bartender and continued. "A herd of broads from the church were hanging around the house, fussing over Genny and the baby."

"They like to do that, don't they?" George laughed. "Got nothin' better to do than get into everyone else's business."

"It wasn't a bad thing." Randall pressed his lips together. "Except, she got a little spoiled. And now, they've moved on to the next best thing. The Holcomb family had a baby last week." He rubbed the back of his neck. "Can't handle not being the center of attention. She can feel sorry for herself all day long, but I'm not gonna give her an audience."

It'd been a while since he'd had a proper drink. He sat for a moment, savoring the relief.

Naturally, his eye went to the women in the bar. Only one caught his attention, but she wasn't quite right. Lipstick too red, a copious amount of rouge on her cheeks, squeezed into her dress, she had a jaded look about her.

George noticed her, too. "She's not a bad ride. If you like the desperate type."

"I'm not looking, man." Randall had an image to keep, and no one, not even his buddy, needed to see anything different.

He tossed some money onto the bar. "I'm calling it a night. This should cover it."

Mac acknowledged him with a nod.

"See you tomorrow night," George slapped Randall's shoulder.

"We'll see."

CHAPTER 71

MARY

He didn't see her until it was almost too late. Bits of gravel skated between his tires and the dirt road as he pumped his brakes and forced the steering wheel to the left.

Giving his racing pulse a second to calm down, he sat with his hands on the wheel. Dust, stirred up by the haphazard stop, took on a life of its own and traveled down the road in the same direction he'd been heading.

Something between a child and a woman, she sat with her forehead pressed into her bent knees. A bicycle, the front wheel bent, lay near her.

"Are you okay?" Squatting in front of her, Randall touched her shoulder.

Lifting her face, revealing the bluest eyes he'd ever seen, she nodded. "I don't know what happened. I was riding, and then I wasn't."

"Let's get you home." He held out his hand.

She hesitated, and he realized she wasn't likely to get into the car of a complete stranger.

"I'm Randall. I live a few houses away."

Pensive, she replied, "I'm Mary."

He opened the passenger door for her. "Pleased to meet you, Mary. Can I give you a ride home?"

"My bike," she said. "I can't leave it."

"Don't worry," he reassured. "It'll fit in the back."

With a little finagling, he was able to put the bike in and close the trunk. He brushed his hands together in a brisk fashion to get most of the dust off and opened the driver's side door.

"Where do you live?"

"Just up the road." She pointed and said, "I'll show you."

"Shouldn't you be in school?"

"I missed the bus." She looked uncomfortable.

"Your mother couldn't take you?"

"She's…" Hesitant, she said, "not home."

"Your dad?"

"Gone. He left when I was a baby."

"I'm sorry to hear that."

"Don't be. I don't remember him." Her smooth face took on a hardened edge. "It's the next house on the right."

Barely wide enough to pass through, the drive was hidden in a thicket of saplings strangled by vines. The rundown shack could hardly be called a house. It reminded him of the hauntingly beautiful photographs he'd seen in a National Geographic piece covering poverty in the Appalachian Mountains.

Only the child in this picture wasn't dirty-faced and shoeless. She was angelic.

"Where do you want the bike?"

"Against the house is fine."

"Do you need a ride to school? I'm heading to work. I can drop you on the way."

She twisted a loose tendril of hair with her fingers. "I'm not sure."

"I won't bite." He chuckled. "We're neighbors," he added.

On the drive into town, he felt a sense of pure joy. Occasionally, he glanced at her, sitting next to him, and found himself overwhelmed with elation. Petite, delicate hands clasped demurely around her crossed legs. The breeze from the open window carried the scent of her freshly washed hair.

The high school was a few blocks from his office. He eased his car into the drive.

"Oh no, I'm not in high school yet." A subtle shade of pink spread across her cheeks and onto the tip of her nose. "Not until next year."

"Let's see…" He did a mental calculation. "That would make you around thirteen or fourteen."

Pleased, she nodded. "Almost fourteen."

Almost fourteen was the age of being still untainted by the world, the age in which one still had hope and trust. Almost fourteen meant she was pure.

"Will you take the bus home?"

"I usually do. I only missed it this morning because my mom wasn't home and forgot to set my alarm."

"What time does your mother come home? I might stop and introduce myself. It's good to know your neighbors, don't you think?"

***

She stayed on his mind all during the workday, and when it was time to leave, he took the long way home just to drive by her house. There was something about her that captivated him.

A dinged-up Pontiac was parked at the edge of the driveway to her home, leaving no room to pull in. He couldn't help but wonder if it'd been left there to keep others out.

He considered parking out front, but the dirt road was narrow, to begin with, and the shoulder was nearly non-existent. Disappointed, he continued driving to his house.

"You're in a good mood." Genny smiled at him during supper. "Did something special happen today?"

"Nothing special; just had an exceptionally good day." This was true, but it was also true that something special had indeed happened. Something that was just for him.

She wouldn't understand. Best to keep it to himself.

***

He drove in her direction the very next morning, in hopes of seeing her either waiting for the bus or riding her bike. Slowing down in front of her house, he looked to see if there were any cars in the drive. It was empty, so he turned in.

Insects, gnats of some sort, swarmed around his head as he walked toward the little shack. He swatted them away and knocked on the door. Not expecting anyone to be home, he had turned to leave just as the door opened.

Dressed in a ratty bathrobe, hair in curlers, she was an older, worn-down version of her daughter. The features were similar—the upturned nose, wide blue eyes, full lips. She didn't have the same shine, the softness of the child.

"Can I help you?"

Intimidated by her skeptical demeanor, he struggled to keep a smile on his face. "I wanted to introduce myself. I'm your neighbor."

Arms crossed, she said nothing.

"I'm Randall Carter. I...uh...my family and I live just down the road." He held out his hand for a shake.

Reluctantly, she took his hand and reciprocated. "Judy. Nice to meet you."

"Your daughter, Mary, may have mentioned me? She missed the bus yesterday, and I gave her a ride to school. Just wanted to introduce myself properly."

"No, she didn't mention any of that."

Judging from the scowl on her face, she wasn't happy about it.

"She probably didn't want to bother you at work."

Chewing on the inside of her cheek, she seemed to be debating something in her mind.

"I won't keep you. I just wanted to say hello."

"Thank you for taking her." Her voice was stiff, but her lips turned up slightly into a guarded smile. "Can I offer you a cup of coffee for your trouble?"

Glancing at his wristwatch, he pretended to be thinking about it. "I have a few minutes. Thank you, that would be nice."

Despite its rundown condition, the interior of the home was surprisingly clean. He took the seat that she offered. Pleasant small talk was a crucial skill for work, and he'd become quite good at it. It was a power to be able to charm others. It was a necessity if he were to get closer to Mary.

When he'd finished his coffee, he stood up and said, "I'd best be going. Thank you for the coffee and the warm welcome."

Disappointment flashed across her face. He was on the right path, and this made it easy to give her a genuine smile.

"You're welcome any time." She had the same endearing dimples as Mary.

"Here." He handed his business card to her. "Feel free to call if you ever need anything. Must be rough by yourself."

She gave a tired smile and said, "Thank you. I appreciate that. We do fine by ourselves most of the time, but there are days."

CHAPTER 72

GROOMING

It was a thin line he'd managed to balance on. Judy trusted him. He knew women, and it was clear to him that Judy looked forward to his visits. She'd begun to lean on him, allowing him to fix small things around the house. He was always careful to pay more attention to her than to Mary.

"That should hold up for a while." He climbed down the ladder and began to pack away his tools. "We'll need to do something stronger than a patch before the spring rains hit, but your bedroom should be dry now."

"Would you like to stay for dinner?"

"I appreciate the offer, but I'd best get home. Genny will have dinner ready."

"Well, maybe some other time." Her disappointment was apparent.

"I'd take you up on a cup of coffee, though."

Judy smiled. "Great! Mary will be home soon. She'll be happy to see you. It's been a while."

He sat down in the chair nearest to the door and watched her make coffee. Worn by the hard years that life had handed to her, she was still a decent-looking woman. There was a soothing quality about her movements.

"Maybe this is too intrusive, but what happened to Mary's father?"

Facing away from him, her expression hidden, she stood still for a moment before replying. "He couldn't handle the responsibilities of a family. Decided that leaving would be easier for him."

"How long has that been?"

"Eleven, maybe twelve years now." She shrugged. "His loss."

"Does Mary miss him?"

"I don't think she remembers him," she sighed. "I still miss him. I wonder how our life together would've turned out if Mary hadn't come along."

"Seems sad for Mary. For you, too. Being on your own and all."

"Definitely not how I'd hoped our lives would've turned out." She smiled. "But we manage. And the kindness of strangers has carried us through the years. It's better now that I've got a decent job."

The screech of the bus brakes announced Mary's arrival. She skipped into the kitchen and tossed her book bag onto the counter. Dressed in a plaid skirt and a button-up white shirt, she smiled at him in a way that tugged at his heart.

"There are cookies in the pantry," Judy said. "How was school?"

Her smile faded. "It was okay. But I'm not doing so well in math."

"I'd be happy to help you with your homework," Randall offered.

"That's a relief," Judy said. "I've never been good at math. She's better than me. I'm no help at all."

And so, it began. Each day, after school, Randall dropped by to help her with homework. He liked the way that she looked at him, the way that she trusted him.

"Guess what?" Mary glowed. "Wanna see my math test?"

She waited, barely able to contain her excitement, while he looked over the paper she'd handed to him.

"You aced it! This calls for a celebration!" He hugged her and suggested, "How about I take you for ice cream?"

"We should wait for Mom. She'll be home soon."

"I'm not gonna be able to stick around that long. Genny will be expecting me for dinner. Gotta keep the wife happy."

Mary thought for a moment. "Mom's working late tonight. I guess I could leave her a note."

"She'll be fine with it, I'm sure."

Feeling impatient to leave before her mother arrived, he waited for her to pencil a message to Judy.

In the car, the same excitement pumped through his veins as he'd felt the first time he'd taken her to school. He glanced at her from time to time, taking in her innocent beauty.

The soda shop was packed. He recognized several of the cars in the parking lot.

"I'll be right back. Do you want chocolate or vanilla?"

"Can't we go in?" she asked. "It's been a long time since I've been in a soda shop."

"No," he answered, shaking his head. "I don't think it's a good idea. We'll be waiting for a seat, and I need to get home soon."

"Chocolate, I guess."

"Hey, why the sad face? It won't be long. I promise." He patted the hand resting on her lap. "We'll go inside another time."

She smiled. "Okay. Next time."

It didn't take long to get a single cone. "Here you go. One chocolate ice cream for the little lady. Get started before it melts on you."

She'd devoured the ice cream before they reached the edge of town. "Ouch! I have a headache from the cold."

He chuckled. "You ate it too fast. It'll feel better in a minute or two."

"Look." He pointed at a billboard. "Have you ever been there?"

"The caves? I don't think so."

"We should go someday."

"I'd like that!" she exclaimed.

Her excited smile was like a summer day to his soul.

"One of my favorite places to go is the lake. Have you seen it?"

"No." She shook her head and frowned. "We haven't done much of anything. At least not anything in this town. Mom's always working, and she doesn't have the time. She's too tired on her days off."

"We can go right now," Randall proposed. Eager, he wanted to make her happy.

"Don't you need to hurry?"

"I've got a few minutes. We won't stay long."

The lake was empty, save for a few devoted fishermen. He found a spot that had been cleared for camping and parked.

"What do you think?"

"It's pretty." She fidgeted with the pendant on her necklace, and he could sense her nervousness.

"Do you want to get out and walk around?"

"I think we should be getting back. My mom might worry."

He brushed a loose strand of hair from her face and tucked it behind her ear. "You're with me. She's not going to worry."

She stiffened slightly as he touched her pendent, turning it over in his fingers. "It's nice. Where'd you get it?"

"For Christmas. My mom." Her voice barely a whisper; he felt her breath becoming uneven.

Gentle, he let go of her pendent, his fingers lingering for a moment longer on her chest.

Something between fear and excitement shone in her eyes. Frozen, she didn't look away.

"You dropped a little." He pointed at her lap.

"What?"

"Ice cream, on your skirt. Don't worry. We can get it out. Your secret's safe with me." Randall winked and smiled.

He pulled a handkerchief from his breast pocket. "I'll be right back."

Squatting at the edge of the lake, he dampened the handkerchief. He was lightheaded with anticipation. Too innocent to know how to show him, she wanted him as much as he wanted her.

"May I?"

She nodded.

With his left hand, he placed a folded napkin on the underside of her skirt, directly beneath the stain. Using the dampened handkerchief, he rubbed furiously over the top of the chocolate. "See? All gone."

"Thank you." Her bashful demeanor was charming.

"You have a little on your mouth."

She rubbed at the corner of her lips with her thumb.

"No, the other side."

She repeated the action on the other corner of her mouth.

"Did I get it?"

"Almost." He gently rubbed at the chocolate. "I think I got it."

With her face still in his hands, he leaned toward her and kissed her tender lips, soft and slow. He wanted to take his time. She was pure, unblemished. He didn't want to take that away from her.

Yielding to him, she allowed him to continue.

He stopped and asked, "Are you okay?"

Speechless, she nodded.

Caressing her face and neck, he kissed her once more. He moved his hands slowly down to her small, blossoming breasts. He reminded himself to be gentle. He didn't want to frighten her.

"I should get you home. Your mom will be worried."

She was quiet on the way back. Disturbed that he couldn't read her mood, paranoia rumbled around in his head. What if he'd misread her? Physically, she'd responded as he'd hoped. But what if he'd gotten it all wrong? Something akin to fear twisted at his stomach. He couldn't stand to be on the downside of things.

The driveway was empty, but that didn't mean Judy wasn't home. As far as he could tell, Judy didn't have a car of her own. He'd never bothered to ask details about her circumstances. It didn't interest him beyond Mary.

He parked the car and turned off the ignition. Turning to Mary, he asked, "Are you feeling okay?"

Timid, she said, "I don't know."

"People won't understand. You realize that, don't you?"

Uneasy, she agreed. "I know."

"What we have…it's special." He reached for her hand. "I don't want to let anyone else ruin it."

"But what about your wife? It's wrong."

"She doesn't understand me. It's going to take some time to sort things out."

"I should go inside. It's getting late." Her hands shook as she grasped the passenger door handle.

He pulled her back into his embrace and whispered in her ear. "Don't ruin this for us."

Her clean scent still lingered in his car as he pulled into his own driveway. He wanted more, and he wasn't going to let anything get in the way.

CHAPTER 73

THE WOLF

"Randall! What a surprise!" Judy smiled and waved for him to come inside. "What brings you here? It's been a while."

In fact, it hadn't been more than a few days since his last visit to Mary, but it was clear to him that Judy was none the wiser. Although he hadn't told Mary to keep secrets from her mother, it was good to know that she was capable of discretion.

"Weather's getting colder." He smiled and rubbed the back of his neck. "Thought I'd check on you ladies—see if you need anything."

"That's really kind of you. We're getting along okay, but I'm going to need a little help to make sure the furnace is working."

"I'd be happy to take a look."

"Can I offer you a cup of coffee first?"

The eager shine in her eyes made it difficult to feel annoyed. He held a small amount of affection for her, especially when she made an expression that reminded him of Mary.

"I'll take you up on that." He grinned in the way that melted most women.

Mary's absence disturbed him, but he made small talk with her mother for a few minutes before asking about her.

"Oh, she's not feeling well. She got off the bus and crawled into bed."

"Does she need to see a doctor?"

"I'm sure it's nothing. Probably tired from the day." Judy handed him a steaming cup of coffee and added, "She's been a little moody lately. I suppose she's getting to that age."

"I wouldn't know yet," he chuckled. "My daughter's still a baby."

Judy's face relaxed, and it occurred to him that he'd found another point of trust with her. Women loved to talk about babies, and even more, they loved when men talked about babies with them.

"Here." He pulled out his wallet and fished around for the photo. Worn around the edges from the hands of clients and co-workers alike, the picture of Lillian never failed to bring a round of congratulations.

Handing the photo to her, he said, "This is my baby, Lillian. We call her Lilly."

"She's precious!" Judy giggled and exclaimed, "What a little darling!"

"That, she is. Growing like a weed, too."

"We'd love to meet your family sometime. Mary and I should cook dinner for you."

Bringing Genny and the baby over was the last thing that he wanted to do.

It was apparent by her expression that she expected a response from him.

He rubbed the stubble on his chin and lied to her. "That would be nice. I'll talk to my wife."

This seemed to satisfy her, and he felt a fleeting relief. The coffee in his cup had grown cold. He swallowed the last bit and got up from the chair to place the empty cup near the sink.

"I'll get that," she fussed. "You do enough around here."

She stood near him—close enough to touch, close enough to smell her perfume. He could sense her desire for him. Unwelcomed images paraded through his mind. Judy was attractive enough, and even though she had a decade or more on him, he thought about what she would feel like, naked, lying next to him. There was something about her that appealed to him—a motherly quality that he had longed for so many years ago.

But he wasn't putting the time in to get close to Judy.

"Ah," he sighed and took a step backward, just out of her reach. Holding out the empty cup, he said, "I should get home."

"Of course." She turned to the sink and began to scrub the cup with a dishcloth. Looking over her shoulder, she said, "I'll let Mary know that you stopped by."

She was sulking. A small pilot light of impatience ignited in the back of his skull. If she knew his intentions, she would be jealous. What was the saying? Hell hath no fury like that of a scorned woman, or something to that effect. This knowledge kept his irritation in check.

"If you don't mind, I'll be over tomorrow afternoon to check on the furnace."

Judy shrugged her shoulders. "Sure, if it's convenient for you."

"Have a good evening. Tell Mary that I hope she feels better soon."

He paused outside of Mary's bedroom. Judy was still clinking around in the kitchen, so he felt safe to tap on the door.

"Mary." He spoke quietly. "Are you okay?"

She opened the door. Mary's face was puffy as if she'd been crying for days.

"I'm fine. I... um...I have my..." Her words dwindled as she seemed to search for the right way to say it. "I'm having my time of the month."

The flush on her face tugged at his emotions. She was embarrassed. He wanted to hold her, but he didn't dare—not with her mother in the house.

"I'll be back tomorrow afternoon. I hope you feel better soon."

"My mom works late, I think."

With his hand on the door frame, he leaned in toward her and whispered, "I'll be here as soon as I can get away."

The following morning started with a series of annoyances. Genny and the baby were red-faced, presumably both from crying. He ate the breakfast that Genny made while doing his best to avoid yet another conversation about the little amount of help that Genny had with the baby.

It was always directed at him, but she didn't have the balls to come right out and say it. He wasn't sure which was worse, being accused of neglecting his fatherly duties or being drawn into her manipulative self-pity. Either way, he couldn't get out of the house fast enough.

He slipped on his blazer and planted a perfunctory kiss on her forehead. "See you tonight."

"You're leaving now?" she asked. "I was hoping you could watch the baby so I could take a shower."

She needed one. It was all he could do to get close enough to kiss her. A fog of sweat, sour milk, and baby spit-up surrounded her. It was disgusting.

"Sorry. I'm already late." He glanced at his wristwatch and frowned. "Put her in the crib. She'll be fine."

Randall devoted the exact amount of time that it took to warm up his car to reassure himself he was indeed a good father. Genny didn't have a clue how bad it could be for her and Lilly. She had no idea what it was to suffer because he provided for them. He got up every single day and made a living, paid the bills on time, and put food on the table. She had no right to complain. He was doing more than his part.

His mood lifted a little as he neared Mary's house. Judy's car was still in the driveway, which meant she'd be working the late shift. Feeling encouraged, he hummed along with the songs on the radio as he drove to his office.

Other than the handyman, the office was empty. He checked his schedule. It was perfect. The last meeting was at two o'clock. There was no reason he wouldn't be free by three o'clock at the latest.

Using the hour before his first client, Randall reviewed the applications needed for the day. By the time nine o'clock rolled around, everything was laid out and ready to go.

Around noon, George poked his head in Randall's doorway. "Got any plans for lunch?"

"No," Randall said without looking up. "I'm working through. I need to get out of here early today."

"Big plans with the missus tonight?"

"Yeah." He grinned. "Something like that."

"I take it things are better at home?"

Randall chuckled and said, "You could say that."

George raised an eyebrow. "So, no drinks tonight?"

"You got it." He turned his attention back to the contract on his desk. "Maybe later this week."

Mrs. Fischer, a rotund woman with hair fashioned into the shape of a helmet, which did nothing to take away from her rather large cheeks and sagging neck, arrived ten minutes late to the two o'clock appointment.

"I'm so sorry for the delay," she warbled. "Ava, my poodle, got loose from the yard. It took a full five minutes to catch her."

Perhaps, he thought, *you should eat less and walk more.* "Not a problem, Mrs. Fischer. This shouldn't take too long." He examined the checklist in front of him.

"Let's see. Do you have the photographs of the valuables to be insured?" He tapped his pen onto the pad of paper in front of him and said, "We'll just go through them, and you can give me a brief description."

"Oh, yes. I've even brought the history behind each piece." Her eyes sparkled beneath false lashes and a truckload of eye shadow. She rubbed her hands together, and he imagined that she looked just the same way when she sat down in front of a plate full of food. A vision of Jack Sprat's greedy, fat wife popped into his brain.

"That won't be necessary. We'll only need the description and the appraised value."

"Oh, well, I'd assumed you'd be interested to know the background." Disappointment caused her bulbous cheeks to sink nearly to the level of her turkey neck.

He waved away her obvious displeasure over his lack of curiosity. "I'm sure it's very fascinating, but we're short on time. Unfortunately, I have another appointment right after yours."

She seemed satisfied with this and began the process of handing pictures of her prized possessions across the desk.

"Are these from a Polaroid camera?"

"Absolutely," she huffed. "I don't trust the developers. I'm not about to hand over a shopping list to those thieves."

"Shopping list?" He frowned. "I'm not sure what you mean."

"I wouldn't put it past them to burglarize my home if they knew I had valuables."

Shaking his head, he said, "I don't think you need to worry about something like that."

"Well, you can think whatever you like, but I'm not taking any chances!" Her voice had risen beyond a warble to a full-fledged shrill. "Are these photographs unacceptable? There should be no reason you can't use them."

"Relax, Mrs. Fischer. They're fine. I was fascinated by the camera. My wife recently had a baby girl. Naturally, we want to capture all those sweet little moments with her. Seems like it would be nice if we didn't have to take the film for developing."

Her shoulders relaxed down to a position below the tips of her sagging earlobes. "The camera has been worth every penny. I ordered mine from the Sears and Roebuck catalog several years ago, but I'll bet you could find it at the department store."

"Thank you, Mrs. Fischer. I'll do that!"

Randall rushed her through the process and managed to wrap up the appointment five minutes early. By three o'clock, he was in his car, driving to Mary's house.

CHAPTER 74

THE CALM BEFORE THE STORM

Judy slipped her headset off and began to wipe the small counter. She hoped to get home before he left. It was silly of her, she knew, to get excited about a man so much younger than herself. *And married, don't forget that part.*

"Judy, can you stay for five more? Amy's not here yet." The head operator rolled her eyes and growled out an exasperated sigh. "These young girls—they have no sense of time."

Judy nodded, put her headset back over her head, and connected the next line. "Operator, how may I assist you?"

Amy arrived within a few minutes and tapped Judy on the shoulder. "I'll take the next one," she mouthed the words.

She restrained herself from hugging Amy and rolled the chair away from the desk. "Thanks! Have fun with it. It's been hectic."

Outside, the sky was a dark swirl of grays, making it feel much later than five o'clock. The air smelled of impending rain, and she thought of better times with Mary's father.

Rainy days had been her favorite because he couldn't work on those days. Before Mary, before the burdens of being adults, they'd loved nothing more than to lie next to each other and listen to the drizzle on the tin roof of their little cottage. Those were the days of laughter and endless lovemaking. This was the part of her that was now missing, the piece of her that made her feel alive.

A loud crack of thunder sounded as she parked in the driveway behind Randall's car, and the beginnings of a rain shower announced itself with tiny spits and splats on her windshield. A charge of electricity moved through her core at the thought of his touch.

Inside, the little house was dark. She switched on the lamp next to the sofa and then the kitchen light. Noticing the dishes stacked next to the sink, she wondered if Mary was still suffering from cramps. It wasn't like her to slack on her chores.

"Mary? Where are you?" She called out in the direction of Mary's bedroom. "Are you feeling bad?"

She dropped her purse onto the table and went to Mary's room. Tapping on the closed door, she asked, "Can I get you anything? A cup of tea?"

Judy waited for a moment before opening Mary's door. Randall sat next to Mary's bed. Startled by his presence, she managed not to scream. Hair ruffled out of place; he looked as though he'd been sleeping.

"What are you doing in here? Is she all right?" A twisting and turning sensation pushed around in her gut. She rushed to the opposite side of the bed from where Randall sat.

He chuckled and answered, "She's fine. I was sitting with her because she felt sick. But she seems okay. I must have dozed off."

She reached under the edge of the bedspread, where Mary's face was hidden and felt her forehead. A thin layer of sweat coated Mary's brow, but it was difficult to decide whether she was warm with a fever. Pulling the cover back to get a better look at her face, Judy was disturbed to see Mary's bare shoulders.

"Where are your clothes?" she demanded. "Why aren't you dressed?"

Randall stood and said, "I didn't realize. She was buried under the blankets when I came in."

"Why are you in here?" she asked again. Fear and anger snaked their way up from the pit of her belly into her heart. She glared at him and waited for an answer.

"She was crying out for you."

His expression was impossible to decipher. Was it guilt? *Don't be ridiculous*, she argued. *He's been nothing but kind.*

The racing of her heart settled, and she forced a weak smile. "Thank you for checking on her. I can take it from here."

"I'll go take a look at the furnace." His face was flushed.

Judy wondered if she'd made him uncomfortable. It was conceivable, she rationalized, that he hadn't considered how his actions might have been construed. After all, his daughter was just a baby.

She waited until he'd left the room. Grabbing Mary's shoulder, she scolded, "You need to get dressed. It's indecent of you to lay in bed naked."

Mary didn't acknowledge her words, but Judy was certain she understood them.

CHAPTER 75

CLOSE CALL

He would be more careful next time. It had been too close for comfort. Randall had managed to button his collar one second before Judy barged in. Even worse, his tie was still in Mary's room. There was no practical way to retrieve it without drawing suspicion.

Although his impulse was to leave immediately, he went through the process of inspecting the furnace. When he finished, Judy was in the kitchen, chopping potatoes.

"Well?" she asked. "How did it look?"

"The pilot ignited just fine, but your left burner is a little rusty. Might want to tell the landlord about it."

She snorted. "I doubt he'll take it seriously. I told him about the leak in the roof last spring. If it weren't for you, my bedroom would still be damp."

"I'd better get home. The wife won't be happy if I'm late."

Without looking up from the cutting board, she said, "Thank you for checking the heater."

The exchange was awkward. *You're just paranoid. She didn't see anything.*

It took exactly one minute from the time the nose of his car left the edge of Mary's driveway until he'd parked in front of his own house. Through the kitchen door, he could see Genny's movements.

If he were lucky, she would be making one of the four meals that she'd managed to master. More likely, she would be slopping together yet another disaster, and he would be forced with the impossible choice of honesty or pretending that he liked it in order to keep the peace.

He turned off the car and sat for a moment, reflecting on the time with Mary. Afraid that she would somehow be able to read his thoughts, he hadn't dared to think of it with Judy nearby.

He'd been gentle enough for the first time, and he was sure he hadn't gone too far. Remembering her nervous responses, an electric current crackled through his brain.

Unsure of herself, inexperienced, her reception of his caresses had been simple and sweet. Embarrassed by her time of the month, she'd pulled away from his attempts to touch her there. It wouldn't have bothered him, but it wouldn't have been ideal either. Too messy. Too difficult to clean up afterward.

It couldn't have been a better start. He was sure of it.

CHAPTER 76

SHAME

Mary pulled the bedspread back over her face and listened to the *thump-thump* hammering sound of her heart. Why hadn't she stopped him?

Minutes, perhaps thirty or more, passed, and the hot, stale air made her feel as if she were being smothered. She pushed the blankets down to her chin and took a deep breath, filling her lungs with the cool air of her dark bedroom.

She'd asked for it. That's what people would say if she were to tell. That's what her mother would say.

Tears mingled with the perspiration on her temples as she imagined the look of disappointment on her mother's face.

Only dirty girls lie naked with boys, let themselves be touched in that way. Now, she was ruined, spoiled.

She thought about the neighbor girl who'd babysat her after school when she was much younger. Mary had loved her.

"Why can't she watch me anymore?" She'd demanded to know.

"She's been sent away."

"But why? Where did she go?"

"She's at a home for bad girls, a place where girls who make bad choices go."

Baffled that her beloved babysitter could've done something so dreadful to be sent away, Mary persisted. "What did she do?"

Her mother had frowned for a bit before answering. "She let a boy take her clothes off and touch her privates."

Mortified, Mary hadn't dared to ask any more questions.

Suddenly ice cold, the sweat felt like a winter rain on her skin. Her stomach churned over the possibility that she could be sent away for the things that she'd let Randall do to her.

CHAPTER 77

THE LAST DAY

"Mr. Carter, You have a call on line four."

"Can you take a message? I'm knee-deep in a proposal that should've been finished this morning." Covered with loose papers, his desk looked as if it had been ransacked by a burglar.

"She said it's urgent. Wouldn't give me her name."

He massaged at the irritation in his right temple. The receptionist was a pain in his ass. An overbearing little bitch, she acted as if she were a conductor, orchestrating a master plan for the whole damned office. Even worse, the boss-man treated her like she'd invented sliced bread.

"Fine. I'll take it." He put the receiver against his ear and pressed line four. "This is Randall Carter. How can I help you?"

"It's me." Mary's voice came through in a whisper.

"You can't call me here. Ever. I thought you understood that." Still holding the phone against his ear, he stood up and stretched to shut the door to his office. "What is it?"

She sniffled into the phone. "I need to talk to you."

Oh, for God's sake; was she crying?

"I don't have time today."

"I've been waiting for you all week. Why haven't you been around?"

He didn't appreciate the demanding attitude. "I've been busy." He started to explain, then stopped himself. Mary was a child. She had no idea about the pressures of life. It was wasted breath to defend his absence.

"Please!" she begged. "I need to tell you something."

Exasperated, he sighed. "Okay. I'll be there around four."

"You can't come here. Meet me at the old barn next to our house."

He stared at the mountain of paperwork on his desk. His stomach churned. With every element of his being, he wished he'd never met her.

Turning his attention back to the scattered documents, he forced the sense of unease to retreat into the secret place in his mind. Soon, the fear of being caught by her mother, the nauseating worry that Genny would find out, and the ruminations on how best to erase Mary's existence from his life faded away.

At three o'clock, he tucked the finished proposal into a folder bearing the agency's logo and slid it into a large manila envelope for mailing. He slipped on his jacket and collected his briefcase and Polaroid camera. Stopping at the reception desk, he placed the proposal into the outgoing mail.

Without bothering to wait for the receptionist to finish her phone call, he said, "I have a prospect at four. I won't be back today."

She nodded and made a note on her desk calendar.

***

Mary was already waiting in the doorway of the weathered barn when he pulled into the drive. Judging from the overgrown weeds surrounding it, the property hadn't been used in years.

A mixture of relief and apprehension flashed across her delicate features. She looked tiny against the frame of the large door. He felt a pang of sorrow, understanding that he wouldn't be around to see her grow to womanhood.

Don't be a fool, son. You've pushed it long enough. Time to cut loose. Don't you have enough sense to know when you've gone too far?

In fact, he did know when he'd gone too far, and he didn't need his dad's voice interrupting this last time with her. It should be untainted by all the insidious things that threatened to send him over the edge.

He wrapped his arms around her slight frame and breathed in the scent of her hair. Mary burrowed her face into his chest, and he could feel her trembling.

"*Shhh,*" he soothed. "What's the matter?"

"I'm scared. I don't want to be sent away for…" Her muffled words faded into the crisp fabric of his shirt.

"Sent away for what?" Was she pregnant? He'd been careful. It wasn't possible. He untangled her arms from him and held her by her shoulders to better see her expression. "What are you being sent away for?"

Tears rolled down her cheeks, and she struggled to speak. Taking in big gulps of air, she uttered the words, "For doing bad things with you."

"Who knows? Who did you tell?" He realized that he was shaking her shoulders and let go of her. It wouldn't be good for him if he were to accidentally hurt her.

"No one! I didn't tell anyone." She covered her reddened face with her hands and sobbed. "I didn't. Just like you said."

"Why in the hell are you worried about it, then?" A crushing weight squeezed at his core. God help him if she ever spoke a word of this. He would be destroyed. What had he been thinking?

You weren't thinking, son. I told you to keep it in your pants. You just had to get your dick wet. If dumb was dirt, you'd be a whole damned acre. Should've thought about it a little longer. Calm your ass down and think. There's an easy fix for all this mess.

"Because," she wailed. "What if my mom finds out? What if she knows what you did to me?" Her words sounded a little like a threat.

"I'm not going to tell her." Incensed, he labored to control the volume of his voice. "Are you? It sounds to me like you're thinking about tattling."

"I swear I won't," she cried and shook her head. "Never."

"I don't believe you. I'm going to need a little insurance."

"I don't know what that means." She looked miserable.

"Insurance." He repeated the word slowly, emphasizing the syllables. "Something that will reassure me that you're not going to talk."

Her eyes widened with fear. "I don't have any money."

"I don't want money. You're going to give me something better." He winked and smiled. "Wait here."

He grabbed the camera from the front seat of his car and opened the trunk. He'd yet to show Genny the afghan his secretary had crocheted for the baby. It would work nicely.

The warped wooden door protested with a creak and a moan as he shoved it open. "Follow me."

Mary stayed several steps behind him as he surveyed the interior of the dim, musty barn. It had a distinct odor of damp dirt and decomposing hay.

"This will do." He pointed to the feed room.

He spread the blanket over a stack of hay. "Take your clothes off."

"No, please, no!" she begged. "It's dirty in here. I don't want to do this."

"If you don't, I'm going to tell your dear mama how you tried to seduce me. Imagine her dismay when she hears all about her little tramp of a daughter."

"You can't say that to her," she cried.

Her words came out in the form of a hiccupping, wailing sound, and he knew that she was frightened. He felt some satisfaction in the core of his steeled heart. After all the kindness he'd shown her, the little whore had every intention of squealing to her mother. Good thing he had his thinking cap on.

"I *will* say that to her. That, and more." He smiled. "That's why you're going to take your clothes off and do as I say. If you don't, I'll be paying her a visit shortly. I'll tell her all about how you threw yourself at me, how I told you no, and how you begged me not to tell her what a little slut her daughter is."

He put his hand on the back of her neck and pulled her into him, covering her soft lips with his mouth. "Take your clothes off," he whispered into her ear. "Now."

She nodded and began to undress. Her hands trembled as she struggled with the buttons.

Picture perfect, the horror in Mary's eyes was intoxicating. Vulnerable, helpless, she stood exposed in little cotton panties with daisies printed on them and a modest, white brassiere with a tiny blue bow sewn right between the cups. He'd never wanted her more.

The Art of Picking Flowers

The most beautiful flowers in the garden
Have yet to fully ripen
Small, firm, and bright
And not quite open

Baby shampoo and honeysuckle perfume
The taste of cherry Chapstick
Sleeping beauty never resists
She knows no other
And I am her god

There is nothing so seductive
As the unripened flower

~

The story continues in *Hidden in the Dark: Every Family Has Secrets - Some Are Worth Dying For...*

Grab it here https://www.amazon.com/Hidden-Dark-Every-Family-Secrets-ebook/dp/B06W2FZHSK or search Amazon for 'Hidden in the Dark' by RaShell Lashbrook

ABOUT THE AUTHOR

RaShell Danette Lashbrook was born in Wellington, Kansas, the eldest daughter of Lyle and Marcia Pope Lashbrook. Her parents threw the television away when she was just two years old, so she spent her childhood in the little town of Mulvane, Kansas reading, exploring, biting her nails, and picking her nose.

Her deep love of reading always fueled a small flame of desire to write, but it wasn't until 2012 that she began to practice the craft of throwing words onto paper and rearranging them repeatedly.

She is blessed to share her life with her six magnificent children and their friends, parents that anyone would be envious of, the best siblings in the whole world, and a "top-shelf" circle of close friends and extended family.

RaShell's fascination with many different subjects has served her well in her writing. She prefers to think of her dabbling as "research." Her lasting passions have been organic gardening, music, cooking, murder, mysteries, aliens, and mental disorders.

Made in the USA
Monee, IL
22 July 2021